Praise for #1 *New York Times* bestselling author

LISA JACKSON

"Bestselling Jackson cranks up the suspense to almost unbearable heights in her latest tautly written thriller."
—*Booklist* on *Malice*

"When it comes to providing gritty and sexy stories, Ms. Jackson certainly knows how to deliver."
—*RT Book Reviews* on *Unspoken*

"Provocative prose, an irresistible plot and finely crafted characters make up Jackson's latest contemporary sizzler."
—*Publishers Weekly* on *Wishes*

"Lisa Jackson takes my breath away."
—*New York Times* bestselling author Linda Lael Miller

LISA JACKSON

RUMORS:
The McCaffertys

Recycling programs for this product may not exist in your area.

ISBN-13: 978-0-373-77803-4

RUMORS: THE McCAFFERTYS

Copyright © 2012 by Harlequin Books S.A.

The publisher acknowledges the copyright holder of the individual works as follows:

THE McCAFFERTYS: THORNE
Copyright © 2000 by Susan Crose

THE McCAFFERTYS: MATT
Copyright © 2001 by Susan Crose

www.Harlequin.com

Printed in U.S.A.

CONTENTS

THE McCAFFERTYS: THORNE

Prologue

Last summer

"The truth of the matter, son, is that I've got a request for you," John Randall McCafferty stated from his wheelchair. He'd asked Thorne to push him to the fence line some thirty yards from the front door of the ranch house he'd called home all his life.

"I hate to ask what it is," Thorne remarked.

"It's simple. I want you to marry. You're thirty-nine, son, Matt's thirty-seven and Slade—well, he's still a boy but he is thirty-six. None of you has married and I don't have one grandchild—well at least none that I know of." He frowned. "Even your sister hasn't settled down."

"Randi's only twenty-six."

"High time," J. Randall said. A shell of the man he'd once been, J. Randall nonetheless gripped the arms of his metal chair, often referred to as "that damned contraption," so tightly his knuckles bleached white. An old afghan was draped over his legs though the temperature hovered near eighty according to the ancient thermometer tacked to the north side of the barn. Across his lap was his cane, another hated symbol of his failing health.

"I'm serious, son. I need to know that the McCafferty line won't die with you boys."

"That's an archaic way of thinking." Thorne wasn't going to be pushed around. Not by his old man. Not by anyone.

"So be it. Damn it, Thorne, if ya haven't noticed I don't have a helluva lot of time left on this here earth!" J. Randall swept his cane from his lap and jabbed it into the ground for emphasis.

Harold, J. Randall's crippled hunting dog, gave off a disgruntled woof from the front porch and a field mouse scurried into a tangle of brambles.

"I don't understand you," J. Randall grumbled. "This could have been yours, boy. All yours." He swept his cane in a wide arc and Thorne's gaze followed his father's gesture. Spindly legged colts frolicked in one pasture while a herd of mottled cattle in shades of russet, black and brown ambled near the dry creek bed that sliced through what was commonly referred to as "the big meadow." The paint on the barn had peeled, the windows in the stables needed replacing and the whole damned place looked as if it were suffering from the same debilitating disease as its owner.

The Flying M Ranch.

John Randall McCafferty's pride and joy. Now run by a foreman as he was too ill and his children too busy with their own lives.

Thorne regarded the rolling acres with a mixture of emotions running the gauntlet from love to hate.

"I'm not getting married, Dad. Not for a while."

"What's the wait? And don't tell me you need to make your mark. You've done it, boy." Old, faded blue eyes rolled up to look at him, then blinked when rays from a blinding Montana sun were too much. "What're ya worth now? Three million? Five?"

"Somewhere around seven."

His father snorted. "I was a rich man once. What did it get me?" His old lips folded back on themselves. "Two wives who bled me dry when we divorced and a bellyful of worry about losin' it all. No, money isn't what counts, Thorne. It's children. And land. Damn it all—" biting his lower lip, J. Randall dug deep into his pocket "—now where in tarnation is that— Oh, here we go."

Slowly he withdrew a ring that winked in the sunlight and Thorne's gut twisted as he recognized the band—his father's first wedding ring; one he hadn't worn in over a quarter of a century. "I want you to have this," the old man said as he held out the gold band with its unique silver inlay. "Your mother gave it to me the day we were married."

"I know." Thorne, sensing he was making a serious mistake, accepted the ring. It felt cold and hard in his fingers, a metal circle that held no warmth, no promise, no joy. A symbol of broken dreams. He pocketed the damn ring.

"Promise me, boy."

"What?"

"That you'll marry."

Thorne didn't bat an eye. "Someday."

"Make it soon, will ya? I'd like to leave this earth knowin' that you were gonna have a family."

"I'll think about it," Thorne said and suddenly the small band of gold and silver in his pocket seemed to weigh a thousand pounds.

Chapter 1

Grand Hope, Montana
October

Dr. Nicole Stevenson felt a rush of adrenaline surge through her blood as it did each time accident victims were rushed into the emergency room of St. James Hospital.

She met the intensity in Dr. Maureen Oliverio's eyes as the other woman hung up the phone. "The copter's here! Let's go, people!" The hastily grouped team of doctors and nurses responded. "The paramedics are bringing in the patient. You're on, Dr. Stevenson."

"What have we got?" Nicole asked.

Dr. Oliverio, a no-nonsense doctor, led the way through double doors. "Single-car accident up in Glacier Park, the patient's a woman in her late twenties, pregnant, at term. Fractures, internal damage, concussed, a real mess. Membranes have ruptured. We'll probably need to do a C-section because of her other injuries. While we're inside, we'll repair any other damage. Everybody with me? Dr. Stevenson's in charge until we send the patient to O.R."

Nicole caught the glances of the other doctors as they adjusted masks and gloves. It was her job to stabilize the patient before shipping her off to surgery.

The doors of the room flew open and a gurney, propelled by two paramedics, flew through the doors of the emergency room of St. James Hospital.

"What have we got here?" Nicole asked the nearest paramedic, a short red-faced man with clipped graying hair and a moustache. "What are her vital signs? What about the baby?"

"BP normal, one-ten over seventy-five, heart rate sixty-two but dropping slightly..." The paramedic rattled off the information he'd gathered and Nicole, listening, looked down at the patient, an unconscious woman whose face once probably beautiful was now bloody and already beginning to bruise. Her abdomen was distended, fluid from an IV flowed into her arm and her neck and head were braced. "...lacerations, abrasions, fractured skull, mandible and femur, possible internal bleeding..."

"Let's get a fetal monitor here!" Nicole ordered as a nurse peeled off.

"On its way."

"Good." Nicole nodded. "Okay, okay, now, let's stabilize the mother."

"Has the husband been notified? Do we have a consent?" Dr. Oliverio asked.

"Don't know," a grim-faced paramedic replied. "The police are trying to locate her relatives. According to her ID, her name is Randi McCafferty and there's no indication of any allergies to meds on her driver's licence, no prescription drugs in her purse."

Oh, God! Nicole's heart nearly stopped. She froze. For a split second her concentration lapsed and she gave herself a quick mental shake. "Are you sure?" she asked the shorter of the two paramedics.

"Positive."

"Randi McCafferty," Dr. Oliverio repeated, sucking in her breath. "My daughter went to school with her. Her father's dead—J. Randall, important man around these parts at one time. Owned the Flying M Ranch about twenty miles out of town. Randi, here, has three half brothers."

And Thorne's one of them, Nicole thought, her jaw tensing.

"What about the husband or boyfriend? The kid's got a father somewhere," Dr. Oliverio insisted.

"Don't know. Never heard of one."

"We'll figure out all that later," Nicole said, taking charge once more. "Right now, let's just concentrate on stabilizing her and the baby."

Dr. Oliverio nodded. "Let's get that fetal monitor on here! STAT."

"Got it," a nurse replied.

"BP's falling, Doctor—one hundred over sixty," a nurse said.

"Damn." Nicole's own heart began to pound. She wasn't going to lose this patient. *Come on, Randi,* she silently urged. *Where's that good ol' McCafferty fight? Come on, come on!* "Where's the anesthesiologist?" Nicole demanded.

"On his way."

"Who is he?"

"Brummel." Dr. Oliverio met Nicole's gaze. "A good man. He'll be here."

"The monitor's in place," a nurse said just as Dr. Brummel, a thin man in rimless glasses, pushed his way through the doors. "What have we got here?" he asked as he quickly scanned the patient.

"Woman. Unconscious. About to deliver. Single-car accident. No known allergies, no medical records, but we're checking," Nicole said. "She's got a skull fracture, multiple other fractures, pneumothorax—so she's already entubated. Her membranes have ruptured, the kid's on his way, and there might be more abdominal injuries."

"The mother's BP is stabilizing—one hundred and five over sixty," a nurse called, but Nicole didn't relax. Couldn't. In her estimation Randi McCafferty's life wasn't yet certain.

"Keep your eye on it. Now, what about the baby?" Nicole asked.

"We've got trouble here. The baby's in distress," Dr. Oliverio said, eyeing the readout of the fetal monitor.

"Then let's get it out of there."

"I'll be ready in a minute," Dr. Brummel said from behind his mask as he adjusted the breathing tube. Satisfied, he glanced up at Nicole. "Let's go."

"We've got a neonatalogist standing by."

"Good." Nicole checked Randi's vital signs one last time. "Patient's stable." She glanced at the team, then met Dr. Oliverio's eyes with her own. Randi McCafferty was in an uphill battle for her life. As was the baby. "All right, Doctors, the patients are all yours."

Thorne drove like a madman. He'd gotten the call from Slade less than three hours earlier that Randi was in a car accident in Glacier Park, here in Montana.

Thorne had been in Denver at the time, in a private business meeting at the offices of McCafferty International and he'd left abruptly. He told his secretary to handle everything and rearrange his schedule, then he grabbed a duffel bag he kept packed in a closet and had driven to the airfield. Within the hour he was airborne, flying the company jet directly to a private airstrip at the ranch. He hadn't bothered checking with his brothers again, instead he'd just taken the keys to a pickup that was waiting for him, tossed his duffel bag into the truck then taken off for Grand Hope and St. James Hospital where Randi was battling for her life.

He stepped on the accelerator, took a corner too fast and heard the tires squeal in protest. He didn't know what was going on; the phone call from his brother Slade had been broken up by static and eventually disconnected as cell service wasn't the greatest here. But he did understand that Randi's life was in question and that the name of the admitting doctor was Stevenson. Other than that, he knew nothing.

Night-darkened fields flew by. The wipers slapped sleet from the windshield and Thorne's jaw grew hard. What the devil had happened? Why was Randi in Montana when her job was in Seattle? What had she been doing in Glacier Park, how serious were her injuries—was she really in danger of losing her life? A piece of information that finally pierced his brain from his conversation with Slade burrowed deep in his brain. Hadn't his brother said something about Randi being pregnant? No way. He'd seen her less than six months ago. She was single, didn't even have a steady boyfriend. Or did she? What did he really know about his half sister?

Not a helluva lot.

Guilt ripped through him. *You should have kept in contact. You're the oldest. It was your responsibility. It wasn't her fault that her mother seduced your father over a quarter of a century before and broke up John Randall's first marriage. It wasn't her fault that you were just too damned busy with your own life.*

Dozens of questions burned through his conscience as he saw the lights of the town glowing in the distance.

He'd have his answers soon enough.

If Randi survived. His fingers clenched around the wheel and he found himself praying to a God he'd thought had long ago turned a deaf ear.

Thorne McCafferty.

The last person on earth Nicole wanted to deal with. But, no doubt, he'd be here. And soon. As she tore off her surgical gloves, she told herself to buck up. He was just another worried relative of a patient. Nothing more.

Nonetheless Nicole didn't like the idea of facing him again. There were too many old wounds, too much pain she'd never really resolved, too many emotions that she'd locked away years ago. She'd realized when she moved here after her divorce that she wouldn't be able to avoid Thorne forever. Grand Hope, despite its recent growth, was still a small town and John Randall McCafferty had been one of its leading citizens. His sons and daughter had grown up here.

So she'd have to face Thorne again. Big deal. It was only a matter of time. Unfortunately the situation—with his sister struggling for her life—wasn't the best of circumstances.

Nicole stuffed her stethoscope into her pocket and braced herself. Not only would she have to face Thorne again, but Randi McCafferty's other distraught brothers as well—men she'd known in a lifetime long, long ago when she'd dated their older brother. Her time with Thorne had been short, though. Intense and unforgettable, but thankfully short. His younger brothers, who had been caught up in their own lives at the time, might not remember her.

Don't believe it for a minute. When it comes to women, the McCafferty men were almost legendary in their conquests. They'd known all the girls in town.

Another painful old scar ripped open because Nicole had come to face the fact that she had been nothing more than another one of Thorne McCafferty's conquests, just another notch in his belt. A poor, shy, studious girl who had, for a short period one summer, caught his eye.

An archaic way of thinking, but oh, so torturously true.

Through a high window she saw the movement of stormy gray clouds that reflected her own gloomy thoughts. Though it was only October the weather service had been predicting snow.

She'd been in the ER all day, had nearly finished her shift when Randi McCafferty had been brought in.

Nicole's feet ached, her head pounded and the thought of a shower was pure heaven—a shower, a glass of chilled Chardonnay, a crackling fire and the twins cuddled with her under the quilt in her favorite rocker as she read them a bedtime story. She couldn't help but smile. "Later," she reminded herself. First she had serious business to attend to.

Randi, still in recovery, wasn't out of the woods yet, nor would she be for a while. Comatose and fighting for her life, Randi would spend the better part of the next week in ICU being monitored, her vital signs watched twenty-four hours.

The good news was that the baby, a robust boy, had survived the accident and a quick Cesarean birth. So far.

Sweaty and forcing a smile she didn't feel, Nicole slipped into her lab coat and pushed open the doors to the waiting room where two of Randi McCafferty's brothers sat on chairs, thumbing through magazines, their cups of coffee ignored on a corner table. They were both tall and lanky, handsome men with bold features, expressive eyes and worry written all over their faces.

Looking up as the doors opened, they dropped their magazines and climbed hastily to their feet.

"Mr. McCafferty?" she asked, though she'd spotted them instantly.

"I'm Matt," the taller of the two said as if he didn't recognize her. Maybe that was for the best. Keep the situation as professional as possible. Over six feet, with dark-brown eyes and near-black hair, Matt was dressed in jeans and a Western-cut plaid shirt with the sleeves rolled up. Cowboy boots covered his feet and a stir-stick, chewed flat, was wedged firmly in the corner of his mouth. "This is my brother Slade."

Again, no hint of recognition lit Slade's gaze. The youngest of the McCafferty brothers, he'd been tagged as the hellion. He was shorter than Matt by less than an inch and a thin scar jagged down one side of a face distinguished by hawkish features and deep-set, startling blue eyes. Wearing a flannel shirt, faded jeans and beat-up tennis shoes, he shifted nervously from one foot to the other.

"I'm Dr. Stevenson. I was on duty when your sister was brought into the ER."

"How's she doin'?" Slade asked anxiously. His eyes narrowed a bit as he looked at her and she realized he'd started the recognition process. It would take a while. It had been years since she'd seen him, her name was different, and there were dozens of women he would have to sift through unless she missed her guess.

She didn't have time for any of that now. Her job was to allay their fears while explaining about Randi's condition. "The surgery went well, but your sister was in pretty rough shape when she was brought in, comatose but in labor. Dr. Oliverio delivered your nephew and he seems healthy, though he'll be given a complete examination by a pediatrician here on staff.

"Randi's prognosis looks good, barring unforeseen complications, but she's survived an incredible trauma." As the brothers listened grimly, Nicole described Randi McCafferty's injuries—concussion, punctured lung, broken ribs, fractured jaw, nearly shattered femur—the list was long and grave. Concern etched in both brothers' features, storm clouds gathering in their eyes. Nicole explained the procedures that had been used to repair the damage, using as many lay terms as possible. Matt's dark skin paled slightly and he winced at one point, looking out the window and chewing the stir-stick until it was thin as parchment. On the other hand, the younger brother, Slade, stared her straight in the face, his jaw clenching, his blue eyes rarely blinking.

As she finished, Slade let out a soft whistle. "Damn it all to hell."

Matt rubbed the stubble on his chin and stared at her. "But she will make it. Right?"

"Unless she takes a turn for the worse, I think so. There's always a question with head injuries, but she's stabilized."

Slade frowned. "She's still in a coma."

"Yes. You understand that I'm the emergency room physician, and other doctors have taken over your sister's care. Each of them will contact you."

"When?" Slade demanded.

"As soon as they can."

She managed a reassuring smile. "I'm going off duty soon. Randi's other doctors will want to talk to you as well. I came out first because I knew you were anxious." *And because, damn it, I have a personal connection to your family.*

"Anxious doesn't begin to cover it," Matt said and glanced at his watch. "Shouldn't Thorne be getting here by now?" he asked his brother.

"He said he was on his way." Slade's gaze swung back to Nicole. "Our oldest brother." His eyebrows knit a bit. "He'll want a full report."

"No doubt," she said and Matt's eyes narrowed. "I knew him. Years ago."

She could almost see the wheels turning in the McCafferty brothers' minds, but the situation with their sister was too imminent, too dire, to be distracted.

"But Randi, she's gonna be okay," Matt said slowly, doubts shadowing his brown eyes.

"We're hopeful. As I said, she's stabilized, but there's always a question with head injuries." Nicole wished she could instill more confidence, allay their worries, but couldn't. "The truth is, it's gonna be touch-and-go for a while, but she'll be monitored around the clock."

"Oh, God," Slade whispered and the words sounded more like a prayer than a curse.

"I—we appreciate everything you and the other doctors have done." Matt shot his brother a look meant to silence him. "I just want you to know that whatever she needs, specialists, equipment, whatever, we want her to have it."

"She does," Nicole said firmly. In her estimation the staff, facilities and equipment at St. James were excellent, the best she'd seen in a town the size of Grand Hope.

"And the baby? You said he's okay, right?" Matt asked.

"He seems fine, but he's being observed for any signs of trauma. He's in pediatric ICU, as a precaution for the next few hours, just to make sure that he's strong. From all outward appearances, he's healthy and hale, we're just being doubly cautious especially since your sister was in labor and her water had broken before she got to the hospital. Dr. Oliverio will have more details and of course the pediatrician will get in touch with you as well."

"Damn," Slade whispered while Matt stood silent and stern.

"When can we see Randi?" Matt asked.

"Soon. She's still in Recovery. Once she's settled in ICU and her doctors are satisfied with her condition, she can have visitors—just immediate family—for a few minutes a day. One at a time. Again, her physician will let you know."

Matt nodded and Slade's fist clenched, but neither argued. Both brothers' jaws were square and set, the McCafferty resemblance impossible to ignore.

"You have to understand that Randi's comatose. She won't respond to you until she wakes up and I don't know when that will be—oh, here we go. One of Randi's doctors." Spying Dr. Oliverio walking down the hallway, Nicole took a few minutes to introduce the McCafferty brothers, then, excusing herself, made her way to her office.

It was a small room with one window. It barely had enough space for her desk and file cabinet. She usually transcribed her own notes and after shrugging out of her lab coat, flipped on the computer and spent nearly a half an hour at the keyboard writing a report on Randi McCafferty. As she finished, she reached for the phone. Dialing her home number by rote, she massaged the back of her neck and heard the strains of piped-in music for the first time since she'd walked into the hospital hours before.

"Hello?" Jenny Riley answered on the second ring. Jenny, a student at a local community college, watched Nicole's twins while she worked.

"Hi. It's Nicole. Just wanted to know what was going on. I'll be outta here in about—" she checked her watch and sighed "—probably another hour. Anything I should pick up on the way?"

"How about a ray or two of sunshine for Molly?" Jenny quipped. "She's been in a bad mood ever since she woke up from her nap."

"Has she?" Nicole grinned as she leaned back in her chair so far that it squeaked in protest. Molly, more precocious than her twin sister, was known to wake up grumpy while Mindy, the shier half of the two girls, always smiled, even when rousted from a nap.

"The worst."

"Am not!" a tiny, impertinent voice disagreed.

"Sure you are, but I love you anyway," Jenny said, her voice softer as she turned away from the phone.

"Am not the worst!"

Still grinning, Nicole rested a foot on her desk and sighed. The struggles of the day melted away when she thought of her daughters, two four-year-old dynamos who kept her running, the reasons she'd stayed sane after her divorce.

"Tell them I'll bring home pizza if they're good." She listened as Jenny relayed the message and heard a squeal of delight.

"They're pumped now," Jenny assured her and Nicole laughed just as there was a sharp rap on the door before it was pushed open abruptly. A tall man—maybe six foot three or four—nearly filled the frame. Her heart plummeted as she recognized Thorne.

"Dr. Stevenson?" he demanded, his face set and stern before recognition flared in his eyes and for the briefest of seconds she saw regret chase across his face.

"Look, Jenny, I've got to go," she said into the receiver as she hung up slowly, righted her chair and dropped her feet to the floor.

"Nikki?" he said, disbelieving.

Nicole stood but on her side of the desk, her barely five-foot-three-inch frame no match for his height. "Dr. Stevenson now."

"You're Randi's doctor?"

"The ER physician who admitted her." Why, after all the time that had passed and all the pain, did she still feel a ridiculous flutter of disappointment that he hadn't, in all the years since she'd last seen him, ever looked her up? It was silly. Stupid. Beyond naive. And it had no business here; not when his sister was fighting for her life. "I'm not her doctor, you understand. I helped stabilize her for surgery, then the team took over, but I did stop to speak with your brothers out of courtesy because I knew they'd been waiting a long time and the surgeons were still wrapping things up."

"I see." Thorne's handsome face had aged over the years. No longer were any vestiges of boyhood visible. His features were set and stern, matched only by the severity of his black suit, crisp white shirt and tie—the mark of a CEO of his own little empire. "I didn't know—didn't expect to find you here."

"I imagine not."

His eyes, a deep, troubled gray, held hers in a gaze that she knew was often daunting but now seemed weary and worried sick. "Did you see your brothers in ICU?" Nicole asked.

"I came directly here. Slade called, said a Dr. Stevenson was in charge, so when I got here, I asked for you at the information desk." As if reading the questions in her eyes, he added, "I wanted to know what I was dealing with before I saw Randi."

"Fair enough." She waved him into the office and motioned to the small plastic chair on the other side of the desk. "Have a seat. I'll tell you what I know, then you can talk to Randi's other doctors about her prognosis." As she reached for her lab coat, she leveled a gaze at him that had been known to shrink even the cockiest of interns. She wanted him to understand. She was no longer the needy little girl he'd dated, seduced and tossed aside. "But I think we should get something straight right now. As you can see this is my private office. Usually people knock, then wait for an answer, before they come barging in."

His jaw tightened. "I was in a hurry. But—fine. Next time I'll remember."

Oh, Thorne, there's never gonna be a next time. "Good."

"So she's in ICU?" Thorne asked.

"Yes." Nicole sketched out the details of Randi's emergency arrival to St. James, her conditions and the ensuing procedures. Thorne listened, his expression solemn, his gray eyes never leaving her face.

Once she was finished, he asked a few quick questions, loosened his tie and said, "Let's go."

"To ICU? Both of us?"

"Yes." He was on his feet.

Nicole bristled a bit, ready to fight fire with fire until she spied the hint of pain in his gaze and a twinge of some other emotion that bordered on guilt.

"I suppose I can do that," she agreed, hazarding a glance at her watch. She was running late, but being behind schedule came with the territory. As did dealing with worried relatives of her patients. "Let me make sure she's out of Recovery first." Nicole made a quick phone call, discovered that Randi had been transferred and explained that she and the patient's brother were on their way. For the duration of the short conversation she felt the weight of Thorne McCafferty's gaze upon her and she wondered if he remembered anything about the relationship that had changed the course of her life. Probably not. Once his initial shock at recognizing her had worn off, he was all business. "Okay," she said, hanging up. "All set. Matt and Slade have already seen Randi and the nurse on duty wasn't crazy about a third visitor, but I persuaded her."

"Are my brothers still here?"

"I don't know. They told the nurse they'd be back but didn't say when." She adjusted her lab coat and rounded the desk. He had the manners to hold the door for her and as they swept down the hallways he kept up with her fast pace, his long strides equal to two of hers. She'd forgotten that about him. But then she'd tried to erase every memory she'd ever had of him.

A foot taller than she, intimidating and forceful, Thorne walked the same way he faced life—with a purpose. She wondered if he'd ever had a frivolous moment in his life. Years before, she'd realized that even those stolen hours with her had been all a part of Thorne's plan.

At the elevator, Nicole waited as a gurney carrying a frail-looking elderly woman connected to an IV drip was pushed into the hallway by an aide, then she stepped inside. The doors shut. She and Thorne were alone. For the first time in years. He stood ramrod stiff beside her and if he noticed the intimacy of the elevator car, he didn't show it. His face was set, his shoulders square, his gaze riveted to the panel displaying the floor numbers.

Silly as it was, Nicole couldn't remember having ever been so uncomfortable.

The elevator jerked to a stop and as they walked through the carpeted hallways, Thorne finally broke the silence. "On the telephone, Slade mentioned something about Randi not making it."

"There's always that chance when injuries are as severe as your sister's." They'd reached the doors of the Intensive Care Unit and she, reminding herself to remain professional at all times, angled her head upward to stare straight into his steel-colored eyes. "But she's young and strong, getting the best medical care we can provide, so there's no need to borrow trouble, or voice your concerns around your sister. She's co-matose, yes, but we don't know what she does or doesn't hear or feel. Please, for her sake, keep all your worries and doubts to yourself." He seemed about to protest and by instinct, Nicole reached forward and touched his hand, her fingers encountering skin that was hard and surprisingly callused. "We're doing everything we can, Thorne," she said and half expected him to pull away. "Your sister's fighting for her life. I know you want what's best for her, so whenever you're around her, I want you to be positive, nurturing and supportive. Okay?"

He nodded curtly but his lips tightened a bit. He wasn't and never had been used to taking orders or advice—not from anyone. "Any questions?"

"Just one," he said slowly.

"What?"

"My sister is important to me. Very important. You know that. So I want to be assured that she's getting the best medical care that money can buy. That means the best hospital, the best staff, and especially the best doctor."

Realizing she was still holding his hand, she let go and felt a welling sense of disappointment. It wasn't the first time her ability had been questioned and certainly wouldn't be the last, but for some reason she had hoped that Thorne McCafferty would trust her and her dedication. "What are you trying to say?" she asked.

"I need to know that the people here, the doctors assigned to Randi's care are the best in the country—or the whole damned world for that matter."

Self-impressed, rich, corporate bastard.

"That's what everyone wants for their loved ones, Thorne."

"The difference is," he said, "I can afford it."

Her heart sank. Why had she thought she recognized a bit of tenderness in his eyes? Foolish, foolish, idealistic woman. "I'm a damned good doctor, Thorne. So are the others here. This hospital has won awards. It's small but attracts the best, I can personally assure you of that. Doctors who have once practiced in major cities from Atlanta to Seattle, New York to L.A., have ended up here because they were tired of the rat race...." She let her words sink in and wished she'd just bitten her tongue. Thorne could think whatever he damn well pleased.

"Let's go inside. Now, remember, keep it positive and when I say time's up, don't argue. Just leave. You can see her again tomorrow." She waited, but he didn't offer any response or protest, just clenched his jaw so hard a muscle jumped. "Got it?" she asked.

"Got it."

"Then we'll get along just fine," she said, but she didn't believe it for a minute. Some things didn't change and she and Thorne McCafferty were like oil and water—they would never mix; never agree.

She pressed a button and placed her face in the window so that a nurse inside could see her, then waited to be admitted. As the electronic doors hummed open, she felt Thorne's gaze center on the back of her neck beneath the upsweep of her hair. Without making a sound, he followed her inside. She wondered how long he'd obey the hospital's and the doctor's terms.

The answer, she knew, was blindingly simple.

Not long enough.

Thorne McCafferty hadn't changed. He was the type of man who played by his own rules.

Chapter 2

Oh, God, this couldn't *be Randi.* Thorne gazed down at the
small, inert form lying on the bed and he felt sick inside—
weak. Tubes and wires ran from her body to monitors and
equipment with gauges and digital readouts that he didn't understand. Her head was wrapped in gauze, her body draped
in sterile-looking sheets, one leg elevated and surrounded by
a partial cast. The portions of her face that he could see were
bruised and swollen.

His throat was thick with emotion as he stood in the tiny
sheet-draped cubicle that opened at the foot of the bed to
the nurses' station. His fists clenched impotently, and a quiet,
damning rage burned through his soul. How could this have
happened? What was she doing up at Glacier Park? Why had
her vehicle slid off the road?

The heart monitor beeped softly and steadily yet he wasn't
reassured as he stared down at this stranger who was his half
sister. A dozen memories darted wildly through his mind and

though at one time, when she was first born, he'd been envious and resentful of his father's namesake, he'd never been able to really dislike her.

Randi had been so outgoing and alive, her eyes sparkling with mischief, her laughter contagious, a girl who wore her heart on her sleeve. Guileless and believing that she had every right to be the apple of her father's eye, Randi Penelope McCafferty had bulldozed her way through life and into almost anyone's heart she came across—including those of her reluctant, hellions of half brothers who had sworn while their new stepmother was pregnant that they would despise the baby who, as far as their tunnel-visioned young eyes could see, was the reason their own parents had divorced so bitterly.

Now, twenty-six years later, Thorne cringed at his ill-focused hostility. He'd been thirteen when his half sister had summoned the gall to arrive, red-faced and screaming, into this world. Thorne had been thoroughly disgusted at the thought of his father and the younger woman he'd married actually "doing it" and creating this love child. Worse yet was the scandal surrounding her birth date, barely six months after J. Randall's second nuptials. It had been too humiliating to think about and he'd taken a lot of needling from his classmates who, having always been envious of the McCafferty name, wealth and reputation, had found some dark humor in the situation.

Hell, it had been a long time ago and now, standing in the sterile hospital unit with patients barely clinging to life, his own sister hooked up to machines that helped her survive, Thorne felt a fool. All the mortification and shame Thorne had endured at Randi's conception and birth had disappeared from the first time he'd caught his first real glimpse of her little, innocent face.

Staring into that fancy lace-covered bassinet in the master bedroom at the ranch, Thorne had been ready to hate the baby on sight. After all, for five or six months she'd been the source of all his anger and humiliation. But Thorne had been instantly taken with the little infant with her dark hair, bright eyes and flailing fists. She'd looked as mad to be there as he'd felt that she'd disrupted his life. She'd wailed and cried and put up a fuss that couldn't be believed. The sound that had been emitted from her tiny voice box—like a wounded cougar—had bored right to the heart of him.

He'd hidden his feelings, kept his fascination with the baby to himself and made sure no one, least of all his brothers and father knew how he really felt about the infant, that he'd been beguiled by her from the very beginning of her life.

Now, as he watched her labored breathing and noticed the blood-encrusted bandages that were placed over her swollen face, he felt like a heel. He'd let her slip away from him, hadn't kept in touch because it hadn't been convenient for either of them and now she lay helpless, the victim of an accident that hadn't yet been explained to him.

"You can talk to her," a soft, feminine voice said to him and he looked up to see Nicole looking at him with round, compassionate eyes. The color of aged whiskey and surrounded by thick lashes, they seemed to stare right to his very soul. As they had when he was twenty-two and she'd been barely seventeen. God, that seemed a lifetime ago. "No one knows if she can hear you or not, but it certainly wouldn't hurt." Her lips curved into a tender, encouraging smile and though he felt like a fool, he nodded, surprised not only that she'd matured into a full-fledged woman—but that she was a doctor, no less, and one who could bark out orders or offer compassionate whispers with an equal amount of command. This was Nikki Sanders, the girl who had nearly roped his heart? The one girl who had nearly convinced him to stay in Grand

Hope and scrape out a living on the ranch? Leaving her had been tough, but he'd done it. He'd had to.

As if sensing he might need some privacy, she turned back to the chart on which she was taking notes.

Thorne dragged his gaze from the curve of Nikki's neck, though he couldn't help but notice that one strand of gold-streaked hair fell from the knot she'd pinned at her crown. Maybe she wasn't so buttoned-down after all.

Grabbing the cool metal railing at the side of Randi's hospital bed, he concentrated on his sister again. He cleared his throat. "Randi?" he whispered, feeling like an utter fool. "Hey, kid, can you hear me? It's me. Thorne." He swallowed hard as she lay motionless. Old memories flashed through his mind in a kaleidoscope of pictures. It had been Thorne who had found her crying after she'd fallen off her bike when she'd been learning to ride at five. He'd returned home from college for a quick visit, had discovered her at the edge of the lane, her knees scraped, her cheeks dusty and tracked with tears, her pride bitterly wounded as she couldn't get the hang of the two-wheeler. After carrying her to the house, Thorne had plucked the gravel from her knees, then fixed the bent wheel of her bike and helped her keep the damned two-wheeler from toppling every time she tried to learn.

When Randi had been around nine or ten, Thorne had spent an afternoon teaching her how to throw a baseball like a boy—a curveball and a slider. She'd spent hours working at it, throwing that damned old ball at the side of the barn until the paint had peeled off.

Years later, Thorne had returned home one weekend to find his tomboy of a half sister dressed in a long pink dress as she'd waited for her date to the senior prom. Her hair, a rich mahogany color, had been twisted onto the top of her head. She'd stood tall on high heels with a poise and beauty that had shocked him. Around her neck she'd worn a gold chain with the same locket J. Randall had given Randi's mother on their wedding day. Randi had been downright breathtaking. Exuberant. Full of life.

And now she lay unmoving, unconscious, her body battered as she struggled to breathe.

Nicole returned to the side of the bed. Gently she shone a penlight into Randi's eyes, then touched Randi's bare wrist with probing, professional fingers. Little worry lines appeared between her sharply arched brows. Her upper teeth sank into her lower lip as if she were deep in thought. It was an unconsciously sexy movement and he looked away quickly, disgusted at the turn of his thoughts.

From the corner of his eye he noticed her making notations on Randi's chart as she moved to the central area where a nurses' station had full view of all of the patients' beds. Like spokes of a wheel the separated "rooms" radiated from the central desk area. Pale-green privacy drapes separated each bed from the others and nurses in soft-soled shoes moved quietly from one area to the next.

"Why don't you try to speak with her again?" Nicole suggested quietly, not even glancing his way.

He felt so awkward. So out of place. So big. So damned healthy.

"Go on," she encouraged, then turned her back on him completely.

His fingers tightened over the rail. What could he say? What did it matter? Thorne leaned forward, closer to the bed where his sister lay so still. "Randi," he whispered in a voice that nearly cracked with emotions he tried desperately to repress. He touched one of her fingers and she didn't respond, didn't move. "Can ya hear me? Well, you'd better." Hell, he was bad at this sort of thing. He shifted so that his fingers laced with hers. "How ya doin'?"

Of course she didn't answer and as the heart monitor beeped a steady, reassuring beat, he wished to heaven that he'd been a better older brother to her, that he'd been more involved with her life. He noticed the soft rounding of her abdomen beneath the sheet stretched over her belly. She'd been pregnant. Now had a child. A mother at twenty-six. Yet no one in the family knew of any man with whom she'd been involved. "Can... can you hear me? Huh, kiddo?"

Oh, this was inane. She wasn't going to respond. Couldn't. He doubted she heard a word he said, or sensed that he was near. He felt like a fool and yet he was stuck like proverbial glue, adhering to her, their fingers linked, as if someway he could force some of his sheer brute strength into her tiny body, could by his indomitable will make her strong, healthy and safe.

He caught a glance from Nicole, an unspoken word that told him his time was up.

Clearing his throat again, he pulled his hand from hers, then gently tapped the end of her index finger with his. "You hang in there, okay? Matt, Slade and I, we're all pulling for you, kid, so you just give it your best. And you've got a baby, now—a little boy who needs you. Like we all do, kid." *Oh, hell, this was impossible. Ludicrous.* And yet he said, "I, uh, I— we're all pullin' for you and I'll be back soon. Promise." The last word nearly cracked.

Randi didn't move and the back of Thorne's eyes burned in a way they hadn't since the day he learned his father had died. Shoving his hands into the pockets of his coat, he crossed the room and walked through the doors that opened as he approached. He sensed, rather than saw Nicole as she joined him.

"Give it to me straight," he said as they strode along a corri-

dor with bright lights and windows overlooking a parking lot.
Outside it was dark as night, black clouds showering rain that
puddled on the asphalt and dripped from the few scraggly trees
that were planted near the building. "What are her chances?"

Nicole's steps, shorter by half than his own, were quick. She
managed to keep up with him though her brow was knitted,
her eyes narrowed in thought. "She's young and strong. She
has as good a chance as anyone."

An aide pushing a man in a wheelchair passed them going
the opposite direction and somewhere a phone rang. Piped-
in music competed with the hum of soft conversation and the
muted rattle of equipment being wheeled down other corridors. As they reached the elevator, Thorne touched Nicole
lightly on the elbow.

"I want to know if my sister is going to make it."

Color flushed her cheeks. "I don't have a crystal ball, you
know, Thorne. I realize that you and your brothers want pre-
cise, finite answers. I just don't have them. It's too early."

"But she will live?" he asked, desperate to be reassured. He,
who was always in control, was hanging on the words of a
small woman whom he'd once come close to loving.

"As I said before, barring any unforeseen—"

"I heard you the first time. Just tell me the truth. Point-
blank. Is my sister going to make it?"

She looked about to launch into him, then took a deep
breath. "I believe so. We're all doing everything possible for
her." As if reading the concern in his eyes, she sighed and
rubbed the kinks from the back of her neck. Her face softened a bit and he couldn't help but notice the lines of strain
surrounding her eyes, the intelligence in those gorgeous am-
ber-colored irises and he felt the same male interest he had
years ago, when she was a senior in high school. "Look, I'm
sorry. I don't mean to be evasive. Really." She tucked an er-

rant lock of hair behind her ear. "I wish I could tell you that Randi will be fine, that within a couple of weeks she'll be up walking around, laughing, going back to work, taking care of that baby of hers and that everything will be all right. But I can't do that. She's suffered a lot of trauma. Internal organs are damaged, bones broken. Her concussion is more than just a little bump on her head. I won't kid you. There's a chance that if she does survive, there may be brain damage. We just don't know yet."

His heart nearly stopped. He'd feared for his sister's life, but never once considered that she might survive only to live her life with less mental capabilities than she had before. She'd always been so smart—"Sharp as a tack," their father had bragged often enough.

"Shouldn't she see a specialist?" Thorne asked.

"She's seeing several. Dr. Nimmo is one of the best neurosurgeons in the Northwest. He's already examined her. He usually works out of Bitterroot Memorial and just after Randi's surgery he was called away on another emergency, but he'll phone you. Believe me. Your sister's getting the best medical care we can provide, and it's as good as you're going to get anywhere. I think we've already had this conversation, so you're just going to have to trust me. Now, is there anything else?"

"Just that I want to be kept apprised of her situation. If there is any change, any change at all in her condition or that of the child, I expect to be contacted immediately." He withdrew his wallet and slid a crisp business card from the smooth leather. "This is my business phone number and this—" he found a pen in the breast pocket of his suit jacket and scribbled another number on the back of his card "—is the number of the ranch. I'll be staying there." He handed her the card and watched as one of her finely arched brows elevated a bit.

"You expect *me* to contact you. Me, personally."

"I—I'd appreciate it," he said and touched her shoulder. She glanced down at his hand and little lines converged between her eyebrows. "As a personal favor."

Her lips pulled into a tight knot. Color stained her cheeks. "Because we were so close to each other?" she asked, gold eyes snapping as she pulled her shoulder away.

He dropped his hand. "Because you care. I don't know the rest of the staff and I'm sure that they're fine. All good doctors. But I *know* I can trust you."

"You don't know me at all."

"I did once."

She swallowed hard. "Let's keep that out of this," she said. "But, fine...I'll keep you informed."

"Thanks." He offered her a smile and she rolled her eyes.

"Just don't try to smooth-talk or con me, Thorne, okay? I'll tell it to you straight, but don't, not for a minute, try to play on my sympathies and, just to make sure you're getting this, I'm not doing it for old times' sake or anything the least bit maudlin or nostalgic, okay? If there's a change, you'll be notified immediately."

"And I'll be in contact with you."

"I'm not her doctor, Thorne."

"But you'll be here."

"Most of the time. Now, if you'll excuse me, I've really got to run." She started to turn away, but he caught the crook of her elbow, his fingers gripping the starched white coat.

"Thanks, Nikki," he said and to his amazement she blushed, a deep shade of pink stealing up her cheeks.

"No problem. It comes with the job," she said, then glanced down at his fingers and pulled away. With clipped steps she disappeared through a door marked Staff Only. Thorne watched the door swing shut behind her and fought the urge to ignore the warning and follow her. Why he couldn't imagine. There was nothing more to say—the conversation was finished, but as he tucked his wallet back into his pocket, he experienced a foolish need to catch up with her—to catch up with his past. He had dozens of questions for her and he'd probably never ask one. "Fool," he muttered to himself and felt a headache begin to pound at the base of his skull. Nicole Stevenson was a doctor here at the hospital, nothing more. And she had his number. Big-time. She'd made that clear enough.

Yes, she was a woman; a beautiful woman, a smart woman, a seemingly driven woman, a woman with whom he'd made love once upon a time, but their affair was long over.

And she could be married, you idiot. Her name is Stevenson now, remember?

But he'd checked her ring finger. It had been bare. Why he'd bothered, he didn't understand; didn't want to assess. But he was satisfied that she was no longer another man's wife. Nonetheless she was off-limits. Period. A complicated, beguiling woman.

He stepped onto the elevator, pounded the button for the floor of the maternity level and tried to shove all thoughts of Nikki Sanders—Dr. Nicole Stevenson—from his mind.

But it didn't work; just as it hadn't worked years before when he'd left her. Without so much as an explanation. How could he have explained that he'd left her because staying in Grand Hope, being close to her, touching her and loving her made his departure all that much harder? He'd left because he'd had a deep sense of insight that if he'd stayed much longer, he would never have been able to tear himself away from her, that he never would have gone out into the world and proved to himself and his father that he could make his own mark.

"Hell," he cursed. He'd been a fool and let the only woman who had come close to touching a part of him he didn't want to know existed—that nebulous essence that was his soul—

get away from him. He'd figured that out a couple of years later, but Thorne had never been one to look back and second-guess himself. He'd told himself there would be another woman someday—when he was ready.

Of course he'd never found her.

And he hadn't even worried about it until he'd seen Nikki Sanders again, remembered how it felt to kiss her, and the phrase *what if* had entered his mind. If he'd stuck by her, married her, had children by her, his father wouldn't have gone to his grave without grandchildren. "Stop it," he growled to himself.

Nicole let out her breath as she walked through the maze that was St. James. She was still unsettled and shaken. Used to dealing with anxious, sometimes even grieving relatives, she hadn't expected that she would have such an intense and disturbing reaction to Thorne McCafferty.

"He's just a man," she grumbled, taking the stairs. "That's all."

But she met men every day of the week. All kinds from all walks of life and none of them caused anywhere near this kind of response.

Was it because he had been her first lover? Because he nearly broke her heart? Because he left her, not because of another woman, not because he had any good reason, just because she didn't mean enough to him?

"Fool," she muttered under her breath as she pushed open the door to the floor where her office was housed.

"Excuse me?" a janitor who was walking down the hall asked.

"Nothing. Talking to myself." She offered the man an embarrassed smile and continued to her office, where she plopped into her desk chair and stared at the monitor of her computer. The notes that had filled her head only an hour earlier seemed scattered to the wind and she couldn't budge thoughts of Thorne from her brain. In her silly, very feminine mind's eye she saw him with the clarity of young, loving eyes. Oh, she'd adored him. He was older. Sophisticated. Rich. One of the McCafferty scoundrels—bad boys every one, who had been known to womanize, smoke, drink and generally raise hell in their youths.

Handsome, arrogant and cocky, Thorne had found easy access to her naive heart. The only daughter of a poor, hard-working woman who pushed for and expected perfection, Nicole had, at seventeen, been ripe for rebellion. And then she'd stumbled onto Thorne.

She'd fallen stupidly head over heels in love, nearly throwing all of her own hopes and dreams away on the rakish college boy.

Blowing her bangs out of her eyes she shook her head to dislodge those old, painful and humiliating memories. She'd been so young. So mindlessly sophomoric, caught up in romantic fantasies with the least likely candidate for a long-term relationship in the state.

"Don't even think about it," she reminded herself, moving the mouse of her computer and studying the screen while memories of making love to him under the star-studded Montana sky swept through her mind. His body had been young, hard, muscular and sheened in sweat. His eyes had been silver with the moon glow, his hair unkempt.

And now he was some kind of corporate hotshot.

Like Paul. She glanced down at her hands and was relieved to see that the groove her wedding ring had once carved in her finger had disappeared in the past two years. Paul Stevenson had been climbing the corporate ladder so fast, he'd lost track of his wife and young daughters.

She suspected Thorne wasn't much different.

When she'd moved back to Grand Hope a year ago, she'd known his family was still scattered around the state, but she'd thought Thorne was long gone and hadn't expected to come face-to-face with him. According to the rumors circulating through Grand Hope like endless eddies and whirlpools, Thorne had finished law school, linked up with a firm in Missoula, then moved to California and finally wound up in Denver where he was the executive for a multinational corporation. He'd never married, had no children that anyone knew of, and had been linked to several beautiful, wealthy, career-minded women over the years, none of whom had lasted on his arm too long before they'd been replaced with a newer model.

Yep. Thorne was a lot like Paul.

Except that you're still attracted to him, aren't you? One look, and your gullible heart started pounding all over again.

"Stop it!" she growled and forced herself to concentrate. This wasn't like her. She'd been known to be single-minded when it came to her work or her children and she found the distraction of Thorne McCafferty more than a little disconcerting. She couldn't, *wouldn't* fall victim to his insidious charms again. With renewed conviction, she ignored any lingering thoughts of Thorne and undid the clasp holding her hair in place. No doubt she'd have to deal with him later and at the thought her heart alternately leaped and sank. "Great," she told herself as she finger-combed her hair. "Just...great."

Right now facing Thorne again seemed an insurmountable challenge.

Twenty minutes later Thorne was still smarting from the tongue-lashing he'd received from a very sturdily built and strong-willed nurse who allowed him one glimpse of Randi's infant, then ushered him out of the pediatric intensive care unit. Thorne had peered through thick glass to an airy room where two newborns were sleeping in plastic bassinets. Randi's boy had lain under lamps, a shock of red-blond hair sticking upward, his tiny lips moving slightly as he breathed. To his utter surprise, Thorne had felt an unexpected pull on his heartstrings and he'd promptly advised himself that idiocy ran in the McCafferty family. Nonetheless Thorne had stared at the baby, so tiny, so mystifying, so innocent and unaware of all the turmoil he had caused.

As he'd left the pediatric unit Thorne wondered about the man who had fathered the child. Who was he? Shouldn't he be contacted? Was Randi in love with him? Or...had she hidden her pregnancy and the fact that she was involved with someone from her brothers for a reason?

Thorne didn't care. He'd find out about the kid's father if it killed him. And he couldn't sit idle just waiting for Randi to recover. No, there was too much to do. Ramming his hands into his coat pockets, he took a flight of stairs to the first floor.

"Think," he ordered himself and a plan started forming in his mind. First he had to make sure that both Randi and her child were on the road to recovery, then he'd hire a private investigator to look into his sister's life. Wincing at the thought of prying into Randi's private business, he rationalized that he had no choice. In her current state, Randi couldn't help herself. Nor could she care for her child.

Thorne would have to locate the baby's father, interview the son of a bitch, then set up a trust fund for the kid.

Already planning how to attack the "Randi situation" as he'd begun to think of it, he shouldered open a door to the parking lot. Outside, the wind raged. Ice-cold raindrops beat down from a leaden sky. He hiked his collar more closely around his neck and ducked his head. Skirting puddles, he strode toward his vehicle—a Ford pickup that was usually garaged at the ranch's airstrip.

Then he saw her.

Running to her car, her briefcase held over her head, Dr. Nicole Stevenson—Nikki Sanders once upon a time—dashed toward a white four-wheel-drive that was parked in a nearby lot.

Rain ran down his neck and dripped off his nose as he watched her. Her hair was no longer pinned to the back of her head, but caught in the wind. Her stark white lab coat had been replaced by a long leather jacket cinched firmly around her waist.

Without thinking, Thorne swept across the puddle-strewn lot. "Nikki!"

She looked up and he was stunned. "Oh. Thorne." With raindrops caught in the sweep of her eyelashes and her blond-streaked hair tossed around her face in soft layers, she was more gorgeous than he remembered. Raindrops slipped down sculpted cheekbones to a small mouth that was set in a startled pout.

For a split second he thought of kissing her, but quickly shoved that ridiculous thought from his mind.

She jabbed her key into the SUV's lock. "What're you doing lurking around out here?"

"Maybe I was waiting for you," he said automatically—actually *flirting* with her. For the love of God, what had gotten into him?

He saw her eyes round a bit, then one corner of her mouth lifted in sarcasm. "Try again."

"Okay, how about this? I just got finished dealing with Nurse Ratched up in Pediatrics and was tossed out on my ear."

"Someone intimidated you?" One eyebrow lifted in disbelief. "I don't think so." If she'd been teasing him before,

she'd obviously thought better of it and her smile fell away.
She yanked open the door and the interior light blinked on.
"Now...was there something you wanted?"

You, he thought, then chided himself. What the devil was
he thinking? What they'd shared was long over. "I didn't get
your home number."

"I didn't give it to you."

"Because of your husband?"

"What? No." She shook her head. "There is no husband,
not anymore." She was standing between the car and open
door, waiting, her hair turning dark with the rain. His heart
raced. She was single. "You can reach me here," she said. "If
it's an emergency, the hospital will page me."

"I'd feel better if I could—"

"Look, Thorne," she said pointedly. "I understand that
you're a man used to getting your way, of being in charge, of
making things happen, but this time you can't, okay? At least
not with me, not any more, nor with St. James Hospital. So,
if there's nothing else, you'll have to excuse me." Her eyes
weren't the least bit warm and yet her lips, slick with rainwa-
ter, just begged to be kissed.

And, damn it, he reacted. Knowing that she'd probably slap
him silly, he grabbed her, hauled her body close to his and
bent his head so that his lips were suspended just above hers.
"Okay, Nikki," he said as he felt her tense. "I excuse you."
Then he kissed her, pressed his mouth over hers and felt a second's surrender when her lips parted and her breath mingled
with his as rain drenched them both. The scent of her perfume teased his nostrils and memories of making love to her
over and over again burned through his brain. Dear God, how
she'd responded to him then, just as she was now. He was lost
in the feel of her and old emotions escaped from the place

where he'd so steadfastly locked them long ago. With a groan, he kissed her harder, deeper, his arms tightening around her.

Her entire body stiffened. She jerked her head away as if she'd been burned. "Don't," she warned, her voice husky, her lips trembling a bit. She swallowed hard, then leaned back to glare up at him. "Don't ever do this again. This—" she raised a hand only to let it fall "—this was uncalled-for and...and entirely...*entirely* inappropriate."

"Entirely," he agreed, not releasing her.

"I mean it, Thorne."

"Why? Because I scare you?"

"Because whatever you and I shared together is over."

He lifted a doubting eyebrow as rain drizzled down his face. "Then why—?"

"Over!" Her eyes narrowed and she pulled out of his embrace. Though he wanted nothing more than to drag her close again, he let her go and tamped down the fire that had stormed through his blood, the pulse of lust that had thudded in his brain and caused a heat to burn in his loins. "I don't know what happened to you in the past seventeen years, but believe me, you should take some lessons in subtlety."

"Should I? Maybe you could give them to me."

"Me?" She let out a whisper of a laugh. "Right. Just don't hold your breath."

She slid into the interior of the car and reached for the door handle. Before she could yank the door closed, he said, "Okay, maybe I was outta line."

"Oh? You think?"

"I know."

"Good, then it won't happen again." She crammed her key into the ignition, muttered something about self-important bullheaded men, twisted her wrist and sent him a look that was meant to cut to the quick. The SUV's engine sputtered, then died. "Don't do this to me," she said and he wondered if she was talking to him or her rig. "Don't do this to me now." She turned the key again and the engine ground but didn't catch. "Damn."

"If you need a ride—"

"It'll start. It's just temperamental."

"Like its owner."

"If you say so." She took a deep breath, snapped her seat belt into place and grabbed the handle of her door. "Good night, Thorne." She yanked the door closed, turned the key again and finally the rig roared to life. Pressing on the gas pedal, she revved the engine and rolled down the window. "I'll let you know if there are any changes in your sister's condition." With that she tore out of the parking lot and Thorne, watching the taillights disappear, mentally kicked himself.

He'd been a fool to grab her.

And yet he knew he'd do it again.

If given half a chance.

Yep, he'd do it in a heartbeat.

Chapter 3

"God help me," Nicole whispered, trying to understand why in the world Thorne would embrace her so intimately and more to the point, why didn't she stop him. *Because you wanted him to, you idiot.*

As she wheeled out of the parking lot, she glanced in the rearview mirror, and saw him standing beneath a security light. Tall, broad-shouldered, bareheaded, rain dripping from the tip of his nose and the hem of his coat, he watched her leave. "Cocky son of a gun," she muttered, flipping on her blinker and joining the thin stream of traffic. She hoped Thorne Almighty McCafferty got soaked to the skin. She switched her windshield wipers to a faster pace to keep up with the rain. Who was he to barge in on her, to question her and the hospital's integrity and then…and then have the audacity, the sheer arrogance, to grab her as if she were some weak-willed, starry-eyed, spineless…ninny!

Oh, like the girl you once were, the one he remembered?

She blushed and her fingers curled around the steering wheel in a death grip. She'd worked hard for years to overcome her shyness, to become the confident, scholarly, take-charge emergency room physician she was today and Thorne McCafferty seemed hell-bent to change all that. Well, she wouldn't let him. No way. No how. She wasn't the little girl he'd left a lifetime ago—her broken heart had mended.

As she braked for a red light, she flipped on the radio, fumbled with the stations until she heard a melody that was familiar—Whitney Houston singing something she should know—and tried to calm down. Why she let Thorne get to her, she didn't understand.

She cranked the wheel and turned into a side street where the neon lights and Western facade of Montana Joe's Pizza Parlor came into view.

She pulled into the lot, raced inside and waited in line between five or six other patrons whose raincoats, parkas and ski jackets dripped water onto the tile floor in front of the take-out counter. A gas flame hissed in the fireplace in one corner of the room that was divided by fences into different seating areas. Pickaxes and shovels and other mining memorabilia were tacked to bare cedar walls and in one corner, Montana Joe, a stuffed bison, stared with glassy eyes at the patrons who were listening to Garth Brooks's latest hit while drinking beer and eating hot, stringy pizza made with Joe's "secret" tomato sauce.

As Nicole stood in line and dug into her wallet to check how much cash she was carrying, she couldn't help but overhear some of the conversation of the other patrons. Two men in front of her were discussing the previous Friday's high school football game. From the sound of it the Grand Hope Wolverines were edged out by an arch rival in a nearby town though there was some dispute over a few of the calls. Typical.

Other conversations buzzed around her and she heard the

name McCafferty more often than she wanted to. "Terrible accident...half sister, you know...pregnant, but no mention of a father and no husband...always was bad blood in that family...what goes around comes around, I tell you..."

Nicole grabbed a menu from the counter and turned her attention from the gossip that swirled around her. Though Grand Hope had grown by leaps and bounds in the past few years and had become a major metropolis by Montana standards, it was still, at its heart, a small town, where many of the citizens knew each other. She placed her order, lingered near the jukebox and listened to three or four songs ranging from Patsy Cline to Wynona Judd, then, once her name was called, picked up her pizza and refused to think about any member of the McCafferty family—especially Thorne. He was off-limits. Period. The reason she'd responded to his kiss was simple. It had been over two years since she'd kissed any man and at least five since she'd felt even the tiniest spark of passion. She didn't even want to think how long it had been since she'd been consumed with desire—that particular thought led her back to a path that she didn't want to follow, a path heading straight back to her youth and Thorne. She was just susceptible right now, that was all. Nothing more. It had nothing to do with chemistry. Nothing.

Once in her SUV again, she twisted on the key and the engine refused to fire. "Come on, come on," she muttered. She tried again, pumping the gas frantically and mentally chiding herself for not taking the rig into the shop for its regular maintenance. "You can do it," she encouraged and finally, on the fourth attempt, the engine caught. "Tomorrow," she promised, patting the dash as if comforting the vehicle, as if that would help. "I'll take you in. Promise."

On the road again, Nicole drove through the side streets to her little cottage on the outskirts of town. Her stomach rumbled as the tangy scents of melting cheese and spicy sauce filled the rig's interior and her mind, damn it, ran back to Thorne and the feel of his lips on hers. He was everything she despised in a man: arrogant, competitive, in control and determined—a real corporate Type A and the kind of man she had learned to avoid like the plague. But beneath his layer of pride and his take-charge mentality, she'd caught glimpses of a more complex man, a gentler soul who stumbled through the awkwardness of talking to his comatose sister. He'd tried to communicate with Randi, the back of his neck flushing in embarrassment, his steely gray eyes conveying a sense of raw pain at his sister's condition—as if he somehow blamed himself for her accident.

"Don't read more into it than there is," she warned herself as she cranked the wheel and braked in her driveway. She pulled to a stop in front of her garage and made a mental note that between helping at preschool, the twins' dance lessons, the housework and the grocery shopping, she should call a roofer for a bid on the sagging roof.

Juggling her briefcase and boxed pizza, she made a mad dash to the back porch and was able to unlock the door, then shove it open with her hip.

Patches, her black-and-white cat, streaked through the opening and Nicole nearly tripped on the speeding feline. Tiny footsteps thundered through the house. "Mommy! Mommy! Mommy!" the twins cried, flying pell-mell into the kitchen and sliding on the yellowed linoleum as Patches slunk down the bedroom hallway. Molly and Mindy were dressed in identical pink-and-white-checked sleepers that zipped up the front and covered their feet in attached slippers. Their hair was wet and curled in dark-brown ringlets around cherubic faces and bright brown eyes.

Nicole slid the pizza onto a counter, knelt and opened her

arms wide. The four-year-old imps nearly bowled her over. "Miss me?" she asked.

"Yeth," Mindy said shyly, nodding her head and smiling.

"You got pizza?" Molly demanded. "I'm hungry."

"I sure do. Lots of it." She dropped kisses on each wet head, then standing once again, she stripped out of her coat and hung it in a tiny closet near the eating alcove.

Jenny Riley appeared in the archway separating the kitchen from the dining room. Tall and willowy, with long straight black hair and a nose ring, the twenty-year-old had been the twins' nanny since Nicole had moved to Grand Hope.

"How were they today?" Nicole asked.

"Miserable as usual," Jenny said, her green eyes twinkling, sarcasm lacing her words.

"Were not!" Molly said, planting her little fists on her hips. "We was good."

"Were," Nicole corrected. "You were good."

"Yeth," Mindy said, nodding agreement with her precocious sister. "Real good."

Jenny laughed and bent down to retie the laces of her elevated tennis shoes, "Oh, okay, I lied," she admitted. "You were good. Both of you. Very good."

"It's not nice to lie!" Molly said with a toss of her wet curls.

"I know, I know, it won't happen again," Jenny promised, straightening and slinging the strap of her fringed leather purse over her shoulder.

"Want a piece of pizza?" Nicole offered. Using her fingers and a spatula she'd grabbed from a hook over the stove, she slid piping hot slices onto paper plates. The girls scrambled onto the booster seats. Nicole licked a piece of melted cheese from her fingers and looked questioningly at Jenny.

"No thanks, Mom's got dinner waiting and—" Jenny winked broadly "—I've got a hot date after."

"Oooh," Nicole said, licking gooey cheese from her fingers. "Anyone I know?"

"Nope. Not unless you're into twenty-two-year-old cowboys."

"Only in the ER. I have been known to treat them upon occasion."

"Not this one," Jenny said with a wide grin and slight blush. "Tell me more."

"His name is Adam. He's a hired hand at the McCafferty spread. And...I'll fill you in more later."

Nicole's good mood vanished at the mention of the McCaffertys. Today, it seemed, she couldn't avoid them for a minute.

"Gotta run," Jenny said as Molly reached across the table to peel off pieces of pepperoni from her sister's slice of pizza.

Mindy sent up a wail guaranteed to wake the dead in every cemetery in the county. "No!" she cried. "Mommeee!"

Grinning, Molly dangled all the pilfered slices of pepperoni over her open mouth before dropping them onto her tongue. Gleefully she chewed them in front of her sister.

"I'm outta here," Jenny said and slipped through the door as Nicole tried to right the wrong and Patches, appearing from the hallway, had the nerve to hop onto the counter near the microwave.

"You, down!" Nicole said, clapping her hands loudly. The cat leaped to the floor and darted in a black-and-white streak into the living room. "Everyone seems to have an attitude today." She turned her attention back to the twins and pointed at Molly. "Don't touch your sister's food."

"She's not eating it," Molly argued while chewing.

"Am, too!" Big tears rolled down Mindy's face.

"But it's hers and—"

"And we're s'posed to share. You said so."

"Not your food...well, not now. You know better. Now,

come on, there's no real harm done here." Nicole picked off pepperoni slices from another piece of pizza and placed them on the half-eaten wedge that sat on Mindy's plate. "Good as new."

But the damage was done. Mindy wouldn't stop sobbing and pointing a condemning finger at her twin. "You, bad!"

Molly shook her head. "Am not."

Nicole shot her outspoken daughter a look meant to silence her, then picked Mindy up and, consoling her while walking toward the hallway, whispered into her ear, "Come on, big girl, let's brush your teeth and get you into bed."

"Don't wanna—" Mindy complained and Molly cackled loudly before realizing she was alone. Quickly she slid out of her chair and little feet pounding, ran after Nicole and Mindy. In the bathroom, the dispute was forgotten, tears were wiped away and two sets of teeth were brushed. As the pizza cooled, mozzarella cheese congealing, Nicole and the girls spent the next twenty minutes cuddled beneath a quilt in her grandmother's old rocker. She read them two stories they'd heard a dozen times before. Mindy's eyes immediately shut while Molly, ever the fighter, struggled to stay awake only to drop off a few minutes later.

For the first time that day, Nicole felt at peace. She eyed the fire that Jenny had built earlier. Dying embers and glowing coals in deep ashes were all that remained to light the little living room in shades of gold and red. Humming, she rocked until she, too, nearly dozed off.

Struggling out of the chair she managed to carry her daughters into their bedroom and tuck them into matching twin beds. Mindy yawned and rolled over, her thumb moving instinctively to her mouth and Molly blinked twice, said, "I love you, Mommy," then fell asleep again.

"Me, too, baby. Me, too." She kissed each daughter and

smelled the scents of shampoo and baby powder, then walked softly to the door.

Molly sighed loudly. Mindy smacked her little lips.

Folding her arms over her chest Nicole leaned against the doorjamb.

Her ex-husband's words, "You'll never make it on your own," echoed through her mind and she felt her spine stiffen. *Right, Paul,* she thought now, *but I'm not on my own. I've got the kids. And I'm going to make it. On my own.*

Every minute of that painful, doomed marriage was worth it because she had the girls. They were a family—maybe not an old-fashioned, traditional, 1950s sitcom family, but a family nonetheless.

She thought fleetingly of Randi's baby, tucked away in the maternity ward, his father not yet found, his mother in a coma and she wondered what would become of the little boy.

But the baby has Thorne and Matt and Slade. Between the three of them, certainly the boy would be taken care of. Every one of the McCafferty brothers seemed interested in the child, but each one of them was a bachelor—how confirmed, she didn't know.

"Not that it matters," she reminded herself and glanced outside where rain was dripping from the gutters and splashing against the window. She thought of Thorne again, of the way his lips felt against hers, and she realized that she had to avoid being alone with him. She had to keep their relationship professional because she knew from experience that Thorne was trouble.

Big trouble.

He was making a mistake of incredible proportions and he knew it, but he couldn't stop himself. Driving through the city streets and silently marveling at how this town had grown, he'd decided to see Nikki again before returning to the ranch. She'd probably throw him out and he really didn't blame her as he'd come on way too strong, but he had to see her again.

After watching her wheel out of the parking lot after their last confrontation, he'd walked back into the hospital, downed a cup of bitter coffee in the cafeteria, then tried to track down any doctor remotely associated with Randi and the baby. He'd struck out with most, left messages on their answering machines and after talking to a nurse in Pediatrics and one in ICU, he'd called the ranch, told Slade that he'd be back soon, then paused at the gift shop in the hospital lobby, bought a single white rose and, ducking his shoulders against the rain, ran outside and climbed into his truck.

"This is nuts," he told himself as he drove across a bridge and into an established part of town, to the address he'd found in the telephone directory when he'd made his calls to the other doctors. Bracing himself for a blistering reception, he parked in front of the small cottage, grabbed the single flower and climbed out of the car.

Jaw set he dashed up the cement walk, and before he could change his mind, pressed on the door buzzer. He'd been in tighter spots than this. He heard noises inside, the sound of feet. The porch light snapped on and he saw her eyebrows and eyes peer through one of the three small windows cut into the door. A moment later they disappeared as, he supposed, she dropped to her flat feet from her tiptoes.

Locks clicked. The door opened. And there she stood, all five feet three of her wrapped in a fluffy white robe. "Is there something I can do for you?" she asked without a smile. Her eyes skated from his face to the flower in his hands.

He nearly laughed. "You know, this seemed like a good idea at the time but now...now I feel like a damned fool."

"Because?" Again the lift of that lofty eyebrow.

"Because I thought I owed you an apology for the way I came on earlier."

"In the parking lot?"

"And the hospital."

"You were upset. Don't worry about it."

"I wasn't just upset. I was, as I said before, out of line, and I'd like to make it up to you."

Her chin lifted a fraction. "Make it up to me? With…that?" she asked, one finger pointing to the single white bud.

"To start with." He handed her the flower and thought, beneath her hard posturing, he caught a glimpse of a deeper emotion. She held the flower, lifted it to her nose and sighed.

"Thanks. This is enough…more than you needed to do."

"No, I think I owe you an explanation."

She tensed again. "It was only a kiss. I'll live."

"I mean about the past."

"No!" She was emphatic. "Look, let's just forget it, okay? It's been a long day. For both of us. Thanks for the flower and the apology, it's…it's very nice of you, but I think it would be best—for everyone, including your sister and her new baby— if we both just pretended that nothing ever happened between us."

"Can you?"

"Y-yes. Of course."

He couldn't stop one side of his mouth from twitching upward. "Liar," he said and Nicole nearly took a step backward. Who was he to stop by her house and…and *what? Apologize? What's the crime in that? Why don't you ask him in and offer him a cup of coffee or a drink?*

"No!"

"You're not a liar?"

"Not usually," she said, recovering a bit. She felt the lapel of her bathrobe gap and it took all of her willpower not to clutch it closed like a silly, frightened virgin. "You seem to bring out the worst in me."

"Ditto." He leaned forward and she expected him to kiss her again, but instead of molding his lips to hers, he brushed his mouth across the slope of her cheek in the briefest of touches. "Good night, Doctor," he whispered and then he turned and hurried down the porch steps to dash through the rain.

She stood in the glow of the porch lamp, her fingers curled possessively around the rose's stem and watched him steer his truck around in her driveway before he drove into the night. Forcing herself inside, she closed and bolted the door. She didn't know what was happening, but she was certain it wasn't going to be good.

She couldn't, wouldn't get involved with Thorne again. No way. No how. In fact, she'd toss the damned flower into the garbage right now. Padding to the kitchen she opened the cupboard under the sink, pulled out the trash can and hesitated. How childish. Thorne was trying to make amends. Nothing more. She touched the side of her cheek, then placed the rosebud in a small vase, certain it would mock her for the next week.

"Don't let him get to you," she warned, but had the fatalistic sensation that it was already too late. He'd gotten to her a long, long time ago.

Thorne parked outside of what had once been the machine shed and eyed the home where he'd been raised, a place he'd once vowed to leave and never return. Though it was dark and the rain was coming down in sheets, he saw the house looming on its small rise, warm patches of light glowing from tall, paned windows. It had been a haven at one time, a prison later.

He grabbed his briefcase and the overnight bag and wondered what had come over him. Why had he stopped at Nikki's? There was more than just a simple apology involved and that thought disturbed him. It was as if seeing her again sparked something deep inside him, something he'd thought had burned out years before, a smoldering ember he hadn't known existed.

Whatever it was, he didn't have time for it and he didn't want to examine it too closely.

Lights blazed from the stables and he recognized Slade's rig parked near the barn. As he ducked through the rain he remembered the first time he'd seen Nicole—years ago at a local Fourth of July celebration in town. He'd been back from college, ready to enter law school in the fall, randy as hell and anxious to get on with his life. She'd only been seventeen, a shy girl with the most incredible eyes he'd ever seen as she'd staked out a spot on a hill overlooking the town and waited for darkness and the fireworks that were planned.

Funny, he hadn't thought of that night in a long, long time. It seemed a million years ago and was tangled up in the other memories that haunted this particular place. As he walked up the front steps he remembered nearly drowning in the swimming hole when he was about eight, hunting pheasants with his brothers and pretending the cold silence between his parents really didn't exist. But the memories that were the clearest, the most poignantly bright, were of Nikki.

"Yeah, well, don't go there," he warned himself as he yanked open the screen door. He walked inside and was greeted by the smells of his youth—soot from the fireplace, fresh lemon wax on the floors, and the lingering aroma of bacon that had been fried earlier in the day and still wisped through the familiar hallways and rooms. He dropped his briefcase and bag near the front door and swiped the rain from his face.

"Thorne?" Matt's voice rang loudly through the century-old house. The sound of boots tripping down the stairs heralded his brother's arrival onto the first floor. "I wondered when you'd show up." Forever in jeans and a flannel shirt with the sleeves rolled up, Matt clapped his brother on the shoulder. "How're you, you old bastard?"

"Same as ever."

"Mean and ornery and on your way to your next million-dollar deal?" Matt asked, as he always did, but this time the question hit a nerve and gave him pause.

"I can only hope," he said, unbuttoning his coat, though it was a lie. He was jaded with his life. Bored. Wanted more. He just wasn't sure what.

"How's Randi?" Matt asked, his face becoming a mask of concern.

"The same as when you saw her. Nothing new to report since I called you from the hospital."

"I guess it's just gonna take time." Matt hitched his chin toward the living room where lamplight filtered into the hallway. "Come on in. I'll buy you a drink. You look like you could use one."

"That bad?"

"We could all use one today."

Thorne nodded. "So where's Slade?"

"Feeding the stock. He'll be in soon. I was just on my way to help him, but since you're here, I figure it won't hurt him to finish the job by himself." Matt flashed his killer smile, the one that had charmed more women than Thorne wanted to count.

Matt had been described as tall, dark and handsome by too many local girls to remember. The middle of the three Mc-Cafferty brothers, Matt's eyes were so deep brown they were nearly black, his skin tanned from spending hours outdoors, and the shadow covering his jaw was as dark as their father's had once been.

Sinewy and rawhide tough, Matt McCafferty could bend

a horseshoe at a forge as well as he could brand a mustang or rope a maverick calf. Raw. Wild. Stubborn as hell.

Matt belonged here.

Thorne didn't.

Not since his parents had divorced.

"Look at you." Matt gave a sharp whistle. One near-black eyebrow cocked as he fingered the wool of Thorne's coat. "Since when did you become a fashion statement?"

Thorne snorted in derision. "Don't think I am. But I happened to be at work when Slade got hold of me." Thorne hung his coat on an aging brass hook mounted near the door. The long wool overcoat seemed out of place in the array of denim, down and sheepskin jackets. "Didn't have time to change." He pulled at the knot in his tie and let the silk drape over his shoulders. "Tell me what's going on."

"Good question." Together they walked into the living room where the leather couches were worn, an upright piano gathered dust, and two rockers placed at angles near blackened stones of the fireplace remained unmoving. His great-grandfather's rifle was mounted over the mantel, resting on the spikes of antlers from an elk killed long ago. "There's not a lot to tell."

Matt opened the liquor cabinet hidden in cupboards beneath a bookcase filled with leather-backed tomes that hadn't been read in years. "What'll it be?"

"Scotch."

"Straight up?"

"You got it…well, I think."

Matt scrounged around in the cabinet and with a snort of approval withdrew a dusty bottle. "Looks like you're in luck." He reached farther into the recesses of the cabinet, came up with a couple of glasses and, after giving them each a swipe with the tail of his shirt, poured two healthy shots. "I could get ice from the kitchen."

"Waste of time. Unless you want it."

Matt's smile was a slow grin. "I think I'm man enough to handle warm liquor."

"Figured as much."

Thorne took the drink Matt offered and clicked the rim of his glass to his brother's. "To Randi."

"Yep."

Thorne tossed back his drink, unwinding a bit as the aged liquor splashed against the back of his throat then burned a fiery path to his stomach. He rotated his neck, trying to relieve the kinks in his neck. "Okay, so shoot," he said, as Matt lit tinder-dry kindling already stacked in the grate. "What the hell's going on?"

"Wish I knew. Near as the police can tell, Randi was involved in a single-car accident up in Glacier Park. No one knows for sure what happened and the cops are still lookin' into it, but, from what anyone can piece together, she was alone and driving and probably hit ice, or swerved to miss something—who the hell knows what, a deer maybe, your guess is as good as mine. The upshot is that she lost control and drove over the side of the road. The truck rolled down an embankment and—" he studied the depths of his glass "—she and the baby are lucky to be alive."

Thorne's jaw tightened. "Who found her?"

"Passersby—Good Samaritans who called the local sheriff's department."

"You got their names?"

Matt reached into his back pocket and withdrew a piece of paper that he handed to Thorne. "Jed and Bill Swanson. Brothers who were on their way home from a hunting trip. The deputy's name is on there, too."

He read the list of names and numbers, his eyes lingering for a second when he came to Dr. Nicole Stevenson.

"I figured we should keep a list of everyone involved."

"Good idea." Thorne tucked the piece of paper into his pocket. "So do you have any idea what Randi was doing at Glacier or anywhere around here for that matter? The last I heard she was in Seattle. What about her job? Or the father of the baby?"

Matt finished his drink. "Don't know a damned thing," he admitted.

"Well, that's gotta change. The three of us—Slade, you and I—we've got to find out what's going on."

"Fine with me." Matt's determined gaze held his brother's.

"We'll start tonight." The gears were already turning in Thorne's mind. "As soon as Slade gets in, we'll start making plans. But first things first."

"Randi and the baby's health," Matt guessed.

"Yep. We can start digging around in her private life as much as we want, but it doesn't mean a damned thing if she or the baby don't pull through."

"They will." Matt was cocksure as the front door banged open and Slade appeared.

"Thanks for all the help," the youngest brother grumbled as he marched into the room smelling of horses and smoke. He found a glass and poured himself a stiff shot.

"You managed," Matt guessed.

Thorne rolled up his sleeves. "Why are you so sure that Randi and her boy will be okay?"

One side of Matt's mouth lifted. "Because they're McCaffertys, Thorne. Just like us—too ornery not to pull through."

But Thorne wasn't convinced.

Chapter 4

"Don't want to dance," Molly insisted as Nicole shepherded both her daughters from the preschool and into the SUV. The rain had stopped in the night and an October sun peered through high, thin clouds.

"Why not?"

"Don't like it." Molly climbed into her car seat and started hooking the straps together while Mindy waited for her mother to snap her into place.

"Next year you can play soccer and we've got swim lessons in the spring. Until then, I think we'll stick with dance. I already paid for the lessons and they won't hurt you."

"I like to dance," Mindy said, casting her more outspoken sibling a look of pure piety. "I like Miss Palmer."

"I *hate* Miss Palmer." Molly crossed her chubby arms over her chest and glowered at the back of the passenger seat as Nicole slid behind the steering wheel.

"It's not nice to hate." Mindy lifted her eyebrows imperiously and glanced knowingly at her mother. The angel, making sure Nicole knew that Molly was being the embodiment of evil.

"*Hate*'s a pretty strong word," Nicole said and started the SUV. The engine fired on the first try. "Atta girl," she added and Mindy nodded, thinking her mother was praising her. Dark curls bounced around her head as she sent her twin a holier-than-thou look of supreme patience.

"Quit that! Mommy, she's *looking* at me."

"It's okay."

"I want ice cream," Molly insisted.

"Right after dance."

"I *hate* dance."

"I know, I know, we've been over this before," Nicole said adjusting the heat and defrost. Sun or no sun, the air was still cold. She drove over a small bridge and past a strip mall to the older side of town where an old brick grade school had been converted into artists' quarters. She parked, took the girls inside, and rather than stay and watch them go through their routine, she drove to the service station where the mechanic looked under the hood of the SUV, lifted his grimy hat and scratched his head.

"Beats me," he admitted, shifting a toothpick from one side of his mouth to the other. An elderly man with a barrel body and silver beard stubble, he frowned and wiped the oil from his hands. "Seems to be working just fine. Why don't you bring it in next week and leave it—can you? We'll run diagnostics on it."

She made an appointment, mentally crossed her fingers, rounded up the girls and managed to stop at the grocery store and ice-cream parlor before they had a total meltdown.

"Why doesn't Daddy live with us?" Mindy asked as they pulled into the driveway of their house.

Nicole parked and pocketed her keys. "Because Mommy and Daddy are divorced, you know that. Come on, let's get out of the car."

"And Daddy lives far away," Molly said, drips of bubble-gum ice cream falling from her chin.

"He don't come and see us. Bobbi Martin's daddy comes and visits her."

"Would you like for your father to visit?" Nicole had opened the back door and was unsnapping the straps to Mindy's car seat.

"Yeth."

"Nope." Molly shook her head. "He don't like us."

"Oh, Molly—" Nicole was about to argue and then saw no reason to defend Paul. He'd had no interest in the twins since the divorce. Sending Nicole child support payments seemed to fulfill all his requirements as a father; at least in his opinion. "You just don't know your father."

"Is he going to come see us?" Mindy asked, her eyes bright, her ice-cream cone forgotten. The single scoop of cookies-'n'-cream was melting into her fingers.

"I don't know. He doesn't have any plans to, not yet. But, if you like, I could call him."

"Call him!" Mindy swiped at the top of her cone with her tongue.

"He won't come." Molly didn't seem upset about it; she was just stating a fact. "You can have the rest," she said, handing her mother the cone and bolting from the rig. She tore off across the wet grass to the swing set.

"Can't you undo this yourself?" Nicole asked lifting the safety bar of the car seat.

"You do it." Mindy smiled impishly, then, still clutching her cone, slid out of the car.

You're spoiling her, Nicole told herself as she juggled the grocery sacks and carried them into the house. *You're spoiling them both, trying to be father and mother, feeling sorry for them because, they, like you, are growing up without their father.*

Was it her fault? She had a lot of reasons for moving away from San Francisco, for wanting to start over. But maybe in so doing, she was robbing her daughters of a vital part of their lives, of the chance to know the man who'd sired them.

Not that he'd shown any interest when they still lived in the city. He'd never seen the girls for more than a couple of hours at a time and his new wife had been pretty clear that she saw his twins as "baggage" she didn't want or need.

So Nicole wasn't going to beat herself up about it. The twins were doing fine. Just fine.

Patches, who had been washing his face on the windowsill, hopped lithely to the floor. "Naughty boy," Nicole whispered, but added some dry food to his dish, unpacked the groceries and watched her girls through the back window. They were playing on the teeter-totter, laughing in the crisp air as clouds began to gather again. Nicole pressed the play button on the answering machine.

The first voice she heard was Thorne McCafferty's.

"Hi. It's Thorne. Call me." He rattled off his phone number and Nicole's stomach did a flip at the sound of it. Why he got to her after all these years she didn't understand, but he did. There was no doubt about it. She knew that he'd been her first love, but it had been years, *years* since then. So why did he still affect her? She glanced to the windowsill where she'd placed the bud vase with its single white rose—a peace offering, nothing more.

Sighing, she wished she understood why she couldn't shake Thorne from her thoughts. She wasn't a lonely woman. She wasn't a needy woman. She *didn't* want a man in her life—at least not yet. So why was it that every time she heard his voice those old memories that she'd tucked away escaped to run and play havoc through her mind?

"Because you're an idiot," she said and finished unloading the car. She remembered seeing him for the first time, the summer before her senior year in high school. He'd been alone, dusk was settling, the sky still glowing pink over the western hills, the first stars beginning to sparkle in the night. The heat of the day hung heavy in the air with only a breath of a breeze to lift her hair or brush her cheeks. She was sitting on a blanket, alone, her best friend having ditched her at the last minute to be with her boyfriend and suddenly Thorne had appeared, tall, strapping, wearing a T-shirt that stretched over his shoulders and faded jeans that hung low on his hips.

"Is this spot taken?" he'd asked and she hadn't responded, thinking he had to be talking to someone else.

"Excuse me," he'd said again and she'd twisted her face up to stare into intense gray eyes that took hold of her and wouldn't let go. "Would it be all right if I sat here?"

She couldn't believe her ears. There were dozens of blankets tossed upon the bent grass of the hillside, hundreds of people gathered and picnicking as they waited for the show. And he wanted to sit *here*? Next to her? "Oh, well…sure," she'd managed to reply, feeling like an utter fool, her face burning with embarrassment.

He'd taken a spot next to her on her blanket, his arms draped over half-bent knees, his spine curved, his body so close to hers she could smell some kind of cologne or soap, barely an inch between his shoulder and hers. Suddenly she found it impossible to breathe. "Thanks," he said, his voice low, his smile a flash of white against a strong, beard-shadowed chin. "I'm Thorne. McCafferty."

She'd recognized the name, of course, had heard the rumors and gossip swirling about his family. She had even met his younger brothers upon an occasion or two, but she'd never been face-to-face with the oldest McCafferty son. Never in her life had she felt the wild drumming of her heart just because a man—and that was it, he wasn't a boy—was regarding her with assessing steely eyes.

Five or six years older than she, he seemed light-years ahead of her in sophistication. He'd been off to college somewhere on the East Coast, she thought, an Ivy League school, though she couldn't really remember which one.

"I imagine you do have a name." His lips twitched and she felt even a bigger fool.

"Oh…yes. I'm Nicole Sanders." She started to offer him her hand, then let it drop.

"Is that what you go by? Nicole?"

"Yeah." She swallowed hard and glanced away. Clearing her throat she nodded. "Sometimes Nikki." She felt like a little girl in her ponytail and cutoff jeans and sleeveless blouse with the shirttails tied around her waist.

"Nikki, I like that." Plucking a long piece of dry grass from the hillside he shoved it into his mouth and as Nicole surreptitiously watched, he moved it from one sexy corner to the other. And he was sexy. More purely male and raw than any boy she'd ever been with. "You live around here?"

"Yeah. In town. Alder Street."

"I'll remember that," he promised and her silly heart took flight. "Alder."

Dear God, she thought she'd die. Right then and there. He winked at her, stretched out and leaned back on his elbows while taking in the back of her head and the darkening heavens.

As the fireworks had started that night, bursting in the sky in brilliant flashes of green, yellow and blue, Nicole Frances

Sanders spent the evening in exquisite teenage torment and, without a thought to the consequences, began to fall in love.

It seemed eons ago—a magical point in time that was long past. But, like it or not, even now, while standing in her cozy little kitchen, she felt the tingle of excitement, the lilt, she'd always experienced when she'd been with Thorne.

"Don't go there," she warned herself, her hands gripping the edge of the counter so hard her fingers ached. "That was a long, long time ago." A time Thorne, no doubt, didn't remember.

She waited until she'd fed and bathed the girls, read them stories, and then, dreading talking to him, punched out the number for the Flying M Ranch.

Thorne picked up on the second ring. "Flying M. Thorne McCafferty."

"Hi, it's Nicole. You called?" she asked while the twins ran pell-mell through the house.

"Yeah. I thought we should get together."

She nearly dropped the phone. "Get together? For?"

"Dinner."

A *date?* He was asking her out? Her heart began to thud and in the peripheral vision she saw the rose with its soft white petals beginning to open. "Was there a reason?"

"More than one, actually. I want to talk to you about Randi and the baby, of course. Their treatment, what happens if we can't find the baby's father, convalescent care and rehabilitation when Randi's finally released. That kind of thing."

"Oh." She felt strangely deflated. "Sure, I suppose, but her doctors will go over all this with you."

"But they're not you." His voice was low and her pulse elevated again.

"They're professionals."

"But I don't know them. I don't trust them."

"And you trust me?" she said, unable to stop herself.

"Yes."

The twins roared into the room. "Mommy, Mommy—she hit me!" Molly cried, outraged, while Mindy, eyes round, shook her head solemnly.

"Not me."

"Yes, she did."

"You hit me first." Molly began to wail.

"Thorne, would you excuse me. My daughters are in the middle of their own little war."

"Oh, I didn't realize." He paused for a second as she bent on one knee, stretching the phone cord and giving Molly a hug. "I didn't know you had children."

"Two girls, dynamos. I'm divorced," she added quickly. "Nearly two years now."

Was there a sigh of relief on his end of the conversation, or did she imagine it over Molly's sobs?

"I'll talk to you later," he said.

"Yes. Do." She hung up and threw her arms around both girls, but her thoughts were already rushing forward to thoughts of Thorne and being alone with him. She couldn't do it. Even though he'd tried to apologize for leaving her and she'd spent years fantasizing about just such a scenario, she wouldn't risk being with him again. It wasn't just herself and her heart she had to worry about now, she had the girls to consider. And yet…a part of her would love to see him again, to smile into his eyes, to kiss him… She pulled herself up short. What was she thinking? The kiss in the parking lot had been passionate, wild and evoked memories of their lovemaking so long ago, but it was the kiss on her cheek that had really gotten to her, the soft featherlike caress of his lips against her skin that made her want more.

"Stop it," she told herself.

"Stop what?" Mindy looked at her mother with wounded, teary eyes. "I didn't do it!"

"I know, sweetie, I know," Nicole said, determined not to let Thorne McCafferty bulldoze his way into her life...or her heart.

Thorne walked into the barn and shoved thoughts of Nicole out of his mind. He had too many other problems, pressing issues to deal with. Besides Randi's and the baby's health, there were questions about her accident and, of course, the ever-present responsibilities he'd left behind in Denver—hundreds of miles away but still requiring his attention.

The smells of fresh hay, dusty hides and oiled leather brought back memories of his youth—memories he'd pushed aside long ago. As the first few drops of rain began to pepper the tin roof, Slade was tossing hay bales down from the loft above. Matt carried the bales by their string to the appropriate mangers, then deftly sliced the twine with his jackknife. Thorne grabbed a pitchfork and, as he had every winter day in his youth, began shaking loose hay into the manger.

The cattle were inside lowing and shifting, edging toward the piles of feed. Red, dun, black and gray, their coats were thick with the coming of winter, covered with dust and splattered with mud.

After a day of being on the phone, the physical labor felt good and eased some of the tension from muscles that had been cramped in his father's desk chair. Thorne had called Nicole, his office in Denver, several clients and potential business partners, as well as local retailers as he needed equipment to set up a temporary office here at the ranch. But that had just been the beginning; the rest of the day he'd spent at the hospital, talking with doctors or searching for clues as to what had happened to his sister.

For the most part, he'd come up dry. "So no one's figured out why Randi was back in Montana?" he said, tossing a forkful of hay into the manger. A white-faced heifer plunged her broad nose into the hay.

"I called around this afternoon while you were at the hospital." The three brothers had visited their sister individually and checked in on their new nephew. Thorne had hoped to run into Nicole. He hadn't.

"What did you find out?"

"Diddly-squat." Another bale dropped from above. Slade swung down as well, landing next to Thorne and wincing at the jolt in his bad leg. His limp was still as noticeable as the red line that ran from his temple to his chin, compliments of a skiing accident that had nearly taken his life, though the scars on the outside of his face were far less damaging than those that, Thorne imagined, cut through his soul. "I talked to several people at the *Seattle Clarion* where she wrote her column, whatever the hell it is." Slade yanked a pitchfork from its resting place on the wall.

"Advice to the lovelorn," Thorne supplied. Drops of frigid rain drizzled down the small windows and a wind, screaming of winter, tore through the valley.

"It's a lot more than that," Matt said defensively. "It's general advice to single people. Things like legal issues, divorce settlements, raising kids alone, dealing with grief and new relationships, juggling time around career and kids, budgeting… hell, I don't know."

"Sounds like you do," Thorne said, realizing that Matt had maintained a stronger relationship with their half sister than he had. But then that hadn't been difficult.

"I take a paper that prints her column. It's been syndicated, y'know. Picked up by a few independents as far away as Chicago."

"Is that right?" Thorne felt a sharp jab of guilt. What did he know about his sister? Not much.

"Yeah, she adds her own touch—her quirky humor—and it sells."

"Since when did she become an expert?" Slade wanted to know.

"Beats me." Matt scratched the stubble on his chin. "Looks like she could've used some pearls of wisdom herself."

Thorne kicked at a bale, causing it to split open. Why hadn't Randi come to him, explained about the baby, confided in him if her life wasn't going well? His back teeth ground together and he reminded himself that maybe she didn't know things weren't on track, maybe this baby was planned. "Okay, so what else did you find out?" he asked, refusing to wallow in a sea of guilt.

Slade lifted a shoulder. "Not a hell of a lot. Her co-workers, of course, all figured out she was pregnant. She couldn't really hide it. But none of them admitted to knowing the father's name."

"You think they're lying?" Thorne asked.

"Not that I could tell."

"Great."

"No one even thinks she was dating anyone seriously."

"Looks serious enough to me," Matt grumbled.

Slade reached across the manger and pushed one cow's white face to the side so a smaller animal could wedge her nose into the hay. "Move, there," he commanded, though the beast didn't so much as flick her ears. Wiping his hand on the bleached denim of his jeans, he said, "Randi's editor, Bill Withers, said that she'd planned to take a three-month maternity leave, but he'd assumed she'd stay in town, because she told him that as soon as she was on her feet and she and the baby were settled in, she was going to work out of her condominium. She had enough columns written ahead that they'll run for a few weeks. Then, she'd be back at it again, though she didn't plan to start going into the office until after the first of the year."

"So there was no trouble at work?"

"None that anyone is saying, but I get the feeling that there was more going on than anyone's willing to admit."

"Par for the course. Reporters, they're always ready to snoop into anyone else's business—they've already been calling here, you know. But ask them about what they know and all of a sudden the First Amendment becomes the Bible." Matt snorted and picked up the used strands of baling twine. "Does anyone at her office know anything about her accident?"

"Nope." Slade dusted his hands. "They were shocked. Especially the ones she was supposedly closest to. Sarah Peeples, who writes movie reviews gasped and nearly fell through the floor, from the sound of her end of the conversation. She couldn't believe that Randi was in the hospital and Dave Delacroix, he's a guy who writes a sports column for the paper, thought I was playing some kind of practical joke. Then once he figured out I was on the level, he got angry. Demanded answers. So, basically, I drew blanks."

"It's a start," Thorne said as they finished up. The wheels had been turning in his mind from the moment he'd heard about Randi's accident; now it was time to put some kind of plan into action. Slade forked the last wisps of hay into the manger. "I'll catch up with you," he said as he traded his pitchfork for a broom. "Pour me a drink."

"Will do." Thorne followed Matt outside and dashed through rain cold enough that he knew winter was in the air.

Once in the house again, Matt built another fire from last night's embers and Thorne poured them each a drink. As they waited for Slade, they sipped their father's Scotch and worried aloud about their headstrong sister and wondering how they would take care of a newborn.

"The problem is, none of us know much about Randi's life," Thorne said as he capped the bottle.

"I think that's the way she wanted it. We can beat ourselves up one side and down the other for not being a part of her life, but that was Randi's choice. Remember?"

How could he forget? At their father's funeral in May, Randi had been inconsolable, refusing any outward show of emotion from her brothers, preferring to stand in an oversize, gauzy black dress apart from the rest of the family, while a young preacher, who knew very little of the man in the coffin, prayed solemnly. Most of the townspeople of Grand Hope came to the service to pay their respects.

She had to have been four months pregnant at the time. Thorne would never have guessed as they paid their last respects on the hillside. But then he'd been lost in his own black thoughts, the ring his father had given him the summer before hidden deep in his pocket.

John Randall hadn't been a churchgoing man. Under the circumstances, the young minister whose eulogy had been from notes he'd taken the day earlier, had done a decent enough job asking that the blackheart's soul be accepted into heaven. Thorne wasn't certain God had made such a huge exception.

"Randi's kept her life pretty private."

"Haven't we all?" Matt remarked.

"Maybe it's time to change all that." Thorne ran a hand through the thin layer of dust that had collected on the mantel.

"Agreed." Matt lifted his glass and nodded.

The front door banged open. A gust of cold wind blew through the hallway and Slade, wiping the rain from his face,

hitched himself into the living room. He shrugged out of his
jacket and tossed it over the back of the couch.

"Any word on Randi?" Making his way across the braided
rug, Slade found an old-fashioned glass in the cupboard and
without much fanfare, poured himself a long drink from the
rapidly diminishing bottle of Scotch.

"Not yet. But I'll check the answering machine." Matt
crossed the room and disappeared down the hallway leading
to the den.

"She'd better pull out of this," Slade said, as if to himself.
The youngest of the three brothers, Slade was also the wildest. He'd left a trail of broken hearts from Mexico to Canada,
if rumors were to be believed and never had really settled
down. While Matt had his own ranch, a small spread near
the Idaho border, Slade had put down no roots and probably
never would. He'd done everything from race cars, to ride
rodeo, and do stunt work in films. The scar running down
one side of his face was testament to his hard, reckless lifestyle
and Thorne had, at times, wondered if the youngest McCafferty son harbored some kind of death wish.

Slade stood in front of the fire and warmed the backs of his
legs. "What're we gonna do about the baby?"

"We take care of him until Randi's able."

"Then we'd better get this place ready," Slade observed.

"The orthopedist called earlier," Matt said, entering the
room. "As soon as some of the swelling has gone down and
Randi's out of critical condition, he'll take care of her leg."

"Good. I put a call in to Nicole. I want to meet with her so
that she can tell me about Randi's doctors and her prognosis,
rehab, that sort of thing."

"Nicole?" Matt replied, his eyes narrowing as if struck by
a sudden memory. "You know she mentioned that you knew
each other, but I'd forgotten that you were an item."

"It was only a few weeks," Thorne clarified.

Slade rubbed the back of his neck. "I hardly remember it."

"Because you were off racing cars and chasing women on the stock car circuit," Matt said. "You weren't around much when Thorne got out of college and was heading to law school. It was that summer, right?"

"Part of the summer."

Slade shook his head. "Let me guess, you dumped her for some other long-legged plaything."

"There was no other woman," Thorne snapped, surprised at the anger surging through his blood.

"No, you just had to go out and prove to Dad and God and anyone else who would listen that you could make it on your own without J. Randall's help."

"It was a long time ago," Thorne muttered. "Right now we've got to concentrate on Randi."

"And that's why you called Dr. Stevenson?" Obviously Matt wasn't buying it.

"Of course." Thorne sat on the arm of the leather couch and knew he was lying, not only to his brothers but to himself. It was more than just wanting to discuss Randi's condition with her; he wanted to see Nicole again, be with her. The strange part of it was, ever since seeing her again, he wanted to see more of her. "Now, listen," he said to his brothers. "Something we'll have to deal with and pronto is finding out who the father is."

"That's gonna be tough considerin' Randi's condition." Slade rested a shoulder against the mantel and folded his arms over his chest. "Just how long you plannin' on stickin' around, city boy?"

"As long as it takes."

"Aren't there some big deals in Denver and Laramie and

wherever the hell else you own property—things you need to oversee?"

Thorne resisted being baited and managed a guarded grin, the kind Slade so often gave the rest of the world. "I can oversee them from here."

"How?"

"By the fine art of telecommunication. I'll set up a fax, modem, Internet connection, cell phone and computer in the den."

Matt rubbed his chin. "Thought you hated it here. Except for a few times like that summer after you graduated from college you've avoided this ranch like the plague. Ever since Dad and Mom split, you've spent as little time here as possible."

Thorne couldn't argue the fact. "Randi needs me—us."

Matt added wood to the fire and switched on a lamp. "Okay, I think we need a game plan," Thorne said.

"Let me guess, you'll be the quarterback, just like in high school," Slade said.

Thorne's temper snapped. "Let's just work together, okay? It's not about calling the shots so much as getting the job done."

"Okay." Matt nodded. "I'll be in charge of the ranch. I've already talked to a couple of guys who will help out."

Slade walked to the couch and picked up his jacket. "Good enough. Matt should run the place, he's used to it and I'll pitch in if we need an extra hand. Thorne, why don't you give Juanita a call? Maybe she can help with the baby. She's had some experience raising McCaffertys, after all, she helped Dad with us."

"Good idea, as we'll need round-the-clock help," Thorne decided.

"We'll get it. Now, the way I think I can help best is by concentrating on finding out all I can about what was going on in our sister's life, especially in the past year or so. I have a friend who's a private investigator. For the right price, he'll help us out," Slade said.

"Is he any good?" Thorne asked.

Slade's expression turned dark. "If anyone can find out what's going on, it'll be Kurt Striker. I'd bet my life on it."

"You're sure?"

Slade's gaze could've cut through steel. "I said, I'd bet my life on it. I meant that. Literally."

"Call him," Thorne said, persuaded by his usually cynical brother's conviction.

"Already have."

Thorne was surprised that Slade had already started the ball rolling. "I want to talk to him."

"You will."

"I'll keep on top of the doctors at the hospital," Thorne said. "I'll can do most of my business here by phone, fax and e-mail, so I won't have to go back to Denver for a while."

Matt held his gaze for a long second and for the first time in his life Thorne realized that his middle brother didn't approve of his lifestyle. Not that it really mattered. "Then let's just get through this," Matt finally said, as if he suddenly trusted Thorne again, as he had a long time before.

"We will."

"As long as Randi cooperates," Slade said.

"She's a fighter." Thorne's reaction was swift and he recognized the irony of his words. Phrases such as *she's really strong, she'll make it,* or *she's too ornery to die,* or *she's a fighter,* were hollow words, expressed by people who usually doubted their meaning. They were uttered to chase away the person's own fears.

"Look, I'm going to take inventory of the feed," Matt said.

"I'll check the gas pump, see what's in the tank." Slade

snagged his jacket with one finger and the two younger brothers headed for the front door.

Thorne watched them through the window. Slade paused to light a cigarette on the porch while Matt jogged across the lot, disappearing into the barn again.

As kids they'd been through a lot together; depended upon each other, but as men, they'd gone about their own lives. Thorne had become the businessman, first law school and a stint with a firm before branching out on his own. His father had been right. He'd wanted to prove himself and the measure of a man's success, he'd always thought, was the size of his bank account.

For the first time in his life he wondered if he'd been wrong. Thinking of Randi battling death and her newborn son just starting his life gave him pause as he walked down the hallway where family portraits graced the walls. There were pictures of his father and mother, his stepmother and all four McCafferty children. Thorne in his high school football uniform and his graduation cap and gown, Matt riding a bucking bronco in a local rodeo, Slade skiing down a steep mountain and Randi in her prom dress, standing next to some boy Thorne couldn't begin to name. He stopped, touched that framed photo and silently vowed that he'd do anything, *anything* to make sure she was healthy again. He'd heat a cup of coffee, then call Nicole. She might have more news on his sister. That was the only reason he was calling her, he reminded himself as he walked into the kitchen and snapped on the lights. From the corner of his eye, he caught sight of his reflection in the windows. For a split second he imagined a mite of a woman with wide gold eyes and a fleeting smile at his side, then pulled himself up short.

What was he thinking? Nicole was Randi's ER admitting physician and that was it. Nothing more. Yet, ever since he'd first seen her in her office at the hospital, her heels propped on her desk, and her chair leaned back as she cradled the phone between her ear and shoulder, he hadn't been able to force her from his mind. It hadn't helped that when he'd caught up with her in the parking lot, he'd seen her not as Randi's doctor, but as a woman—a beautiful, bright and articulate woman. He hadn't been able to stop himself from kissing her and he'd been thinking about it off and on ever since. Nicole Sanders Stevenson was all grown-up, educated and self-confident—more intriguing now than she had been as a girl of seventeen. Despite her small stature she was a force to be reckoned with—way too much trouble for any man.

And yet...

The wall phone jangled. Snapped out of the ridiculous path of his thoughts, he grabbed the receiver on the second ring. "McCafferty ranch," he said. "Thorne McCafferty."

"So you are there!" a sharp female voice accused, and Thorne envisioned Annette's pretty face in a scowl. He'd dated her for a few months, but had never really connected with her. "What in the world happened? We were supposed to meet the mayor last night!" Annette's tone brought him up sharp and he gave himself a quick mental shake. He'd never called her. Never once thought of her after leaving his office yesterday.

"There was a family emergency."

"So you couldn't pick up a phone? You have a cell phone and you're on one right now...oh, listen, I don't mean to go off on you." She took in a deep, audible breath. "Your secretary told me that your half sister was in some kind of wreck and I'm sorry for her, I really am. I hope she's okay...?"

"She's in a coma."

"Oh, God." There was another long, weighty pause. "Well, I, um, understand, I really do. Dear Lord, how awful. I know you had to get back there in a hurry, Thorne. That's understandable and I made your apologies to my father and the mayor, but it seems to me that you could have called me yourself."

"I should have."

"Yeah…oh, well." She sighed. "Dad was disappointed."

"Was he?" Thorne drawled, imagining Kent Williams's reaction. The shrewd old man was probably in a stew as he'd wanted to invest with Thorne and was hoping they could cozy up with members of the city council and get an edge on a zoning ordinance that was up for review. "Thanks for giving him my apologies. You didn't have to do that. I would have called him."

"And me, would you have called me?"

"Yes."

"Eventually."

"Right." No reason to lie. "Eventually."

"Oh, Thorne." She let out a world-weary sigh and some of the shrewishness in her voice disappeared. "I miss you."

Did she? He doubted it and their relationship had always left him feeling alone. "It looks like I'm going to be in Montana a while."

"Oh." There was hesitation in her voice. "How long?"

"A few weeks, maybe months. It all depends on Randi."

"But what about your work?"

"What about it?"

"It's—it's your life."

Was my life, he wanted to say. Instead, added, "Things have changed."

"Have they?" Silent accusations sizzled over the wires.

"Afraid so."

"What does that mean?" But she knew. It was obvious. "You know, there are other men who are interested in me. I've put them on hold because of you."

"I'm sorry."

She waited and the silence ticked between them. "So, what're you telling me, Thorne?" she asked. "That it's over? Just like that? Because your sister is in the hospital?"

"No, Annette," he admitted, "it's not because of Randi. You and I both know that this wasn't going anywhere. I was up front about that at the beginning."

"I thought you'd change your mind."

"It didn't happen."

"So I should start seeing other men."

"It wouldn't be a bad idea."

"Okay." Again a frosty pause. "I'll think about it," she said.

"Do."

"And you, too, Thorne," she said with a renewed amount of spunk. "You think about what you're giving up." She hung up with a click and he replaced the receiver slowly, wondering why he didn't feel any sense of loss. But then he never had; not with any woman. Not even with Nikki way back when, and she'd been the most difficult. But he hadn't trusted her with his heart and when it came time to take off for law school, he'd left Grand Hope, his family and Nicole Sanders and never once looked back. Until now. While away at school, whenever he'd thought of her, which was often at first, he steadfastly turned his mind to other things. Eventually he'd quit thinking about her altogether and he'd lived by the axiom that women weren't a priority in his life.

But now, as he stared out the window into the dark, wet night, he felt a change inside him, a new kind of need. He reached for the phone as it rang again sharply.

Annette. He should have known she wouldn't give up without a fight.

"Hello," he said, as the receiver reached his ear.

"Thorne? This is Nicole." Her voice was cold and professional.

He knew in a heartbeat that Randi's condition had worsened. Fear clutched his heart and for the first time in his life he felt absolutely helpless. Oh, God. "It's my sister," he stated.

"No. Randi's still stable, but I just got a call from the hospital because they couldn't get through to you—your line was busy." Nicole hesitated a beat and before she got the words out, Thorne experienced an anguish the like of which he'd never felt before. He sagged against the wall as she said, "It's the baby."

Chapter 5

"What about him?" Thorne clutched the receiver in a death grip. His heart thudded in dread. For the love of Mike, how could one little baby, Randi's son whom he'd never even held, make such a difference in his life?

He heard the back door open and Matt, unbuttoning his sheepskin jacket, strode in. "Slade's still—"

Thorne silenced his brother with a killing glance and a finger to his lips.

"What about the baby?" he repeated, bracing himself and he saw Matt's dark complexion pale.

"He's lethargic, experiencing feeding problems and respiratory distress, his abdomen is distended, his temp has spiked—"

"Just cut to the chase, Nicole. What's he got? What went wrong?" Thorne was pacing now, stretching the telephone cord as Matt's eyes followed his every move.

Nicole hesitated a beat and Thorne found it hard to breathe.

"Dr. Arnold thinks the baby might have bacterial meningitis. He's going to call you later and—"

"Meningitis?" Thorne repeated.

"No way!" Matt broke his silence.

"How the hell did that happen?"

"When Randi came into the hospital, her membranes had already ruptured—"

"What? Ruptured?"

Matt swore under his breath, then looked up, his gaze locking with that of his older brother. "Let's go," Matt said. "Right now. To the damned hospital!" Thorne cut him off with a quick shake of his head. He had to concentrate.

Nicole was talking again—her voice calm, though he sensed an urgency to her. "Her water had broken in the accident and there's a chance that there was contamination, the baby was exposed to some source of bacteria."

"This Dr. Arnold? Is he there? At the hospital now?"

"Yes. He'll call you with more information—"

"We're on our way."

"I'll meet you there," she said as he slammed the receiver down.

"What the hell's going on?" Matt demanded.

"The baby's in trouble. It doesn't sound good." Thorne was already striding to the front hall where he yanked his coat from a hook and shoved his arms down the sleeves. Matt was right on his heels. The two men half ran to Thorne's truck, but before he climbed into the passenger side, Matt said, "Wait a minute, I'd better tell Slade that we're on our way to the hospital—"

"Make it fast," Thorne ordered, but Matt was already running toward the barn. He disappeared inside. Thorne jabbed his key into the ignition, the truck roared to life and he glared at the barn, willing his brother to return.

Less than a minute later Matt, head ducked, holding on to the brim of his Stetson, dashed through the rain. Thorne was already throwing the pickup into gear by the time Matt opened the door and slid inside.

"He's gonna follow us."

"Good."

Thorne stepped hard on the accelerator, though he didn't know why. The urge to get to the hospital, to do *something* pounded through him. What had gone wrong?

Rain poured from the sky and the twin ruts of the lane glistened in the glow of the headlights as water spun beneath the tires.

"Okay, now what happened?" Matt demanded, his face tense in the dark interior.

"Something went wrong."

"What?"

"Everything." Thorne squinted against oncoming headlights, shifted down and turned onto the main road cutting through the pine-forested canyons and rolling acres of farmland surrounding the Flying M. In clipped words, Thorne repeated his conversation with Nicole.

Matt's jaw clenched. "Why was Nicole the one who called? Why not the pediatrician?"

"He couldn't get through, but I'll have more phone lines installed. Tomorrow. And I'd asked Nicole to phone me if there was any change. She said Dr. Arnold would call us, but I'm not going to hang around and wait. I want answers and I want them now."

The ranch was nearly twenty miles from town. Thorne pushed the speed limit and the truck's tires sang against the wet pavement.

They arrived at the hospital in record time. Thorne was out of the truck like a shot. Matt kept up with him, stride for stride. They sprinted across the dark parking lot, flew through the automatic doors of the lobby, then took the stairs two at a time to the second floor.

This time, Thorne didn't allow any nurse to tell him what to do. The poor woman, a slight blonde with a tentative smile tried to ward them off. "Excuse me, you can't come in here," she said, pointing to a sign that read Authorized Personnel Only.

"Where's the McCafferty baby?" Thorne demanded.

"Who are you?"

"I'm the baby's uncle and so is he," Matt said, hooking a thumb toward Thorne. "We're Randi McCafferty's brothers."

"The only family the baby has right now," Thorne explained, "as our sister is in Intensive Care and we haven't located the child's father." That wasn't a lie. Not really. He just didn't bother to add that they had no idea who the father was. Slicing Matt a look warning him not to elaborate, Thorne continued. "I want to see my nephew."

"He's in his crib," the nurse said patiently. "And he's being monitored closely." Her lips pursed and she motioned toward the glassed-in room where the baby, lying seemingly peacefully under a warm lamp, with a monitor strapped to him, was sleeping. Tubes were inserted into his small body and he breathed with his tiny mouth open. Another nurse hovered near his plastic bed. The blonde nurse continued, "Dr. Arnold has seen him and should be right back—oh, here he is now." She was obviously relieved to pass the responsibility of dealing with Thorne and Matt to a small man with wire-rimmed glasses, slightly stooped shoulders and a ring of wild white hair.

"Dr. Arnold?" Thorne asked, pinning the shorter man with his gaze.

"Yes."

"I'm Thorne McCafferty. This is my brother, Matt. The baby's mother is our sister. What the hell's going on?"

"That's what we're trying to find out," Dr. Arnold said calmly, obviously not offended by Thorne's sharp words and demanding attitude. "The baby's suffering from bacterial meningitis, probably contracted at the site of the accident as your sister's amniotic sac had already ruptured." Thorne's chest tightened. He felt a muscle in his jaw work as the doctor explained in finer detail what Nicole had already told him on the phone. Slade, white-faced, jaw set, fists coiled, arrived and was introduced quickly and brought up to speed.

"So how dangerous is this?" Thorne demanded.

"Very." The doctor was solemn. "We're a small hospital but luckily, we've got a state-of-the-art intensive pediatric unit."

Matt got straight to the point. "Is the baby going to make it?"

"I wish I could tell you that he's out of the woods, but I can't." The doctor's eyes, behind his glasses, were solemn. "The mortality rate for this kind of meningitis is high, somewhere between twenty to fifty percent—"

"Oh, God," Matt whispered.

"However, your nephew's survival chances are good here because of the staff and equipment. Already the baby's on antibiotic therapy and a mechanical ventilator along with compulsive fluid management."

"What?"

"An IV to minimize the effects of cerebral edema. Even if the baby is to survive, there's a chance that he might be deaf, blind or have some retardation."

"Damn," Slade mumbled and ran a hand over his chin and was suddenly pale as death, his scar more visible.

Thorne was thunderstruck. He stared at Randi's baby and

felt, for the first time in his life, impotent. Frustration burned through his bloodstream.

"Isn't there anything else you can do?" Matt asked, lines of worry sketching his brow.

"There must be," Thorne added.

"Believe me, we're doing everything possible." Dr. Arnold's voice was steady.

"If there's anything he needs, anything at all—equipment, specialists, whatever—we'll pay for it." Thorne was adamant. "Money isn't an issue here."

The doctor's lips pulled together just a fraction. His spine seemed to stiffen and his voice was clipped. "Money isn't the problem right now, Mr. McCafferty. As I said we have the best equipment available, but this hospital is always looking for endowments and benefactors. I'll see that your name is on the list. Now, if you'll excuse me, I want to check on my patient."

He punched a code into a keypad and the doors marked Authorized Personnel Only opened. Dr. Arnold disappeared for an instant before he stepped into the neonatal nursery and was visible through the thick glass of the viewing window. Thorne's teeth clenched, anger and impotence burned in his brain. There had to be something he could do to help Randi's boy. There had to be! He stared at the pediatrician hard, but if Dr. Arnold felt Thorne's eyes upon him, he didn't so much as flinch or glance up. Instead he focused on the baby, carefully examining the fragile little boy who was Randi's only child—John Randall McCafferty's sole grandchild.

"He's got to pull through," Matt said, his fists balling in determination. "If he doesn't and Randi wakes up to find out that he didn't make it—"

"Don't say it! Don't even think it! He's gonna be fine. He's got to!" Slade slashed Matt a harsh glance filled with his own

private hell. Not too long ago he'd lost a girlfriend and an un-
born child. "He'll make it."

"Will he?" Matt wasn't convinced. "Here? I mean, I know
this is a good hospital—the best around—but maybe he needs
specialists, the kind that you find in bigger cities at teaching
hospitals in L.A. or Denver or Seattle."

"We'll check it out," Thorne agreed. "I'll find out the best
in the country."

"Right now it would be a mistake to move him." Nicole's
voice came from somewhere down the hallway.

Thorne hadn't heard her approach but saw her reflection
in the glass, a pale ghost in jeans and ski jacket, a filmy image
that pulled strangely on his heartstrings. "Trust me on this
one, Thorne, the baby's in good hands."

He turned and stared into a face devoid of makeup except
for a bit of lipstick, her hair falling freely to her shoulders, her
gold eyes quietly reassuring. She looked younger than she had
before, more like the girl he remembered, the one he'd thought
he'd loved, the one he'd so callously left behind. "Sorry it
took me a while to get here, I had to round up a babysitter."

"You have a child?" Matt asked.

"Two. Twin girls. Four years old." Her serious face brightened at the mention of her daughters and Thorne tried to ignore the ridiculous spurt of jealousy that ran through his blood
that another man had fathered her daughters, then he gave
himself a swift mental shake. What the hell was he thinking?
"And I'd trust them to Geoff—er, Dr. Arnold."

"Good enough for me," Matt allowed, though his face was
still tense.

"Nothin' else we can do but have some faith in the guy,"
Slade agreed, then cursed softly in frustration.

"There are always other options," Thorne disagreed.

"None better." Nicole's voice brooked no argument. Her

face was a mask of certainty. She had absolute trust in this man and again, ludicrously, Thorne felt a prick of jealousy that she would have such unflagging confidence in another male. "Let me talk to Geoff and see what's up." Nicole punched a code into the door lock. "I'll just be a minute." The electronic doors opened. Nicole slipped through.

Slade shifted from one foot to the other. Scowling through the glass, he eyed the two doctors and finally said, "I think I'll go check on Randi, then head back. You can fill me in when you get home."

Matt nodded curtly. "I'll come with you." He glanced at Thorne. "I'll catch a ride back to the ranch with Slade."

"Fine," Thorne said. "Call Striker again. Tell him I want to talk to him. ASAP."

"What about?" Slade asked.

"The kid's father for starters."

"Okay, I'll try to find Kurt."

"Don't try. Do it."

Slade's eyes flared and he slanted Thorne a condescending, don't-push-me-around smile. "Don't worry, brother. I'll handle it." With that he turned and walked away.

"Hell, you can be an insufferable bastard," Matt growled. "You might be used to barking orders at your office and everyone hustles to do what you want, but back off a bit, okay? We're all in this together. Slade'll call Striker."

"Will he?" Thorne's eyes narrowed. "It seems to me he's made a lot of promises in his life that he somehow managed to forget."

"He's straightening out."

"Good, 'cause he sure as hell has messed up his life."

"Not all of us are blessed with the Midas touch," Matt reminded him. "And, as far as I can see, you're not in much of a position to start slinging arrows." Matt glanced through the glass to Nicole. "Somethin' about the lady doctor that's got you riled?"

Thorne didn't respond.

"Thought so." Matt's smile was positively irritating. "Well, good luck. She doesn't much look like a filly that's easy to tame."

"This has nothing to do with her."

"Right. I forgot. You never get too involved with a woman, now, do ya?" Matt gave an exaggerated wink, pointed his finger at Thorne's chest, then sauntered down the hall after Slade.

Irritated as hell Thorne waited, watching Nicole and Dr. Arnold through the glass, hating the feeling that he was powerless, that the baby's life was out of his control, and that his brother had seen through his facade of indifference when it came to Nicole Sanders Stevenson. The truth of the matter was that she'd already gotten under his skin. He'd kissed her last night not certain of her marital state, not really giving a damn, then taken a flower to her doorstep like some kind of junior high kid suffering some kind of crush. Afterward he'd called her and manipulated the facts just to get a date with the woman. He'd never acted this way before. Never. Didn't understand it. Yes, she was beautiful and beyond that she was smart. Sassy and clever. But deeper still, he sensed a woman like no other he'd ever met. And he'd lost her once. Given her up all for the sake of making a buck.

He was still mentally kicking himself up one side and down the other when Nicole emerged. Her brow was creased, her eyes shadowed with concern.

"How bad is it?" Thorne asked.

Little lines appeared between her eyebrows and he braced himself for the worst. "It's not good, Thorne, but Dr. Arnold is doing everything he can here. He's also linked by computer to other neonatologists across the country."

Thorne's jaw was clenched so hard it ached. "What can I do?"

"Be patient and wait."

"Not my strong suit."

"I know." The ghost of a smile crossed her lips as they walked down the stairs and outside together. Nicole flipped up her hood and held it tightly around her chin. They dashed through puddles to her SUV while sleet pelted from the sky in icy needles.

"Thanks for calling me and letting me know about J.R.," he said as they reached the rig.

"J.R.? That's the baby's name?"

"He doesn't really have one. But I've been thinking that he should be named after my father since Randi is still in a coma and well…who knows what she'll call him when she wakes up." *If she wakes up. If the baby survives.* "Anyway, I appreciate the call."

"No problem. I said I would." She fumbled in her purse, found her keys and unlocked the door.

"Yeah, but you didn't have to go to the trouble of getting a babysitter and driving down here." It had touched him.

"I thought it would be best." She flashed him a small grin. "Believe it or not, Thorne, some of the doctors here, including Dr. Arnold and me, really care about our patients. It's not a matter of clocking in and out on a schedule so much as it is about making sure the patient not only survives but receives the best care possible."

"I know that."

"Good." She blinked against the drops of water running down her face and a twinkle lighted her gold eyes. "Okay, so now you owe me one."

"Name it," he said so softly that she barely heard the words, but when she looked into his face and saw an unspoken message in his eyes, her throat caught and she was suddenly touched in the most dangerous part of her heart. She remembered his kiss, just yesterday in this very parking lot, and she couldn't forget all the passion that was coiled behind the press of his lips against hers. And that was just the start of it. She knew that within the past day and a half her life had changed irrevocably, that she and Thorne had rediscovered each other and it scared the devil out of her, so much that she couldn't think about it. Not now. Not ever. "Careful, McCafferty," she said, clearing her throat. "Giving me carte blanche could be dangerous."

"I've never been one to steer clear of trouble."

"I know." She sighed, remembering how many of her friends had tried to warn her off Thorne way back when. The McCafferty boys were known as everything from rogues to hellions who always managed to find more than their share of trouble. "Look, I've got to go—"

He grabbed the crook of her elbow. "I meant it when I said thank you, Nicole. And I really am sorry."

"For—?"

"For taking off on you way back when."

Her heart jolted a bit when she realized his thoughts had taken the same wayward path as her own. As the wind ripped the hood from her head, she warned herself not to trust him. "That was a long, long time ago, Thorne. We—well, I was a kid. Didn't really know what I wanted. Let's just forget it."

"Maybe I can't."

"Well, you did a damned fine job of it for a lot of years."

"Not as fine as I'd hoped," he said. "Look, I'd just like to set the record straight."

"Now?" She glanced away from him and felt her pulse skyrocketing as the sleet ran down her neck. "How about another time? When we're both not in danger of freezing?"

His fingers gave up their possessive grip and she yanked open the door. Hoisting herself behind the wheel, she pulled the door shut and plunged her key into the ignition. With a flick of her wrist, she tried to start the engine. It ground, then died. She pumped the gas, all too aware that Thorne hadn't moved. He stood outside the driver's door, his bare head soaked, his long coat dripping, as she tried again. The engine turned over slowly, revved a bit and then sputtered out.

Three more flicks of her wrist.

Three more grinding attempts until there was no sound at all. "No," she muttered, but knew it was over. The damned rig wasn't going to move unless she got behind it and started pushing. "Great. Just…great." And Thorne was still standing there, like a man without a lick of sense who wouldn't come in out of the freezing rain.

He opened the door. "Need a ride?"

"What I need is a mechanic—one who knows a piston from a tailpipe!" she grumbled, but reached for her purse and slid to the ground. "Failing that, I suppose a ride would be the next best thing." She locked the SUV, abstained from kicking it and turned. He took her hand in his, linking cold, wet fingers through hers as they dashed to his pickup. She told herself not to make any more of this than what it was, just an old friend offering help. But she knew better.

Once inside the cab, she swiped water from her face and directed him through town as the defroster chased away the condensation on the windows. He drove carefully, negotiating streets that were slick with puddles of ice as the radio played softly.

"So tell me about yourself." Headlights from slowly passing cars illuminated the bladed angles of his face and she reminded herself that he really wasn't all that handsome, that he was a corporate lawyer, for God's sake, the kind of man she wanted to avoid.

"What do you want to know?" she asked.

"How you got to be a doctor."

"Medical school."

He arched a brow and she laughed. "Okay, okay, I know what you mean," she admitted, glad to have broken some of the ice that seemed to exist between them. "Guess I wanted to prove myself. My mother always told me to aim high, that I could achieve whatever I wanted and I believed her. She insisted I have a career where I didn't have to rely on a man." And Nicole knew why. Her own father had taken off when she was barely two and no one had seen or heard from him since. No child support. No birthday cards. Not even a phone call at Christmas. If her mother knew where he was, she'd never said and her answer to all of Nicole's questions had never wavered. *"He's gone. Took off when we needed him most. Well, we don't need him now and never will. Trust me, Nicole, we don't want to know what happened to him. It really doesn't matter one way or another if he's dead or alive."* At that point in the speech she'd usually bend on a knee to look her young daughter straight in the eye. Strong maternal fingers had held firm to Nicole's small shoulders. "You can do anything you want, honey. You don't need a deadbeat of a father to prove that. You don't need a husband. No—you'll do it all on your own, I know you will and you can do and be anything, *any*one you want. The sky's the limit."

In the last few years Nicole had wondered secretly if her need to succeed, her driving ambition, her quest to make her mark was some inner need to prove to herself that she could make it on her own and that the reason her father left had nothing to do with her.

Of course at seventeen, after meeting Thorne McCafferty, she'd fallen head over heels in love and been ready to chuck all her plans—her dreams and her mother's hopes—for one man...a man who hadn't cared enough for her to explain what had gone wrong.

Until now.

She sensed it coming. Like the clouds gathering before a storm, the warning signs that Thorne hadn't given up his need to explain himself were evident in the set of his jaw and thin line of his mouth.

He waited until the second light, then slowed the truck and turned down the radio. "I said I wanted to explain what happened."

"And I said I thought it could wait."

"It's been nearly twenty years, Nikki."

She closed her eyes and her heart fluttered stupidly at the nickname she'd carried with her through high school, the only name he'd called her. "So why rush things?" *Don't be taken in, Nicole. He used you once and obviously he thinks he can do it again.*

He let her sarcasm slide by. "I was wrong."

"About?" she said in a voice so low, she thought he might not have heard her.

"Everything. You. Me. What's important in life. I thought I had to go out and prove myself. I thought I couldn't get entangled with anyone or anything—I had to be free. I thought I had to finish law school and make a million dollars. After that I thought I'd better keep at it."

"And now you don't?" She didn't believe him.

"And now I'm not sure," he admitted, his fingers drumming on the steering wheel as the interior of the cab started to fog.

"Sounds like midlife crisis to me."

He shifted down and took a corner a little too fast. "Easy answer."

"Usually right on."

"You really believe that?"

She leaned back in the seat and stared out the window to the neon lights of the old theater, and wondered why she was in this discussion. "Let's just say I've experienced it firsthand."

"Oh."

"And I swore to myself that the next midlife crisis I was going to suffer through was going to be my own."

He parked at the curb in front of her little bungalow and she reached for the door handle. "I suppose I could ask you in for some coffee, or cocoa or tea or something."

"You could."

She hesitated, one hand on the door handle. "Then again, maybe it wouldn't be such a good idea."

"And why's that?"

She tilted up her chin a bit. "Because this is getting a little too personal, I think."

"And you'd rather keep it professional."

"It would be best for everyone. Randi—the baby—"

To her surprise one side of his mouth lifted in a sexy, damnably arrogant slash of white. "Is that the reason, Doctor, or is it that you're scared of me?"

No, Thorne, I'm not scared of you. I'm scared of me. "Don't flatter yourself."

"Why should I stop now?" He reached for her, dragged her close and started to kiss her, only to stop short, his mouth the barest of whispers from hers. His breath fanned her face. "Good night, Nikki." Then he released her. She opened the door and nearly fell out of the truck. Embarrassment washed up her cheeks as she strode to the door and felt him watching her, waiting until she made it inside. Then he threw his truck into gear and took off, disappearing through the veil of silvery sleet.

Chapter 6

"Damn!" Thorne slammed down the receiver and stared out the window to a winter-crisp day where evidence of last night's storm still glistened on the grass and hung from the eaves in shimmering icicles. A headache pounded behind his eyes. He'd been on the phone all morning, guzzling cups of coffee as bitter as a spinster's heart.

He'd bedded down in his old room, the one that had abutted his folks' suite and his brothers had, by instinct, claimed the bedrooms where they'd been raised. But when he'd awoken this morning he'd been alone in the house.

During the intervening hours, he'd called the hospital, hoping for a report of improvement in Randi and the baby's condition. As far as he could tell, nothing had changed. His sister was still comatose and the baby, though stable, was still in danger. He'd hooked up his laptop computer to the antiquated phone lines and looked up everything he could on little J.R.'s condition. From what he could determine, everything that

could be done to counteract the meningitis was being done
at St. James. He'd even managed to call the office, check in
with Eloise and tell her that he hoped a portable office would
be set up here, in his father's den, by the end of the day. He
wondered what John Randall would've done in a similar situation and, thinking about his father, removed the gift he'd
been given from his pocket. The ring winked in the sunlight
and Thorne folded his hand over the silver-and-gold band.

"I want you to marry. Give me grandchildren." John Randall's
request seemed to bounce off the walls of this old pine-paneled
room that still smelled faintly of the elder McCafferty's cigars
and Nicole's image came to mind, the only woman he'd ever
dated that he'd considered as a mother for his children. And
that thought had scared him nearly twenty years ago. It still
did because nothing had changed. Oh, there had been a lot
of women since he'd dated her; Thorne hadn't been celibate
by any means, but no one woman had come close to touching his heart.

Until he'd seen Nicole again.

Not that he wanted a wife or mother for his children or—

What was he thinking? Wife? Children? Not him. Not
now. Probably not ever…and yet…the reason he was thinking this way was probably because of his father's dying request,
his father's wedding ring, and the fact that his own mortality
wouldn't go on forever. Randi's situation was proof enough
of that.

Oh, for the love of God. Enough with these morbid
thoughts. He looked around this room again and wondered
how many deals had been concocted here in the past. How
many family or business decisions dreamed up while John
Randall had puffed on a black market Havana cigar, rested
the worn heels of his boots on the scarred maple desk and

leaned back in a leather chair that had been worn smooth by years of use?

This damned metal band had been his father's wedding ring, a gift from Larissa, Thorne's mother, on their wedding day. John Randall had worn it proudly until Larissa had found out about Penelope, the younger woman whom her philandering husband had been seeing. The woman who had broken up a marriage that had already been foundering. The woman who had eventually given John Randall his only daughter.

And now Thorne's mother, too, was dead, a heart attack just two years ago taking her life.

Thorne slid the ring into his pocket and reached for the phone again. He dialed Nicole's number and hung up when her answering machine picked up. Drumming his fingers on the desktop he wondered if she'd managed to get her car towed, if she'd found another means of transportation and how, as a single mother of four-year-old twins she was getting along. "Not that it's any of your business," he reminded himself, bothered nonetheless. He wondered about her marital state—about the man who had been her husband, then forced himself to concentrate on the problems at hand—there were certainly enough without borrowing more. Nicole was a professional, a mother, and a levelheaded woman. She'd be fine. She had to be.

He heard the sound of the front door opening and the heavy tread of boots. "Anyone here?" Slade yelled, his uneven footsteps becoming louder.

"In the den."

Slade appeared in the doorway. He was wearing beat-up jeans, a flannel shirt and a day's worth of whiskers he hadn't bothered to shave. A denim jacket with frayed cuffs was his only protection against the weather. He held a paper coffee cup in one hand. "Good mornin'."

"Not yet, it isn't."

Slade's countenance turned grim. "Don't tell me there's more bad news. I called the hospital a couple of hours ago. They said there was no change."

"There isn't. Randi's still in critical condition and the baby's holding his own." Thorne rounded the desk and snapped off his laptop, turning off his link to the outside world—news, weather and stock reports. "I was talking about everything else."

"Such as?"

"To begin with, your friend Striker hasn't returned any of my calls, Randi's editor at the *Clarion* is always 'out' or 'in a meeting.' I think he's avoiding me. I've talked to the sheriff's department, but so far there's nothing new. A detective is supposed to call me back. The good news is that the equipment I ordered for this office is due to arrive today, and the phone company's gonna come in and install a couple of lines. I've talked to an agency specializing in nannies as we'll need one when J.R. gets home—"

"J.R.?" Slade repeated.

"I call the baby that."

"After Dad?" Slade asked, obviously perplexed.

"And Randi."

Slade gave out a long, low whistle. "You have been busy, haven't you?"

Thorne elevated an eyebrow and remembered that this was his youngest brother, the playboy, a man who had never settled down to any kind of responsibility.

"All I've had time for this morning is a call into Striker and a couple of cups of weak coffee down at the Pub'n'Grub. I ran into Larry Todd down there."

"Why does his name sound familiar?"

"Because he was the man who ran this place when Dad became ill."

Thorne settled into his father's chair and leaned back until it squeaked in protest.

"Get this. Randi kept Larry on when she inherited the bulk of this place."

Thorne remembered, though he hadn't paid much attention at the time. He'd been in negotiations for the Canterbury Farms subdivision at the time and had been dealing with land use laws, an environmental group, the city council and an accounting nightmare because one of his bookkeepers had been caught embezzling off the previous project. On top of all that, John Randall had died and Thorne, though he'd known his father was dying, had been stricken by the news and assuaged by grief. He hadn't cared much about the sixth of the ranch he'd inherited and had left Randi, who owned half of the acres and the old ranch house, to run the place as she saw fit.

"But just last week, Randi called Larry up, told him she didn't need him any longer and that she'd pay him a couple of months' severance pay."

Thorne's head snapped up. "Why?"

"Beats me. Larry was really ticked off."

"When did this happen?"

"A day before the accident."

"Did she hire anyone else?"

"Don't know. I just found out about it."

"Someone would have to come and look after the stock."

"You'd think." He saw movement outside the window and watched Matt hiking the collar of his jacket more closely around his neck as he made his way to the back door. Slade frowned. "Guess I'd better help out with the cattle. I told Larry we'd hire him back, but he's pretty mad. I thought Matt might talk to him."

"Let's see."

They convened in the kitchen where Matt had set his hat on the table and had flung his jacket over the back of a ladder-back chair. He was in the process of pouring himself a cup of coffee. "There's nothing to eat around here," he grumbled as he searched in the refrigerator, then the cupboard. He dragged out an old jar of instant creamer and poured in a healthy dose as Slade and Thorne filled him in on everything they'd already discussed.

"We need Larry Todd back on the payroll," Thorne said to Matt. "Slade ran into him today and thought you might talk to him."

Matt studied the contents of his cup and nodded slowly. "I can try. But he called me after Randi let him go, and to say he was a little ticked off is an understatement."

"See what he wants," Thorne suggested.

"I'll give it a shot."

"Convince him."

"I'll try." Matt slowly stirred his coffee. "But Larry's been known to be stubborn."

"We'll deal with that. I've got a call in to Juanita to see if she'll come on board again," Thorne said.

"She might be working for someone else by now. Randi let her go after Dad died." Matt hoisted himself onto the counter and his feet swung free.

"Then we'll have to make it attractive enough that she'll come back."

"Might not be that easy," Slade said, sipping coffee from his paper cup. "Some people feel obligated to stay with their employer."

"Everyone can be bought."

Slade and Matt exchanged glances.

Thorne didn't waver. "Everyone has a price."

"Including you?" Matt asked.

Thorne's jaw hardened. "Yep."

Slade snorted in contempt. "Hell, you're a cynic."

"Aren't we all?" Thorne said, undeterred. "And we'll need a nurse. When Randi and the baby get here, we'll need professional help." He was running through a mental checklist. "I'll call a law firm I used to deal with."

"A law firm?" Slade shook his head. "Why in the world would we need lawyers?"

"For when we find the boy's father—he might want custody."

"He should probably get it, at least partial," Matt allowed.

"Maybe, maybe not. We don't know a thing about this guy."

Slade rolled his eyes and tossed the remains of his coffee into the sink. "For the love of Mike, Thorne, don't you trust anyone?"

"Nope."

"If Randi chose this guy, he might be all right," Matt conceded.

"So then where is he? Assuming he knows that she was pregnant, why the hell hasn't he appeared?" The same old questions that had been plaguing Thorne ever since learning of his sister's accident gnawed at him. "If he's such a peach of a guy, why isn't he with her?"

"Maybe she doesn't want him." Slade lifted a shoulder. "It happens."

"Any way around it, we'll need to see about our rights, the baby's rights, Randi's rights and—"

"And the father's rights." Matt pointed out before taking a long swallow of coffee. "Okay, I've got to run into town and go to the feed store. While I'm there I'll pick up some supplies and hit the grocery store for a few things. When I get back, I'll call Larry."

Slade reached into his pocket for a pack of cigarettes. "I'll ride into town with you," he said to Matt. "I want to talk to the sheriff's department, find out what they know about Randi's accident."

"Good idea," Thorne agreed. "I've called but haven't heard back."

"Figures. Look, I've left a message with Striker, but I'll phone him again," Slade promised, shaking out a cigarette and jabbing the filter tip into the corner of his mouth. "What's your game plan?"

"I'm setting up my office in the den, already scheduled equipment delivery and then I'm going to run into town myself. Visit Randi and the baby." He didn't add that he intended to see Nicole again.

"Yeah. I figured we'd stop by the hospital, too," Matt allowed. "If you get any calls from Mike Kavanaugh, tell him I'll call him back."

"Who's Kavanaugh?" Thorne asked.

"My neighbor. He's looking after my spread while I'm here."

Slade crumpled his empty coffee cup and threw it into the trash. "How long will he take care of it?"

Matt shrugged into his jacket and squared his hat on his head. "As long as it takes." He locked gazes with his brothers. "Randi and the baby come first."

Nicole ground the gears of the rental car and swore under her breath. She wheeled into the parking lot of the hospital and told herself to trust that the mechanics looking at the SUV could find the problem, get the part, fix whatever was wrong, and return it to her soon, without it costing an arm and a leg.

She had half an hour before she was actually on duty and planned to use the time to check on Randi McCafferty and the baby before taking over in the ER.

Setting the emergency brake, she switched off the rental, grabbed her briefcase and told herself that her interest in Randi and the baby was just common courtesy and professional concern, that oftentimes she looked in on patients once they'd been moved from the ER. This wasn't about Thorne. No way. The fact that he was related to Randi was incidental.

She argued with herself all the way through the physicians' entrance and in the elevator to her office.

"Something wrong?" a nurse she'd known since she'd arrived at St. James asked as she passed the nurses' station in the west wing.

"What?"

"You look worried. Are the twins okay?"

"Yes, I mean Molly has a case of the sniffles, but nothing a little TLC and a couple of Disney movies won't cure. I guess I was just thinking."

"Well, smile a little when you think," the nurse said with a wink.

"I'll try."

She made her way to the Intensive Care Unit, where she looked at Randi's chart. "Any change?" she asked.

"Not much," Betty, the ICU nurse, said with a shake of perfectly coiffed red curls. "Still comatose. Unresponsive, but hanging in there. How's the baby?"

"Not good," Nicole admitted as she glanced into Betty's concerned gaze. "I'm on my way to check on him now."

Betty's lips folded in on themselves. The gold cross suspended from her neck winked against her skin. "A shame," she said.

"Where there's life, there's hope." Nicole glanced over Randi's chart, then headed down to Neonatal Pediatrics where little J.R., as Thorne called him, was struggling for his life. As she stared at the tiny baby, hooked up to tubes and monitors, her heart ached. She remembered the birth of her own twins, the elation of seeing each little girl for the first time, the feeling of relief that they were both so perfect and healthy. She'd been jubilant and even Paul, at that time, had seemed happy. He'd looked at her with tears in his eyes and told her, "They're beautiful, Nicole. As beautiful as their mother."

His kind words still haunted her. Were they the last he'd ever spoken to her? Surely not. There had to have been a few more compliments and tender glances before the toll of two high-powered jobs and rambunctious daughters had robbed the marriage of whatever gel had bound it together. Naively Nicole had believed that children would bring Paul and her closer together—of course she'd been wrong. Bitterly so.

"Has Dr. Arnold been in today?" she asked the nurse on duty.

"Twice."

"Good." *Come on, J.R.,* she thought watching the tiny fingers curl into fists. *Fight. You can do it!*

But the baby looked so frail, so small and his vital signs hadn't improved.

"Has the family been in?"

"All three uncles at one time or another."

Nicole had suspected as much. If anything, the McCafferty brothers seemed determined to see that their sister and her son improved, if only by their sheer, collective will. If only it was that easy. "I'll be back later," she said and walked into the hallway, nearly bumping into Thorne in the process. She glanced up to his worried gray eyes and she felt her heart turn over for him as he so obviously loved this little baby.

"How's he doing?"

"The same," she said, turning to look through the glass at the baby. "I thought you'd already been in."

"Couldn't stay away," he said, then cleared his throat. "I

had business in town and thought I'd stop by again." He stared at the tiny baby and for an instant Nicole wondered what it would have been like if she and Thorne had had a child together. If things had turned out differently, would they have become parents? Bittersweet were the thoughts, for certainly if she and Thorne had both stayed in Grand Hope, she wouldn't have become a doctor nor would she have her own precious daughters.

"J.R.'s a fighter," she said, touching the back of Thorne's hand. "Try not to worry."

One side of his mouth lifted in a cynical smile. "That seems to be impossible."

"Anything's possible, Thorne," she said and wondered why she felt compelled to comfort him. He turned his hand around and clasped her fingers in his.

"Do you really believe that?"

"With all my heart." Their gazes locked and she thought she might drop right through the floor. The hospital seemed to recede in a fine mist and she felt as if she and he were alone in the universe. Oh, God, this was so wrong....

Her pager buzzed and she dropped his hand. Digging in her pocket, feeling heat wash up her neck, she found the beeper and read the message. "I've got to run." She looked up at him again. "Have faith, Thorne. J.R. will pull through." Why she'd said something she couldn't possibly know as truth, she didn't understand, but she turned quickly on her heel and hurried to the emergency room where she was due to start her shift.

She was immediately accosted by an admitting nurse. "When it rains it pours. Been quiet here for hours, but now we're swamped. You can start with room three. We've got a seven-year-old girl who fell off her horse. Looks like she might have broken her wrist."

"On my way."

"After that, there's a teenager with a sinus infection, and a toddler with a pea wedged up her nose. An RN tried to help, but the mother wants a doctor to look at it." The nurse rolled her eyes. "New mother. This is her first."

"Reassure her that the nurse can handle the extraction and I'll check it out after I'm done with the others."

"Will do—uh-oh." The nurse frowned as she looked over Nicole's shoulders.

"What?"

"Bad news. It's the press. They've been nosing around here ever since the McCafferty accident, but I thought it would die down by now." From the corner of her eye Nicole saw a van for a local news station roll to a stop just outside the windows of the waiting room. "Someone must've gotten wind that the baby was in distress."

"Great."

The nurse's mouth curved into a pained expression. "It doesn't take much in Grand Hope to cause a stir, does it?"

"Never has," Nicole said. The McCafferty family had always been a subject of interest to the townspeople as John Randall had been a flamboyant, once rich man who had actually run for local politics. His public and private life had been the subject of more than one wagging tongue—and his sons had been wild as teenagers, always getting into trouble; but, as the town had grown and the McCafferty children had become adults and spread like seeds in the wind, they had garnered less interest.

"I'd better go see what's up," the nurse said.

Nicole had more important things to do than worry about the press. She pulled the chart of the girl with the broken wrist from the door, scanned the information and, managing a smile, forced all thoughts of Thorne's family from her mind as she spied a frightened blonde girl with a tearstained face sitting on the edge of the examining table. Dirt and grass stains were ground into her bib overalls and her mother, a petite woman with worried eyes behind thick glasses stood as Nicole entered.

"You're Sally," Nicole said to the girl who nodded slowly.

"Yes, yes. And I'm her mother. Leslie Biggs. She was riding her horse and fell off just as they got back to the barn. I was on the porch when I saw it, heard her cry...." The mother's voice, gruff and soft, fell away.

"I fell off a horse when I was about your age," Nicole told her new patient.

"Did you?" The girl sniffed, her eyes rounded, but there was a hint of suspicion in her words, as if she expected the doctor to try to cajole her into a good mood.

"Yeah, but I was lucky, I didn't hurt anything except my pride. I was showing off for a boy, thought I could make my pony jump over a pile of firewood and he balked. Stopped dead short. I kept going. Landed in a cow pie." She sent the mother a quick glance. "I think a basic law of physics was involved."

"Ick." The new patient giggled then cried out as Nicole gingerly touched her swollen arm.

"Yep. I never landed a date with Teddy Crenshaw after that. Nope. In fact, he told the story all over school."

"What a creep."

"I thought so. Talk about embarrassing. Now, let's see what we've got here. Looks like we're going to need some X rays..."

Dead tired, Nicole, finished with her shift, rounded the corner to her office and spied Thorne, big as life, leaning one broad shoulder against the frame of her locked door. He was less intimidating in casual slacks and a sweater, a leather coat unzipped and gaping open.

She nearly missed a step and her stupid heart fluttered as she caught the intensity of his silvery gaze. Lord, what was it about the man that always put her on edge? The plain truth of the matter was that the man bothered her. He always had. He reminded her of a runaway train on a downhill track, a locomotive that gathered speed to race headlong toward his destination. "You work here now?" she joked.

"Seems like it."

"Seriously, have you been here the whole time?"

"No." He flashed her the remnant of a smile. "Believe it or not, I do have a life of my own. I came back looking for you."

"For me?" She didn't know whether to be flattered or wary. "So you just waited at my office? How'd you know I'd be showing up here? Sometimes I take off directly from the ER."

"Lucky guess."

She arched an eyebrow as she unlocked her door. "Somehow I don't think you ever rely on luck."

"So I called."

"Mmm." The door opened and she stepped inside. He was right behind her. "I assume you've seen your sister and the baby again."

"Yep."

"Any change?"

"Not that anyone's saying."

"I've got a call in to Dr. Arnold."

"So do I."

Rounding her desk, she slid into her chair and said, "Let me check my messages." Thorne waited, standing in the doorway and she waved him inside as she listened to several quick recordings—one from the mechanic. They'd located a part and would start working on the SUV as soon as it arrived. The second call was from Jenny saying she was taking the twins to the park, two more were from specialists she'd consulted with and finally a quick message from Dr. Arnold, giving her an update. She called him back, got his machine again and left another message.

Hanging up, she shrugged. "Nothing. The baby's stable. His condition hasn't worsened and Dr. Arnold is guardedly optimistic." She noticed Thorne's eyebrows slam together, saw his jaw set in frustration.

"There must be something more you can do."

She bristled slightly. "You know that Dr. Arnold's in contact with other physicians and pediatric units across the country—linked up by computer."

"Maybe it's not enough."

"So what do you suggest?"

"You're the doctor."

"Then trust me. Trust Dr. Arnold."

"I guess I don't have much choice," he admitted, rubbing his jaw and scowling.

"There are always choices, Thorne. Just not good ones. Moving the baby to another hospital would be a big mistake."

"Like I said, no other choices."

Feeling as if he were questioning the integrity of the hospital, she wanted to argue, but she didn't. He was upset, understandably so. A man who was used to being in charge, in control of every facet of his life, reduced to the mere mortal status.

"Have a little faith," she told him.

If only he could. As Thorne gazed into Nicole's amber eyes, he felt only a slight case of well-being. But he told himself not to be seduced into a lull, just because he was starting to care for this woman. He couldn't afford to become complacent, not while his sister was battling for her life and the baby was struggling for his. There had to be something more that he could do. "I'll try," he said and caught a shadow of a smile tug at the corners of her lips.

For a second he thought of the kiss they'd shared so recently, the intimate linking of their hands this afternoon and how it had felt years ago, to make sweet, sensuous love to her. The turn of his thoughts was insane, here in this sterile office, with the sounds of the hospital vibrating behind him, and yet he couldn't keep his mind from straying to a simpler, more innocent time when he and Nicole had made love in the long hay ready to be cut, while the Montana sun had shone on two naked bodies glistening with sweat, flushed from the heat of recent lovemaking and supple with youth. He'd kissed her then and she, giggling, had struggled to her feet, dashed through the waist-high grass and down a soft slope to the creek where she'd splashed through the shallow water and he, chasing after her, had caught her before she'd scrambled up the opposite bank. He'd kissed her again, the cool water swirling and eddying around her knees and then he'd cradled her body, drawn her down and made love to her in the creek, where the sunlight pierced the branches of aspen and pine to sparkle on the clear surface.

Finches and tanagers had fluttered in branches, singing over the babble of the creek and butterflies and water skippers had joined a few bees hovering near the water, but all Thorne really remembered was the silky feel of Nicole's skin against his, the play of her muscles and the taste of her mouth as she kissed him wildly.

Now, staring at her he felt those same male stirrings that had been forever with him when he was near her. No longer a tanned girl running naked through a country field, she was a woman, a doctor dressed in a lab coat, seated in an office that boasted of the professional woman she'd become.

Surrounded by tomes of medical information, a sleek computer, certificates and degrees decorating the walls, Nicole Stevenson had come a long way since she'd been Nikki Sanders, a smart, pretty high school girl with big dreams and little else. As if she, too, in that split second remembered their reckless, jubilant lovemaking, she cleared her throat. "Well, good, then that's that."

"When are you finished here?"

"Just about done," she admitted, and straightened a few files that were scattered over her desk. A forgotten, half-drunk cup of coffee, stained with peach-colored smudges from her lipstick sat unattended near her computer. On a small bookcase, along with medical books, were several picture frames that showed off photos of her daughters smiling and bright-eyed as they posed for the camera.

"So those are your daughters," he guessed, surveying the snapshots of the sprites.

She nodded, her eyes glowing with parental pride. "Molly and Mindy and yes, I can tell them apart."

He laughed. "But no one else can."

"Just their father," she admitted and seemed suddenly uncomfortable. "Or at least he could at one time. It's been a while since he spent much time with them."

"Why?"

She hesitated, sighed and picked up one of the framed photos. "Lots of reasons. Time. Distance. Space...but I'd say the most important was disinterest. Don't quote me, though, I'm just the ex-wife who carries a grudge." She set the picture back on the bookcase, ran her finger over the surface as if checking for dust and straightened. "But I'm sure you didn't come here to hear me complain about my divorce."

"Actually I stopped by to see if you needed a ride. Your rig's not in the lot."

"Towed earlier. And thanks." She was touched that he'd thought of her, then reminded herself not to trust him. He'd left her once before, destroyed all her silly schoolgirl fantasies. "But I've got a rental."

"When will the SUV be ready?"

"That's the sixty-four-thousand-dollar question, I'm afraid. Don't know yet."

"Well, if you need another vehicle we've got more than we need at the ranch and I'd give you a ride anytime."

His eyes held hers for a split second and the back of her throat went dry. Unspoken messages—all male—filled his gaze.

"Thanks. I'll let you know."

"Do. And there's one more thing."

"What?" she asked, looking up.

"Would you have dinner with me?"

"What?" To his amusement, she actually looked shocked.

Thorne's lips curved into a satisfied smile. "I just asked you for a date. For Saturday night. This shouldn't come as a big surprise. I think we talked about it a few days ago." He folded his arms across his wide chest and smiled. "So, Doctor, what do you say?"

Chapter 7

"I just don't want the rug pulled out from under me again," Larry Todd said. He was tall, about six-three or six-four, with straight blond hair that fell over piercing green eyes. Somewhere between forty-five and fifty, he stood military straight on the porch, a thick jacket zipped to his neck as a raw wind chased down the valley.

"I'll draw up a contract for a year," Thorne assured him. "By that time Randi should be in charge again. Then you can deal with her."

Frowning slightly, Larry gave a sharp nod. "Okay." He slid a glance at the three brothers who had spent the day showing him around the place that he already knew like the back of his hand. If anything, Larry had pointed out the flaws in the ranch—the stretches of fence that needed to be repaired, the way the soil was eroding on the north side, why it would be a good idea to sell off some of the timber on the lower slopes of the foothills, pointing out that buying a new bailer wasn't necessary this year, while investing in a larger tractor was a necessity. He knew about a neighbor's bull—a prize-winner that could be traded for one on the ranch to mix up the genes of the herd. Why Randi had seen fit to let him go was beyond Thorne.

"So, how is that sister of yours?" Larry asked and, despite his falling out with Randi, deep grooves of concern stretched across his brow.

"Still in a coma." Slade kicked at a small dirt clod with the toe of his boot.

"But she'll pull through."

"The doctors think so," Thorne replied.

"And the baby?"

The men exchanged glances. Thorne said, "We had a scare. He's still not out of the woods, but he's doin' better."

"Good. Good." Larry tugged at the hem of his gloves, fitting the rough leather more tightly around his fingers as the phone blasted from inside the house. "Draw up that contract and we'll talk again."

He took the steps toward his pickup as Thorne heard Juanita shout his name.

"Mister Thorne. Telephone!" she yelled and all three brothers smiled. It was good to have her back. They'd grown up with her heartfelt convictions, flashing dark eyes and stern sense of right and wrong.

Thorne stepped inside the house. "Boots off!" Juanita's voice rang from the vicinity of the kitchen. She appeared, round-faced, her black hair now shot with strands of wiry gray, wiping her hands on the edge of her apron. "It's your secretary."

"I'll take it in the den." Thorne snapped up the receiver and listened as his secretary gave him an update on his ongoing projects. The development he was working on with Annette's dad had hit a snag with the planning commission, there was threat of a framers' strike and a real estate agent he worked with was "frantic" to talk to him.

By the time he got off the phone his brothers had settled into the living room. They stood in stocking feet, warming the backs of their legs against the fire. Their jeans were grimy and they smelled of horses and dirt. A silver belt buckle—the one their father had won at a long-forgotten rodeo—held up Matt's Levi's and the watch John Randall had worn for as long as Thorne could remember was strapped to Slade's wrist. So they all carried mementos of the man who had sired them—personal gifts he'd bestowed upon them with strings attached—just like the ring Thorne had gotten. Thorne wondered what promises John Randall had wrung from his younger brothers, but he didn't bother to ask.

"What's this about you having a date?" Slade asked, a crooked grin slashing through the dark stubble surrounding his chin.

Thorne met his brother's curious gaze steadily. "I thought I'd take Nicole out to dinner. That's all."

"Sure." Slade wasn't convinced.

A cat-who-ate-the-canary smile was pasted to Matt's square jaw and he shifted the toothpick he'd been sucking on from one side of his mouth to the other. "She isn't exactly your type, is she?"

"Meaning?"

"Kinda down-to-earth, for you." Matt said, obviously amused. "A woman with as much brains as beauty."

"The settlin' down kind," Slade added.

Thorne refused to be galled by his brothers' needling. Neither one had much room to talk when it came to affairs of the heart. "It's just a date," he said, but sensed that there was more involved. He'd had hundreds of dates in his life, spent hours with lots of women and yet tonight seemed different—

a little more serious. Maybe it was because Nicole worked at the hospital where his sister and her son were still recovering, but that wouldn't explain the slight elevation in his pulse at the sight of her, the restless nights when he dreamed of making love to her or the fact that he was breaking one of his own cardinal rules: Never Go Back.

Never in his life had he dated a person with whom he'd once before been involved. He figured there was just no rhyme or reason to it. If a love affair hadn't worked out in the past, why would a second try guarantee success? The old adage, Once Burned, Twice Shy, said it all. And yet here he was, planning a date with a woman who had been his lover long ago. He frowned for a second, remembering that he'd seduced her— taken her virginity and after a few short, hot-summer weeks, left her to her own devices.

It hadn't been that he'd grown tired of her; quite the opposite. The more he'd been with her, the more he'd wanted to be with her and it had scared the daylights out of him. At that point in his life he'd had too much to do, too many ambitions yet to be fulfilled. He didn't have time for a serious relationship or a girl he could have easily thought of as his wife.

The truth of the matter was that his feelings for Nicole had terrorized him. But then, he'd been little more than a boy at the time. Now, things had changed.

"If it's just a date, then why all the secrecy, and why did you ask me to—"

"Just take care of it, okay?" Thorne snapped.

"Okay, okay," Matt said holding his hands up, palms outward. "You got it. Two horses, saddled and waiting."

"What?" Slade clucked his tongue. "Horses? Have you flipped? You're taking out a *doctor*. One who practiced in *San Francisco* before she came here. She's a classy, sophisticated lady."

"But not the kind I regularly date?" Thorne threw back at him.

"Not the kind to jump on a horse in the middle of the winter." Slade shook his head as if his brother had gone stark, raving mad.

"Maybe I'm not taking a doctor out," Thorne said, though he didn't feel the need to explain himself. "Maybe I'm taking out an old friend. Nikki Sanders."

"Who's now a mother, divorced and an M.D."

"Well, you boys stay put and hold down the fort, would you? I'll handle Nikki."

"Or she'll handle you," Matt predicted. "Now listen, be careful with her, all right? She doesn't seem to be the love-'em-and-leave-'em type."

"And we might need to get hold of you. If there's any change in Randi or the baby's condition," Slade clarified.

"I'll have the cell phone with me."

Slade nodded. "Good. Just in case there's any trouble."

"There won't be!" Matt was insistent.

"Let's hope not," Slade said, unconsciously running a finger over the scar running down his cheek. "We've all had enough of that to last a lifetime."

Thorne couldn't disagree. For the past few years, it seemed as if bad luck had become a part of the family legacy. John Randall had lived life full, made and lost fortunes, enjoyed good health and believed that it was his God-given right to be good-looking, rich and powerful. He'd stepped on those who'd gotten in his way, cast off a good woman for a younger model, sired three sons and a daughter; but when fate had turned on him, shredding his fortune, stripping him of a fickle woman, robbing him of his health, he'd been shocked, flabbergasted that his luck had eluded him and the gods of fortune had seen fit to turn on him and laugh, mock him for his pitiful arrogance, in the end leaving him a shell of the man he'd once been.

His death hadn't ended the downward spiral. Randi had lost her mother less than a year earlier. Slade had suffered his own personal loss and Randi's accident, her coma and the illness of her newborn all seemed to be part of a cruel twist of fate.

But it was about to stop. It had to. Randi and little J.R. would recover. The mystery over the boy's paternity and her accident would be solved. Thorne would settle down, marry, have himself some kids.... He pulled up short as he reached the top of the stairs. How had his thoughts gotten so far out of line. Married? Kids?

"Not in this lifetime," he told himself, but felt the pressure of his father's wedding ring deep in the pocket of his slacks and had the vague suspicion that Dr. Nicole Stevenson might change his mind. The truth of the matter was that it was already happening. Even now, he couldn't wait until he saw her again.

Why had she ever agreed to something as foolish as a date? Nicole wondered as she flung on her favorite black dress, then wrinkled her nose in distaste at her reflection in the full-length mirror. The short silk was far too sophisticated for Grand Hope, and yet Thorne was used to big-city women who attended charity balls and gala events.

Her bed was littered with other outfits, everything from black jeans and casual sweaters to this damned dress. "It's just for a few hours," she chided herself as she felt like a damned schoolgirl getting ready for a date with the most popular guy in school. Gritting her teeth, she settled for gray wool slacks, a fitted navy cowl-necked sweater, sterling hoop earrings and black boots. "The everywhere outfit."

"Hey, Mommy. You beau–ti–ful," Mindy said as she slid into the room in her slipper-footed pajamas and drew up short.

Molly was on her heels, sliding headlong into the bed and sniffing loudly from her cold.

"Thanks," Nicole said. "But you're prejudiced."

"What's that mean?" Molly asked suspiciously.

"That you like me just because I'm your mommy."

"Yeth." Mindy nodded, running in circles around the free-standing mirror and Molly raced ever faster, sliding on the hardwood floor.

"Careful," Nicole said.

"Are they bothering you? Girls, come on into the kitchen," Jenny called. "Let's make some popcorn."

"They're fine," Nicole yelled back.

Molly gave chase to her twin, around and around the mirror. Both girls scampered gaily, laughing and shrieking as Nicole twisted her hair onto her head, applied a few strokes of mascara, a light dusting of eyeshadow and a slash of lipstick, then eyed her reflection again. She was struck by her image. Not because she was drop-dead gorgeous, but because there was a light in her eyes, a bit of anticipation, that startled her. For all intents and purposes, she looked damned close to a woman in love.

"Don't even go there," she told herself as she saw headlights flash through the panes of her bedroom window. *Thorne.* Her stomach did a quick nosedive.

"Go where?" Molly asked.

"You don't want to know."

"Where you going?" Mindy asked.

"Out." Nicole bent down to hug them both, careful not to let Molly's runny nose brush against her sweater.

"Here, let's take care of that," she offered, reaching onto

the bureau for a tissue, but Molly shrieked, shook her head violently and scampered off.

"It's okay."

Nicole caught her in the kitchen where Jenny was popping the corn and the smell of butter and sharp reports of the kernels popping reminded Nicole of a rifle range. There was a hard knock on the door and both twins slipped away and ran into the living room as fast as their little legs would carry them.

"I get it!" Mindy cried.

"No, me!" Molly shoved her out of the way, her springy curls flying wildly. Nicole caught up with her just as Mindy, without looking through the window, threw the door open. Cold air breezed through the house. Thorne stood on the stoop and Nicole, straddling a wiggling Molly managed to wipe her nose amid violent protests and wails.

"Sorry," she said, looking over her shoulder, her hair falling out of its clasp. "Come on in."

"No! No! Mommy, no!" Molly screamed.

Thorne entered as Nicole straightened, wadded the used tissue and blew her bangs from her eyes. Molly, her pride wounded, ran to her room while Mindy, sucking on a finger, looked up at the tall stranger with wide, suspicious eyes. "My daughter, Mindy," Nicole said, "and the tornado that just screamed down the hall is Molly."

"Am *not* a 'nado!" Molly protested.

Thorne couldn't swallow a smile. "And here I thought you were skinning live cats from the sound of it."

"I *hate* you, Mommy!" Molly screamed and slammed her door.

Nicole ignored the outburst and tucked her hair into place. "I'm so glad you got to see my parenting skills in action."

The door down the hall opened again. "I mean I really, *really* hate you!" Bang! The door slammed shut.

"Excuse me." Nicole's smile was forced. "I have to go deal with my daughter."

"Me, too." Mindy followed after her as Nicole headed down the hallway. She felt Thorne's eyes on her back and wished to God that he would have come at just about any other hour of the day. Why did the girls have to act up now? She tapped softly on the door. Molly's sobs were theatrically loud as Nicole entered and found her four-year-old draped dramatically across one of the twin beds.

Stepping over scattered dolls, clothes and toy cars, Nicole crossed the room. "Oh, honey, come on, it's not that bad."

"Is…is…too," Molly said, hiccuping through her tears.

Nicole gathered her into her arms, straightened and began rocking slowly, cradling her daughter's head into the crook of her neck, mindless of the damage of tears to her sweater. "Shh, shh, sweetheart," she whispered as Mindy, not wanting to be left out, wrapped her chubby little arms around one of her legs and eyed the doorway where Thorne appeared, his shoulders nearly touching each side. An amused smile played upon his lips and he folded his arms across his chest.

"Who he?" Molly asked crossly, her little face drawn into a frown.

"A…a friend. Mr. McCafferty."

"Thorne," he corrected and Molly's expression turned sour.

"Like on roses?"

"Just about."

Mindy giggled. "It's funny."

"Is it?" Thorne's eyes glinted a bit and he bent onto one knee. "Let's just say it's been a pain in my backside ever since I can remember. Lots of kids used to make fun of me. Now, what's your name?"

Mindy bit her lower lip.

"She's Mindy," Molly said looking down at her sister in disdain, her tears and trauma temporarily forgotten.

"And you're…?"

"Molly." Wriggling she struggled down to the floor and looked up at the stranger with her knowing, imperious four-year-old gaze.

"Mr. McCaff—er, Thorne and I are going out."

"You need any help?" Jenny's voice floated into the room and the top of her head was visible over Thorne's shoulder. He stepped into the room and she appeared, arms outstretched toward the twins.

"Jenny, this is Thorne McCafferty," Nicole said and before she could finish the introductions, the twins raced to Jenny's open arms.

"Popcorn?" Molly asked.

"You want some?"

"Yeth." Mindy nodded frantically.

"Good. Let's go into the kitchen and fix up some bowls." Jenny winked at Nicole, muttered a quick "Nice to meet you," and carried both twins out of the room.

"Welcome to my life," Nicole said, turning her palms upward as if to encompass the entire room. "It's kind of hectic."

He nodded slowly. "Between this and the ER, you're on the go most of the time." One side of his mouth lifted. "My guess is that you wouldn't have it any other way."

"Well, that's where you're wrong, Mr. McCafferty. In my ideal world I'm independently wealthy, living on a private tropical island and my nannies watch my children while I lie around a pool in the sun sipping frozen daiquiris and having a hunk of a pool boy named Ramon rub the kinks from my muscles."

He laughed and she giggled.

"You'd die of boredom in two days."

"Probably," she admitted, rolling her eyes. "Crazy as it is, I kinda like my life." She tried to pass him, but he grabbed her wrist and held fast.

"It's not crazy at all."

"No?" Her pulse skyrocketed and she felt the warmth of his fingertips against the soft skin adjacent to her palm.

"It's good." His gaze lingered on hers and for a split second she thought he would kiss her again, right here in the house with the kids only a few feet away. Her knees went weak at the thought. "Not many people appreciate their lives nor do they realize how lucky they are." His gaze slid to her lips and she swallowed hard.

"How about you? Do you know you're a lucky man?"

One dark brow rose insolently and her pulse fluttered crazily. His fingers tightened around her wrist. "At this moment I feel very lucky." His head lowered and his breath caressed her face. "Very lucky indeed." He brushed a kiss across her cheek and she gasped. Then he released her. "I think we'd better go now."

Dear Lord. She nearly sagged against the wall, but rallied. "Just give me a couple of minutes to change—this sweater has had it." She escaped to her room on weak legs, closed the door and drooped against it for a minute. What was wrong with her? He'd just touched her arm, for Pete's sake. He hadn't even kissed her and yet she'd nearly melted, like some idiotic, naive schoolgirl. *Just like the girl you once were when you dated him.*

"Damn it all anyway!" Suddenly angry at herself, she ripped off the sweater, looked down, saw that her slacks hadn't escaped their share of damage as well and sighed. From the depths of her closet she found another sweater—a red V neck and threw it over her head and traded the slacks for a long black denim skirt that buttoned up the front. Muttering under her breath, she undid her hair, swiped a brush through it and though it still crackled with electricity, decided she looked fine—good enough for the likes of Thorne McCafferty. She yanked her favorite black leather jacket from a hook on the back of her door and walked into the kitchen where Thorne, still amused, watched Molly throw pieces of popcorn at her sister while Jenny's attention was distracted.

Mindy shrieked. Jenny responded and Nicole couldn't get out of the house fast enough. She slid into her jacket, cinched the belt tight and planted a kiss on each twin's forehead, then did it again when the girls decided to put up a fuss. As she and Thorne walked onto the porch, the twins were wailing loudly, crying, "Mommy...don't go...Mommy, Mommy, Mommmeee—"

"It's nice to be wanted," Thorne observed, holding open the door of his truck as the wind tore at Nicole's hair.

"Always," she agreed, glancing to the house where two little sad faces were pressed against the windowpanes of the kitchen nook. She waved but neither girl responded other than to appear woefully forlorn. "This will last less than two minutes. As soon as the pickup disappears around the corner, they'll be sweetness and light again."

"You're sure?"

"Positive." She leaned back against the seat and eyed him. "Okay, Mr. McCafferty, so where are we going?"

His smile was a slash of white in the darkness. "You'll see," he said, ramming the truck into reverse and backing down the drive.

"Oh, so now you're being mysterious."

"I'm *always* mysterious."

"In your dreams, McCafferty," she said.

"No, Nikki." He slid a knowing glance in her direction. "In yours."

Chapter 8

"Are you out of your mind?" she asked, shaking her head as Thorne turned into the lane of the Flying M Ranch. The last place on earth she wanted to be was anywhere near the Mc-Cafferty home. Too many old memories haunted the spread, too many long-forgotten feelings threatened to jeopardize her emotional stability.

"I've been accused of just that more often than you'd think."

"I thought we were going to a movie or dinner or..." She let her sentence drift off as she wiped the condensation on the glass and stared through the passenger window to the wintry, star-spangled night.

Frost clung to the blades of grass, reflecting in the beams of the headlights. Dried weeds and brambles clung to the fence-posts and in the fields, illuminated by a pearly moon, the dark shapes of cattle and horses moved silently. The ranch house itself loomed in the distance. Warm patches of light glowed from a few of the windows and the security lamps gave the outbuildings an eerie bluish tinge.

Thorne parked near the garage and pocketed the keys.

"Don't tell me, you're doing the cooking," she muttered sarcastically.

"Hell, no. Wouldn't want to poison you." He climbed out of the cab, rounded the front of the truck and opened the door for her.

"Then what?"

"You'll see."

"Once again the enigmatic soul," she observed, taking the hand he offered and hopping down to the gravel that crunched under her boots as they walked, hand in hand, to the stables. Her heart was drumming by this time, her sense of anticipation spurred by an adrenaline rush that she found difficult to ignore. What the devil did he have in mind?

He threw open the door to the stables and drew Nicole inside. They weren't alone. There, hitched to the top rail of their stalls were two horses, bridled, saddled, liquid eyes watching them approach. "You're crazy," she whispered.

"You think?"

"Certifiably."

"Come on, Doc. Where's your sense of adventure? Take your pick. The General here, is docile as a lamb," Thorne said, indicating the tall chestnut gelding with a crooked blaze. "Or, if you'd prefer, you can have Mrs. Brown, but I've got to warn you, like most women, she's got a temperamental streak."

"Chauvinist," she said.

"Always." His grin was expansive as she, refusing to back down, deftly untied the reins of Mrs. Brown's bridle. The horse's dark eyes appraised her. "It's been a while since I've been in the saddle," Nicole admitted to the high-strung mare as she patted the animal's soft muzzle, "but I think you and

I will get along just fine." Mrs. Brown tossed her dark head and the bridle jangled loudly.

"You're sure?" Thorne was skeptical.

"Positive."

"It's your funeral."

"Then be sure to send flowers."

"I think I already did. Well, at least one flower." Thorne laughed as he tied a thick pack and roll to the back of The General's saddle, then clucked his tongue. They led the horses through a back door that opened to a group of paddocks that led to a field crisp with hoarfrost.

"This is absolutely insane," Nicole thought aloud as she undid a few more buttons of her skirt and swung into the saddle. Mrs. Brown sidestepped and fidgeted while the staid General waited patiently as Thorne mounted.

"Where, exactly, are we going?" she asked, holding tight to the reins so that her horse wouldn't immediately spring to the lead. "And don't tell me 'you'll see.'"

"Take a guess."

"I couldn't," she lied because deep in the very most inner part of her she knew the answer, as certainly as if he'd said the words. Through a series of gates they walked, the animals anxious, the moon a shining platter over the dark hills, the creek running through the foothills. Nicole's heart thudded and she bit her lip as, at the final gate, Thorne kneed the gelding and The General broke into a gentle lope. Ever eager, Mrs. Brown bolted, stretching her shorter legs, trying desperately to take the bit in her teeth.

"Take it easy, girl. All in due time." Leaning forward Nicole patted her mount's shoulder but as the words passed her lips she wondered if she was talking to the horse or giving herself some hard but necessary advice. What was this all about, this moonlit ride alone with Thorne?

Wind streamed through her hair. Cold air brushed her cheeks. Her skirt billowed behind her and exhilaration lifted her spirits. Oh, so easily, she could be swept away in the romance, the pure cheeky thrill of this night ride. But she wouldn't.

Because of Thorne. The man wasn't trustworthy. He'd proved it once before and she would be a fool of the highest order if she were ever to give her heart to him again.

"Never," she vowed aloud.

"What?" He turned his head and astride the taller horse, his face thrown into relief, his hair rumpled in the wind, he appeared more dangerous and dark than ever. No longer a corporate big shot, but a forceful man, as wild and unbending as this sweep of harsh Montana land.

"Nothing. It—it's nothing," she said and, in an effort to get away from the questions he might hurl at her, kicked her little mare and gave the animal her head.

Mrs. Brown exploded forward. Her hooves pounded. Her legs stretched and retracted. Faster and faster, flying past the larger horse as if he were plodding.

Nicole laughed out loud and cast all caution to the wind. The moonlit night played with her heart and mind. The wind brought tears to her eyes and tangled her hair. She felt freer and younger than she had in years—a girl in the rush of love. Over the rise she rode with the gelding bearing down on them. She cast one glance over her shoulder and spied Thorne, hunched forward, his eyes drawn like a rifle bead on her, his mouth a line of satisfied determination.

"Oh, God," she whispered, then shouted, "hi-ya!" and slapped Mrs. Brown's shoulder with the reins. The little horse shot forward even faster, the ground whirling by in a rush. Over the flat land, across a rise, onward until the trees surrounding the creek appeared— great, black towers bordering the field and looming ever closer. Nicole drew back on the reins and heard The General snorting and blowing as Thorne, too, pulled his mount to a stop.

Nicole tried to catch her breath.

How long had it been since she'd been here? Seventeen years? Eighteen? But it had been summer then, a time of youth and hot, breathless days, when the touch of Thorne's lips against the nape of her neck was as sensual and welcome as a cool breeze.

Her throat swelled at the thought of their lovemaking, so hot, so uninhibited, so long ago. Why had he brought her here now, in this shadowy night with winter as close at hand as summer had been years before?

He climbed off his horse and stood on the frozen ground looking up at her. "Need help?"

"No…I…" She cleared her throat and gave herself a swift mental shake. For God's sake, she wasn't the tongue-tied teenager she once had been. She was a grown woman, a mother, a doctor for crying out loud! "I'm fine," she said, inwardly cringing at the lie because the truth of the matter was that she wasn't fine at all. In fact she was far from it, but she swung down from the saddle and landed on the hard ground only inches from him and determined not to show one sign that any part of him intimidated her. Dusting her hands, she hoped to appear more collected than she felt. "So…why did you bring me here? Just for old times' sake?"

"Something like that."

"Gee, and I didn't think you were nostalgic."

"Maybe you were wrong about me."

Her throat tightened. "I…I, uh, don't think so." She offered him a smile filled with a bravado she didn't really feel. Her skirt was tugged by a gust of wind that rattled through the leafless trees and shivered the longer blades of grass. "I'm just surprised that you seem to feel a need for a trip down memory lane."

"Don't you want to sometimes?" His voice was low, his eyes silver with the moonlight and her breath was suddenly trapped in the back of her throat.

"No." She shook her head. "As a matter of fact, I think it would be a bad idea."

"Oh?" His arms surrounded her and he drew her close, his nose touching hers. "Well I think it's a damned fine one." His lips found hers and she gasped, her mouth opening and granting his tongue easy access. She told herself that she was being foolish, that being with him was emotional suicide, that getting involved with a man named McCafferty was sure to break her heart all over again and yet she couldn't stop herself. Emotions old and new enveloped her and desire swept through her veins. As if of their own accord her traitorous arms wound around his neck, her eyes closed and she sank against him.

Oh, Thorne…it's been so long....

His lips were sweet warm pressure, his hands big and strong as they splayed against her back, and the combination of the cold starry night and his hot skin was seductively erotic. A small moan escaped her throat only to be answered by his own husky groan.

Don't do this, Nicole, she told herself to no avail. She sensed the horses wandering off, heard, over the ever increasing drumming of her heart, the soft plop of their hooves and the chink of their bridles as they tried to pluck at the frozen blades of grass. Somewhere in the distance an owl hooted and a gentle breeze rushed through the dry leaves of the aspen trees guarding the creek.

"I've wanted to do this from the first time I saw you again," Thorne admitted, his fingers catching in her hair. He tugged, pulling her face away so that he could stare at her. His features were shadowed, his eyes a silver reflection of the moonlight.

"From the first time you saw me again."

"Yes."

"At the hospital?"

"At the hospital."

"Liar." Her breath fogged in the air.

"Never." He kissed her again and this time she responded without the shackles of the past. She kissed him with the same abandon she had as a young girl. It felt so right to have his strong arms drag her to the ground, so natural to turn her head so that his lips and tongue found that spot in the curve of her neck that caused her entire body to convulse.

Warm, liquid sensations streamed through her. Her blood heated, her heart thudded and he kissed her as if he would never stop.

She felt the knot of her belt loosen, noticed when her jacket opened and his hands reached beneath the hem of her sweater. Her back arched as his skin brushed against hers and as he kissed her he scaled her ribs with warm-tipped fingers.

A dozen reasons to deny him screamed through her mind. Twice as many silenced her doubts. Why not make love to this man? What would it hurt? It wasn't as if she'd never lain with him before, never felt the seduction of his kiss or the power of his body joining with hers.

His tongue was sweet persuasion as his fingers found the few buttons that were still holding her skirt closed. She gasped as his fingers brushed the bare skin of her thighs. *Stop him, Nicole! Are you nuts? You can't make love to him. You can't!* And yet as certain as it was that the sun would rise over the eastern horizon, she knew that she would love him again.

Within minutes both her skirt and sweater were disposed of, dropped in a pool on the ground and Thorne was lying above her, kissing her, touching her, causing the blood in her veins to tingle and dance. When she opened her eyes, she looked into a face she'd once loved, a face etched by the years, a face of bladed angles and hard edges, yet in the depths of his eyes and the set of his mouth she saw regret—the tiniest hint of remorse.

The ice around her heart cracked and she blinked against the sting of sudden unwanted tears. Through their soft sheen she saw the moon above him, a bright, frigid disk surrounded by thousands of twinkling stars and she heard the soft babble of the creek.

"I never said I was sorry." His voice was a hoarse whisper.

"Shh." She placed a finger to his lips. "You don't have to say—ooh."

He drew her finger into the warmth of his mouth.

"Oh, no—"

But she didn't pull away as his hot, wet tongue drew anxious circles on her skin as he sucked.

"Thorne—please—"

She intended to deny him but didn't get that chance.

In a heartbeat he released her finger and kissed her hard. Any thoughts of refusal were suddenly stripped away. Her hands found the zipper of his jacket and the buttons of his wool shirt underneath. Her skin tingled, her blood was on fire.

They kissed and touched. Callused fingers caressed her bare skin and she, too, touched him intimately, kissing him and tugging at his clothes, touching him as his jacket and pants fell away. Her fingers traced the deep ridges of his muscles, thrilling to the hard, tight flesh beneath his skin. She kissed the thatch of springy hair upon his chest and was rewarded with the same heart-stopping sensuality as he traced the fragile bones at the hollow of her throat with his tongue, then lowered himself to her breasts where he caressed one button-hard nipple and suckled at the other.

"You're more beautiful than I remembered," he claimed, his breath cool against her hot flesh.

Don't listen to this, don't believe him.... But already she was lost.

Heat burned through her and her mind spun in delicious circles of lovemaking. Deep in the most private part of her she tingled and became moist. Desire thrummed in her blood and seemed to shimmer in the crisp winter air. His breathing was as heavy as her own, his skilled hands rubbing and touching and creating a maelstrom that caused her to gasp.

"I've dreamed of this," he said, lowering his face and kissing her abdomen.

Deep inside she convulsed. Her fingers shot through his hair. Lower still he slid, his tongue rimming her navel. She bucked upward, then quivered with the want of him and bit her lower lip as he kissed the inside of her thigh. Her eyes were closed but as his fingers found the feminine folds of her womanhood and he touched the most sensitive spot within her, she groaned. His fingers were bold, his breath feather soft and seductive, his tongue quick. She arched again and cried out, her fingers digging into the cold, hard dirt as the first spasm hit. Her eyes flew open and the sky seemed to blur—stars and moon blending in pearlescent shards as sensation after sensation rocked her. She was dragging in each breath, spiraling downward, floating....

His fingers dug into her buttocks. He held her close and assailed her again and again, his tongue working exquisite magic, sending her soaring again and again until she was certain her heart and lungs would burst.

"Thorne..."

He came to her. While she was gasping, barely able to move, the sweat of her body drying in the cold night air, he moved upward, spreading her bare legs with his own, kissing her abdomen, her breasts, her throat.

"Now?" she whispered, her blood stirring again.

"Mmm." He kissed her and she responded, felt the male hardness of him pressed against her mound.

"But—"

"Now. You can do it, Nikki." His mouth cut off any further protest. With one quick thrust he claimed her. "We can do it."

She stared up at him and as their gazes locked, he moved, slowly at first, taking his time as the fires within her stoked all over again. Her skin broke out with perspiration and liquid heat seared her. She heard a roaring in her ears, felt the pressure build again. Her mind spun in endless circles and she caught his rhythm, meeting each of his thrusts, opening to him, clinging to him.

Faster and faster. She closed her eyes, thought she was dreaming, cried out and heard his own answering scream as with one final stroke he fell against her, flattening her breasts, his face buried in the crook of her neck. "Oh, Nikki. Sweet, sweet Nikki."

The old ache in her heart reopened at the sound of his breathless voice. She held tight to him, feeling afterglow seep through her bones.

Finally her heart slowed and she could breathe again.

She'd never felt like this—never with Paul, only with Thorne.

"Well, well, well," he whispered. "That was—" he looked down at her "—worth the wait."

"Oh, was it?" She cocked an insolent eyebrow and imagined that her eyes glowed with a wicked light. "Was it good for you—"

"Don't!" He shook his head and laughed, the deep timbre of his voice ringing in the hills. "Just don't, okay?"

"Just checking."

"Or being a wise guy." He kissed her on the lips then and rubbed her arms. "Cold?"

"Not yet."

"You will be, but I've got something for that." Without bothering with his clothes, he rolled off her, climbed to his feet and whistled to the horses. The General's head shot up and he came close enough that Thorne loosened the saddlebag. From its depths he withdrew a thermos, a bottle and an insulated pack. "I'm afraid to ask what you're doing." Shivering a bit, Nicole slipped into her sweater and skirt.

"You're getting dressed?"

"If you haven't noticed, it's subfreezing out here." She glanced at the creek where ice glinted between the exposed roots of the trees at the water's edge.

"You're tough. You can take it."

"You be the macho one, okay?"

"Always." She tried not to stare at his nakedness, refused to notice the play of his shoulder muscles, or the expanse of his chest or the dark juncture of his legs. Instead she concentrated on his actions which included spreading a small tablecloth, handing her a foil-wrapped package and opening the thermos.

"What is this?"

"Juanita's speciality. Soft tacos and Spanish coffee."

"What? Are you crazy?"

"You keep bringing up my sanity, but believe me, I'm as sane as you are. Eat." He sat on the bare ground and she shifted her eyes away from his long, muscular thighs to accept a speckled enamel cup with steaming coffee laced with alcohol.

"I don't believe this." She unwrapped her soft taco and took a bite. A delicious blend of flavors exploded in her mouth. She sipped from her cup and felt the hot liquid slide down her throat. "Tell me this isn't how you treat all the women in your life."

"Nope. Only one." He stared at her for a long minute and she, avoiding looking into his eyes, buried her nose in her cup and drank a long sip.

"So I guess I'm special?" she teased.

"Very." He was still looking at her.

Another long swallow and bite. She wanted to believe him with all the naivete of her lost youth, but didn't dare. "So special it took eighteen years and a tragedy to force you to face me again?"

He was about to take a drink, but stopped short, his cup halfway to his lips. Somewhere nearby one of the horses snorted. "Maybe I didn't make myself clear earlier," he said. "I started to apologize for the past, but you stopped me."

"I know, you don't have to—"

"Sure I do, Nikki. I've got a lot of excuses, but that's all they are and not very good ones at that. This is the here and now. I would hope that you would take me at face value."

"Well that's damned hard to do when you're sitting there naked as a jaybird and I'm having one devil of a time concentrating on your face, if you know what I mean."

"I know exactly," he said, setting his cup aside. Her heart stopped for she knew what was coming. In a split second, he'd grabbed her again, kissed her as if he never intended to stop and, stripping her of her clothes, made love to her all over again.

Nikki, the romantic young girl who still resided deep in the most hidden parts of her, was in heaven at the thought of a love affair with Thorne McCafferty.

But Nicole, the grown woman, knew she'd just crossed a threshold into certain emotional hell.

Chapter 9

"Barring any unforeseen complications, the baby's going to pull through." Dr. Arnold's voice was a balm but Thorne, in his relief, wanted to jump right through the ceiling of the den where he'd taken the call. For hours he'd been trying to concentrate on alterations to a contract he'd been faxed by Eloise, or playing phone tag with his real estate agent and tax attorney, but all the while he'd been worried about his sister and the baby.

Then there was Nicole. Always at the edges of his mind. It had been two days since their first night together by the creek and he'd had to rein himself in rather than chase her down, but he had too much to think about to rush headlong into a passionate love affair.

"…so as long as he continues to improve, I would guess that he can come home in about three days. Since your sister isn't ready to be moved yet, I assume that you've made arrangements for his care."

"Absolutely," Thorne said, though the truth of the matter was that he hadn't made much headway in finding a suitable nanny and the upstairs room that he planned to become the nursery was a long way from being ready for a newborn.

"Well, if you have any questions, give me a call. I'll be checking in on the baby every few hours, just to make sure that he's turned the corner and the nursing staff will notify me of any change."

"Thanks," Thorne said and felt as if a weight as heavy as any he'd ever felt in his life had been lifted from his shoulders. "Thank God," he whispered and leaned his head on the desk. He couldn't imagine what would have happened if little J.R. hadn't survived; he'd never allowed his thoughts to wander down that dark and painful path.

Maybe things were finally turning around. He shoved his paperwork aside and walked in stocking feet out of the den. In the past week he'd changed his habits, giving up the strict regimen he'd adhered to in Denver and loosening up. Randi's condition and the baby's tenuous hold on life had turned his thoughts away from corporate takeovers, mergers, land deals and developments. He'd had less interest in oil leases and start-up software companies than he'd had on this ranch—the land he'd once disdained.

What about Nicole? Isn't she one of the reasons you've found life here idyllic?

Rubbing his jaw, he realized that he hadn't shaved this morning and that it didn't bother him. As he walked down the hall to the kitchen he wondered if he was getting soft or getting smart.

"I tell you I don't want any strangers in this house!" Juanita's voice was firm.

"Thorne's interviewing nannies…they're all referred by an agency I think."

"One that only wants to make money. And what does he know about taking care of babies?"

"Good point."

"My ears are burning," Thorne said as he strode into the kitchen and caught Slade's eye.

Juanita was elbow deep in flour, throwing her weight into a rolling pin that was stretching a disk of dough. Every once in a while she stopped to sprinkle the dough with cornmeal or flour and her expression was thunderous. "That baby, he needs his mother and Señorita Randi—she would not want someone she does not know or trust taking care of her son!" Juanita took off a few seconds and made the sign of the cross. "I have told you this before."

"I haven't hired anyone yet."

"Good." Juanita rattled off a stream of rapid-fire Spanish that Thorne was grateful he didn't understand.

Slade chuckled and shook his head. He reached into the pocket of his shirt and withdrew a folded piece of paper. "Larry Todd's signed on," he said. "I'm goin' to meet him in about—" he checked his watch "—half an hour."

"Good."

"Later this afternoon Kurt Striker is gonna pay us a visit. Will you be around?"

Thorne's head snapped up. "You bet I will. Has he found out anything else?"

"Nothing that I know of, but we'll see." Slade wandered to the back door where his boots were waiting. Nearby Harold, their father's half-crippled dog, lay on a rag rug. Harold thumped his tail and Slade rewarded him by scratching him behind the ears while Juanita slid a warning glance toward dog and man.

"I just washed the floors."

"I know, I know."

Harold, suitably abashed, rested his head between his paws and stared up at her with sorrowful eyes.

"Stay." Juanita pointed at the dog with her rolling pin.

"He's not moving," Slade said.

"Good news," Thorne said and caught Juanita's and Slade's attention.

"Señorita Randi?"

"The baby. He's pulling out of it."

Slade let up a whoop and Juanita prayed and crossed herself, her dark eyes filling with tears of relief. "I knew it," she said.

"Does Matt know?" Slade asked, unable to stop grinning, his eyes rimmed in red.

"Don't think so. I just got the call. Why don't you tell him?"

"Damned straight, I will."

"Good." Thorne ran a hand over his chin. "I'll run into town—got to talk to some local attorneys about Randi, then I'm gonna stop by the hospital. I'll meet you and Striker back here later," Thorne said.

"Fair enough." With a nod and a crisp salute to Juanita, the "warden" as he sometimes called her, Slade disappeared through the back door.

"Thank goodness for the baby," Juanita said as she turned back to her dough. "As for that one." She hitched her head toward the door that was closing behind Slade. "He is too… *irrespetuoso*…too—" She waved one hand frantically in the air, sending a cloud of flour around her head.

"Too irreverent."

"*Sí. Irrespetuoso* for his own good."

"You're the one who once referred to Randi's mother as a witch."

"That was years ago and is irreverent—"

"Irrelevant."

"It is fact."

"If you say so."

"I do."

"He's had his own demons to deal with."

"*Sí.*" Her lips pursed and she plunged her hands into the bowl of cornmeal and went about her task, though both she and Thorne considered his youngest brother and the personal pain that Slade had endured.

His thoughts dark, Thorne slipped back to the office, called Eloise and checked in. Her voice was professional and bright, but Thorne didn't miss the stress of the office.

"Buzz Branson's been calling twice a day," Eloise informed him. "Your accountant would like to go over the projected profit and loss on the Hillside View development and Annette Williams left her number twice." His conscience twinged at the mention of Annette's name, though he thought they'd reached an understanding the last time they'd spoken. Obviously not.

"If anyone calls back, give him—or her—the number here," Thorne said. "If I'm not in they can leave a message on the answering machine."

"Will do. Now you probably want to know that there's still talk of a strike by the local carpenters' union. It could involve one of the framing crews, and one of the partners in Tech-Link is under investigation by the IRS."

Thorne let out a long whistle. "You're just full of good news, aren't you?"

"Wouldn't want you to feel unloved," Eloise said wryly.

"Don't worry. As I said, give them the new number—it's connected to two lines and an answering machine, so I'll get any messages. You've got it."

"Will do," she promised and he hung up feeling more dispassionate about his business than he had in years. He looked out the window to the gleaming acres of raw land where he'd grown up. Hooking his thumbs into the belt loops of his jeans, he leaned a shoulder against the window frame and watched a herd of cattle lumber across the winter-dry acres. Shaggy red, black and mottled gray coats moved slowly and every once in a while a lonesome calf bawled.

Thorne had loved it here as a kid, turned his back on it disdainfully when he'd approached adulthood and spent the next twenty years avoiding the place. Now, it got to him. Just as a certain lady doctor did. *You're losing it, McCafferty,* he thought without a trace of despair. *Whatever that edge was that separated you from your brothers and your old man, it's getting dull with age.*

And he couldn't let that happen.

Rather than dwell on his changing attitude, he strode to the stairs and climbed upward to his room. Some of his clothes had arrived and he thought he'd best shake himself out of this maudlin nostalgia that had gripped him ever since seeing Nicole again. He unpacked his favorite gray suit, starched white shirt and burgundy tie, then he headed to the bathroom to shower and shave.

"She hasn't responded yet?" Nicole asked the RN on duty in ICU. Randi McCafferty lay still, unmoving, her monitors in place, the bandages removed from her face. She was healing slowly, at least externally, but she looked worse than ever. Her skin was discolored and scabbed over, her cheeks still swollen.

"No. We even talked to her and one of the brothers—the one with the dark eyes—"

"Matt."

"Yes, he stopped by earlier and talked to her for fifteen minutes, but there wasn't the slightest bit of response." She held Nicole's gaze. "Sometimes it takes a while. Dr. Nimmo isn't concerned yet and he's the best neurosurgeon around."

That much was true, and the other doctors who were attending to Randi, Dr. Oliverio, an orthopedist and an OB-GYN, were outstanding as well. "I know, but I was just hoping. Since the baby's doing better, it would be nice…"

Again she looked down at Thorne's sister. *Wake up, Randi! You've got so much to live for!*

"Unfortunately the press keeps snooping around. Several people from the local paper have called and one woman tried to get in here. She posed as the patient's sister."

"Randi doesn't have a sister," Nicole said, irritated.

"We knew that." The nurse smiled. "Security took care of her."

Nicole wished the reporters would leave Randi and her baby alone. She realized the mystery surrounding Randi's accident and pregnancy was a big deal in this small town, but it seemed blown out of proportion. The patients needed to recover—without the eagle eye of the press scrutinizing them.

"Well, let me know if there's any change." Nicole touched Randi's fingers with her own. "Come on," she encouraged, "you can do this. You've got a little baby who needs you and three brothers who are worried sick."

She made her way down to her office and sighed. It had been a long night in the ER, made more difficult because of her lack of sleep from a few nights before.

After making love by the creek and eating the cold meal, she and Thorne had ridden the ridge at midnight then returned to the ranch. She hadn't gotten home until well after one and then had slept poorly, thinking of Thorne, tossing, turning and pounding her pillow in frustration.

The next day hadn't been any better and last night Molly, complaining of bad dreams and a sore throat had crawled into bed with her. Again, she'd slept poorly and one of the main reasons was Thorne. She'd remembered kissing him, touching him and making love to him in the cold winter air. Worst of all she thought she might be falling in love with him all over again.

"Foolish, foolish woman," she said, skirting a janitor's cart and rounding a corner of the corridor. She didn't have time to fall in love with any man, much less one who had walked away from her in the past. No, she couldn't fall in love with Thorne. Wouldn't! Gritting her teeth, she forced her mind away from the sexy eldest McCafferty brother and concentrated on the tasks at hand. Her shift in the ER didn't start for nearly two hours, but she had catch-up work to do, patient notes to write on her computer, some calls to make to colleagues, and, as always, she wanted to check on the twins.

At the thought of her girls she smiled though she was concerned as Molly had developed a cough and this morning had been barking up a storm. The trouble with being a doctor was that she knew what complications might develop and she was always worried sick whenever either one of them showed the least sign of illness. "Get a grip," she told herself as she entered her office and shed her lab coat, hanging it over the back of her chair.

To ease her mind she put a quick call in to Jenny and the twins, then switched on her computer and checked her e-mail before writing her patient notes and returning the patient and colleague calls that she retrieved from her voice mail. Her stomach rumbled as she hadn't eaten for hours, but she ignored the hunger pangs and kept working.

Over an hour later she took a break and stopped by the neonatal care unit where little J.R. blinked up at her under the warm lights. "How 'ya doin', little guy?" she whispered as he focused on her. Carefully she picked the baby up and held him to her chest. Tears came to her eyes as she smelled the baby scent of him, felt him snuggle against her, his tiny body swaddled and warm. "You just hang in there, sweetie. Your momma's gonna be so glad to see you when she wakes up."

Soft little coos hung in the air and Nicole thought her heart would break for the poor child whose mother was struggling for life and whose father was nowhere to be found—completely unknown. But J.R. did have his uncles, three rugged men who loved him dearly.

"Got time to feed him?" one of the nurses asked and Nicole couldn't resist. With practiced hands she held baby and bottle and smiled as she watched him suckle hungrily. It felt so right to hold him and she realized how much she wanted another child.

Thorne's child? her wayward mind taunted. *Is that what you want? Isn't he the man you think you're falling in love with? The confirmed bachelor who left you before?*

She blinked hard and fought a powerful wave of emotions as she slowly rocked and cradled little J.R. Was it so wrong to want another baby?

Forget it, you've got the twins; that's enough for a single parent. Would you really want to raise another one without a father?

But Molly and Mindy did have a father, though Paul didn't really seem to give a damn. He rarely called them, never came to visit, wasn't interested in hearing about them. He was remarried now to a professional woman like himself, one who swore she didn't want to be tied down with children. But she was young. Nicole expected she might change her mind.

"There you go," she said softly as the baby quit drinking to stare up at her. "You are precious." She kissed the top of his downy curls and glanced through the plate glass window. Thorne was on the other side, his gaze centered on her, his expression unreadable. Dressed in a business suit, crisp white shirt and perfectly knotted tie, he appeared more unapproachable than he had been, more hard-edged. The terms *shark* and *corporate raider* slid through her mind and she reminded herself he wasn't her kind of man; she'd learned that lesson well.

Nonetheless she felt a flush of scarlet climb up the back of her neck at being caught in such a tender moment. Managing a weak smile she lay the baby back into his crib and hesitated when he began to cry. "Shh. You're all right," she assured the infant.

The nurse stepped forward. "I'll take it from here," she said as Nicole slipped through the door and joined Thorne in the hallway.

"Didn't expect you here," she said, stuffing her hands into the pockets of her white coat.

"Had business in town. Thought I'd check on Randi and the baby."

"He's much better."

Thorne managed a smile. "I see that. I just wish my sister would respond."

"She will. In time."

"I hope." He didn't seem convinced. "Can I buy you lunch?"

She thought about the work in her office. She'd finished most of it and she was hungry. Why not? *Because it would be best if you gave him up right now. He's not in love with you—you're just a convenient distraction while he's in town. But he's going to leave, Nicole. You know it. His life is in Denver.*

"I have to be in the ER in a few minutes."

"So how about a cup of coffee in the cafeteria?" His smile was irresistible.

"Okay. You've twisted my arm," she said with a laugh. To-

gether they walked through the hallways, passing nurses with
medication carts, aides helping patients walk and an assort-
ment of visitors looking for loved ones.

The cafeteria was a madhouse, and over Thorne's protests
that she should eat something more substantial, she grabbed
a carton of vanilla yogurt, a cranberry-pecan muffin and a
cup of black coffee while he ordered a turkey sandwich and
cup of soup.

Once served, Thorne carried the tray to the end of a Formica-topped table where a few pages of the morning newspaper were scattered. Several nurses were talking at the next
table—one of them had obviously just gotten engaged and the
others were gushing; clusters of visitors had gathered in several
groups and several of her colleagues were debating the addi-
tion of another wing and trauma unit.

Nicole slid into a seat near a shedding ficus tree and Thorne
sat opposite her. A few of her colleagues cast curious glances in
her direction, but for the most part they were left alone. "I was
hoping you could help me," he said, unwrapping his sandwich.

"How?" She bit into her muffin.

"As I said before, when J.R.'s released we'll need a nanny."

She swallowed and grinned up at him. "Don't tell me the
three McCafferty brothers can't handle one baby."

"We're all busy."

"Mmm." She dipped her spoon into her yogurt.

"I don't think it's gonna be like the movie *Three Men and a
Baby* at the Flying M."

"No?" She laughed. "The thought conjures up some interesting scenarios. Thorne McCafferty, CEO, president of the
Chamber of Commerce and…diaper changer. Matt McCaf-

ferty, calf roper, horse brander and…baby burper. Slade Mc-
Cafferty, daredevil and—"

"Okay, okay, I get the idea." His lips twitched and his gray
eyes sparkled.

"Good." She winked at him.

"So you've had your fun," he said around a bite of sandwich.

"It's just nice to be with a man of sooo many talents," she
teased.

"Only you would know."

The laughter died from his eyes and Nicole nearly dropped
her spoon. Thoughts of making love to him flitted through
her mind. Heat climbed up the back of her neck and she swallowed hard at the thought of their recent lovemaking.

"If I recall—"

"Enough, okay? I get it," she whispered, not wanting anyone to overhear the conversation. "Truce."

"Then you'll help me find a nanny."

"I guess I don't have much choice."

"Good. I accept your white flag."

"I didn't surrender, just suggested a truce!"

His eyes glittered with wicked mischief. "Whatever you
say."

Still flushed, she managed to change the subject and make
small talk through the rest of the meal. Why did she let him
get to her? Bait her? Tease her? Flirt outrageously with her?
What was it about him that she found downright irritating
and incredibly sexual? Good lord, she was becoming one of
those foolish, man-crazy women she abhorred! Glancing at
her watch, she realized she was running out of time. "Duty
calls," she said, standing.

He scraped his chair back. As she discarded the remains of

her lunch in the trash bin, he walked with her stride for stride and she was aware how distinctive he looked, a tall man in a long black coat amidst doctors and nurses in white lab coats or green scrubs, or visitors in an array of cotton, denim, rawhide or flannel. There were a few business types as well, salesmen, for the most part, but none were as tall or as arrogantly self-important as was Thorne McCafferty in his crisp white shirt, silk tie and expensive suit. His presence demanded notice and noticed he got.

At the table where the nurses sat, more than one pair of interested eyes watched him as he held open one of the double doors leading to the hallway, while his other palm rested against the small of her back, as if he needed to guide her through. It was a simple gesture, maybe even a polite, automatic movement on his part, but she stepped away from him as they entered the corridor and was thankful that he dropped his arm to his side. The less personal contact they had, the better.

And yet…

"Has anyone located J.R.'s father?" she asked. "He might have a say in what kind of care the baby gets."

"Not yet." His eyes turned as cold as a blast of winter. "But I'll find him." She didn't doubt it for a moment. Thorne McCafferty was an intimidating force, a man who, if he chose to hunt someone down, would leave no stone unturned in his quest. As she pushed the elevator call button, he touched her shoulder.

She started to step inside, but he took hold of the crook of her arm and pulled her against him. To her surprise he kissed her. Hard. So hard, her knees nearly gave way.

"What was that all about?" she asked, as he finally released her.

"Just something to remember me by."

As if I don't have enough.

Thrusting his hands into the pockets of his coat, he turned and walked toward the front of the building. Nicole, stripped of her breath and dignity in one fell swoop, entered the elevator car. Gratefully, the doors whispered shut and she was alone. *So she wouldn't forget him?*

Well, he needn't worry. Sighing, Nicole leaned against the back wall of the car. Thorne McCafferty was impossible to forget.

Chapter 10

Kurt Striker looked like the television version of an ex-cop turned private detective—hard features, deep-set eyes that, when they weren't pinning you in his cold, green glare, moved restlessly, his gaze taking in everything.

He shook Thorne's hand in a strong grip that he released quickly. In a jean jacket, matching Levi's, scratched boots and collarless shirt, he stood on the back porch, watching the clouds roll across the western hills. Slade smoked. Kurt didn't seem to mind as he squinted into the distance. Growling deep in his throat, Harold rounded the end of the porch and with a wag of his tail, slowly climbed the steps to settle at Slade's feet.

"Good to finally meet you," Thorne said.

Kurt nodded and Thorne noticed a few flecks of gray in his otherwise brown hair. "Thought you'd want to know what I've found out."

So there was some information. Good. "Anything." Thorne hitched his head toward the kitchen. "Let's go inside and talk."

Slade took last one pull on his cigarette, then flipped it into an empty metal can that rested on a weathered bench. Together they walked into the house where the sharp scent of pine from some kind of cleanser mixed with the aroma of roasting pork.

"Boots off! Muddy boots on the porch," Juanita called from deep in the recesses of the pantry.

"Eyes in the back of her head," Slade grumbled, checking the scuffed leather of his hiking boots. "Forget it."

"Mine're clean," Kurt said.

Juanita was on a new subject as she emerged from the pantry. Carrying two plastic bags of small onions and red potatoes, she kicked the pantry door shut, then dropped both sacks onto the butcher block and shook her head. Pointing an accusing finger at Thorne, she said, "That woman—that Annette. She called again. Insists you phone her, today." With a roll of her expressive eyes, she muttered something in Spanish.

Thorne couldn't hide his irritation. "Next time let the machine answer."

"I did. But I heard it record. I was dusting." Juanita's back was as stiff as an ironing board, her chin elevated a fraction as if she expected Thorne to reprimand her for eavesdropping. "And that is not the worst of it, another reporter called today. Wants to talk to you. *Dios!*" She clucked her tongue, threw up her hands and shook her head as if she couldn't understand the folly of it all.

"I'll talk to them later," Thorne said. Then he turned to Kurt. "Let's go into the living room."

Juanita opened the bag of onions and began peeling them deftly. "Would you like something to eat? A *bocado?* Something to drink?"

"Snacks would be fine. And beer," Thorne said as they walked down the hall. While Slade and Striker made their way to the living room, Thorne shed his jacket, rolled up the sleeves of his shirt and followed.

"So, what've you got?" he asked once they were all in the living room.

Striker stood near the windows. His forehead was creased, his eyes serious. "I don't think your sister was involved in a single-car accident." Thorne's eyes narrowed on the other man. "I suspect another car or truck or some kind of rig was involved."

"Wait a minute. Doesn't this go against everything the police have told us?" Thorne was thunderstruck. He glanced at Slade to back him up.

"That's what I heard." Slade was kneeling at the fireplace, striking a match to the paper and dry kindling.

"It's only a theory at this point," Striker admitted. "But there does seem to be a discrepancy. A few paint scratches on her back fender. No skid marks, no other evidence, but I think it's a distinct possibility another vehicle was involved."

The fire crackled to life and Slade tossed a thick chunk of oak onto the hungry flames. Juanita carried in a tray of three long-necked bottles of beer and a basket of chips. As soon as she disappeared, Striker crossed the room and settled into a corner of the worn leather couch facing the fireplace. Both he and Slade picked up bottles. Thorne didn't. He wasn't interested in anything other than the story the detective was concocting.

"What does the sheriff's department have to say?" he asked, ignoring the fact that his gut was clenching hard, his head pounding. Striker's hypothesis wasn't good news. Not at all. If someone had run Randi off the road or even hit her accidentally, it meant hit-and-run was involved—or worse. It could have been intentional.

"They're not saying much. Though they're still considering all the possibilities. The trouble is, they don't have any eyewitnesses and as Randi's in no condition to tell them what happened, they're not jumping to any conclusions."

"But you seem sure."

Green eyes found his and held. "I said it was just a theory. I'm not sure about anything."

"What about the baby's father?"

"Got a few leads, but haven't talked to the guys yet."

"Who are they?"

"Men she was seen with about a year ago. Seems your sis didn't have a steady boyfriend, at least not recently. She hung out with people she worked with at the paper, and friends she knew from school, but no one she knew realized she was in any serious romance. She never told any of her friends about the guy, whoever he is." He took a long swallow from his beer. "But there are some men who dated her that I'm trying to track down, one's a guy named Joe Paterno, a photojournalist who did some freelance stuff for the *Clarion*. Then there was a lawyer by the name of Brodie Clanton—he's connected to big money in Seattle. His grandfather was a judge at one time. The last guy's a cowboy type she met while helping someone with an interview."

"His name?"

"Sam Donahue."

"I knew a Sam Donahue," Slade said as he took up a position near the bookcase, leaned his hips against the liquor cupboard and crossed his ankles. "When I rode the circuit a while. Matt knows him, too, if he's the guy I'm thinking of. Big. Blond. Tough as nails."

"That's the one."

"*He* was involved with Randi?" Thorne couldn't believe his ears.

"Appears so. Haven't quite caught up with him yet."

Slade scowled and look a long swallow from his bottle. "Donahue was bad news. In and out of jail, I think."

"You're right."

"Hell," Thorne snarled.

"The more I learn about little sis, the more I feel like I didn't know her at all." Slade shook his head.

"None of us did," Thorne said as the front door opened and slammed shut. Matt, bringing in a rush of cold wind, strode into the living room and caught the tail end of the conversation.

"None of us did what?" he asked, yanking off his gloves and looking from one man to the next. His face was ruddy with the cold and he tossed his hat onto the cushion of a vacant armchair.

Slade introduced him to Kurt Striker and caught him up with the conversation as he grabbed the last bottle of beer and twisted off the cap. "Sam Donahue?" He snorted. "No way. The guy's not Randi's type."

"Oh, so you're the expert now. Tell us, who is Randi's kind of guy?" Thorne demanded, more frustrated than ever.

"I wish I knew," Matt admitted. "Hell."

"What else have you got?" Thorne asked the private detective.

"Not much more, except that your sister wasn't having such a great time at her job, either. Though everyone at the paper's been tight-lipped, some of her co-workers thought she'd gotten into some hot water with the editors."

"How?" Thorne asked, his eyebrows slamming together.

"Good question. I've got copies of all the columns she wrote for the past six months, but those are only the ones that were in print. According to her friend Sarah Peeples who writes movie reviews, Randi had about two weeks' worth of columns that she'd written but hadn't yet been printed. No one has seen them. And there was talk of some kind of project she was working on, though the paper denies it. Again, no one's seen any copies of it."

"Except maybe Randi."

"And she's not talkin'," Matt observed, his mouth a grave line as he leaned against the bookcase and the fire crackled and hissed.

"She writes advice to the heartbroken for God's sake!" Slade interrupted.

"And what else?" Striker thought aloud.

Matt frowned down at his beer. "Now wait a minute. You said that Randi's vehicle *might* have been struck, but no one knows if it was intentional or not. It's a pretty big leap to go from a single-car accident because the driver hit black ice to some kind of...what? Attempted murder?"

"All I'm saying is that there might have been another vehicle involved and if there was, the driver is, at the very least, guilty of hit-and-run. From there it only gets worse."

"*If* she was hit." Matt's gaze fastened on the private investigator. He was obviously skeptical.

"Right."

"I think we're making big assumptions here."

"Just checkin' out all the possibilities," Slade argued. "We owe it to Randi."

"God, I wish she'd wake up." Matt straightened and shoved a hand through his hair in frustration.

"We all do." Thorne looked from one brother to the other. "But until she does, we've got to keep trying to figure this out." To Striker, he said, "Keep at it. Talk to anyone you can. We need to find the father of Randi's baby. If there's any way you can find out the blood type of the men she was involved with, we could at least eliminate some of the possibilities."

"Already doin' it," Striker admitted.

"How do you do that?" Matt said.

Kurt sent him a look silently telling him he didn't want to know.

"Just handle it." Thorne wasn't sure he liked Kurt Striker, but he believed the man would do what had to be done to dig up the truth. That was all that mattered. He didn't even care if the law was bent a little, not if Randi's life was truly endangered by someone with a grudge. But *who?*

Striker nodded. "Will do. And I'm gonna try to find those missing columns. I don't suppose any of you know if she had a laptop computer?"

Slade lifted a shoulder, Matt shook his head and Thorne frowned.

"Nothin's on her desktop."

"How do you know that?" Matt asked.

"I checked."

"You broke into her apartment?" Matt looked from one of his brothers to the next. "Hey—isn't that illegal? Randi'll kill us if she ever finds out."

"Or someone doesn't take care of that first." Striker took a long, final tug on his long-necked bottle.

"Wait a minute...." Matt stared at Thorne incredulously. "Don't you think we're leaping to conclusions, here? I mean she had a wreck, she got hurt, but I don't see that there's any hint of foul play."

"You don't know there isn't."

"But why? Everyone she ever met liked her and as Slade said, she gave advice to the lovelorn for crying out loud. Not exactly cloak and dagger stuff. It's not like she was writing scandal sheets or political exposes."

"It was more than just lovelorn cra—stuff," Slade clarified. "Her column was about single people—"

"Right. I know," Matt snapped.

"But the point of it is that none of us really knew what she was doing with her life, did we?" Thorne pushed up his sleeves. "She didn't even tell us she was pregnant. Now, there's a chance someone, either by accident or intent, was involved in her accident. We just have to find out who."

"And *why*." Matt threw up a hand in exasperation. "Don't we need a motive?"

"Not if it was an accident and someone was just scared to come forward." Slade drained his bottle.

Matt's back was up. "Well then, looking into her computer records and breaking into her apartment wouldn't be necessary, would they?"

"Hey! Anything's worth a try!" Slade shot to his feet and walked up to his brother. "Don't you think we should look into everything?" Slade's color was high, his jaw set, just the way it had been when they'd been kids growing up and were about to start throwing punches.

Matt held his ground. Even managed that slow, go-ahead-and-try-it smile that both his brothers found so damned irritating.

"We don't know a lot," Slade said through clenched teeth. "Kurt's gonna help us get to the bottom of it. You got a problem with that?"

A muscle worked in Matt's jaw and his brown eyes narrowed on his younger brother. "No problem. I just want what's best for Randi and J.R., you know that. And some son of a bitch is responsible for her condition. I want him found and nailed. You bet I do. But that's what the sheriff's department is for."

"Unless they're sittin' on their butts," Slade said.

"Right. But I don't think we should go on a witch hunt until we're sure there's a witch."

Kurt stood. "Don't worry. If there is one, I'll find him... or her."

"Good." Slade took a step back.

"That settles it. Do what you have to," Thorne said, then walked Striker to the door where they shook hands again. The phone rang as the door shut behind the investigator. "I'll get it," Thorne said, striding to the den. He had work to do and couldn't let his brothers' tempers deter him.

"Hello?" he nearly shouted.

"Boy, are you in a bad mood." Annette's voice sang through the wires.

He felt instantly weary. "Just busy."

"When are you coming back to Denver?" Good old Annette. She didn't beat around the bush.

"Don't know," he admitted, resting one hip on the corner of his father's desk and letting his leg swing free. The thought of returning to his office and the penthouse and the whirl that was his life in the Mile-High City held little appeal right now.

"So you like being a cowboy again?" she asked and laughed without a trace of acrimony—as if nothing had changed between them.

"Believe it or not, I do like it here," he said with complete honesty. "Don't think I'm much of a cowboy."

"Oh, darn, and I was just pressing my denim skirt and checked blouse."

"Was there something you wanted?"

"Mmm. Actually there was. Daddy's forgiven you."

Thorne doubted it.

"And he still wants to work with you."

"So, why didn't he call me?"

"Because I wanted to. To make sure there were no hard feelings."

"None on this end." And yet he didn't trust her.

"Good. And don't worry, Daddy will call you himself. Let

me know when you're in town. Oh, and Thorne—take off the bolo, it's not your style."

"I'm not wearing a tie of any kind."

"Oh, dear. That's worse yet. Well, so long, pardner," she said with a laugh. There was a click on the other end of the line and he was left holding the receiver and wondering why she'd bothered to call.

"Doesn't matter," he reminded himself because he didn't feel a thing for her; never had. Nor had he experienced any special bond with the women he'd dated in the past few years. Until he'd seen Nicole again. From the moment he'd first laid eyes on her in the hospital, he'd been taken with her. He wondered what she was doing right now, considered dialing the number he'd already committed to memory, then reminded himself that he had other things that had to be done.

For the next two hours he returned phone calls, e-mails and faxes, but his concentration wasn't as focused as it usually was and thoughts of his sister and her baby kept sneaking into his mind.

When he'd finally hung up from a call with his attorney Thorne leaned the desk chair back so far it protested. Drumming his fingers on the curved arm, he stared through the window into the night. A dozen questions burned through his brain. Why was Randi in Montana? Who was the baby's father? Did the accident involve another vehicle? Would Randi and the baby be okay? When would she come out of the coma?

He had no answers to any of those and another thought, one he'd kept steadfastly at bay, burrowed into his brain. He wondered what Nicole was doing tonight. "Forget it," he growled at himself, but his mind kept wandering back to the night they'd made love, their bodies glistening with sweat under the cold winter stars. When could he see her again? He glanced at the phone, mentally cursed and wondered how she'd managed to get under his skin.

He remembered taking her into his arms in the parking lot of the hospital and her small gasp of surprise as he'd kissed her; he remembered the way she'd moaned when he'd made love to her by the creek; and he remembered seeing her hold the baby in the nursery, looking down at the child's tiny face, smiling and whispering to the infant, so naturally as if she were his mother. The effect on Thorne had been immediate and heart stopping.

If he didn't know better, he'd think he was falling in love. But that was ridiculous. He wasn't the kind of man to fall into that kind of trap.

He wasn't ready to tie himself up with one woman, not yet. He had too much to do.

Oh, yeah? And what's that? Make another million or two? Turn a losing company into a winning corporation? Develop another subdivision? Go back to an empty penthouse in a city where your only friends are business associates?

Standing, he raised his arms over his head and stretched, his spine popping a bit. Of course he'd return to Denver and resume his life. What was the other option? Stay here? Marry Nicole?

He froze. *Marry Nicole?* Dr. Stevenson? Impossible! No way! And yet the thought held a seductive and dangerous appeal.

"This is ridiculous," Nicole told herself as her shift ended and she opened the door to her office. Thankfully it had been a slow day in the emergency room, with only a broken hip, an asthma attack, a dog bite, a case of severe appendicitis and two kids with contusions and concussions in a bicycle-car mishap. In the lulls between patients she'd been able to catch up on her notes, check on some of the patients she'd admitted earlier including Randi and J.R., and think about Thorne McCafferty.

She'd been thinking about him a lot lately. Too much. She sat in her desk chair and twiddled a pen. They'd talked on the phone a couple of times since they'd made love near the creek and, of course, he'd come for lunch that day and run into her at the hospital time and again when he'd been visiting his sister. He'd always stopped by to see her and consequently a few rumors had already started and some of her co-workers had winked at her whenever he'd appeared.

"Forget him," she told herself, knowing it was impossible. He was getting to her all over again, even though he'd taken off on her once before. He'd given no excuses, just taken off and bailed out to chase after dreams of making his mark in the world, leaving her heartbroken. In spite of this, she was fascinated by the man. Stupidly fascinated, she reminded herself. She couldn't take a chance on letting him hurt her again.

She finished her paperwork, then perused photocopies of a few of Randi McCafferty's columns that Clare Santiago, Randi's OB-GYN, had given her. Out of curiosity about her new patient and the hoopla created by the local press, Clare had found some of the articles on the Internet and printed them out.

Now, as Nicole scanned the columns, she smiled. Randi gave advice freehandedly. With tones of irony and sarcasm, she dished out levelheaded counsel to single people who had written to her concerning their love lives, work problems, past relationships, or troubles juggling hectic schedules. Randi borrowed literary clichés, old adages and peppered the column with hip slang; but most of the advice was given tongue-in-cheek and showed off her clever, if sometimes cutting, wit. Nicole actually laughed at a few of the passages, and wondered if any of Randi's headstrong older brothers had ever been on the receiving end of her razor-sharp tongue.

If only the woman lying in ICU could talk. Tucking the articles into a file, Nicole decided to call it a day. She snapped off her computer and desk lamp, then stretched and walked into the hallway. Before she'd go home, she would look in on Thorne's sister—the silent, comatose woman whose advice had touched millions.

Outside the doors of ICU, Nicole found Slade and Matt McCafferty waiting impatiently.

"Hi." Matt was standing near a post and quickly removed his hat.

Slade, seated in a chair in the small waiting area, quickly tossed aside a battered magazine and climbed to his feet.

"I thought I'd check on your sister before I went home."

"There's no change," Slade grumbled. "I was just in there and the doctors are talking about setting her broken bones now that the swelling's gone down." He looked down at his hands as they worked the brim of his hat. "She looks like hell."

"But improving," Nicole countered. "These things take time."

"Well, I wish she'd wake up." Matt's brow was furrowed with deep lines of worry. He motioned toward the closed doors. "Thorne's with her now."

"He is?" Why did her heart do a stupid little flip at the mention of his name?

"Yep." Slade checked his watch, stared at the face a second and his lips rolled in on themselves. "He should be out soon if you want to talk to him."

One side of Matt's lips curved upward. "So what is the deal with you and Thorne?"

"Is there a deal?" she said, matching his grin.

"I'd say so." Slade gave a quick nod. "Never seen Thorne so...content."

"He's not content," Matt said, shaking his head. "Hell, that guy doesn't know the meaning of the word. But he is less restless. Not as quick to jump down someone's throat. Distracted."

"Is that right—"

The doors flew open and Thorne, in jeans and a leather bomber jacket, burst through. His face was a thundercloud, his jaw set, his eyes narrowed until his gaze landed full force on Nicole.

"Something wrong?" she asked.

"Yeah, there's something wrong." He hitched a thumb toward the doors swinging shut behind him. "She's still in a coma and looks like hell. The doctors keep saying she's doing as well as can be expected, but I don't know if I can believe them. It's been over a week since she was brought in here."

"Everything that can be done is being—"

"Is it?" he demanded and she was aware of how much taller he was than she. "How do I know that?"

"I thought we'd been through this—the competency of the staff, the efficiency of the hospital, the time it takes the body to heal—"

"Enough." He glared down at her, then rammed his hands through his hair in frustration. "Hell!"

"What is it you want?" she demanded.

"You mean other than my sister and her child to be well, the baby's father located, the truth about her accident figured out, and world peace?"

"Is that all?" She lifted an imperious eyebrow and held his arrogant, demanding and ultimately irresistible gaze fast.

"No. I could use a cup of coffee, too!"

"Well, I'll find one for you, just as soon as I heal your sister and finish the last-minute details on the world peace thing," she snapped, hearing a snicker behind her. Turning on her heel, she found Slade trying and failing to swallow a smile. "Something funny?"

"Nothin' at all. In fact I'm enjoyin' the show. Not often someone puts ol' Thorne in his place."

"Is that what she's doing?" Thorne asked, then before Nicole could protest, grabbed her by the crook of the elbow and propelled her down the hallway. "You two," he called over his shoulder, "can leave. I'll catch up with you later."

"Wait a minute. What do you think you're doing?" she demanded as he forced her around a corner to a tiny alcove with a window seat and two potted plants.

"This." He didn't waste time, just lowered his head and kissed her so hard she couldn't breathe.

Her bones began to melt and she told herself this was insane, that he had no right to manhandle her anywhere, but especially not here, in the hospital where she was working. Yet there was a part of her that responded to his spontaneity, the thrill of a man wanting her enough to drag her into the comparative privacy of the alcove.

His mouth was pure magic—warm, insistent pressure. She kissed him back, her lips parting to accept his tongue, her heart pounding a wild, frantic cadence as her beeper went off.

She jerked back and saw the amusement in his eyes. "Couldn't resist," he said by way of explanation as she reached into her pocket for her pager.

"Maybe you should learn to exercise some control." She checked out the digital display of numbers and recognized Dr. Oliverio's extension.

"Ha." He let out a short laugh. "I don't have a helluva lot of that around you," he admitted. "Nor, *Doctor,* do you."

"You surprised me, that's all. Look, I have to go."

"Emergency?"

"I don't know," she admitted, "but I'd better check it out."

His grin was pure mischief as he pulled her to him and kissed her soundly again. "I'll call you later."

"Fine." She turned and found two aides walking down the hallway and pretending they hadn't seen anything, but the smiles they tried to disguise and the twinkle in their eyes as they exchanged knowing glances convinced her otherwise.

Clearing her throat she marched down the corridor toward her office and reminded herself, for what seemed the fiftieth time, she wasn't going to get involved with Thorne McCafferty.

But a little voice inside her head had the audacity to insinuate that it was too late. She was already more involved than any sane woman would allow herself to be.

Chapter 11

"I'll let you know," Thorne said, raining what he hoped appeared to be a patient smile on the woman seated in his father's favorite recliner. Her name was Peggy, she'd moved to Missoula from Las Vegas this past year and was now in Grand Hope. As far as he could tell her experience with young babies had been limited to raising her own children, who were now grown, and spending a few years as an aide in a day-care center. Her other jobs had included working as a supervisor in a cannery in California and as a maid for a hotel while she'd lived in Nevada. She was pleasant enough, he supposed, but he wasn't convinced she was the woman for the job of living at the ranch and taking care of little J.R. "I'm still interviewing."

She smiled as she stood and tossed her shaggy graying hair over her shoulders. "Well, let me know. You've got my number."

"It's on the résumé."

She stuck out her hand and he clasped it, noticing that she

wore a ring on every finger. Her makeup was thick, her fingernails long and polished a deep maroon. "Thanks." She strolled out of the living room, her slim hips rolling beneath tight jeans. At the door front, he handed her a battered suede coat and a heavy fringed purse. She slung the strap over her shoulder and headed out the door.

Boots pounded on the stairs. "Well?" Matt asked as he appeared from the second story. He looked expectantly at his brother. "Found someone?"

"Not yet." Thorne glanced through the window and watched Peggy climb into a huge station wagon that had enough grime on it that some wise guy had written Wash Me on the back windshield. She paused to light a cigarette and blow out a geyser of smoke before putting the car into gear and gunning the engine. No, Peggy Sentra wouldn't do. Nor would the other two women he'd already met.

"You interviewed three people."

"And I'll probably have to talk to a dozen or so more." The three women he'd seen, Peggy and the two others, had barely made an impression on him other than they were entirely unsuitable to take care of his newborn nephew and were a far cry from what he'd expected. "I've already left a call on the voice mail of the agency."

"Little J.R.'s coming home tomorrow."

"I know, I know," Thorne snapped. "And I guess the four of us, you, Slade, Juanita and I will just have to juggle the duties until we find someone."

"Hey, whoa there," Matt said, holding up both hands palms outward. "I'm gonna be out tomorrow—got to fix the fence on the north end of the property before we move the herd. Slade, Adam Zolander and Larry Todd are supposed to help me. The day after that I've got to run back to my own spread, so you'd better count me out until I get back."

Thorne frowned, but didn't argue. Matt owned a ranch near the Idaho border, a place he'd barely been able to afford, and yet he'd scraped together enough money for a down payment and talked the previous owner into taking a contract on the rest. Matt was known to work sixteen or eighteen hour days—all for that scrap of hilly land and a small run-down farmhouse. Thorne had never understood Matt's connection with the land, his need to ranch his own place, but there it was. Whereas Thorne had learned at an early age that acreage was valuable because it held its worth or could be developed and sold for a profit, Matt seemed to believe that he was somehow linked to the soil.

"All right. You're out."

"And so is Slade tomorrow, so, unless you can con Juanita into changing diapers and burping the baby, looks like you're the chosen one, the nanny." Chuckling, he grabbed his hat. "And the nursery's just about ready. I got the crib and changing table and bureau together, but we still need some staples—formula, diapers, baby powder and sleepers."

"Already ordered," Thorne said.

"Good."

Laughing to himself, Matt threw on his jacket, then walked outside. Thorne headed back to the den. Time for Plan B.

The phone rang and Nicole, already reaching for her keys, grabbed the receiver instead. "Hello?"

"Hi." Recognizing Thorne's voice she leaned against the window and smiled to herself. Why her lips curved upward, she didn't understand, but she didn't fight it as she stared into the night-darkened backyard. The girls clamored around her and to quiet them she pressed the index finger of her free hand to her lips.

"I need your help."

"*You* need *my* help?" She smothered a smile. There was something amusing about the CEO of McCafferty International asking for any kind of advice or aid.

"Absolutely. J.R.'s being released from the hospital tomorrow and that'll be quite a change around here."

She eyed her two dynamos. "You have no idea."

"I thought maybe you could give me some pointers."

"Oh, sure." She laughed as she watched Molly chase after Mindy with a rubber snake. Mindy shrieked in mock horror. "Don't you know that I do this motherhood thing day by day?"

"Can we discuss it over dinner?"

"I have the girls."

"Bring 'em."

She laughed out loud. "I don't think you understand what you're asking."

"Probably not, but maybe it's time I learned. I could pick you up and—"

"No, we'd better meet. I finally got the SUV back and it's ready to go *and* equipped with safety seats. Besides that I have been known to cut out early if the twins—" she was eyeing the girls as they streaked by with her I'm-the-mom-and-you'd-better-listen-to-me scowl "—make the mistake of acting up, which I'm *sure* won't happen tonight. They wouldn't dare."

Mindy bit her lower lip, but Molly ignored the warning and wriggled the fake-looking snake in her sister's face. "I already told the girls I'd take them to the Burger Corral. It's on the corner of Third and Pine."

"I know where it is," he said dryly. "I grew up here. But I was thinking of something a little quieter."

"Believe me, when you've got four-year-olds, you don't want quiet."

Molly was tugging at the edge of her jacket. "Come *on,* Mommy."

"Look, if you want to meet us, do," she invited. "We're on our way right now."

"I'll be there in half an hour."

Nicole hung up and told herself she wasn't thinking clearly. Hadn't she already told herself not to get involved with Thorne, that just because they'd shared a few kisses and quiet conversations and made love wasn't any reason to put on her old pair of rose-colored glasses again—the ones with the cracked lenses from trusting Thorne McCafferty before? But there was something about the man she found so damned irresistible it was dangerous. More than dangerous—emotional suicide. "Come on, kids, put your jackets on."

The phone rang again almost instantly and Nicole picked up thinking that Thorne had changed his mind. "Want to back out?" she teased.

"I think it's a little too late for that now, isn't it?" Paul's voice was a damper on her good mood and she steeled herself for what was certain to be a tense conversation.

"I was expecting someone else to call."

"Then I'll make it short." His voice had all the warmth of a blue norther and Nicole wondered how she'd ever once thought she'd loved the man.

"Okay."

"It's about visitation rights."

"What about them?" she asked, her fingers clenching the receiver in a death grip, the knot in her stomach tightening as it always did when she and Paul began to argue—which was nearly every time they spoke.

"I know that I'm supposed to have the girls every other Christmas and each summer."

"That's right." Her heart began to pound. She couldn't believe it but thought he might actually be angling for custody. Oh, Lord, what would she do if she lost the twins?

"But Carrie and I are going to visit her folks in Boston over the holidays and this summer we've planned a trip to Europe. Her company is sending her to a convention in Madrid and we thought we'd take the opportunity to see France, Portugal and England while we're there. So, there would be four weeks right in the middle of summer where we couldn't take the twins."

As if parental responsibility were an option.

She glanced at her daughters, now struggling into their jackets and her heart broke when she thought about them growing up without a father.

"You know we'd *love* to have them if it were possible, but Carrie's got to think of her career."

"Of course she does."

"Just like you do, Nicole. Like you always have." There it was: the inevitable dig. What was deemed noble for Carrie was somehow disgraceful for Nicole because she was a mother. She let the little barb slide. No reason to reduce the conversation to hot words at this point. "Don't worry about it," she said, though her throat was thick. "It would probably be best if they stayed with me."

"Actually, I think so. It would be hard on Molly and Mindy to uproot them and drag them here to the apartment. They're not used to a big city or being confined to a few rooms. With both our jobs it would make it really difficult and——"

"Look, I understand, but I've got to run. Do you, uh, want to speak to the girls?" She couldn't stand to hear one more minute of his rationalizations for giving up his children. They were his daughters, for God's sake! So precious. So wonderful. And they deserved better.

"Oh." A pause. "Sure."

Without much enthusiasm, she put each of the twins on the phone, let them speak to the stranger who had sired them and within three minutes was back on the phone. "I'm already late and I've really got to run now, but we'll work the visitations out."

"I knew I could count on you." The words echoed through her mind and she toyed with the question of what he would do if he couldn't rely on her.

"I'm glad you understand." Relief was heavy in his voice.

"Goodbye, Paul." She hung up incensed and helped Mindy zip up her jacket. "Come on, kids, let's roll."

"You mad, Mommy?" Mindy asked as Nicole slung the strap of her purse over her shoulder. Catching sight of her reflection in the window, she understood her daughter's concern. Her eyebrows were slammed together, her mouth pursed tight at the corners.

"Not anymore. Come on, let's get into the car." She opened the door and the twins swarmed through, their chubby legs flashing, their shoes pounding on the back porch, their laughter and giggles ringing through the night air.

"I get shotgun!" Molly cried.

"No, me—" Mindy started to pout.

"You're both in the back seat, in your car seats and you know it," Nicole said. "Remember?"

"But Billy Johnson gets to ride in the front seat," Molly said. Billy was a wild-haired boy in their preschool.

"So does Beth Anne."

Another friend.

"Well, you don't." Nicole helped strap them into their respective seats, then climbed behind the wheel. She paused long enough to reapply her lipstick, then twisted on the ignition and grinned as the SUV roared to life. As she put the rig into reverse she felt a twinge of apprehension about meeting Thorne again. Whether she liked it or not she was in some kind of relationship with him and that thought worried her.

"It's not a date," she told herself.

"What?" Molly demanded.

"Nothing, sweetie, now you girls figure out what you want to get for dinner," she said and silently added, *and I'll try to figure out what to do with Thorne McCafferty.*

Within fifteen minutes she'd driven to the small restaurant, parked in the crowded lot, then shepherded her girls to a corner booth near the soda fountain. With the efficiency of the mother of twins, Nicole helped the girls out of their jackets and let them wander to the video games where a group of boys who looked about eight or nine were trying to best each other and the sounds of bells, whistles and simulated gun reports punctuated the buzz of conversation, clatter of flatware and rattle of ice cubes from the self-serve soda machine.

Somewhere, above it all, there was the hint of music, some old Elvis Presley hit, she thought, but couldn't remember. She recognized some of the customers—the couple who owned a small market around the corner, a boy she'd stitched up when he'd cracked his head inline skating, a young mother who worked at the preschool where her twins were enrolled.

She ordered a diet cola for herself and milk shakes for the girls, then waited nervously until she spied Thorne push open one of the double glass doors. Tall, broad-shouldered, a determined expression on his bladed features, he glanced around the interior until his gaze landed full force on her. Her breath caught as if she were a silly schoolgirl and she mentally chided herself. *Get over it. He's just a man.* What was it about him that caused her idiotic heart to turn over at the sight of him? She waved and he strode through the maze of tables and booths.

"Where are—?" he started to ask before he spied the twins standing on chairs and peering over the shoulders of the boys working the video games. "Oh."

"They'll be back. I'm just lucky they don't understand they need money to work the machines."

"Then they'll break you."

"Exactly."

Hanging his leather jacket on a peg already holding one of the twins' coats, he glanced around the open restaurant, then slid onto the bench opposite her. "Not exactly what I had in mind when I called," he admitted, "but it'll do."

"Oh, will it?" she mocked.

"I haven't been here since high school."

"Fond memories?" She managed to keep her tone light though there had been times when she'd sat in this very booth hoping that Thorne McCafferty would call or return to Grand Hope. It hadn't happened.

"Some fonder than others." His gaze touched hers for a second. Picking up a plastic-coated menu, he elaborated, "I had the first date of my life here with Mary Lou Bennett when I was a freshman in high school. I was scared to death and then another time—" his eyes narrowed a fraction "—I got into a fight with a kid a couple of years older than me. What was his name? A real tough…Mike something or other…Wilkins… that was it. Mike Wilkins. He beat the tar out of me in the parking lot."

"He beat you up?"

"Yep. But I hate to admit it." He lifted an eyebrow. "Oh, yes, Dr. Stevenson, I wasn't always the tough guy you see before you."

"What happened?" she asked, fascinated. She'd never heard this story before.

"The police came and hauled us both in. Took our statements and those from the kids that had collected around the fight. My dad had to come down and claim me and I was nearly kicked out of school and thrown off the football team, but, as usual, John Randall managed to pull some strings. The worst punishment I ended up with was a black eye, a couple of loose teeth and some pretty bad damage to my ego."

"Which you probably deserved."

"Probably." One side of his mouth lifted in a self-deprecating grin. "I was a little cocky."

"Was?"

He snorted a laugh.

"What was the fight about?" she asked, surprised at his candor.

"What else? A girl. I was hitting on his girlfriend and for the life of me I can't remember her name, but she had red hair, a cute little smile and a few other attributes as well."

"And that's what attracted you—her 'attributes'?"

"And the fact that she was Mike Wilkins's girlfriend." His gray eyes twinkled. "I've always liked a challenge and a little competition never hurt, either."

At that moment Molly came running up. "I want a quarter."

"Why?"

"'Cause that kid—" she pointed an accusatory finger at a boy of eight or nine with spiky blond hair and freckles "—he says I need one to play the games."

Nicole shot Thorne a knowing look. "Well, we don't have any time right now. Go and get your sister and let's order."

"No!" Molly's lower lip stuck out petulantly. "I want a quarter."

"Listen, not tonight, okay? Now, come on—" Nicole glanced up at Thorne and sighed. "Excuse me for a second, would you?" She climbed out of the booth, made her way to the video machines and peeled Mindy from the chair on which she'd been standing. Mindy put up her kind of low-keyed fuss while Molly, ever more vocal, was bordering on being obnoxious.

"I want a quarter!" she demanded, stomping her little foot imperiously.

"And I told you that we couldn't come here unless you behaved." Nicole managed to get both girls onto booster chairs, one on her side of the booth, the other next to Thorne.

"I want French fries," Molly stated.

"Oh, do you? Now there's a surprise."

"And a hot dog."

"Me, too," Mindy agreed. They managed to stay in their seats until the waitress, a slim teenaged girl in black slacks, crisp white shirt and red bow tie took their order. Then they were off again, making a beeline for the video machines as the restaurant filled up and conversation buzzed through the air.

"See what you're in for?" Nicole's gaze followed her children. "I might have two the same age, but you'll have a newborn to deal with."

"Just until Randi can take over." He frowned and then settled back.

"I take it no one's been able to locate the baby's father?"

"Not yet. But we will." Determination pulled at the corners of his mouth.

She was disappointed that he seemed so anxious to cast off his responsibility of temporary father, but, as the waitress returned with their drink order, she reminded herself that he was, after all, a confirmed bachelor, a man more interested in making money than making babies.

Thorne noticed the play of emotions that crossed her face and the way her teasing smile suddenly disappeared.

"The reason I called you was that I need your help," he admitted. "We need a babysitter until Randi's well enough to take care of J.R."

"Oh."

He tried not to notice the sexy way her front teeth settled

against her lower lip as she watched her girls, or the seductive way her blouse gaped at her neckline, showing off just the hint of cleavage. She glanced at him and in that second, when her gold eyes met his, he felt the incredible urge to kiss her again—just as he always did.

"It shouldn't be that hard to find someone suitable. I'm willing to pay whatever it takes."

"Money isn't the issue."

"Of course it is."

She rolled those expressive eyes and unwrapped her straw. "You still don't get it, do you? It's not about money." Taking a long sip from her soda she thought for a minute. "That's always been your problem, you know. Don't you understand that you can't go out and *buy* love? You can't expect to find the most loving, caring babysitter just by offering her a few more dollars. People are who they are. They don't change when you wave a check in front of their faces."

"I know that, but most people perform for money."

"You don't want someone to perform, you want someone who cares. There's a big difference. I'm not saying you don't pay them well, of course you do. But first you find the caring, warm, loving person. Then you pay them what they're worth to you."

"Is that what you did?"

"Absolutely. I located Jenny through an advertisement I ran in the local paper. After interviewing a dozen or so women and looking at day-care centers, she called, we met and the rest is history. She's a part-time college student and the nicest woman you'd ever want to meet. She's warm, affectionate, wholesome and has a great sense of humor, which you need with kids. We work it out so that our schedules mesh. It takes some doing, but it can be accomplished." The waitress came with their trays of food and Thorne helped Nicole round up the girls. Just as they sat down, Nicole's pager went off. She glanced at the readout and frowned. "Look, I've got to make a call," she said. "I've got a cell phone out in the car—would you mind watching the girls just a minute?"

Thorne lifted a shoulder.

"No, Mommy," one of the twins cried.

"I'll be right back. Promise. Mr. McCafferty will help you open the ketchup packets for your French fries."

"Sure," Thorne said, though the thought of being with two four-year-old dynamos was a trifle daunting. Nicole slid out of the booth, then clipped across the tile floor. The twins looked ready to bolt after her, but Thorne distracted them with their milk shakes. He unwrapped their plastic straws then pushed them deep into their cups.

While one twin tried to suck up the milk shake the other was busy trying to open ketchup packages. Again he assisted and then squirted the red sauce over the fries. "Nooo!" the little girl wailed. "I want to dip!"

"What?"

"I want to dip. I don't want it on the top." Her little face was screwed up in a scowl as she glared at her basket. The other twin was sucking like crazy, trying to draw the too thick milk shake up her straw.

"It don't come," she complained.

"Just try harder."

"I am!"

"I don't like it," the first one insisted and Thorne seeing no other answer, took her hot dog, put it in his basket, then placed his cheeseburger in her basket and switched them. He handed her an opened packet of ketchup.

"You do it any way you want. Now—" he took the milk shake from the other girl's hands and opening in the lid, used the straw to swirl the chocolatey goo "—that should help," he said, replacing the lid and straw. "If it doesn't work, just give it a little time, it'll melt."

"Where's Mommy?" number one asked as she plopped a French fry into a pool of ketchup that she'd created.

"In the car making a call."

"Is she coming back?"

"I think so," he said and winked. The pixies tore into their food, pulling off the buns and squeezing more mustard and ketchup onto their hot dogs than was necessary but Thorne, not used to being around children of any age, decided to let them do what they wanted. By the time Nicole returned, they had condiments on their faces, hands, clothes and even in their hair.

"Everything all right?" he asked.

"Minor emergency—nothing serious. I handled it. Oh, what happened?" she asked, eyeing her daughters.

"They ate."

"Didn't they give you bibs?" Her eyes fell to the tray where two plastic bibs were tucked.

"Didn't see 'em."

Sighing, she wiped one face, then the other before finally turning her attention to her own dinner. "You have a lot to learn," she said, biting into her hamburger.

"That's why I need a nanny."

"Or two," she said.

"As I mentioned, I was hoping you could help me out in that department."

"How?"

"Either you or your sitter might be able to give me the names of people who would be interested in a part-time or full-time job taking care of the baby. At least until Randi's on her feet and able to care for him."

"It's a possibility," she said, touching a napkin to the corner of her lips, then automatically wiping a smudge from one of her daughter's cheeks.

"Don't!" the little girl cried.

"Oh, Molly, don't be such a grump." Nicole was undeterred and soon, despite much cringing and grumbling, the little girl's face was condiment-free and they were all digging into their food again.

Thorne watched Nicole with her daughters, how she joked with them and played with them even when she was disciplining them. She didn't raise her voice, always paid attention when they spoke and pointed out their mistakes with a wink and a smile. It didn't always work. The precocious one challenged her mother and the shier little girl sometimes didn't speak and offered Nicole a cold shoulder, but throughout the meal one thing was clear—Nicole Sanders Stevenson, M.D., was one helluva mother.

Not that it mattered. He wasn't looking for a woman who could raise children. Hell, he wasn't even looking for a woman period.

Yet, for a reason he couldn't name he still carried that damned ring his father had given him in his pocket.

Chapter 12

Thorne had never felt so awkward in his life. He'd just fed the baby and burped him and heard soft little sighs against his shoulder as he walked from the den to the living room and wondered how the hell he was going to get J.R. into his crib without waking him. The baby, bright-eyed and healthy, seemed the most content while being held, which was a worry.

A natural athlete, Thorne had been able to handle a wet football, rope a calf, ride a horse, or crack a baseball over the fence, but when it came to holding, feeding, burping and diapering a tiny infant, he was all thumbs.

Not that his brothers were any better at it. Matt had spent his life on the ranch and had dealt with everything from newly hatched chicks to orphaned lambs and foals who were rejected by the mares that gave them birth. He'd helped bring litters of puppies and kittens into this world. But when it came to helpless human babies, he, too, seemed out of place and incompetent. Slade was the worst. Although fascinated beyond belief with the baby, he seemed terrified to hold J.R. That part was downright ridiculous in Thorne's estimation, though Matt was amused that his daredevil of a brother was frightened of the infant.

J.R.'s eyes blinked open.

Uh-oh.

Within seconds he started to put up a fuss and Thorne tried not to panic. "You're all right," he said, wondering how it was that mothers seemed to have some kind of natural rhythm while holding and swaying slightly as they held a child. He'd seen that same natural reaction through the glass window of the hospital when Nicole had cradled and fed the baby.

He tried to sway, felt like an ass and the baby started crying in earnest, wailing and turning red in the face. "Now, it's okay," Thorne reassured the child when he had no idea whatsoever was wrong with him. "Hang in there."

Juanita's footsteps echoed down the stairs. "I'm coming, I'm coming," she said to Thorne's utter relief.

A second later she appeared. "He is tired."

"He *was* asleep."

"Then why didn't you put him in his *cuna?*"

"Because I couldn't get to his *cuna,*" Thorne said, emphasizing the Spanish word, "without waking him up."

"But you woke him up anyway." She lifted a graying eyebrow as the baby cried louder than Thorne thought was possible.

"Believe me, I wasn't trying to."

"Here, let me have him. Come on, little one," she said softly, prying him from Thorne's stiff fingers. She began to murmur softly in Spanish as she carried the infant from the room and to Thorne's mortification the baby started to quiet. Within minutes silence prevailed and Juanita, walking softly, returned.

"How do you do that?"

"Practice," she said and smiled.

"Maybe I need lessons."

"*Dios,* all you brothers do. And probably Señorita Randi as well. How is she going to take care of the baby, write her columns, finish her book and get well?" She shook her head as she headed to the kitchen.

"There is no book," Thorne said, following her down the hallway. "Remember, that was always just her dream. Nothing ever came of it."

"But she said that she would write one. I believed it. She will be rich and famous one day. You will see." She scrounged in the refrigerator, muttered something under her breath and reached inside where she found a package, opened it and looked at Harold who lay on a rag rug near the back door. "I saved this soup bone for you," she told him as the crippled dog climbed to his feet and wagged his tail. "But you take it outside." She tossed the bone to the dog and looked over her shoulder at Thorne. "There is a book."

"I hope so," Thorne said, but nearly dismissed the idea. Randi had talked about writing the Great American Novel ever since she was fifteen. To his knowledge she hadn't written the first sentence much less a chapter or two. There was nothing to it, he told himself, but made a mental note to mention Randi's pipe dream to Striker. Why not? It certainly wouldn't hurt.

Nicole climbed out of the bathtub and stepped into her robe. The twins were asleep, the house quiet. Cinching the belt, she padded to the kitchen and heated a cup of cocoa. Patches, curled on a cushion of one of the café chairs at the table, opened one eye and yawned, showing off needle-sharp teeth before resting his chin on his paws again. The microwave dinged and Nicole picked up her cup to carry into the living room where a fire still burned in the grate. Scarlet coals glowed brightly and the fire popped and hissed.

Sipping from her cup, Nicole settled into a corner of her love seat and flipped through a parenting magazine. She'd just started reading an article on a toddler's stages of life when she noticed the column—advice for the single parent, written by R. J. McKay. Why it caught her eye, she didn't know, but she began reading the text and an eerie sensation crawled up her spine. It was written with a light hand and ironic style that was identical to that in the columns she'd read by Randi McCafferty. But no one had ever mentioned that Randi had expanded her column from newspapers to magazines. Not that it wasn't common.

She sipped her cocoa and started rereading the article when she heard a vehicle ease down the street. The engine slowed, then died in front of her house and when she twisted to peek through the blinds she spied Thorne striding up her front walk.

Her pulse leaped at the sight of him and then she remembered that she was wearing only her robe. On her feet in an instant, she started for the bedroom just as she heard the doorbell ring.

"Damn." She hesitated then walked back to the door and swung it open. Wind ruffled his hair and billowed her skirt as it swept into the room. "Well, Mr. McCafferty, this is a surprise."

A cocksure smile stretched across his lips as his gaze traveled the length of her. "A good one, I hope."

"That depends," she teased, unable to stop herself.

"On?"

"You, of course."

He didn't wait. In half a heartbeat he crossed the threshold, his arms were around her and his cold lips found hers. Icy wind swirled around them and just before she closed her eyes and he kicked the door shut, she saw the first few snowflakes fall from the night-dark heavens.

But the snowfall was instantly forgotten. The pressure of his lips was insistent and her heart went wild, pounding out of control, thundering in her ears.

Warmth invaded her limbs and desire slowly uncoiled deep within her. He backed her against the foyer's wall and she willingly complied, winding her arms around his neck, parting her lips, thrilling to the cool, welcome touch of his skin against hers. He smelled of the outdoors—pine laced with the traces of some musky cologne. His body was hard, tense muscles strong as they pressed intimately against hers. This was a mistake. She knew it, but couldn't resist the sweet seduction of his touch, the tingle his lips evoked.

His hands found her belt and as if he had all the time in the world he continued to kiss her as he loosened the knot. His tongue touched hers, flicking and tasting, causing her head to swim. She could barely breathe as her robe parted and with cold, callused fingers he lifted one breast in his hand. Her nipple puckered expectantly and deep inside she turned liquid.

"Oh, Nicole," he murmured against the shell of her ear. Desire was throbbing through her and emotions she didn't pause to understand raced through her mind. "We're alone?" His voice was low and husky.

"No." She shook her head and had trouble finding her voice. Lust pulsed through her veins. "The twins are here."

"Asleep?"

She nodded as his fingers scraped along the front lapel of her robe, touching her skin so lightly she wanted to scream. "It's…it's all right," she said though she wasn't thinking clearly, couldn't concentrate on anything but the want of him.

"Good." He kissed her again and reaching down, placed an arm beneath her knees and lifted her from her feet. As if

she were nearly weightless he carried her down the short hallway past the girls' room to her bedroom—a private sanctuary
where, heretofore, no man had ever been allowed to enter.

Somehow he managed to close and lock the door before
placing her on the bed. Beneath her old hand-pieced quilt, the
mattress sagged under their combined weight. "Wh-what's got
into you?" she asked as he pushed the robe off her shoulders.

He stopped, his hands unmoving for a second as his silvery
gaze found hers. "You, Doctor." He leaned forward and kissed
her slowly on the lips. "You've gotten into me and I can't seem
to do anything about it but this."

"Would you want to?" she asked and smiled.

"No." He parted the robe and took both her breasts in his
hands. Holding them together he kissed the tops of each before guiding her fingers to his shirt. She needed no further
instruction and began to remove his jacket, sweater and jeans
while he never stopped kissing her, touching her, or causing
her blood to heat and the yearning deep within her most private of regions to become ever more insistent.

Don't do this, that nagging little voice in her head screamed,
but she ignored it.

His fingers tangled in her hair, then moved down her back,
kneading and probing. His body molded to hers. He tasted
of salt and desire and she wanted him as she'd never wanted
another man.

Only he could satisfy her.

Only he could send her soaring to heights she'd only imagined. She kissed him and dug her fingers into his shoulders.

Anxious, strident muscles rubbed against her softer, yielding
flesh. His tongue found and rimmed the hollow of her throat
before seeking darker, deeper clefts that made her bite her lip
to keep from screaming out. Intimate spasms erupted deep
inside before he came to her, parting her legs, kissing her and

holding her close. She arched upward, wanting more, needing release. "Thorne—" she whispered when she thought she'd go mad with desire "—Thorne, for the love of—oh, oooh."

With one forceful thrust he began to make love to her then and didn't stop. As her breathing became shallow and her body sheened with a layer of perspiration, he kissed her, loved her. Over and over he claimed her until the first streaks of daylight pierced through the window shades and she, exhausted, still holding him close, finally drifted off.

The girls awakened a few hours later and the bed was cold and empty, only the faint scent of sex lingering with the sweet, sensual memories of lovemaking stealing through her mind. She glanced at the bureau where the rose he'd given her had faded and died, the petals falling onto the old wood. She hadn't thrown the flower out; couldn't.

She was tired, yes, but felt better than she had in years. She sang in the shower, laughed when the girls fought, dressed with a smile on her face. It was only when she was yanking a brush through her hair that she caught a glimpse of her reflection, and she noticed the curve of her lips and the sparkle in her eyes. "Oh, no," she said, disbelieving.

But she couldn't deny the plain truth that stared her squarely in the face: she was, despite all her warnings to herself, falling head over heels in love with Thorne McCafferty.

Denver held no appeal to him. His apartment seemed as cold and empty as an ice cave and though it was clean, every surface shining, fresh towels hung over the brass towel bars, a lit fire at his fingertips, he felt no sense of homecoming. His closet was filled with suits, sport coats, slacks and three tuxedos; the view from his living room and master bedroom, a spectacular array of the lights of the city. And yet he felt as if he were in a foreign land, an alien in a penthouse that he'd called home for more years than he wanted count.

He'd arrived in town in the morning and gone straight to the office. Somehow he'd survived four meetings before driving here where he intended to change and attend the black-tie affair hosted by Kent Williams. The dinner was for a charitable cause but the business behind the scenes was all about turning a profit. Not that he minded. Thorne was the first man to admit to being interested in making money.

And yet...

He poured himself a glass of Scotch and stared out the panorama of windows. Snow was falling and the lights of the city winked through the veil of flakes. He saw his own reflection in the glass, a tall man in a slightly wrinkled suit, holding a drink he didn't want and feeling more alone than he ever had in his life.

He'd never been one to dislike his own company; in fact, he'd silently laughed at men who needed a woman on their arms, showpieces, accessories, or even wives they adored. It had all seemed so weak and cowardly; but now, as he looked at that pale, distorted, ghostlike image of himself in the window, he imagined Nicole with him. Whether dressed in a sequined evening gown, or a pair of jeans and tennis shoes, or a lab coat over slacks and a blouse, her image seemed perfect at his side.

"Idiot," he muttered and tossed back his drink. He'd go to the damned party, do his business and drive to the airport tonight. The weather service was predicting two feet of snow to be dumped on the Denver area in the next couple of days, but Thorne intended to return to Grand Hope as soon as he could escape the obligations of his position.

There were too many pressing problems in Montana for him to tarry in this soulless suite he'd once considered home.

Home. Ha!

What were all the old sayings?

Home sweet home?

There's no place like home?

Home is where the heart is?

He took one final look around the living room as he strode to the bedroom to dig out one of his tuxedos. One thing was for certain: his heart wasn't here. Nope—it was currently residing in the hallways of St. James Hospital with the stubborn, bright, beautiful emergency room physician he'd once turned his back on—a divorced woman with two children already and no apparent desire to settle down again.

Well, all that was about to change. Thorne was used to taking charge of a situation, of getting what he wanted, and right now as he pulled out the designer tux with the forest-green cummerbund, he wanted Dr. Nicole Stevenson. One way or another he'd have her.

Nicole was dead on her feet. She'd worked overtime as there was a horrible accident involving two cars and a pickup. The wreck had occurred just two miles outside the city limits of Grand Hope. An eighty-year-old man and a teenager hadn't survived; the man's wife and three other teenagers were fighting for their lives. All were in critical condition with head injuries, punctured lungs, cracked ribs, ruptured spleens and all manner of contusions. A middle-aged housewife and her two children that were in the pickup had survived with only minor injuries, but the ER had been a madhouse and every available doctor, nurse, aid and anesthesiologist had been called in. Only now, ten hours after the first ambulance had arrived and they'd dealt with the severely injured, were things finally settling down. The rest of the patients, a woman who had scalded herself, an eight-year-old who had slammed his finger in a car door, three flu cases and a man complaining of dizzy spells had been forced to wait.

But the worst of the chaos was over, the patients stabilized, and relief physicians had arrived. Finally, Nicole could go home. She poured herself a fresh cup of coffee and quickly wrote some notes on her computer before grabbing her jacket, laptop and briefcase and leaving St. James.

The parking lot was a blanket of white as snow had fallen all day long. Six inches had piled in the parking lot and ice and snow had collected on the SUV's windshield. She waited for the defroster and wipers to clear the glass, then drove carefully into town.

She hadn't heard from Thorne since yesterday morning and she was beginning to miss him, though she didn't want to admit how deeply and emotionally entangled she'd become with him and his entire family.

"Oh, don't be a fool," she told herself as she stopped to ease the rig into four-wheel drive. She decided to call Thorne when she got home, tell him about a friend of Jenny's who was interested in the nanny job and just reconnect. After all, in these days of women's liberation, why couldn't she call him rather than sit by the phone or wonder what he was doing?

She made her way home and found her girls already dressed in their pajamas and ready for bed. "Sorry I'm late," she apologized to Jenny after hugging each twin and listening to them babble on about what they'd done during the day. There was talk of a snowman in the backyard and Mindy complained that Molly had hit her with a snowball.

"Did not!" Molly cried, but guilt contorted her little face and she called her sister a tattletale when she finally confessed without a drop of remorse.

"They've been pretty good," Jenny admitted and hugged each girl before leaving. With the twins standing on the love seat, their noses pressed to the window, Nicole watched as Jenny drove off through the storm, the taillights of her battle-scarred station wagon winking bright red against a shower of snowflakes.

It was nearly two hours later, once Molly and Mindy were fast asleep, that she dialed the number of the Flying M. The phone was answered by a woman with a thick Spanish accent.

"McCafferty Ranch."

"This is Nicole Stevenson. I'm looking for—"

"The doctor. *Dios!* Has something happened to Señorita Randi?"

"No, I just wanted to talk to Thorne."

"But Randi, she is the same?"

"Yes. As far as I know."

There was a heavy sigh on the other end of the line. "Thorne, he is not here, but you can speak to Slade."

Disappointment pierced her soul. "No, that's all right. Have Thorne give me a call when he returns."

"He is not coming back for a while," the woman said, then holding her hand over the receiver spoke to someone else and within a few seconds Slade's voice boomed over the wires.

"Is this Nicole?"

"Yes."

There was a moment's hesitation. "Oh. Well, I thought you knew. Thorne's in Denver. We don't expect him back for a few days. We're not really sure but the storm's hit hard there and it looks like he won't be back for a while—uh-oh." In the background she heard a baby start to put up a fuss. "Was there a message I could pass along to him?"

"No, not really," she said, feeling deflated somehow. "I thought he was looking for a nanny and I have the number of a woman who might be a possibility."

The baby was really wailing by this time. "Great. The job

hasn't been filled yet. Why don't you give me the information?"

"Sure. The woman's name is Christina Foster." She gave Slade Christina's number and was about to hang up when she remembered something she'd wanted to tell Thorne but hadn't had the chance. "You know, Slade, I was reading an article in a magazine the other night. It was about single parenting and the byline was for an R. J. McKay. I know this sounds crazy, but it sure read like something your sister might have written."

"Is that so?" Slade was all ears. "You still got a copy of it?"

"Yes."

"I'd like to see it."

"Sure, but as I said, I'm not certain it was written by Randi."

"Nonetheless."

"I'll make you a copy and send it to you."

"Thanks."

She hung up and felt a big case of the blues threatening to overtake her. So Thorne was in Denver. So what?

Why didn't he mention that he was going? Why hasn't he called?

"Stop it," she told herself. She *wasn't* going to be one of those women who sat around and stewed over a man. No way, no how. And yet, as she pulled the blinds and saw one last view of the snowy night, she couldn't help wish that Thorne was here with her, holding her in his arms and making love to her as if he would never stop.

Cradling a cup of coffee, Thorne glowered out the window to the gray morning. Snow was still falling as if it would never stop and the airport was a mess. At another time in his life, he would have kept busy, gone to the office, buried himself in his work, managed his life around the natural disaster that seemed hell-bent on causing him problems. But now he wanted to return to Grand Hope, Montana—to the ranch, to Randi, to little J.R. and especially to Nicole. Grand Hope was where he belonged. With his brothers and sister. With his nephew. With the woman he loved.

Silently he sipped his black coffee and laughed at himself. Thorne McCafferty, once upon a time a confirmed bachelor, now contemplating not just living with a woman for the rest of his life, but marrying her.

Matt and Slade would needle him mercilessly when they found out. But he didn't mind.

His head still ached from the buzz of last night's party. Kent Williams had been attentive and brought several ideas to him—a condominium project in Aspen, single-family court-yard homes in a development just outside of Denver, and an apartment complex in Boulder. He'd been certain they could work something out and all the while Annette had hovered near him, touching him, smiling up at him, showing off her sleek body in a low-cut gown of mauve silk while he spoke to other businessmen and reporters who were covering the event. She'd even managed to loop her arm through his while a so-ciety page reporter had spoken with him and a photographer had flashed his picture.

Thorne hadn't been interested in her advances, but had managed to smile and accept her attentions throughout the night. Only when he was leaving and she suggested that she was available to come to his place for drinks did he pull her into a private alcove of the hotel and tell her in no uncertain terms that it was over. When she'd pouted, he'd had to tell her that he was involved with another woman. She hadn't believed him and had thrown her arms around his neck and tried to kiss him. Only then, when he hadn't responded, had she realized that he was serious.

"I just hope whoever she is she knows what she's got in

you," she'd said icily. "No woman with any heart wants a man married to his work."

He hadn't responded but had silently thought that Nicole didn't even know he loved her; would probably reject him when he proposed. At that thought he smiled for the first time in twenty-four hours. The memory of making love to her had lingered in his mind, but that wasn't all of it. Their lovemaking was wild, raw and passionate, but sex wasn't the driving force. No, he loved Nicole the concerned physician, Nicole the tenderhearted mother, Nicole the brassy woman who stood up to him and joked with him as well as Nicole the sexy lady he wanted to forever warm his bed.

So he was stuck in Denver. Great. He might as well make the most of it. He decided to go into the office, do as much work as he could while he was here and then as soon as the weather broke, he would fly back to the pine-forested slopes of Montana where he belonged.

He showered, changed into a business suit that felt strangely uncomfortable, then he walked the few blocks through the snow-crusted streets to the office. He spent the next hour with Eloise who brought him up to date on his projects. "You know," she said, checking off another item on her list as she sat on one side of his desk and he on the other. "This is working better than I thought."

"What is?"

"You being at the ranch in Montana. I have to admit that I thought it was a crazy scheme when you came up with it."

"The art of telecommunications."

"I suppose."

"Or maybe you just like being in charge when I'm gone."

"Oh, yeah, that's it." A twinkle lit her eyes. "Okay, is there anything else?"

"Yes, get me a florist on the line, would you?"

"You want me to send flowers for you?"

Thorne leaned back in his chair. "No, this time I'll handle it personally."

"Uh-oh. Someone special?"

"Very." He leaned back in his chair and noticed the shocked expression on his secretary's face. "Very special to me."

"Will do." She left his office, buzzed him a few minutes later and told him the florist was on line two. Thorne pulled at his collar and told the man on the other end of the line what he wanted and when he was finished, he grinned widely. That should knock the lady doc's socks off.

The intercom buzzed insistently and when he picked up, Eloise told him that a man named Kurt Striker was on hold.

"Put him through." There was a click. "Striker?"

"Yep. Listen, you told me to let you know if I found out anything about your sister's accident."

All the muscles in the back of Thorne's neck contracted. "I remember."

"Well, I've done some pokin' around."

"And?"

"I think that your sister's accident involved another vehicle—a maroon Ford product, from the looks of it. Either that rig edged her off the road on purpose or clipped her fender, sent her reeling and the driver got so scared he didn't bother to stop. The least it could be is a hit-and-run accident, the worst-case scenario is attempted murder."

Thorne's heart turned to stone. A tic developed over his eye. "You're sure about this?"

"Yep," Striker said, his voice as strong as steel. "I'd be willing to bet my life on it."

Chapter 13

"I guess when your name is McCafferty, there's no way you can keep it away from the press." Maureen Oliverio slapped a copy of the newspaper down on the table and slid into a chair in the cafeteria where Nicole was finishing her lunch.

"Don't tell me, some reporter is writing about Randi again."

"Not just Randi, but the whole damned family." Maureen opened a packet of nondairy creamer and poured the white powder into her cup of coffee. "Page three."

Nicole pushed her cup of soup aside and spread the paper open. As she did, her heart nearly stopped. Yes, there was an article about the McCaffertys and Randi's accident, but the text was more in-depth and gave an overview of John Randall McCafferty, who had once been so influential in the area surrounding Grand Hope. There was also a sketchy story of what his children were doing. There were old snapshots of the McCafferty brothers playing football, a picture of Slade after his skiing accident, a shot of Matt riding rodeo and another picture, one taken just the day before, if the date was to be believed, of Thorne at a charitable fund-raiser in Denver. On his arm was a striking woman who positively glowed in her designer gown and diamonds.

Nicole's world spun for a second. Her throat closed and she tried to deny what was so obvious. Then, gritting her teeth and finding a scrap of her self-esteem she scanned the article before lifting her eyes and reading the concern in Maureen's gaze. "I don't know what possessed me to buy this," the emergency room team leader said, "but I thought you'd like to see it."

"Yes. Thank you." No words were spoken but a moment of understanding passed between them. Maureen wouldn't embarrass her by stating the obvious: that Thorne was dating other women while he was seeing Nicole, and Nicole didn't have to make excuses or defend him. The thread of friend-ship—the woman-bond—between Maureen and Nicole ran too deep for that kind of false pride. They were more than colleagues, more than friends. They belonged to an unspoken sisterhood of single women raising families.

"You can have it."

"Good."

Her pager went off and Nicole read the message—a code that she needed to be in the ER. At the same time Maureen's beeper caught her attention.

"Gotta run," Nicole said.

"Me, too. I'll meet you in the ER."

On her feet in an instant, Nicole tucked the damning news-paper under her arm. What did she expect? Of course Thorne dated other women. He probably had one in every city where he did work. The thought made her stomach turn over. Why, oh, for the love of God, why did she let herself fall in love with him?

At the elevators Nicole gave herself a quick mental shake.

She couldn't be worrying about Thorne or wondering about him or pining over him. She had work to do. Important work. She climbed onto the elevator car, pushed the button for the main floor and once on ground level, swept through the doors to the ER.

"What've we got?" she asked, pulling on a pair of disposable gloves as Maureen appeared through a side door. Tension crackled in the air.

"Plane crash, just outside of town. Some idiot was trying to fly a private jet in this mess," a nurse said as she hung up the phone. "Close enough that he's coming in by ambulance."

"How many injured?" Nicole asked.

"Just the pilot, I think."

"And he's alive?"

"As far as I know."

"Lucky stiff."

At that moment the sound of sirens split the air. "Okay, people, let's get to work!"

The ambulance, siren screaming, roared into the parking lot. Tires and chains squealed. Two paramedics flew out of the back. A police car—lights flashing in red and blue—skidded in behind the ambulance. As the patient was wheeled inside, two deputies from the sheriff's department stormed in.

"What have we got here?" Nicole asked.

"Thirty-nine-year-old man, unconscious, head injuries, broken femur, blood pressure stable at..."

The paramedic rambled on and Nicole heard the vital signs, but her heart was thundering, her legs weak as she stared into the mangled face of the patient and knew, before anyone said a word, that this was Thorne. The overhead lights seemed brighter and started to swim in her eyes. Her heart pounded in her ears and she couldn't breathe. Her legs threatened to give out and she braced herself against the wall.

"Who is he?"

"Thorne McCafferty," she heard through her fog and forced her eyes into the serious gaze of a woman deputy from the sheriff's department. Her name tag read Detective Kelly Dillinger.

"Oh, God," she whispered. "No. No. Oh, God, no—"

"I'll take over," Maureen said from somewhere behind her and the room began to go dark. "Nicole. I said—"

"No, I'll be all right." Her fingers wrapped around the cold metal railing of the gurney as she turned to face Maureen.

"I'll handle it, *Doctor.*" Behind the understanding in Maureen's eyes, was an insistence that warned Nicole she would hear of no argument. Several nurses were staring. All the while Thorne lay still, needing assistance. "You're too involved emotionally, and I'm the team leader," Maureen pointed out.

"All right." Nicole had no choice but to back down. She was shaking and needed to pull herself together. "But as soon as you've examined him, let me know. I'll be in my office and I'll call his family."

"Fine." All business, Maureen Oliverio nodded. "Talk to the detective and I'll see to the patient. Let's go!"

As she watched helplessly, Thorne was wheeled into an examining room.

"What did she mean you were too involved?" the detective asked.

With pale skin and piercing brown eyes she stared at Nicole from beneath the brim of her hat. A few wisps of red hair feathered around her face.

"I—I know the family."

"And Thorne McCafferty specifically?"

"Yes. He and I have dated," she admitted, finally coming to grips with the situation. Her spine found some starch and she was no longer quivering inside but she suspected her face was pale as death. "He's a friend of mine. What happened?" As she talked she peeled off her gloves and tossed them into a waste receptacle.

"His plane went down in the storm and we're investigating the cause of the accident. Probably just the weather, but we have to be sure." Detective Dillinger's lips pursed a bit. "He's lucky to be alive."

Nicole glanced to the examining room and nodded. To think that Thorne might have lost his life. Oh, God. What then? Her heart ached at the thought of it. She cleared her throat and saw a news van wheel into the lot. "Uh-oh."

Looking over her shoulder, the detective recognized the van. Her lips tightened into a frown of disapproval. She nodded to her partner and ordered, "Handle the vultures. And don't tell them the name of the pilot until we talk to his family."

"Got it." The other officer, a lanky man in his early twenties blocked the entrance. The reporter, a petite woman in a bright-blue coat argued as a wiry cameraman stared through the glass.

"Can we talk somewhere a little more private?" Detective Dillinger asked and for the first time Nicole was aware of the curious stares that were cast in her direction.

"Yeah—my office, just let me tell the staff where to reach me." Another doctor agreed to take over for the next half hour while Nicole managed to rein in her wild emotions and escorted the detective upstairs to her office.

"Have a seat," Nicole offered, snatching a stack of books off the chair. She set the books on an empty corner of her desk and settled into her own seat.

"I know this is tough on you right now, and I wouldn't bother you, but since you're close to the McCafferty family maybe you can give me some information."

"As soon as I alert his brothers," Nicole said, her head finally clear again. Somehow she had to put her own emotions aside and don her facade of professionalism, not only for herself, but for Thorne as well. Her fingers were still slightly unsteady, but she picked up the phone. "Matt and Slade need to know that their brother's been in an accident and admitted to St. James." She didn't wait for a response, just dialed the ranch and gave the message to Slade, who shocked, didn't say a word until she was finished.

Then he swore a blue streak. "Damn it all, how can this happen? What kind of a fool gets into a plane in the middle of a blizzard?" he asked, then sighed loudly. "I guess it doesn't matter. Just tell me. Is he gonna make it?"

"Yes—I think so." The thought of Thorne giving up his life was too painful to consider. She cleared her throat and was aware of the detective's eyes silently assessing her and her reaction. "A team of our best doctors is working to stabilize him in the emergency room. From there he'll see specialists."

"Son of a—" Slade began, and then shouted in another direction. "Juanita, can you watch the baby for a while? Thorne's been in an accident and he's at the hospital."

"*Dios!*" the woman cried. "This family, it has a *maldición!*"

"There is no curse, Juanita." Slade's voice was muffled but firm. "Will you watch—"

"*Sí, sí!* I will stay."

"I'll round up Matt," Slade said into the mouthpiece. "We'll be there as soon as we can." He hung up and Nicole, still shaken, slowly set down the receiver. Once again, she found herself staring into the scrutinizing gaze of Detective Kelly Dillinger.

"They're on their way?" she asked.

"Both Matt and Slade."

"Good."

"What is it you want to know?"

"Just a little family history," the detective said, pulling out a notepad. "The reason is simple. First the sister is nearly killed in an accident, has a baby who nearly doesn't make it, remains comatose and leaves a lot of questions unanswered. We can't contact the baby's father as no one seems to know who he is, and we can't talk to her and find out why her car went out of control."

"I thought she hit ice," Nicole said, a needle of dread piercing her heart.

"She did. But the family's insistent that there was another vehicle involved. They hired an independent investigator who's determined to prove that there was some kind of foul play." She took off her hat and red hair spilled around her face in soft layers. "Okay, that's what some families do. It makes them feel better—to pay someone to dig deeper than the police. Or so they think."

"But—was there? Foul play?"

"We don't know," the detective said, her face without expression, her eyes serious. "But I'm trying to find out." She clicked her pen a couple of times, then jotted a quick note. "I wasn't convinced that there was anything to go on, but now there's been another accident involving another member of the family, so I guess I'm just covering all bases."

"But the plane crash, it was an accident." It had to have been. No one would try to harm Thorne—to *murder* him!

"Most likely it was an accident. The storm was bad and those light planes...well..." She cocked her head to one side. "But if it's all just coincidence, then this McCafferty family is having one string of bad luck. If not...then maybe that P.I. knows something the sheriff's department doesn't. I'm here to figure it out."

Nicole's head pounded. Was this possible? Someone out to hurt the McCafferty clan? She swallowed hard and refused to give in to that kind of fear. So far no one had proved anything other than the fact that there had been some accidents. Bad luck, that was it. It had to be.

She checked her watch. Thorne had been in the ER for over thirty minutes. Surely someone knew the extent of his injuries by now. Yet no one had called and she was edgy, her nerves strung tight as piano wires. What if something had gone wrong? Distracted, she tried to answer as many questions as possible and talked with the detective for a few more minutes before she explained that she really had to go back to work.

"That's fine. I'll need to speak to the patient when he wakes up," Kelly Dillinger said, "and I'll want to talk to his brothers." She scraped her chair back, grabbed her hat and together they took the elevator down to the emergency room. The detective hurried out to her police car and Nicole was immediately immersed in her work.

Nicole saw three more patients, a seven-year-old girl who needed five stitches to her forehead after being hit by the end of a twirling baton that had lost its rubber tip and had been wielded by her younger brother, a septuagenarian with a mild case of bronchitis, and an ashen-faced teenager who thought she had a bad case of the flu and showed shock, then horror when tests confirmed that she was nearly three months' pregnant.

By the time Nicole had finished the examinations, the ER was clear. She talked to the nurses and found out that Thorne had been admitted. He was stable and aside from a few contusions and a broken leg that would require surgery once the swelling had gone down, he was healthy.

"Thank God," she whispered as she made her way to his private room. Matt and Slade were camped out at his bedside. Both men wore deep frowns and their eyes were dark with worry.

"I can't believe it," Slade muttered as he walked to the hallway and reached into the inside pocket of his jacket for a crumpled pack of cigarettes. He retrieved the pack, then realized what he was doing and returned it to his pocket. "What in the hell is going on?" He shot an angry glance at Nicole. "Now we got two in this hospital again! The baby just got home and Thorne winds up here!"

"He's going to make it, though. Okay?" Matt muttered. "That's something."

"Damned fool! What was he doin' flyin' in that storm?" Slade closed his eyes and pinched the bridge of his nose as if trying to stave off a headache.

"He thought he should get back—"

Slade's eyes flew open and he dropped his hand only to raise a finger and jab it at Matt's chest. "Because he doesn't have any faith that we can handle the ranch, or the baby or Randi's situation, ourselves. He's got no faith in anyone but himself! A control freak. That's what he is. A damned, corporate control freak."

"Enough!" Matt's face had turned a deep shade of scarlet. "This isn't getting us anywhere."

"I'm going to tell Striker." Slade rammed his fingers through his hair and as if a sudden thought had struck him, turned all of his attention in Nicole's direction. "You said you had some article that Randi might have written?"

"I took a copy and sent it to you."

"Hell, I didn't even think of the mail today." He rubbed the back of his neck in frustration.

"Have you talked to anyone from the sheriff's department?" Nicole asked.

"The sheriff's department?" Matt's eyes narrowed. "Why?"

"They're investigating the accident. I spoke with a Detective Dillinger and she said she wants to talk to you."

"Because—?" Matt asked, but the look in his eyes convinced Nicole that he already knew the answer.

"Because finally someone's starting to believe what Kurt Striker has been saying all along," Slade answered. "I'm going to call him right now."

"And I'll talk to the police." Matt's jaw was hard as granite. "If this isn't just an accident, I'm going to find out who's behind it." He squared his hat onto his head. "You'll call me if there's a change in Thorne's condition?"

"Of course."

As the brothers strode down the hall together, Nicole entered Thorne's darkened room. She told herself that she saw injured people all the time, victims who had suffered horrid accidents and disfigurements, that she could stomach anything. But seeing Thorne lying inert beneath the crisp bedsheets, with an IV running into the back of his hand, his leg elevated in a temporary cast, his face cut and swollen beyond recognition, each breath seeming labored, her heart nearly broke.

"Oh, honey," she whispered, her throat closing in on itself. She loved him. God, how she loved him and he'd betrayed her; been with another woman. She licked her lips and fought tears. There he lay, a broken leg, a concussion, his head bandaged, his features barely recognizable. "I'm sorry it didn't work out," she said, her voice a rasp, her fingers touching the tips of his. "I did love you. Oh, Thorne, if you only knew how much." Sniffing a bit, she cleared her throat. "But then I always was a fool over you. I suppose I always will be." His eyelids didn't so much as flutter. "You get better, y'hear? I'll be back and, damn it, if you do something foolish like take a turn for the worse, I swear, I'll kill you myself." She laughed a bit at her own stupid joke and realized that tears were falling from her eyes. "Oh, look at this. I'm such a moron. *You* make me a moron. I, uh, I've got to go check on the girls."

She dabbed at her eyes with a tissue she found near the bedside. "But I'll be back. I promise." She leaned over the bed and
placed a kiss on his forehead, leaving a lipstick smudge and a
tearstain that she quickly brushed aside. "You know, Thorne,"
she confided, "I was foolish enough to want to spend the rest
of my life with you."

She waited, half expecting him to respond, silently praying
there would be a squeeze on her fingers, rapid eye movement
behind his closed lids, even the barest change in his breathing, but she was disappointed. Like his sister in ICU, Thorne
heard nothing and didn't so much as flinch.

Nicole left the room with a weight as heavy as all Montana
pressing down her shoulders. She wrote her notes in a daze,
then grabbed her coat, changed into boots and headed home.
Outside the snow was still flurrying, swirling and dancing
across the frozen landscape. In gloves and a down ski jacket,
she turned the radio and heater on full blast, but couldn't thaw
the ice in her soul at the thought of Thorne's plane crash and
how close he'd come to losing his life.

*And how would you feel then? If he'd died or was in serious risk
of losing his life? Or paralyzed for the rest of his life?*

She shuddered and tried to concentrate on a song playing
through the speakers, but the lyrics of false love scraped too
close to the bone. Angrily, she snapped off the radio. She was
no longer involved with Thorne. He wanted it that way. It
had been a mistake to get involved with him again but it was
over. Over, over, over! His choice. She braked for a stoplight
and waited impatiently, gloved fingers tapping on the steering wheel as a few brave souls bundled in scarves, boots and
thick winter coats hurried along the snow-covered streets of
Grand Hope. Barren trees lifted naked arms to a night sky
where millions of snowflakes caught in the neon lights of the
city continued to fall.

So what did you expect from him? A marriage proposal? Her wayward mind taunted as the light changed to green and she stepped on the accelerator.

The thought made her laugh without a grain of humor. Then minutes later, still lost in her own thoughts, she turned onto the street where she lived, and promised herself that she would get over Thorne McCafferty once and for all. She had her girls. She had her work. She had a life. Without Thorne. She didn't need him.

The SUV's wheels slid a bit as she pulled into the driveway but she managed to park in front of the garage. Hauling her briefcase and laptop computer with her, she dashed through the short drifts and climbed up the back porch. Stomping the snow from her boots and pulling off her gloves with her teeth, she opened the back door and heard squeals of delight.

"Mommy! Mommy! Come see." Two sets of feet pounded the floor as the girls raced into the kitchen.

Nicole was unzipping her coat, but leaned down to hug each of the twins. Yes, her life was full. She didn't need a man and certainly not Thorne McCafferty.

Patches hopped lithely onto the counter.

"The flowers. Bunches and bunches and bunches of flowers," Molly said, holding her arms as wide as she could.

"Flowers?" Nicole asked and noticed the fragrance of roses that seemed to permeate the air.

"Yeth." Mindy was pulling on one hand, dragging her to the living room. Molly gripped her other.

"You get down!" Nicole ordered the precocious feline as they passed the counter. The cat hopped to the floor as Nicole stepped into the living room and gasped. Jenny was standing near the fireplace and the grate was lit, several logs burning brightly, and all around the room, on every table, in the corners and on the floor, were dozens and dozens of roses. Red, white, pink, yellow—it didn't matter, bouquet after bouquet. "What in the world...?" she whispered.

"There's a card." Jenny pointed to a bouquet of three dozen white long-stemmed roses.

"Read it! Read it!" both girls chimed.

With shaking fingers she opened the small white envelope. It read simply: "Marry me."

Tears burned behind her eyelids. "Do you know who sent these?" she asked.

Jenny smiled. "Don't you?"

Knees suddenly weak, Nicole dropped into a side chair. "Dear Lord..."

"What, Mommy? What?" Mindy asked, her little eyebrows knotting in concern.

"Thorne's in the hospital."

"What?" Jenny's smile fell away and haltingly Nicole told her about the plane crash.

"Oh, my God, well you've got to go back there. You've got to be with him."

"But the girls..."

"Don't worry about them. I can handle them." The twins' faces fell and Jenny added, "We'll have pizza delivered and make popcorn balls and...and a surprise for your mommy."

"But I don't want Mommy to leave," Mindy said.

"Baby!" Molly accused, pointing a tiny finger at her sister.

"Am not!"

"Shh...shh...no one's a baby."

Touched by the dazzling array of flowers, Nicole stared at the soft petals and long stems and her heart pounded with a love she so recently tried to deny. "I—I do have to go back to the hospital," she said, "but I'll be back soon."

Mindy's face began to crumple. "Promise?"

Nicole kissed her daughter's forehead and stood on legs that threatened to give out again. She plucked one crimson rose from its vase and winked at her daughters. "Promise."

Through a veil of pain, he heard the door open and expected that it was the nurse bringing much needed medication.

"Thorne?"

Nicole's voice. His heart leaped, but he didn't move. Nor did she turn on the light as she walked to his bedside. Carefully she laid a long-stemmed rose on his chest. "I—I don't know what to say."

He didn't respond. Didn't move. In his semiconscious state a few hours ago, he'd heard her claims of loving him yet not wanting him, of saying it would never work out, so he'd thought she'd gotten the flowers and had rejected him. He hadn't been able to respond then, didn't know if he could now. He barely remembered the accident. There had been a problem, an engine had died and he'd been forced to land in a field, nearly made it when the plane had crashed into a copse of trees...he was lucky...

"I got the flowers. Dozens and dozens of them. You shouldn't have...oh, Thorne," she whispered, dragging him back to the present, to Nicole. Beautiful, sexy Nicole. "I wish you could hear me. I want to explain...."

Here it comes again. She was going to repeat what she'd said earlier. Without moving he braced himself for the worst.

"I was—am—overwhelmed." She cleared her throat and he felt her fingers find his. "I read the card."

He felt like an idiot. Why had he bared his soul to her? She didn't want him, she'd made that clear enough. He braced himself against the pain.

"And I wish I could make you hear me, that you'd understand just how much I love you. Marry you? Oh, Lord, if you only knew how much I wanted to do just that, but I saw your picture with that woman at the fund-raiser in Denver and I—I thought you weren't ready to settle down, that you never will be and so, I don't know what to do. If there was any chance that we could be together, you and I and the girls, believe me I'd—"

Despite the pain, he forced his hand to move. His head felt as if it might explode, but he grabbed her hand then, held on to it fiercely. The rose dropped to the floor.

"Oh! Dear God—"

"Marry me," he rasped, forcing the words through lips that felt cracked and swollen. Pain screamed through his body but he didn't care.

"But—what? Can you—"

"Marry me." He squeezed her fingers so tightly that she gasped again.

"You can hear me?"

He forced his eyes open, blinked against the fragile light that seemed to blind. "Nicole—would you please just answer?" Somehow he managed to focus on her face—God, it was a great face. "Will you marry me?"

"But what about the other woman, the one in the paper?"

"There is no other woman. Just you." He stared at her hard, willing her to believe him. "And there will always only be you in my life. I swear it."

He watched her swallow hard, bite her lip, fight the indecision.

"I will love you forever," he vowed and then the tears came, slowly at first and then more rapidly, falling from her gorgeous amber eyes. "Marry me, Nicole. Be my wife."

With her free hand, she dashed the tears away. "Yes," she whispered, her voice cracking. "Yes." He yanked hard, pulled her over him and when his lips found hers some of the pain disappeared and he knew that from this day forward he would gladly give up whatever possessions he had, that nothing else came close to the love he felt for her and he would cherish this woman until he gave up his very last breath.

"I love you, Doctor," he vowed as she lifted her head and laughed. "And this time, believe me, I'll never leave you and I'll never let you go."

"Oh, I bet you say that to all the women physicians," she teased, her eyes bright with tears as she picked up the rose and laid it next to him on the bed.

"Nope. Only one."

"Lucky me," she sniffed, leaning down and brushing her lips against his.

"No." Of this he was certain. "Lucky me."

Epilogue

"You're sure you want to live here?" Nicole asked, her gaze roving around the snow-covered acres as she and Thorne sat on the porch while the twins, in matching snowsuits, frolicked in the yard. The old dog, Harold, barked and joined them, acting like a pup, and cattle and horses dotted the landscape. Slade, dressed in a thick buckskin jacket, was walking near the barn, checking the pipes and watering troughs along with the stock.

It was beautiful here and Nicole's heart was full. Though Thorne's leg was casted, there was no keeping him down and they'd planned as soon as he was on his feet again to marry.

"I'll live here as long as Randi lets me."

Randi was the one worry. It had been nearly a month since her accident and she was still unconscious. Though Kurt Striker was still looking into the possibility of a hit-and-run driver forcing her off the road, he hadn't found any suspects and Thorne's plane crash was still under investigation. Was it foul play? Thorne hadn't thought so, or so he'd insisted, citing the fact that he should have had the plane checked out before flying off in the snowstorm. But he'd been anxious to return to Montana. "By the way," he said, "I have something for you."

"What's that?" she asked.

"Something to make our engagement official."

"Oh?" She lifted a wary eyebrow as he winced and dug into a front pocket of his jeans. Slowly he extracted a ring, a band of silver and gold.

"It was my father's, from his marriage to my mom," he explained and Nicole was touched, her throat clogging suddenly as he slipped it onto her finger. "For some sentimental reason, the old man kept it even after the divorce and while he was married to Randi's mother. He gave it to me before he died and now...because of tradition, I guess, I want you to have it." His smile was crooked. "I think we'll have it sized to fit." The ring, an intricate band of gold and silver, was much too big for her finger but she clutched it tight, knowing that it meant so much to Thorne. That he would share it with her said more than words.

"It's beautiful."

"And special."

"Oh, Thorne, thank you," she whispered, then kissed him as he held her close and the old porch swing swayed.

"And you're special to me, Nicole, you and the girls."

She had trouble swallowing over the lump in her throat. Never in her wildest dreams had she thought she'd ever hear those words from Thorne McCafferty, the man who had so callously used her and then walked away.

As if he could read her thoughts, he placed a kiss upon her head. "I know I made a mistake with you and I've kicked myself a dozen times over, but I want to make it up to you, to the twins. I...I never thought I'd want to settle down, to have a family of my own to..." he struggled for a moment, looked across the snow-crusted fields "...to share my life here. On the Flying M. But I do. Because of you." His eyes found hers. "You're the one, Nicole. The only one."

She sighed against him and looked at the ring. God, she loved him. Blinking back tears of joy, she whispered, "I love you."

"Oh, you do, do you?" he said, a slow, sexy smile creeping from one side of his mouth to the other.

"Scout's honor," she said. His grin was infectious and she tossed a sassy smile back his way. "You don't believe me?"

"Maybe..."

"But maybe not?"

"You could prove it."

She laughed and rose to the bait. "And how would I do that?"

His eyes gleamed wickedly. "Oh, I can think of a dozen or two different ways."

"And I can think of a hundred."

He rose awkwardly to his feet and pulled her to hers. "Then let's start, shall we? As my father would say, 'time's a wastin',' and he did say he wanted some grandchildren."

"What about J.R. and the twins?"

"A start, lady, just a start."

"Slow down, Romeo," she said giggling.

"No way, lady. We've only got the rest of our lives."

She threw back her head and laughed huskily. "I do love you, Thorne McCafferty, but if anyone's going to have to do the proving it's you."

"All right." He swept her off her feet and she squealed.

"Thorne, don't! Your leg! For crying out loud, let me go! Put me down!"

He held her tight, his shoulder braced against the side of the house, his strong arms holding her close. "Never," he vowed, then kissed her hard. She closed her eyes, kissed him back and wondered if anyone had the right to feel this happy. As he lifted his head and stared into her eyes, he said again, "I will never let you go, Nicole. Never again."

And she believed him.

★ ★ ★ ★ ★

THE McCAFFERTYS: MATT

Prologue

Early May

"You miserable piece of horseflesh," Matt McCafferty growled as he climbed to his feet, dusted the back of his jeans and glowered at the wild-eyed Appaloosa colt. There was a reason the damned beast was named Diablo Rojo, the orneriest two-year-old on the Flying M Ranch. A challenge. In all his thirty-seven years, Matt had never met a horse he couldn't tame. But he was having second thoughts about Red Devil. Major ones. The horse had spirit. Fire. Not easily tamed. Like a lot of women Matt had run across. "Okay, you bastard, let's start over."

He reached down and picked up his hat. Slapping it hard against his thigh, he squinted into the lowering Montana sun as it started its slow descent behind the western hills. "You and I, Devil, we're gonna come to a reckoning and we're gonna do it this afternoon."

The colt tossed his fiery head and snorted noisily, then lifted his damned tail like a banner and trotted along the far fence line, the empty saddle on his back creaking mockingly. *Damned fool horse.* Matt squared his hat on his head. "It isn't over," he assured the snorting animal.

"It may as well be."

Matt froze at the sound of his father's voice. Turning on the worn heel of his boot, he watched as Juanita pushed John Randall's wheelchair across the parking lot separating the rambling, two-storied ranch house from the series of connecting paddocks that surrounded the stables. Matt didn't harbor much love for his bastard of a father, but he couldn't help feel an ounce of pity for the once-robust man now confined to "the damned contraption," as he referred to the chair.

John Randall's sparse white hair caught in the wind and his skin was pale and thin, but there was still a spark in his blue eyes. And he loved this spread. More than he loved anything, including his children.

"I tried to talk him out of this," Juanita reprimanded as she parked the wheelchair near the fence where Harold, John Randall's partially crippled old springer spaniel, had settled into a patch of shade thrown by a lone pine tree. "But you know how it is. He is too *terco*...stubborn, for his own good."

"And it's served me well," the old man said as he used the sun-bleached rails of the fence to pull himself to his full height. Lord, he was thin—too thin. His jeans and plaid shirt hung loosely from his once-robust frame. But he managed a tough-as-old-leather smile as he leaned over the top bar and watched his middle son.

"Maybe you can talk some sense into him," Juanita said, sending Matt a worried glance and muttering something about *loco,* prideful men.

"I doubt it. I never could before."

The older McCafferty waved Juanita off. "I'm fine. Needed some fresh air. Now I want to talk to Matt. He'll bring me inside when we're through."

Juanita didn't seem convinced, but Matt nodded. "I think I can handle him," he said to the woman who had helped raise him. Clucking her tongue at the absurdity of the situation, Juanita bustled off to the house, the only home Matt had known growing up.

"That one," John Randall said, hitching his chin back to the wayward colt. "He'll give ya a run for your money." He slid a knowing glance at his second-born. "Like a lot of women."

Matt was irritated. He wiped the sweat from his forehead and swatted at a horsefly that got a little too close for comfort. "Is that what you came all the way out here to say to me, the reason you had Juanita push you outside?"

"Nope." With an effort the older man dug into the pocket of his jeans. "I got somethin' here for ya."

"What?" Matt was instantly suspicious. His father's gifts never came without a price.

"Somethin' I want ya to have—oh, here we go." John Randall withdrew a big silver buckle that winked in the bright Montana sun. Inlaid upon the flat surface was a gold bucking bronco, still as shiny as the day John Randall had won it at a rodeo in Canada more than fifty years earlier. He dropped it into his son's calloused hand.

"You used to wear this all the time," Matt observed, his jaw growing tight.

"Yep. Reminded me of my piss-and-vinegar years." John Randall settled back in his wheelchair, and his eyes clouded a bit. "Good years," he added thoughtfully, then squinted upward to stare at his son. "I don't have much longer on this earth, boy," he said, and before Matt could protest, his father raised a big-knuckled hand to silence him. "We both know it so there's no sense in arguin' the facts. The man upstairs, he's about to call me home…that is, if the devil don't take me first."

Matt clenched his jaw. Didn't say a word. Waited.

"I already spoke to Thorne about the fact that I'm dyin', and seein' as you're the next in line, I thought I'd talk to you next. Slade…well, I'll catch up to him soon. Now, I know I've made mistakes in my life, the good Lord knows I failed your mother.…"

Matt didn't comment, didn't want to even think about the bleak time when John Randall took up with a much younger woman, divorced his wife and introduced his three sons to Penelope, "Penny" Henley, who would become their step-mother and give them all a half sister whom none of them wanted to begin with.

"I have a lot of regrets about all that," John Randall said over the sigh of the wind, "but it's all water under the bridge now since both Larissa and Penny are dead." He rubbed his jaw and cleared his throat. "Never thought I'd bury two wives."

"A wife and an ex-wife," Matt clarified.

The old man's thin lips pursed, but he didn't argue. "What I want from you—from all my children—is grandchildren. You know that. It's an old man's dream, I know, but it's only natural. I'd like to go to my grave in peace with the knowl-edge that you'll find yourself a good woman and settle down, have a family, and that the McCafferty name will go on for a few more generations."

"There's lots of time—"

"Not for me, there ain't!" John Randall snapped.

Feeling as if he was being manipulated for the umpteenth

time by his father, Matt tried to hand the buckle back. "If this is some kind of bribe or deal or—"

"No bribe." The old man spit in disgust. "I want you to have that buckle because it means something to me, and since you rode rodeo a few years back, I thought you might appreciate it." He wagged a finger at the buckle. "Turn it over."

Matt flipped the smooth piece of metal and read the engraving on the backside. "To my cowboy. Love forever, Larissa." His throat closed for a minute when he thought of his mother with her shiny black hair and laughing brown eyes, which had saddened over the years of her marriage. From a free spirit, she'd become imprisoned on this ranch and had sought her own kind of solace and peace that she'd never found in the bottles she'd hidden in the old house she'd grown to despise.

Matt's gut twisted. He missed her. Bad. And the old man had wronged her. There were just no two ways about it.

"Larissa had it engraved after I won it. Hell, she was a fool for me back then." The wrinkles around John Randall's mouth and eyes deepened with sadness, and there was a tiny shadow of guilt that chased across his eyes. "So, now I want you to have it, Matthew."

Matt's fingers tightened over the sharp edges of the buckle, but he didn't say a word. Couldn't.

"And I want me some grandbabies. That's not too much for an old man to ask."

"I'm not married."

"Then get yourself hitched." His father gave him a head-to-toe once-over. "Fine, strappin' man like you shouldn't have too much trouble."

"Maybe I don't believe in marriage."

"Then maybe you're a fool."

Matt traced the silhouette of the bucking bronco with one finger. "It could be I learned from the best."

"So unlearn it," John Randall ordered, just as he always did. His way or the highway. Matt had chosen the latter.

"I've got me a horse to break," he said. "And my own place to run."

"I was hopin' you'd be stayin' on." There was a hint of desperation in his father's voice, but Matt stood firm. There was just too much water under the damned bridge—muddy, treacherous water fed by a swift current of lies and deceit, the kind of water a man could slowly drown in. Matt had come to the ranch to mend some emotional fences with the old man and to help the foreman, Larry Todd, for a week or so, but his own spread, a few hundred acres close to the Idaho border, needed his attention.

"I can't, Dad," he said finally as he followed the path of a wasp as it flew toward the back porch. "Maybe it's time to get you inside."

"For God's sake, don't try to mollycoddle me, son. It's not like I'm gonna catch my death out here today." John Randall folded his hands in his lap and looked between the old slats of the fence to the hard pan of the paddock where the Appaloosa, still wearing an empty saddle, pawed the ground, kicking up dust. "I'll watch while you try to break him. It'll be interesting to see who'll win. You or Diablo."

Matt lifted a disbelieving eyebrow. "You sure?"

"Ye-up."

"Fine." Matt squared his hat on his head and climbed over the fence. "But it's not gonna be much of a contest," he said, more to the horse than the man who had sired him. He strode forward with renewed determination, his eyes fixed on the

Appaloosa's sleek muscles that quivered as he approached. Few things in life beat Matt McCafferty.

A high-strung colt wasn't one of them.

Nor was his father.

Nope. His weakness, if he had one, was women. Fiery-tempered, bullheaded women in particular.

The kind he avoided like the plague.

And now his father wanted him to find a woman, tie the knot and start raising a passel of babies.

He nearly laughed as he reached for the reins, and Diablo had the nerve to snort defiantly.

No way in hell was Matt McCafferty getting married. Not today, not tomorrow, not ever. That's just the way it was.

Chapter 1

The following November

She'd met him before.

Too many times to count.

That didn't mean she had to like him.

No, sir.

As far as Detective Kelly Dillinger was concerned, Matt McCafferty was just plain bad news. Pure and simple, cut from the same biased, sanctimonious, self-serving cloth as his brothers and his bastard of a father before him.

But that didn't mean he didn't look good. If you liked the rough-and-tumble, tough-as-rawhide cowboy type, Matt McCafferty was the man for you. His rugged appeal was legendary in Grand Hope. He and his older and younger brothers had been considered the best catches in the entire county for years. But Kelly prided herself on being different from most of the women who wanted to swoon whenever they heard the McCafferty name.

So they were handsome.

So they were sexy.

So they had money.

So what?

These days their reputations had tarnished a bit, notoriety had taken its toll, and the oldest of the lot, Thorne, was rumored to be losing his status as an eligible bachelor and marrying a local woman doctor.

Not so the second brother, Matt. The one, it seemed, she was going to have to deal with right now.

He was muscling open the door to the Grand Hope office of the sheriff's department with one broad shoulder and bringing with him a rush of frigid winter air and snowflakes that melted instantly the minute they encountered the sixty-eight degrees maintained by a wheezing furnace hidden somewhere in the basement of this ancient brick building.

Matt McCafferty. Great. Just...damned great. She already had a headache and was up to her eyeballs in paperwork, a ream of which could be applied to the McCafferty case—no, make that cases, plural—alone. But she couldn't ignore him, either. She stared through the glass of her enclosed office and saw him stride across the yellowing linoleum floor, barely stopping at the gate that separated the reception area from the office, then sweep past the receptionist on a cloud of self-righteous fury. Kelly disliked the man on sight, but then she had her own personal ax to grind when it came to the McCaffertys.

There was fire in McCafferty's brown eyes and anger in his tight, blade-thin lips and the stubborn set of his damnably square jaw. Yep, cut from the same cloth as the others, she thought as she climbed to her feet and opened the door to the office at the same time as he was about to pound on the scarred oak panels.

"Mr. McCafferty." She feigned a smile. "A pleasure to see you again."

"Cut the bull," he said without preamble.

"Okay." He was blunt if nothing else. "Why don't you come in…" But he'd already crossed the threshold and was inside the small glassed-in room, pacing the short distance from one wall to the other.

Stella Gamble, the plump, nervous receptionist, had abandoned her post and was fidgeting at the door, her bright red fingernails catching light from the humming fluorescent tubing overhead. "I tried to stop him, really I did," she said, shaking her head as her tight blond curls bounced around her flushed cheeks. "He wouldn't listen."

"A family trait."

"I'm sorry—"

"It's all right, Stella. Relax. I needed to talk to one of the McCafferty brothers, anyway," Kelly assured her, though that was stretching the truth quite a bit. A conversation with Thorne, Slade or especially Matt wasn't on her agenda right this minute, not when Nathaniel Biggs was calling every two hours, certain that someone had stolen his prize bull last night, Perry Carmichael had reported an odd aura suspended over the copse of oak trees behind his machine shed out on Old Dupont Road and Dora Haines was missing again, probably wandering around the foothills in nineteen-degree weather with a storm threatening to blast in from the Bitterroots by nightfall. Not that the McCafferty case wasn't important—it just wasn't the only one she was working on. "Don't worry about it," she said to Stella. "I'll talk to Mr. McCafferty."

"No one should get by me," the receptionist said, blinking rapidly.

"You're right, they shouldn't," Kelly agreed, and glared at the uninvited guest. "But, as I said, I need to talk to him, anyway, and I don't think he's dangerous."

"Don't count on it," McCafferty countered. Standing near the file cabinet, he looked as if he could spit nails.

The phone rang loudly at Stella's desk.

"I'll deal with this," Kelly said as the receptionist hurried back to her desk and immediately donned her headset.

Kelly closed the door behind her and snapped the blinds shut for privacy, as she didn't want any of the deputies witnessing the dressing-down that was simmering in the air of her postage-stamp-size office.

"Have a seat," she offered, sweeping off the files that were stacked in the single chair on the visitor's side of her metal desk.

He didn't move, but those eyes followed her as she plopped into her ancient desk chair. "I'm tired of getting the runaround," he announced through lips that barely moved.

"The runaround?"

"Yep." He planted his hands between her in-basket and the computer monitor glowing from one corner of the desk and leaned across the reports that were strewn in front of her. "I want answers, dammit. My sister's been in a coma for over a month because of an accident that I believe is the result of someone running her Jeep off the road, and you people, *you people,* are doing nothing to find out what happened to her. For all we know someone tried to kill her that day and they won't stop until they finish the job!"

"That's just speculation," Kelly reminded him, the short fuse on her temper igniting. There was a chance that Randi McCafferty's rig had been forced off the road up in Glacier

Park. With no witnesses it was hard to say. But the sheriff's department was checking into every possibility. "We're trying to locate another vehicle if one is involved. So far, we haven't found one."

"It's been over a month, for crying out loud," he said as she sat on the corner of her desk, watching a battery of emotions cross his face. Anger. Determination. Frustration. And more—a fleck of fear darkened his brown eyes. Fear wasn't an emotion she considered when thinking of any of the roguish, tough-as-rawhide McCafferty men. The three brothers, like their father, had always appeared an intrepid, fearless lot. "And over two weeks have passed since Thorne's plane went down. You think that was an accident, too?"

"It's possible. We're looking into it."

"Well, you'd better look harder," he suggested, his nostrils flaring.

The guy was getting to her. Again. He had a way of nettling her—getting under her skin and irritating her. Kind of like a burr caught beneath a horse's saddle. McCafferty straightened, swept his hat from his head and raked stiff fingers through his near-black, wavy hair. "Before someone actually dies."

"The feds are involved in the plane crash."

"That doesn't seem to be helping a whole helluva lot."

"We're doing everything in our power to—"

"It's not enough," he cut in. Again fire flared in his eyes. "Are you in charge of this investigation, Detective?" he asked, casting a glance at the badge she wore so proudly. He was crushing the brim of his Stetson in fingers that blanched white at the knuckles.

She held on to her patience, but just barely. "I think we've been over this before. Detective Espinoza has been assigned the case. I'm assisting him, as I was the first on the scene of your sister's wreck."

"Then I'm wasting my time with you."

That stung. Kelly gritted her teeth and stood.

"Tell Espinoza I want to talk to him."

"He's not in right now."

"I'll wait."

"It might be a while."

Matt McCafferty looked as if he might explode. He dropped his hat on a nearby folding chair and leaned over her desk again, shoving some file folders out of the way as he pushed his face closer, so that the tip of his nose nearly touched hers. The air seemed to crackle. The smell of wet suede, horses and a faint hint of pine reached her nostrils. Snow had melted on the shoulders of his sheepskin jacket, and there were a few damp spots on his face. His fists opened and closed in frustration on the desktop. "You have to understand, Detective, this is my family we're talking about," he said in a low whisper that had more impact than if he'd raged. "*My* family. Now, the way I see it, my sister was nearly killed, and not only that but she was nine months pregnant at the time."

"I know—"

"Do you? Can you imagine what she went through? She went into labor when her Jeep careered over that embankment and crashed. She was just lucky someone came along and called 911. Between the paramedics and the doctors over at St. James Hospital and a lot of help from the man upstairs, she pulled through."

"And the baby survived," she pointed out, remembering all too clearly the condition of mother and son.

Matt wasn't about to be deterred. Like a runaway freight

train gathering steam, he kept right on. *"After* a bout of men-ingitis."

Her fingers coiled over a pen on the desk. "I understand all this—"

"Fortunately little J.R. is a McCafferty. He's tough. He pulled through."

"So he's fine," she reminded him, trying to keep emotions out of the conversation, which, of course, was impossible.

"Fine?" He snorted. "I guess you might say so, except that he needs his mom, who is still comatose and lying in a hospital room." For a brief second Matt McCafferty actually seemed as if he cared about his nephew, and his brown eyes darkened in concern. That got to Kelly, though she refused to show it. Of course he was worried about the kid—McCaffertys always looked after their own. To the exclusion of all others. "And that's not all, Detective," he added.

"I'm sure not," she drawled, and he scowled at her patron-izing tone.

"It's a miracle that Thorne survived the plane crash and ended up with only a few cuts and bruises and a broken leg."

Amen to that. Thorne was the eldest McCafferty brother, a millionaire oilman who hailed from Denver. He'd been fly-ing the company jet back to Grand Hope, hit bad weather and gone down.

"The way I see it, either the McCaffertys are having one helluva string of bad luck, or someone's out to get us."

"Randi was driving and hit an icy patch. Your brother was flying alone in the middle of a snowstorm. Bad luck? Or bad judgment?"

"Or, as I said, a potential murderer on the loose."

"Who?" she asked, meeting his glare, not backing down an

inch though she was beginning to sweat, and the office, filled by his presence, seemed even smaller than usual.

"That's what I was hopin' you'd tell me."

God, he was close to her. Too close. The desk between them seemed a small barrier.

"Believe me, Mr. McCafferty—"

"Matt. Call me Matt. There're too damned many McCaffertys to call us by our last name."

She wouldn't argue that point.

"And somehow I have the feelin' that you and I, we'll be workin' real close together on this one. I intend to stick to you like glue until you find out who the hell is behind this, so we may as well cut the formalities."

The thought of working closely with anyone named Mc-Cafferty stuck in Kelly's craw, and this one, this damnably sexy, cocksure cowboy, was the most irritating of the lot, but she didn't have much choice in the matter. "All right, *Matt*. As I was saying, we're trying our best here to find out the truth behind both accidents. Everyone in the department is busting their hump to figure this mess out."

"Not fast enough," he growled.

"And none of us, me especially—" she hooked a thumb at her chest "—needs anyone looking over her shoulder." She stuffed the pen in the mug on her desk. "Didn't you hire your own private detective?"

His thin lips tightened a fraction.

"A man by the name of Kurt Striker?" She folded her arms across her chest.

He nodded. "We thought we needed more help."

"So what has he got to say?"

"That he thinks there's foul play," McCafferty said, his eyes narrowing on Kelly as if he couldn't quite figure her out.

Tough. She was used to men distrusting her as a detective because she was a woman, and that's what Matt McCafferty was
saying; she could read it in his eyes. Well, that was just too
damned bad. She wasn't about to be bullied or intimidated.
Not by anyone. Not even one of the high-and-mighty Mc-
Caffertys. Matt's father, John Randall, had once been a rich,
powerful and influential man in the county, and his descen-
dants thought they could still throw their collective weights
around. Well, not here.

"Has Striker got any proof that someone's behind the accidents?" she asked.

Hesitation.

"I didn't think so." She slipped from the desk. "That's it.
Now, listen, I have work to do, and I don't need you barging
in here and making demands and—"

"Striker says there's some paint on Randi's rig. Maroon.
Maybe from the other car when she was forced off the road."

"*If* she was forced off," Kelly reminded him. "She could
have scraped another vehicle in a parking lot at home in Seattle for all we know. And we already know about the paint, so
don't come in here and insinuate that the department is inef-
ficient or incompetent or any of the above, because we're just
being thorough. Got it?"

"Listen—"

"No, you listen to me, okay?" Her temper was stretched to
the breaking point as she stepped around the desk and went
toe-to-toe with him. "This force is doing everything in its
power to try and find out what happened to your sister and
your brother. Everything! We don't take either accident lightly,
believe you me. But we're not jumping off the deep end here,
either. Your sister's Jeep could have hit ice. It's just possible
she lost control of the vehicle, it slid off the road up in Glacier

and she ended up in the hospital in a damned coma. As for your brother, he was taking a big chance with his life flying a small craft in one helluva snowstorm. The engines failed. We'll determine why. We haven't yet ruled out foul play. We're just being careful. The department can't afford to go off half-cocked and making blind assumptions or accusations."

"Meanwhile someone might be trying to kill off my family."

"Who?" she demanded as she rounded the desk again, plopped down in her worn chair and took up her pen. Yanking a yellow legal pad from the credenza behind her, she dropped it on the desk and sat ready, ballpoint pressed against the clean sheet of paper. "Give me a list of suspects, anyone you know who might hold a grudge against the McCafferty clan."

Matt's eyes narrowed. "There are dozens."

"Names, McCafferty, I want names." She hoped she sounded professional, because he was cutting a little too close to the bone with his damned insinuations.

"You should know a few," he said, and though she wanted to, she didn't allow herself to rise to the bait.

"Don't beat around the bush."

"Okay, let's start with your family," he shot out.

Kelly's back went up. "No one in my family has any ax to grind with your brother or half sister." She raised her eyes and met the simmering anger in his.

"Just my dad."

"Lots of people had problems with him. But he's gone. And my family aren't potential murderers, okay? So let's not even go there." She bit out the words but wouldn't give in to the white-hot anger that threatened to take hold of her tongue. The nerve of the man. "Now…" She clicked the pen again. "Who would want to harm your sister, Randi, and your brother Thorne?"

Some of the anger seemed to drain from him. "I don't

know," he admitted. "I'm sure Thorne's made his share of enemies. You don't get to be a millionaire without someone being envious."

"Envious enough to try and kill him?" Kelly said.

"Damn, I'd hope not, but…" He closed his eyes for a second. "I don't know."

That, at least, sounded honest. "He's based out of Denver, isn't he?"

"He was. The corporate headquarters are there."

"But he's moving back here and getting married." It wasn't a question, but Matt nodded and Kelly noticed the way his dark hair shone under the humming fluorescent lamps. He unbuttoned his jacket, revealing a flannel shirt stretched over a broad chest. Black hairs sprang from the opening at the neck. She tore her eyes away, gave herself a swift mental kick for noticing any part of his male anatomy and scribbled down some notes about Thorne, the oldest of the brothers.

"Yeah, he's marrying Nicole Stevenson." Matt managed a half smile that was incredibly and irritatingly sexy. "Lots of people are losing that particular bet."

Kelly understood. Thorne, like his brothers, had been a confirmed bachelor. He, along with Matt and the youngest brother, Slade, had raised holy hell in high school and cut a wide swath through the local girls. Rich, handsome and smart to the point of arrogance, they'd soon been regarded as the most eligible bachelors in the county and thereby broken more than their share of hearts. Matt, in particular, had earned the reputation of being a ladies' man. *Love 'Em and Leave 'Em McCafferty.*

But now it seemed that the first of the invincible and never-to-be-wed brothers was about to fall victim to matrimony. The bride was an emergency room doctor at the local hospital, a single mother with twin girls.

"Okay, so what about your sister?" she asked, trying to keep her mind on business. "Any known enemies?"

Annoyance pulled the smile off of Matt's cocky jaw. This wasn't new territory. Ever since the accident, the sheriff's department had been looking into Randi's life. "I don't know," Matt admitted. "I'm sure she had her share. Hell, she wrote a column for the *Seattle Clarion*."

"Advice to the lovelorn?" Kelly filled in.

"More than that. It's more like general, no-nonsense advice to single people. It's called—"

"'Solo.' I know. I've got copies on file," she said, not admitting that she'd found his sister's wry outlook on single life interesting and amusing. "But most of the advice she gave was about a single person's love life."

"Ironic, wouldn't you say?" Matt said, walking to the far side of the room and shaking his head. Turning, he leaned his shoulders against a bookcase. "She gave out all this advice—the column was syndicated, picked up by other papers as well—and yet she winds up pregnant and nearly dies behind the wheel and no one even knows who the father of her kid is."

"I'd call that more than ironic, I'd call it downright odd." She clicked her pen several times, then motioned to the one empty chair on the far side of her desk. "You could have a seat."

He eyed the chair just as the phone in her office rang.

"Excuse me." Lifting the receiver, she said, "Dillinger."

"Sorry to bother you, but Bob is on the line," Stella said, still sounding nervous from her failed attempt to keep Matt McCafferty in line.

"I'll talk with him." She held up a hand toward Matt as

Roberto Espinoza's voice boomed over the wires. He was out at the Haines farm and was reporting that they'd found Dora, carrying her cat as she trudged through the snow in her house-coat and slippers, following a trail that cut through the woods to a steep slope where, she had explained to Detective Espi-noza, her father had taken her sledding as a girl.

"A sad case," Bob said on a sigh, then added that Dora was now on her way to St. James Hospital by ambulance. The paramedics who had examined her were concerned about ex-posure, frostbite and senility, which could translate into some-thing deeper. Her husband, Albert, was beside himself. "I'm heading over to St. James myself and I'll see you when I'm finished there," Bob added.

"I'll meet you," Kelly said, and glanced at the McCafferty brother filling up a good portion of her office. "When you've got a minute you might want to speak to Matt McCafferty. He's here now." While Matt listened, his expression intense, Kelly explained the concerns of the McCafferty family to her boss.

"Arrogant son of a bitch." Espinoza let out a whistling breath. "As if we're not doing everything humanly possible." She heard the click of a lighter and then a deep sigh. "Tell him to cool his jets. I'll see him as soon as I'm finished dictating a report on Dora."

"Will do." Kelly hung up and relayed the message. "He'll see you soon. In the meantime you're supposed to stay cool."

"Like hell. I've been cool way too long and nothing's being done."

She let that one slide. As far as Kelly was concerned the meeting was over. She stood and reached for her hat and coat, then flipped open the blinds. "I've got work to do, McCafferty.

Detective Espinoza said he'd call you and he will." She opened the door and stood, silently inviting him to leave. "Got it?"

"If that's the best you can do—"

"It is."

He crammed his Stetson onto his head and threw her a look that told her she wasn't about to see the last of him, then she watched as he swung out of her office, past Stella's desk and through the creaking gate. His jeans had seen better days and they'd faded over his buttocks, it seemed, from the glimpse she caught at the hemline of his jacket. He didn't bother with the buttons or gloves; he was probably overheated from the anger she and Bob Espinoza had fired in him. Well, that was just too damned bad.

He shouldered open the door and again a blast of air as cold as the North Pole rushed into the room. Then he was gone, the glass door swinging shut behind him. "And good riddance," Kelly muttered under her breath, irritated that she found him the least little bit attractive and noticing that Stella had forgone answering the telephones or typing at her computer keyboard to watch Matt's stormy exit.

Yep, Kelly thought, squaring her hat on her head and sliding her arms through the sleeves of her insulated jacket. The man was bad news.

Chapter 2

Matt drummed his fingers on the steering wheel of his truck. Snow was blowing across the highway, drifting against the fence line and melting on his windshield. He flipped on the wipers and switched the radio to a local country station, searching for a weather report and settling for a Willie Nelson classic.

Squinting against the ever-increasing flakes, he scowled as he headed out of town toward the Flying M Ranch. Maybe he'd made a mistake, driving like the devil was on his back into town and barreling into the sheriff's department demanding answers.

He hadn't gotten squat.

In fact that red-haired detective had put him in his place. Time and time again. It was unsettling. Infuriating. Downright insulting. Kelly Dillinger had a way of bothering him more than she had the right to. And he couldn't get her out of his mind. Her skin was pale, her eyes a deep chocolate brown, her hair a bright, vibrant red which, in his estimation, accounted for her temperament. Redheads were always a fiery, hot-tempered lot. Then there was her no-nonsense, I-won't-deal-with-any-bull attitude. Like she was a man, for God's sake. That would be the day. Her build was basically athletic, but definitely female. He'd noticed, and kicked himself for it. Her uniform had stretched tight over her breasts and hugged her waist and hips. The woman had curves, damned nice curves, even if she tried her best to conceal them.

He'd always heard that women were attracted to men in uniforms, but he damned well didn't expect it to work in reverse. Especially not with him. Nope. He liked soft, well-rounded women who reveled in and showed off their feminine attributes. He was partial to tight T-shirts, miniskirts or long dresses with split skirts, open enough to show a good long length of calf and thigh. He'd seen slacks and silk blouses that were sexy, but never a uniform, for crying out loud, and espe cially not one of those from the local sheriff's department, but he'd noticed Kelly Dillinger. Angry as he'd been when he'd stormed into the sheriff's department, he'd found it damned hard to keep his mind on business.

But then he'd always had trouble with his libido; around attractive women it had always been in overdrive. Tonight was worse than it had been in a long, long while.

So there it was. He was attracted to her.

But he couldn't be. No way. Not to a woman cop—especially not this one who was working on his sister's case and who, he knew, held a personal grudge against the McCafferty family. But the bare facts of the matter were that he was lying to himself. Even now, just thinking about her, he felt his crotch tighten. He glanced at his reflection in the rearview mirror. "Idiot," he chastised, then shifted down as he approached the Flying M, the ranch that had been his father's pride and joy.

"Great," he grumbled as he cranked the steering wheel and his tires spun a little as they hit a patch of packed snow. The woman was off-limits. Period. If for no other reason than she lived here in Grand Hope, far from his own ranch. If he was going to be looking for a woman, which he wasn't, he reminded himself, he'd be looking for one a lot closer to home. God, where did those thoughts come from? He didn't want or need a woman. They were too much trouble. Kelly Dillinger included.

His headlights caught the snowflakes dancing in front of the truck and a few dry weeds poked through the mantle of white, scraping against the undercarriage as he navigated along the twin ruts leading to the heart of the spread. A few shaggy-coated cattle, dark, shifting shapes against the white background of the snow, were visible, but most of the herd had sought shelter or was out of his line of vision as he plowed down a long lane and rounded a final bend to a broad, flat parking area located between the main house and the outbuildings.

The truck slid to a stop beneath a leafless apple tree near a fence that was beginning to sag in a spot or two.

Matt yanked his keys from the ignition, threw open the door and was across the lot and up the three steps of the front porch in seconds. He only stopped to kick some of the snow off his boots, then pushed open the front door.

A wave of warm heat and the sound of piano keys tinkling out a quick, melodic tune greeted him. He sloughed off his jacket and felt his stomach rumble as he smelled roasting chicken and something else—cinnamon and baked apples. Hanging his jacket and hat on a peg near the front door, he heard the quick, light-footed steps of tiny feet scurrying across the hardwood floor overhead. Within seconds the twins were scuttling down the stairs.

"Unca Matt!" one little dark-haired cherub sang out as she rounded the corner of the landing and flew down the rest of the worn steps.

"How're ya, Molly girl?" Crouching, opening his arms wide, he swept the impish four-year-old off her feet.

"Fine," she said, her brown eyes twinkling at a sudden and uncharacteristic hint of shyness. She sucked on a finger as her sister, blanket in tow, scampered down the steps.

"And how about you, Mindy?" he asked, bending down and hauling the second scamp into his arms. The music was still playing and so he dipped and swooped, dancing with a niece in each arm. He'd only known the little girls over a month, but they, along with Randi's baby, were a part of his family, now and forever. He couldn't imagine a life without Molly, Mindy or the baby.

The girls giggled and laughed, Mindy's tattered blanket twirling as Matt sashayed them into the living room where their mother, Nicole, was seated on the piano stool, her fingers flying over the keys as she played some ragtime piece for all it was worth.

"Is Liberace playing?" Matt asked.

"No!" the girls chimed, throwing back their heads and giggling loudly.

"Oh, you're right. It must be Elton John?"

"No, no!" they screamed in unison, their little noses wrinkling. "It's Mommy."

"And she's a hack," their mother said, twirling around as the final notes faded and the sound of the fire crackling in the grate caught Matt's attention. Nicole's daughters wiggled out of his arms and scrambled to their mother. "But then, you're not exactly Fred Astaire or Gene Kelly."

"Oh, damn, and I thought I was." Matt walked to the fireplace and warmed the back of his legs against the flames. "I'm crushed."

"That'll be the day." Nicole shook her head, her amber eyes bright with mischief.

Harold was lying in his favorite spot on the rug near the fire. He lifted up his head and yawned, stretching his legs before he perked up one ear and snorted, looked as if he might climb to his feet, but didn't bother and let his snout rest upon his paws again.

"Well? What did you find out?" Thorne, on crutches, hitched his way into the room and plopped into the worn leather recliner where he propped up his injured leg. He was wearing baggy khaki pants that covered up the cast running from foot to thigh, and his expression said more clearly than words, "I'm tired of being laid up."

"Nothing. The damned sheriff's department doesn't know diddly-squat."

"You talked to Espinoza?" Thorne asked.

Boots pounded from the back of the house, heralding the arrival of their youngest brother.

"Wait a minute!" Juanita's voice echoed through the hallways. "You take off those boots! I just mopped the floor. *Dios!* Does anyone ever listen to me? No!"

"Hey!" Slade appeared in the archway separating the living room from the foyer and staircase. He didn't bother to answer Juanita, nor did he shed his coat. "Where the hell have you been?" Black eyebrows were slammed together over intense, laser-blue eyes as he stared at Matt. "We've got stock to feed, and Thorne's not a helluva lot of help these days."

"Cool it." Thorne's gaze moved from his youngest brother to Nicole's daughters who, if they'd heard the swearing, were too busy banging on the piano keys to notice. "Matt was down at the sheriff's office."

"They found anything?" Slade asked, his belligerence fading as he walked to the liquor cabinet set into the bookcase and unearthed an old bottle of Scotch. "How 'bout a drink?"

"No, they don't know anything else and yeah, I could use a shot." Matt couldn't hide his irritation that he hadn't gotten more definitive answers.

"None for me." Thorne shook his head. "What did Espinoza have to say?"

"He wasn't around. I talked with the woman."

"Kelly Dillinger," Nicole said as the twins, bored with making their own kind of music, climbed down from her lap and hurried out of the room. A tall woman with brown hair, a sharp wit and a medical degree, Nicole Stevenson was more than a match for his brother. She was smart, savvy, and as an emergency room physician, wasn't used to taking orders from anyone—just the kind of woman to tame Thorne and settle him down.

"She's the one." Matt accepted a short glass from Slade, took a swallow and felt the warm fire of liquor burn a welcome path down his throat. And he shoved any wayward thoughts of Detective Dillinger from his mind. It wasn't easy. In fact it was damned near impossible. That fiery redhead had a way of catching a man's attention. Big time.

"A drink?" Slade asked Nicole as he poured another glass.

"I'd better take a rain check. I'm scheduled at the hospital later," she said, and as her words faded she froze and cocked her head. "Uh-oh, it sounds like someone's waking up."

Matt heard the first cough of a baby's cry, and he was

amazed at how women seemed to have a sixth sense about that sort of thing.

"I'll get him," Nicole said, then turned her head and looked over her shoulder at Thorne. One sleek eyebrow rose as she added, "but you uncles are going to be pulling duty later this evening."

"We can handle it," Thorne said, as if a baby were no problem at all. But then Thorne thought he could handle the world. And he wasn't too far off.

"Yeah. Right." Nicole wasn't buying her fiancé's confident routine. She climbed the stairs to the nursery, and her laughter drowned out the baby's fussy noises.

"So what did the detective say?" Thorne asked Matt as he pushed the recliner into a more upright position.

"Same old runaround. They're looking into all possibilities. They have no evidence of foul play. There are no suspects. When Randi wakes up, then maybe they'll be able to piece more of it together. All a load of bull if you ask me." He downed his drink, irritated all over again. The heat from the fire felt good against the back of his legs, the liquor warmed him on the inside, but he was restless, anxious, needed to take action. He'd been staying at the Flying M for nearly a month, ever since he'd been called and told about his half sister's accident. He'd driven like a madman, camped out and done what he could, but he was frustrated as hell because he felt like he was spinning his wheels. He had his own place to run, his ranch near the Idaho border. His neighbor, Mike Kavanaugh, was looking after the place while he was gone and had hired a couple of high school boys to help out, but Matt was beginning to feel the need to go back and check on the ranch himself.

"Detective Dillinger is a looker, if ya ask me," Slade offered up as he took a swallow from his drink.

"No one did," Matt grumbled.

Slade's chuckle was deep and wicked, and Matt caught the teasing glint in his brother's blue eyes. "Don't tell me you haven't noticed."

Matt snorted. Lifted a shoulder.

"Come on, admit it." Slade wasn't about to give up. "You've always had an eye for the ladies."

"It takes one to know one."

"Enough," Thorne said just as Nicole returned toting the baby. Matt's heart melted at the sight of little J.R., the name the brothers had come up with since Randi was still in a coma, didn't even know she had a son. They figured they could call him Junior or John Randall, like the kid's grandfather. As he had dozens of times, Matt wondered about the baby's father. Who was the guy? Where the hell was he? Why hadn't Randi ever mentioned him?

Matt felt a slash of guilt. The truth of the matter was that he, and the rest of his brothers, had been so caught up in their own lives, they'd lost touch with their half sister, a firebrand of a girl who, for years, had been the bane of her older siblings' existence, the daughter of the woman whom they blamed for wrecking their parents' marriage.

Now, looking down at the baby, his downy reddish-gold hair sticking up at odd angles, Matt felt a bit of pride and something more—something deeper, something that scared him, as it spoke to the need for roots, and settling down and marriage and children of his own.

Nicole handed the bundle to the man she intended to marry. "Here, Uncle Thorne, you deal with J.R. while I see if Juanita needs some help with dinner."

"Me, too. I help," Molly offered, dashing into the room

only to take a spin around her mother and race off toward the kitchen.

"How about you?" Nicole asked Mindy, who was tailing after her more exuberant sister.

"Yeth. Me, too."

"Come on, then," she said, casting one final glance at her soon-to-be husband and shepherding the girls down the hall-way. Harold gave up a disgruntled "woof" and slapped his tail onto the braided rug. Matt swallowed a smile at the sight of his eldest brother—millionaire, CEO of McCafferty International, heretofore international jet-setter and playboy—reduced to juggling a one-month-old infant in his awkward hands while propping up his broken leg.

"Hey, I could use some help here," Thorne grumbled, though he grinned down at the baby.

"Didn't you say something about feeding the stock?" Matt asked Slade.

"That I did." The two younger McCaffertys left Thorne in charge of the infant. Matt thought it was only fitting as he snagged his jacket from the peg near the front door and stepped outside into the frigid air. Seeing as Thorne couldn't help out much with the heavy work around the ranch, he could damned well babysit.

The woman in the hospital bed looked horrible, though by all accounts she was healing. Nevertheless, in Kelly's esti-mation Randi McCafferty had a long way to go. There were tubes and monitors running into and out of her body and she lay on the bed unmoving, thin and pale, her skin still show-ing some signs of discoloration, though some of the bruises and cuts had healed.

"If only you could talk," Kelly said, biting her lower lip. For all the pain the McCaffertys had put on her family, Kelly still didn't like seeing anyone like this. A nurse walked to Randi's bedside and began taking her vital signs. "Has she shown any sign of waking?" Kelly asked.

"I can't really say," sighed the petite woman with shiny black hair, olive skin, eyes rimmed with excessive mascara and a name tag that read Kathy Desmond. "With this one, we might need a crystal ball," she joked as she picked up Randi's wrist and took her pulse, then slipped a blood pressure cuff over her arm. "It seems to me that she should wake up soon. Certainly she's had plenty of eye movement beneath her lids, she's yawned, and one of the night nurses thinks she moved her arm. Whether this means she'll be waking up today, tomorrow or next week, I don't know."

"But soon."

"I would think." The nurse's highly arched brows pulled together. "But I'm not sure."

"I understand," Kelly said, wishing Matt McCafferty's half sister would rouse and open her eyes, be cognizant and clear-headed enough to answer questions about the day her car slid off the road. Had someone intentionally forced her over the embankment? Had she gone into labor and lost control? Had she just hit a patch of black ice that sent her vehicle into a skid? The McCafferty brothers seemed to think there was some person or persons behind the accident. Kelly wasn't convinced. Right now only Randi McCafferty had the answers to what had happened up at Glacier Park and only she knew who was the father of her child.

The nurse left the room and Kelly stepped closer to the unmoving form on the bed. She wrapped her fingers around the cool metal rails, then touched the back of Randi's hand, willing some life into Randi's battered body. "Wake up," she urged. "You've got so much to live for…a new baby, for starters." *And three stubborn, intense half brothers.*

"Besides that you've got a lot of explaining to do when you wake up." She squeezed Randi's hand, but there was no response. "Come on, Randi. Help me out here."

"She can't hear you."

Kelly released the comatose woman's hand quickly and flushed. She recognized Matt McCafferty's voice instantly. Her heart jumped.

"I realize that." Turning, she found him in the doorway, still dressed in the jeans and shirt he'd had on a few hours earlier. His jacket was unbuttoned, his hat in his hands, his face not as hostile as it had been earlier, but there were still silent accusations in his dark eyes. Roguishly handsome and mad as a wet hornet.

"What're you doing here?" he demanded.

"I met Detective Espinoza in the ER, then decided to check on your sister."

"You should be checking out leads, trying to find the bastard who did this to her." Matt stepped into the room, closer. Kelly's nerves tightened and she silently chided herself for her reaction.

He stared down at his sister, and the play of emotions across his bladed features showed signs of a deeper emotion than she would have expected from the rogue cowboy, who had become, according to town gossip, a solitary man. Yes, there was anger in the set of his jaw, quiet determination in his stance, but something else was evident—the flicker of guilt deep in his near-black eyes. At some level Matt McCafferty felt responsible for his sister's condition. He reached over the rails just as Kelly had minutes before and took Randi's small, pale hand in his big, tanned fingers. "You hang in there," he said huskily, his thumb rubbing the back of his sister's hand, only to stop less than an inch from the spot where the IV needle was buried in her skin.

Kelly's throat tightened as she recognized his pain.

"Your little man, J.R., he's needin' ya." Matt cleared his throat, slid an embarrassed glance at Kelly, then turned his attention back to his sister. Obviously he felt more comfortable shoeing horses, mending fence or roping calves than he did trying to come up with words of encouragement to a comatose sibling. And yet he tried. Kelly's heart twisted. Maybe there was more to Matt McCafferty than first met the eye, than rumor allowed. "And the rest of us, we need ya, too," he added gruffly. With a final pat to his kid sister's shoulder, he turned on his heel.

Kelly let her breath out slowly. *Who* was this man and why did she react to him—dear Lord, her hands were sweating, and if she didn't know better, she'd swear her heartbeat accelerated whenever she saw him. But that was crazy. Just plain nuts.

Giving herself a quick mental shake, Kelly followed him through the door into the central hallway to the hub that housed the nurses' station.

"Where's Espinoza?" he asked, sliding a glance her way.

"Probably back at the office. He finished up here on another case, but he's aware that you're concerned. He'll call you tonight, but I don't think he can give you any more information than I have."

"Damn." They walked to the elevator and stepped into a waiting car. She ignored the fact that her pulse had accelerated, and she noticed that he smelled faintly of leather and soap. As the doors to the elevator shut and they were alone, his dark eyes focused on her. Hard. She wanted to squirm away from his intense, silently accusing eyes. Instead she stood her ground as he asked, "So why were you in Randi's room?"

"Just to keep my focus. I hadn't seen her for a while and after your visit this afternoon, I thought I'd see how she was getting along. I've kept in contact with the hospital, of course, gotten updates, but I thought seeing her might make me clearer on some points."

"Such as?"

"Such as why was she up in Glacier Park? Where was she going? Who were her enemies? Who were her friends? Why did she fire the foreman of the ranch a week or so before she left Seattle? What happened at her job? Who's the father of her child? Those kind of questions."

"Get any answers?" he asked sarcastically.

"I was hoping someone in the family might know."

"I wish. No one does." He leaned against the rail surrounding the interior as the elevator car landed and the doors opened to the lobby. He straightened, his jacketed arm brushing hers. She stepped out of the car, ignored the faint physical contact. "What do you know about a book your sister was writing?"

"I'm not sure there is one," he said as they crossed a carpeted reception area where wood-framed chairs were scattered around tables strewn with magazines and a few potted trees had been added to give some illusion that St. James Hospital was more than a medical facility, warmer than an institution.

"Your housekeeper, Juanita Ramirez, said she was in contact with your sister before the accident and that Randi had been working on a book of some kind, but no one seems to know anything more about it."

"Juanita didn't even know that Randi was pregnant. I doubt if she was privy to my sister's secrets," Matt muttered as he made his way to the wide glass doors of the main entrance.

"Why would she make it up?"

"I'm not saying Juanita's lying." The first set of doors opened automatically, and as Kelly stepped into the vestibule, she felt the temperature lower ten or fifteen degrees. Thank God. For some reason she was sweating.

"But maybe Randi fibbed. She'd talked about writing a book since she was a kid in high school, but did she ever? No. Not that my brothers or I ever heard of."

The second set of doors opened and a middle-aged man pushed a wheelchair, where a tiny elderly woman was huddled in a wool coat, stocking cap and lap blankets. Outside the snow was falling, flakes dancing and swirling in the pale blue illumination from the security lamps.

Matt squared his hat on his head, the brim shadowing his face even further. "Talk to anyone and sooner or later they tell you about the book they're gonna write someday. Trouble is that 'someday' never comes."

"Spoken like a true cynic," Kelly observed as she buttoned her coat and felt the chill of Montana winter slap her face and cool her blood, which seemed a few degrees higher than normal.

"Just a reality check. If Randi was writing a book, don't you think one of us, either Thorne, Slade or I, would know about it?"

"Just like you knew all about her job and her pregnancy," Kelly threw back at him, using the same argument he'd given her earlier about the housekeeper's belief that Randi had penned some literary tome.

Matt was about to step off the curb, but stopped and turned to face Kelly. "Okay, okay, but even so. Big deal. So what if she was writing her goddamned version of *War and Peace?* What's

that got to do with the price of tea in China, or more specifically what happened to her up in Glacier Park?"

"You tell me."

"*You're* the cop," he pointed out, his eyes flaring angrily.
"A detective, no less. This is your job, lady."

"And I'm just trying to do it."

"Then try a little harder, okay? My sister's life is on the
line." With that he stepped off the curb, hunched his shoulders against the wind and strode through the blowing snow
to his truck. Kelly was left with her cheeks burning hot, her
temper in the stratosphere, her pride taking a serious blow.

"Bastard," she growled under her breath, and headed to her
own car, an unmarked four-wheel drive. She didn't know who
she was more angry with, the hard-edged cowboy, or herself
for her reaction to him. What was wrong with her? She was
nervous around him, nearly tongue-tied, so...*unprofessional!*
Well, that was going to change, and now!

Once behind the wheel, she twisted on the ignition, flipped
on the wipers and drove to her town house on the west end
of town. With a western facade, the two-storied row house
had been her home for three years, ever since she'd scraped up
enough of a down payment to buy her own place.

She parked in the single garage and climbed up a flight
to the main floor, where she kicked off her boots in the tiny
laundry room, then padded inside. Tossing her keys onto the
glass-topped table that served as her eating area and desk, she
walked into the kitchen and hit the play button on her answering machine while shedding her coat.

"Kelly?" her sister's voice called frantically, bringing a smile
to Kelly's lips as her sibling was nothing if not overly dramatic.
"It's Karla and I was hoping to catch you. Look, it's about six
and I'm still at the shop, but I'm gonna close up soon and pick

up the kids at the sitter's then run out to Mom and Dad's. I thought maybe you could meet me there…call me at the shop or try and reach me out at their place."

Kelly checked the wall clock and saw that it was nearly seven-thirty. There were no other messages so she placed a call to her folks' house and Karla picked up on the second ring.

"Got your message," Kelly said.

"Kelly, great! Mom just pulled this fantastic pork roast from the oven, and from the smell of it, it's to die for."

Kelly's stomach rumbled and she realized she hadn't eaten anything since the carton of yogurt and muffin that had sufficed as lunch.

"We were hoping you could join us."

With a glance at the paperwork on the table, Kelly weighed the options. She wanted to go over every ounce of information she could on Randi McCafferty, but she figured she could wedge in some time for her family first. "Just give me a few minutes to change. I'll be there in half an hour."

"Make it twenty minutes, will ya? My kids are starved and when they get hungry, they get cranky."

"Do not," one of the boys countered, his high voice audible.

"Just hurry," Karla pleaded. "The natives are restless."

"I'll be there in a flash."

"Good idea. Put on the lights and siren, clear out traffic and roar on over."

"I'll see ya." Kelly whipped off her uniform and changed into soft, well-worn jeans and her favorite cowl-necked sweater. She took half a minute to run a brush through her hair, then threw on a long coat and boots and dived into her old Nissan, a relic that she loved. Fifteen years old, a hundred and eighty thousand miles on the odometer and never once had the compact left her stranded. At a stoplight, she applied a fresh sheen of lipstick but still made it to her parents' house, the bungalow where she'd grown up, in fifteen minutes flat.

"Kelly girl!" her father called as he pushed his wheelchair into the dining room where the table was already set. Once tall and strapping, Ron Dillinger had been reduced to using the chair for twenty-five years, the result of a bullet that had lodged in his back and damaged his spinal cord. He'd been a deputy at the time, and had been on disability ever since. "Glad you could join us."

"Me, too, Dad," she said, and bent down to kiss his forehead where thin strands of white hair couldn't quite cover his speckled pate.

"You've been busy, I see," he said, holding up a folded newspaper. "Lots going on."

"Always."

"That's the way I remember it. Even in my day, there weren't enough men on the force."

"Or women."

Ronald snorted. "Weren't any women at all."

"Maybe that's why you weren't so efficient," she teased, and he swatted at her with his newspaper. She ducked into the kitchen and was greeted with squeals of delight from her nephews, Aaron and Spencer, two dynamos who rarely seemed to wind down.

The boys charged her, nearly toppling their mother in the process. "Aunt Kelly!" Aaron cried. "Up, up." He held up chubby three-year-old arms and Kelly obligingly lifted him from the floor. He had a mashed sandwich in one hand and a tiny toy truck in the other. Peanut butter was smeared across the lower half of his face. "You comed."

"That I did."

"Came, she came," Karla corrected him.

"You're such a baby," Spencer needled.

"Am not!" Aaron rose to the bait as quickly as a hungry trout to a salmon fly.

"Of course you're not," Kelly said, swinging him to the ground and wondering just how much peanut butter was transferred to her sweater. "And neither are you," she said to her older nephew, who grinned, showing off the gap where once had been two front teeth. Freckled, blue-eyed and smart as a whip, Spencer enjoyed besting his younger sibling, a half brother. Karla, two years younger than Kelly, had been married twice, divorced as many times, and had sworn off men and marriage for good.

"Here, you can mash the potatoes," Karla said as she snatched a wet dishrag from the sink and started after a squealing Aaron, who took off into the dining room.

"Papa!" Aaron cried, hoping his grandfather would protect him from his mother's obsession with cleanliness.

"He won't save you," Karla said, chasing after her youngest.

Kelly's mother, Eva, was adding a dab of butter and a sprinkle of brown sugar to already-baked acorn squash. The scents of roast pork, herbs and her mother's favorite perfume mingled and rose in the warmth of the kitchen as she shook her head at the melee. "Never a dull minute when the boys are around."

"I see that." Kelly rumpled Spencer's hair fondly, cringed at the wail coming from the dining room, then rinsed her hands and found the electric beaters so that she could whip the potatoes. Over the whir of the hand mixer, Aaron's screams, the microwave timer and comments from Charlie, her parents' pet budgie, who was perched in his cage near the front door, Kelly could barely hear herself think.

"I'll make the gravy," Karla said as she tossed the dirty rag into the sink.

"Mission accomplished?" Kelly glanced down at a more subdued Aaron. His face was clean again, red from being rubbed by the washcloth.

"Yeah, and it'll last all of five minutes. *If* we're lucky."

Kelly's mother chuckled. A petite woman with fluffy apricot curls and a porcelain complexion, she doted on her two grandsons as if they were truly God's gifts, which, Kelly imagined, they were. It was just too bad they had such louses for fathers. Seth Kramer and Franklin Anderson were as different as night and day—their only common trait being that they couldn't handle the responsibilities of fatherhood.

"Are we about ready?" Eva asked, and Kelly clicked off the beaters.

"I think so."

It took another five minutes to carry everything into the dining room, find a booster chair for Aaron, get both boys settled and served up, but soon Kelly was cutting into a succulent slab of herb-seasoned pork. She finally relaxed a little, the tension in her shoulders easing as they ate and talked, just as they had growing up. Except there were two more chairs crowded around the Formica-topped table now, for two boys who were as dear to her as if they'd been Kelly's own.

"So what gives with all that business with the McCaffertys?" her father asked around a mouthful of pork. "I read in the paper there's speculation about foul play."

"Isn't there always?" Kelly asked.

"With that group there is." Eva's eyebrows pulled together, causing little lines to deepen between them.

"Yeah, they're an untrustworthy lot, there's no doubt of that."

"Amen," Karla said as she cut tiny pieces of meat for her youngest son.

Kelly didn't comment. For years the name McCafferty had been tantamount to Beelzebub or Lucifer in the Dillinger home. She saw her mother give off a soft little sigh as Eva poured gravy onto her potatoes. "I suppose it's all water under the bridge," she said softly, but the pain of the old betrayal was still evident in the lines of her face.

Ron scowled into his plate. "Maybe so, but it doesn't mean I have to like 'em."

"John Randall is dead."

"And I hope he rots in his grave."

"Dad!" Karla said sharply, then glanced pointedly at her sons.

"Well, I do. No reason to sugarcoat it. That son of a bitch didn't care a whit about anyone but his own kin. It didn't matter how many years your mother put in working for him, passing up other good jobs, he still cut her loose when times got a little rocky. And what happened to her pension, huh? There wasn't any, that's what happened. Bad investments, or some such crock of—"

"Dad!" Karla said again.

"Karla's right. There's no use discussing it in front of the boys," Eva agreed, but the sparkle in her eyes had faded. "Now, if you'll pass me the pepper..."

And so the subject was gratefully closed for the duration of the meal. Their father even found his smile again over a piece of his wife's lemon meringue pie.

After the plates had been cleared and the dishwasher was humming with a full load, Ron challenged the boys to a game of checkers on a small table near the fire. Aaron climbed onto his grandfather's lap and they played as a team against Spencer, who thought he could beat them both as he'd practiced how to outmaneuver an opponent on a computer.

"The boys could really use a father figure," Karla observed, watching her sons relate to their grandfather as she fished in the closet for her sons' coats and hats. Sadly, she ran a hand through her spiky strawberry-blond hair. "All they've got is Dad."

"They do have fathers," Kelly reminded her.

Karla rolled her expressive green eyes. "Oh, give me a break. They have sperm donors, nothing else. Boy, can I pick 'em. Some people are athletically challenged, I'm love challenged."

"You and the rest of the women on the planet."

"I'm not kidding. I can see when anyone else is making a mistake, but I seem to have blinders on when it comes to my choice in men."

"Or rose-colored glasses."

"Yeah, those, too." She was pensive, running long fingers along the stitching in Aaron's stocking cap. "But then you never take a chance, Kelly. I mean, not on love. You take lots of chances in your career."

"Maybe I've been too busy."

"Or maybe you're just smarter than I am," Karla said with a sigh. "I don't see you making the same mistakes I did."

"You forget I'm a career woman," Kelly said, reaching for her coat. "A cop."

"So am I—a career woman, that is—and don't tell me that being a beautician and owning your own shop doesn't count."

"I wouldn't dream of it," Kelly said, laughing.

"So…when are you going to tuck your badge away long enough to fall in love?"

"As soon as you put down the perm rollers, shampoo and clippers."

"Very funny."

"I thought so." She slipped her arms through the sleeves

of her coat, hiked it up over her shoulders and began working on the buttons.

"I think we both could take some advice from Randi McCafferty. You know she wrote a column for single people?" Karla asked, then added, "Of course you do—what was I thinking? You've been working on the case for weeks." She held up Spencer's coat, then called toward the living room. "Come on, boys. Time to go." Both kids protested and Karla said to Kelly, "I was only kidding about Randi McCafferty's column. The last person I would take any advice from is a McCafferty."

"Maybe they're not all as bad as we think," Kelly said as she reached into her pocket for her keys.

"Oh, yeah? So now they're sprouting wings and halos?" Karla shook her head. "I don't think so."

There was a whoop from the living room as Spencer actually beat Aaron and his grandfather. Aaron burst into tears, and from the twinkle in Ron Dillinger's eyes, Kelly was certain he'd let his eldest grandson win.

"Come on, boys, time to go," Karla called again. In an aside to Kelly, she added, "Getting them out of here is like pulling teeth."

"No!" Aaron cried, refusing to budge from his grandfather's lap while Spencer just ignored his mother, no matter what tack she took. Eventually she wrestled her youngest into his ski coat, hat and mittens while Spencer, lower lip protruding in an exaggerated pout, shrugged into a quilted pullover with a hood.

"You boys be good, now," Eva said as she emerged from the kitchen without her apron. She planted a kiss on each boy's cheek and slipped them each a tiny candy bar left over from Halloween into their hands.

"I be good!" Aaron said, trying to tear off his mittens to get at the bit of chocolate.

"Mom!" Karla admonished.

"I just can't help myself."

"Here, let me get it." Kelly unwrapped the chocolate morsel, then plopped it into Aaron's open mouth.

"He's like one of those nestlings you see on the nature shows," Karla grumbled good-naturedly. "Aren't ya, little eaglet?"

Aaron grinned and chocolate drooled down his chin.

"I've got to get out of here. Come on, Spence." With that she bustled out the door, leaving Kelly to say goodbye to her parents.

"Everything good with you?" her father asked, worry in his dark eyes as he rolled his wheelchair into the foyer.

"Couldn't be better."

"But the boys on the force, they're not giving you any trouble?"

"None that I don't deserve, Dad. This isn't the 1940s, you know. There are thousands of female cops these days."

"I know, I know, but it just doesn't seem like a job for a woman." He held up his hands as if warding off the verbal blow he was certain was heading his way. "No offense."

"Oh, none taken, Dad, none at all. You've just denigrated every woman police officer I know, but am I offended? Oh, no-o-o. Not me."

"Fine, fine, you've made your point," he said with a chuckle. "Just don't let anyone give you a bad time. None of the boys you work with and especially none of the McCaffertys."

"Can't we just forget about them?" Eva asked.

"Impossible." He cranked the wheelchair into the living room and returned with a copy of the *Grand Hope Gazette,* folded to display an article on the third page of the main section, an article about Thorne McCafferty's small plane crash. "And this is after a couple of weeks have passed." He skimmed the article. "Seems as if there's some question as to whether or not there was foul play involved, and this here reporter thinks maybe the plane crash and the sister's wreck might be related. Bah. Sounds like coincidence to me." He glanced up at Kelly, his bristly white eyebrows elevated, inviting her opinion.

"I'm not at liberty to discuss the case."

"Oh, cut the crap, Kelly. We're family."

"And I'll confide in you when I need to, okay? Now... I've got to run. Duty calls."

She bussed each of her parents on the cheeks, then hurried outside to her car. The snow had stopped falling, but because of the dark clouds, she couldn't see a solitary star in the dark heavens. Her breath fogged in the air, her windshield was frozen, and she shivered as she cranked on the ignition.

Like clockwork, the engine fired and she drove away from the warm little bungalow with its patches of golden light and wide front porch. Her parents were aging, more rapidly as the days went by. Her father had never been his robust self after the gunshot blast that had ruined his career and crippled him for life, and her mother, strong woman that she was, had never complained, had taken care of a convalescing, depressed husband and two young daughters. She'd landed a job with John Randall McCafferty as his personal secretary to help make ends meet. John Randall had promised her raises, promotions, bonuses and a retirement plan, but his fortunes had changed, and after his second divorce and a downturn in the economy, he'd been left with nothing but the ranch. Eva had lost her job and all the promises of a substantial nest egg had proved to be empty, the money that was supposed to have been set aside dwindled away by bad investments—oil wells that had run dry, silver mines that had never produced, stock in start-up companies that had shut down within months of opening their doors.

There had been talk of a lawsuit, but Eva hadn't been able to find a local attorney ready to take on a man who had once been a political contender in the area, a man who had been influential and still had connections to judges, the mayor and even a senator or two.

"Don't dwell on it," Kelly told herself. She drove across the town where she'd grown up, wheeled into the parking lot of her row house and used the remote to open her garage door.

Though there hadn't been a lot of money in her family, she'd grown up with security and love from both her parents. That was probably more than any of the McCafferty children could say. She climbed up the stairs to her bedroom on the upper floor, changed into her flannel pajamas and a robe, then made herself a cup of decaf coffee and sat at the kitchen table, scouring the notes she'd taken on Randi McCafferty's accident and Thorne McCafferty's plane crash.

So many questions swirled around John Randall's only daughter and no one, it seemed, could come up with the answers. Kelly had interviewed all the brothers, everyone who worked on the Flying M Ranch, all of Randi McCafferty's friends in the area. All the while she'd kept in contact with the Seattle police, who had handled interviewing Randi's friends and associates there, in the city where Randi had lived and worked. It wasn't usual procedure, but this case was different with Randi being pregnant, giving birth, then lying comatose in the hospital, her half brothers crying foul play.

But until Randi McCafferty came out of the coma, the

mystery shrouding the youngest of John Randall's children would most likely remain unsolved.

Kelly glanced down at the notes she'd taken and two questions loomed larger than the others. First and foremost, who was the father of Randi's son, and second, was she writing a book and what was it about?

Doodling as she sipped her coffee, she thought about the case, then, as a headache began to cloud her mind, she finished her coffee and leaned back in her chair. In her mind's eye she saw Matt McCafferty as he had been at the office and later in the hospital. Chiseled features, dark eyes, square jaw and hard, ranch-tough body. He came on like gang busters, looking as if he was ready to spit nails, but there was more to him, deeper emotions she'd witnessed herself as he'd stood over his sister's bedside. Feelings he'd tried to hide had crossed his features. Guilt. Worry. Fear.

Yes, she decided, there was more to Cowboy Matt than met the eye.

She stretched and yawned, scraped her chair back and started for the bedroom when the phone jangled loudly. She picked it up on the extension near the bed and glanced at the clock. Eleven forty-seven. "Hello?" she said into the receiver, knowing it was bound to be an emergency.

Espinoza's voice boomed over the line. "Kelly? We've got a situation. Meet me down at St. James Hospital ASAP."

"What happened?" she asked, already stripping off her robe.

"It's Randi McCafferty. Someone just tried to pull the plug on her."

Chapter 3

Somewhere a phone was ringing, jangling, intrusive, but the woman, naked to the waist, her uniform tossed over the back of a chair in the unfamiliar room, didn't seem to notice.

Brring!

She walked forward, tossed her long red hair over her shoulder and flashed him a naughty smile. With a wink, she said, "So come on, cowboy, show me what you're made of." Her dark eyes sparked with a wicked, teasing fire and her lips were full, wet and oh so kissable.

Aching, he reached forward to pull her close and lose himself in her.

Brring!

Matt's eyes flew open. He'd been dreaming. About Kelly Dillinger, and he was sporting one helluva proof of arousal. He blinked, the image disappearing into the shadows of the night. Down the hallways of the old ranch house, the phone blasted again. Groggily, he glanced at the digital display of his clock. Nearly twelve. Meaning whoever was calling wasn't waking up the McCaffertys with good news.

Randi. His heart nearly stopped. Slapping on the light, he didn't wait for his eyes to adjust but yanked on the pair of jeans he'd tossed over the foot of the bed and threw a sweatshirt over his head. He was striding barefoot down the hall when the door to the master suite was flung open, and Thorne, wearing boxer shorts, his cast and a robe he hadn't bothered to cinch, was hobbling toward the stairs.

"That was Nicole from the hospital. Someone tried to kill Randi," he said tersely.

"What?"

"Someone put something into her damned IV."

"Hell!" Matt broke out in a cold sweat. His mind began running in circles. "Is she okay?"

"Far as anyone can tell," Thorne said, frowning darkly. By this time they were both working their way toward the center staircase.

"How could that happen?"

"No one's sure yet. It's pandemonium down there. Her heart stopped beating. They had to use paddles."

"Son of a bitch!"

"My thoughts exactly." Thorne stopped at the door to Slade's room and pounded hard, then shoved it open to find their youngest brother half dressed, his hair sticking up at odd angles, his fingers fumbling with the buttons of a flannel shirt.

"I heard the phone ring. Figured it was bad news," Slade muttered.

"You figured right." Thorne filled him in quickly and the youngest McCafferty's expression clouded over.

"For the love of Mike, we told them this would happen!

The police are out to lunch, for God's sake!" He swung a fist in the air. "Who's doing this?"

"And why?" Thorne's gray eyes narrowed with cold fury.

"Let's go." Slade stuffed his shirttails into his jeans.

"We all can't go to the hospital," Thorne pointed out as Slade swore a blue streak and reached for a pair of hiking boots. "Someone's got to stay with J.R. and the girls."

"That's your job," Matt decided. "You're gonna be stepfather to the twins and you're not a helluva lot of use, anyway, what with the bad leg."

"But I can't just stay here and—"

"Don't argue. We've heard it all before," Matt said. "You think you're in charge of 'the Randi situation,' the one calling the shots. But you're laid up, whether you like to admit it or not. So you have two choices. Wake up the baby and Nicole's daughters and drag them out in the freezing cold to a hospital that's sure to be chaos, or stay here and wait for one of us to call or relieve you."

Thorne's gray eyes darkened. Thick black eyebrows slammed together in frustration. "But I think—"

"For once just trust us, okay? We can handle things." Matt was already halfway to his room, where he found his socks, boots and a pair of gloves. He yanked them on as Thorne filled the doorway, his shoulders nearly touching each side of the frame.

"I don't like this."

"Of course you don't. You can't stand not being in charge." Matt tugged on his socks and started with his cowboy boots.

"I'd feel better if—"

"For God's sake, just give it up, okay? I'll feel better if you'd just shut the hell up and stay here with the kids. Coordinate. Take calls. Be Communications Central. Someone will re-

lieve you soon and you can drive yourself to the hospital and
take charge of things there again, okay? Until then, you're on,
'Uncle Thorne.' Now, get out of my way." Matt shouldered
past his older brother, collected Slade and hurried down the
stairs. He didn't have time for any of Thorne's bogus authority trips. Not now. He grabbed his jacket and hat.

His jaw tightened when he thought of Randi lying vulnerable in the hospital. God, you'd think she'd be safe there!

Outside, the snow had started again and it was cold as hell.
Not bothering to button his jacket, he slid behind the wheel
of his pickup and, with the flick of a wrist, twisted on the ignition. Slade climbed into the passenger side. "Let's go."

Matt threw his truck into gear before Slade had a chance
to shut the door.

Who tried to kill his sister?

Why would someone go to such lengths to see that she
was dead?

Did someone want to shut her up?

Was it revenge?

Did it have anything to do with her baby and J.R.'s mystery father?

"What the devil's going on?" he growled, his breath fogging in the frigid air. Worry and fear took turns clawing at his
gut, and his fingers clamped around the steering wheel until
his knuckles showed white. He squinted through the foggy
windshield as the wipers slapped haphazardly over the glass.

What if Randi didn't make it? What if whoever was trying
to kill her was successful?

"I don't know," Slade admitted, reaching into the inside
pocket of his jacket for a crumpled pack of cigarettes as Matt
cranked the wheel at the highway, then gunned the engine.
"But I'm sure as hell gonna find out."

Amen. If nothing else, Matt intended to find out who'd done this to his sister and then he'd beat the living hell out of the bastard.

St. James Hospital was a madhouse. Word had leaked out to the press that someone had tried to murder a patient, and a television van, camera crew and reporters from two stations were already staked out in front of the front doors. Kelly managed to dodge a microphone thrust toward her by muttering a quick "No comment" as she walked outside. Another reporter was camped out in the lobby, and Kelly shoved her way through doors marked Staff Only to avoid him. She flew up the staircase to the third floor, her boots ringing on the steps, her heart pounding as if it were a drum. Outside the doors of the ICU unit, she nearly ran into Detective Espinoza, two deputies from the sheriff's department and a policewoman with the Grand Hope force.

"Okay, so what happened?" she demanded.

"Randi McCafferty went into cardiac arrest, and it looks like someone might have helped her along by slipping something into her IV."

"What?"

"That's what we're trying to determine."

"But Randi's okay?"

"Out of the woods for now," Espinoza said, running a hand around his neck. His uniform, always neatly pressed, was rumpled, his usually spit-polished boots dull under the harsh hospital lights.

"Fill me in."

"One of the doctors here, Nicole Stevenson, stopped by on her break to look in at her soon-to-be sister-in-law. She's engaged to Thorne McCafferty."

"The oldest brother, I know."

"Anyway, Randi was in a private room up on the fourth floor. As Dr. Stevenson stepped off the elevator, she spotted a person in a lab coat emerging from Randi's room. The guy—or it could have been a woman, Dr. Stevenson didn't get that much of a look—anyway, the suspect turned and hurried down the hallway, then cut back into the employee stairwell. Dr. Stevenson didn't think much of it, thought the person was another doctor, until she checked on Thorne's sister. Randi wasn't breathing. Nicole started CPR and yelled for the nurses."

"She didn't recognize the person running away?"

"Can't even say if it was a man or woman." Espinoza snorted. "All she remembers is that the suspect was about five-nine and had brown hair—long for a man, short for a woman. Medium build. She didn't get much of a glimpse of the person's face, but thinks he or she might have been wearing glasses." Espinoza's dark eyes seemed weary. "Not much to go on."

"But better than nothing."

"Unless it's not our guy."

"Or gal," Kelly said.

"Right. Or woman." Espinoza told Kelly that he'd already secured Randi's private room and a crime team was going over it, though the chances of lifting the perpetrator's fingerprints or finding other incriminating evidence were small. Espinoza had also sent the two deputies to check St. James's staff roster and were instructed to interview anyone on duty. The policewoman was posted here, near the ICU, and for the moment, Espinoza thought, Randi was safe.

Rubbing a day's growth of stubble along his jaw, he added, "Whoever struck earlier won't take another chance tonight. He'll lay low for a while. Let things cool off."

"Unless he can't afford to. Obviously he's worried that when Randi wakes up, she'll finger him."

"We'll keep a guard posted," Espinoza said. "If the guy's stupid enough to try again, we'll be ready."

"So what about the patient? Is she still in a coma?" Kelly asked.

Espinoza nodded and glanced at the closed double doors of the ICU unit. "So far. Before the attack a couple of the nurses thought she might be coming around."

"Maybe that's why the perp struck when he did."

"Looks like."

"Then he'll be back." Kelly was certain of it.

The doors to the elevator opened and two of the McCafferty brothers strode through. Kelly's insides tightened and her stupid pulse jumped at the sight of Matt, his jaw thrust forward, his eyes burning bright in their sockets. "What the hell happened?" he demanded as if she were somehow to blame. "Where's Randi?" His head swiveled toward the closed doorway and he took two steps toward the ICU ward.

"You can't go barging in there," Kelly warned, and stuck out her hand as if to physically restrain him.

"Like hell." Matt's gaze sliced clear to her soul. He had one hand on the door and his brother Slade was only a step behind.

"She's right." Espinoza flashed his badge.

"Randi's my sister," Matt said flatly. "And it's gonna take a helluva lot more than a badge to stop me from seeing for myself that she's okay. You people," he snorted, and brushed past Espinoza. Bob stepped forward, but Kelly, recognizing Matt's need to see for himself that his sister was alive, put a hand on Espinoza's arm as the two McCafferty brothers entered the ICU ward.

"The nurses will shoo them out," she said under her breath,

and within seconds, Matt and Slade were back in the hallway. They were more subdued, but the anger in the set of Matt's mouth hadn't disappeared. "This might not have happened," he stated, his brown eyes drilling into hers before centering on Espinoza, "if the police hadn't been sitting on their backsides while a killer was on the loose."

Espinoza's dark gaze flashed fire. "We don't know that."

"Like hell." Matt went nose-to-nose with the detective. Broad shoulders were tense, the cords in the back of his neck stretched taut, his muscles flexed, as if ready for a fight. "Maybe you didn't before, but I'd say that all doubt is gone."

"Things have changed."

"Damned straight. My sister nearly died." His furious gaze burned a path from Roberto Espinoza to Kelly. His lips were blade-thin, bracketed by thin white lines of rage. "Now, let's get on with the investigation."

"Maybe you should let us do our jobs," Kelly snapped, more at her own reaction to the man than at Matt. Just being around him made her tense, edgy, and that silly feminine part that she so long had penned screamed to be set free whenever he was near. Her emotions were a mess. While maintaining her professionalism, she was trying to cut the guy some slack, but he was coming on pretty strong out here in the hushed corridors of St. James Hospital.

"Do your jobs? Let me know when you've started," Matt growled.

"Wait a minute—"

"No." He pushed his nose to within inches of hers and jabbed a finger in the air. His dark skin was red, his nostrils flared, his eyebrows rammed into a single line. "*You* wait a minute. My sister nearly died, got it? *Died*. Twice. I don't think we can give you permission to take your own sweet time."

"We're doing everything possible to find out what happened," she said, squaring her shoulders, not giving in an inch when she wanted nothing more than to put some distance between her body and his, to give herself more room to think.

"Then what about the maroon Ford? Kurt Striker found where Randi's rig was scraped by another vehicle. The paint samples he took from the fender matched any number of Ford products."

"We know that and we're checking into it," Espinoza said firmly as the elevator doors opened and a petite, smartly dressed woman emerged. Kelly recognized the local news reporter in her three-inch heels and tailored suit.

"How'd she get past security and get up here?" Kelly asked, stepping forward, blocking the woman's path. "You'll have to go downstairs," she ordered.

"I'm with the news."

"Jana Madrid. KABO. We've met before." Kelly didn't budge.

"I just want to talk to someone to get the facts." She managed a camera-perfect smile. "You're a police officer. Is it true that there was an attempt on Randi McCafferty's life tonight, here, in the hospital?"

"No comment."

"But—" The reporter was craning her neck, trying to see past the nurses' station to the small crowd clustered around the ICU. "Matt McCafferty's here."

"You know him?" Kelly asked.

"We've met. Yes." Jana's large eyes narrowed and Kelly could almost see the gears turning in the woman's mind. "So someone did make an attempt on his sister's life. If you'll excuse me, I'd like to get a statement from him."

"Later."

"What, exactly, happened here?"

"Leave, Ms. Madrid. Now." Kelly was firm, sensing one of the deputies approaching her to help.

"I just need a few facts for a story," Jana persisted, throwing a friendlier smile in Kelly's direction. "Come on. If a killer's on the loose, the public needs to be aware of it."

"The department will issue a statement at the appropriate time, as will the hospital. Until then I'm not at liberty to answer any questions." Kelly slapped the elevator call button.

"But the people have the right to know."

"The people need to know facts. When we have some. Now, please, either leave the hospital alone, or I'll have someone escort you."

"I'll handle it," the deputy who'd come to assist her offered. Six-three or four-, with his blond hair shaved to barely a quarter of an inch, he stepped forward. About twenty-six and beefy, Mike Benedict was a force to be reckoned with. The reporter hesitated, started to say something, then with a quick appraisal of the no-win situation, frowned.

"Television could help with the investigation, you know. If we got a sketch of a suspect, we could air it to the community, be involved in a community watch. It's the public's right."

"We'll let you know. Now, please," Kelly said firmly, and the woman reluctantly stepped into the elevator. The doors closed and Kelly returned to find Matt McCafferty ready to jump down Espinoza's throat.

"So check the hell faster, would ya? Find out what's going on and arrest the bastard who did this to Randi before she winds up dead!"

From the corner of her eye Kelly caught sight of a slim woman in a white coat striding purposefully along the hallway. Her hair was tossed off her face, and her worried gold eyes,

sculpted cheekbones and full lips were set into a regal countenance. Her name tag read Nicole Stevenson, M.D.

"Where's Thorne?" she asked without preamble. She seemed
cool and sophisticated, but just beneath the surface of her eyes
there was a deeper emotion. Worry. Maybe even fear. Obviously a strong woman, one who was in charge of her life
professionally and personally, she was nonetheless frightened.
Kelly had seen enough trauma to recognize when someone's
calm life had been breached. The killer had broken into Nicole Stevenson's workplace, a spot she considered a haven, and
attacked someone the doctor was close to. Beneath her veneer
of cool professionalism, Dr. Nicole Stevenson was anxious.

"We left Thorne home with the kids," Slade said.

"But I thought he was going to get Juanita or Jenny to stay...
oh, it doesn't matter. I thought I'd check on Randi again,"
Nicole said before her gaze landed on Kelly. "Detective Dillinger." She didn't bother forcing a smile she didn't feel. Obviously she, too, thought the police weren't doing everything
possible to track down Randi's enemies or protect her from
attack.

"Do that—check on Randi," Slade said, shoving a hand
nervously through his rumpled black hair.

"I'll be back in a minute." Nicole swept through the doors
to Intensive Care with the quiet authority of a medical professional on her own turf.

"You questioned her?" Kelly asked Espinoza.

He nodded.

"I think I'll have a few words with her."

"Have at. But she didn't see much. I'll be up on the fourth
floor in the private room where she was attacked," he said,
with one last glance at the McCafferty brothers as he headed
toward the elevators.

"How's your sister doing?" Kelly asked, hitching her chin at the closed doors to ICU.

White lines of irritation were visible at the corners of Matt's mouth, but he'd calmed a bit and the self-righteous fury she'd seen burning in his eyes had faded to some extent. "I guess we should be thankful she's alive."

Slade nodded. "Now, if only she'd wake up."

"That would help," Matt agreed, and slid his jaw to the side. "Why don't you tell me any theories you have?" he said. "Surely you must have some idea who's behind this."

"Ideas, no suspects, no hard evidence." Kelly shook her head thoughtfully. "Not much to go on. How about you? Or you?" She cut a glance toward Slade. "I'll buy you a cup of coffee in the cafeteria."

Matt looked at the closed door to the ICU. "Just as soon as we talk to Nicole."

"You go along," Slade said to Matt, and braced himself against the wall with his shoulders. "I think I'll hang out here and I'll let Nicole know where you are so she can fill you in."

"Fair enough." Matt nodded sharply and fell into step with Kelly as they took the back stairs.

On the first floor, Matt walked directly toward the cafeteria, a path he'd obviously traveled often while his half sister, nephew and brother were patients at St. James. The coffee was complimentary, and they found a quiet table near the windows and a shedding ficus tree.

"I want to know what you guys have," Matt said, sipping from a paper cup, his dark eyes blazing above the rim. "And don't keep anything back. I'm not buying into anything being top secret or any other mumbo-jumbo. I want the facts about my sister."

Kelly had nothing to hide. She took a sip of her coffee and

leaned her elbows on the table, so that she was closer to this middle McCafferty brother and could keep her voice at a lower level. "I'll tell you what I can, but I'm not going to compromise the investigation."

"I'm *family,* for Pete's sake."

"But they're not." Lifting an eyebrow, she scanned the tables, noting that a few nurses sat at one, at another, doctors in scrubs, and at a third, a few people were drinking from cups while others milled nearby. Jana Madrid, the pushy reporter who had pushed her way onto the floor housing the ICU, was among them.

"The press." Matt scowled darkly.

"Some of them. Who else would be up at this hour?"

"Hell."

"So let's just talk in general terms."

"Shoot."

"As I said, we're investigating the possibility that your sister might have been run off the road, and we're checking any vehicles that might have needed body work after the time of the accident, specifically maroon Fords. We've narrowed that down to probably an Explorer. Also, we're checking on the people she worked with and the men she dated...." Kelly let her voice drift off as one of the men near the table of reporters, a thin man with sandy hair, a clipped mustache and an affable smile wended his way through the empty tables in their direction. Not far behind was the petite newswoman.

"Excuse me," the man said, flashing a brilliant smile. "I'm Troy White with KAB—"

"I've seen you on television," Kelly said, cutting the reporter off. "I've already said 'No comment' to one of your associates." She pointed toward Jana Madrid, and the woman took it as a cue to step forward. Inwardly groaning, Kelly leveled her censorious gaze at Troy.

"I'd just like a few words with Mr. McCafferty. You're Matt, right?"

Matt glared at him as if he could see right through the man. "Yep."

"If you don't mind."

"I do." Matt's expression was hard as granite.

"But it'll only take a few seconds." This from Jana, who despite her brashness stood a step behind Troy as if the small man were some kind of shield. Doctors, nurses and the woman behind the cafeteria counter all stopped to watch.

"Another time," Matt said, standing and towering over the shorter man by three or four inches. He was spoiling for a fight, if ever anyone was. His shoulders were bunched, his right hand clenched into a fist, his nostrils flared.

The reporter either didn't pick up on Matt's mood, or didn't give a damn. "Just tell me about Randi. Do you have any idea who would attack your sister?"

"That's it!" Kelly shot to her feet. "Maybe you weren't listening, but Mr. McCafferty here said he didn't want to be bothered, so maybe you'd better wait for your interview until it's more convenient for him." Kelly wedged her angry body between the reporter and Matt and glowered at both reporters, then allowed her gaze to skate across the room to include the cameraman hanging out near the coffeemaker. "Now, if you people aren't careful, I'll personally escort you out of here."

Troy White took offense. His mustache shivered. "Listen, lady, the American people have the right to know—"

"Stuff it, Troy," Kelly said, cutting him off. "I already heard the spiel from Jana here." She glanced at the woman next to him. "Both of you will have to wait for a statement."

Jana's lips pinched. "Let it go," she said, touching Troy's sleeve, though her eyes were fastened to Matt. Despite her professionalism, Kelly felt an unlikely spurt of jealousy squirt through her veins. The woman was pretty, proud and predatory. "We've got enough tape for the morning news," Jana said, and managed a smile that seemed to be trained only on Matt. "Thank you for your trouble."

Troy White somehow managed to grit his teeth and give Kelly and Matt a quick cursory nod. "Another time."

"Call first," Matt warned. He strode out the doors and Kelly caught up with him near the reception area. He slid her a glance as he kept walking. "Look, Detective, I don't need anyone to fight my battles." He glanced down at her small frame. "Especially not a woman."

"I'm a cop," she reminded him as they reached the elevators.

"A female cop."

Stung, she slapped the call button. "But a cop just the same. I can handle myself," she asserted, angry with herself for letting his remarks get under her skin. He was so damned unsettling and his opinion mattered way more than it should.

"I don't remember asking for your help."

The nerve of the man. Of all the pompous, self-serving… Simmering, she turned on him, ready for a fight. "I was just doing my job, okay? I didn't mean to step on your fragile male ego if that's what you're insinuating."

He grabbed her arm. "Nothing about me is fragile." Her heart leaped and blood pounded in her ears as she stared into a face raw with emotion.

The doors to the elevator slid open. Nicole Stevenson nearly collided with them. "Oh! Matt?" She stopped on the tracking and the doors started to close only to open again. The bell chimed. Her surprised gaze moved from the middle Mc-

Cafferty brother's eyes to Kelly's before she glanced down at
Matt's fingers, wrapped so tightly over Kelly's arm.

"Vulture alert," Matt said, dropping Kelly's elbow as if it
were hot. "The press."

"They just don't let up," Nicole muttered. She frowned at
Kelly. "Maybe that's something you should handle."

"I have."

"Just like you and your department handled Randi's safety?"
she asked, then, as if hearing herself, sighed and stepped back
into the elevator car. "Sorry," she said, leaning her shoulders
against the back wall of the elevator. She shoved stiff fingers
through her hair, pushing the locks off her forehead. "That
was uncalled-for." Matt pushed the button to the third floor.
"I'm just worried sick," Nicole admitted. "Not only for Randi,
but for Thorne as well."

"He'll be fine. Tough as nails," Matt said, and offered her
an encouraging smile, hinting at a softer, kinder man beneath
his cowboy-thick skin. There was definitely more to the man
than met the eye, more than he wanted most people to see.
More than Kelly wanted to glimpse. The last thing she needed
was to start softening to any member of the McCafferty family. Especially this man who sent her pulse skyrocketing for
no tangible reason.

"I hope he'll be okay," Nicole whispered.

The rest of the ride was tense silence. On the third floor
Slade was still standing, one shoulder propped against the wall
near the doors to the ICU. A self-imposed security guard.
"Your boss is looking for you," he said to Kelly. There wasn't
a bit of warmth in his laser-blue eyes; he was as cold to her as
the McCaffertys had always been.

"Espinoza?"

"Yeah. He's up on the fourth floor."

"Thanks." Kelly noted that the policewoman was still hanging around. Espinoza was leaving nothing to chance. "I'll need to talk to all of you again."

"You know where to find us," Matt said, and she felt his gaze drilling into her back as she hurried to the stairwell. Inhaling deeply, she forced him from her mind. She couldn't, wouldn't think of him as anything more than the brother of a victim...nothing more.

Jaw set, she took the stairs two at a time. Whether anyone in the McCafferty household believed it or not, she was determined to unearth the slime who had run Randi McCafferty off the road and, when that hadn't killed her, had found the guts to walk into a hospital and try to finish the job. Not that murdering a comatose victim took much bravery.

Kelly couldn't wait to nail the bastard.

Because she wanted to solve the crime, because she wanted to insure Randi's safety and because, damn it, she wanted to prove herself to Matt McCafferty.

Chapter 4

"So the police have nothing," Thorne said the next morning while huddled over a cup of coffee, his broken leg propped on another chair at the scarred kitchen table, the same table where they'd prayed, eaten and fought as kids. The maple surface was nicked and half the original chairs had been replaced, but the biggest change was that John Randall no longer took his seat at the head of the table near the window, where he could rest his elbow on the ledge, sip coffee and stare out at the vast acres of the ranch he loved.

Not that Matt cared. But, in a way, it seemed odd that the old man was missing. "I think the police don't have a clue as to who's behind the attacks."

"Hell." Storm clouds gathered in Thorne's gray eyes and Matt knew that his older brother was silently cussing his broken leg for keeping him housebound. Thorne couldn't stand being cooped up. A control freak from the get-go, he needed to be in charge, to make decisions, to be able to be on the front lines. "Has anyone heard from Striker?" he grumbled.

"Not for a couple of days." Matt stretched one arm over his head and yawned. He'd spent a restless night, tossed and turned, his mind spinning in endless circles of concern for his sister, her baby, and with disturbing thoughts about a certain red-haired cop, the one who seemed determined to infiltrate his dreams and keep him awake at night. He'd woken up this morning and beelined for the shower, turning on the cold stinging spray to chase any remaining thoughts of her from his mind…and body. Why he was attracted to Kelly Dillinger, he couldn't imagine. She was a policewoman, for crying out loud. Not exactly his type.

As Matt drained his cup, Juanita bustled through the back door. A blast of cold air swept through the room and Harold found his way to his favorite spot on the braided rug under the table. Absently Matt leaned over to scratch the old dog behind his ears.

"*Dios,* it's cold out there. *Frío.*"

"That it is, Juanita," Matt agreed, as he'd already trudged to the barn and stables to feed the stock, then checked the troughs, making certain they hadn't iced over. He'd called Mike Kavanaugh, his neighbor, this morning and learned that his own place on the Idaho border was still standing. Mike was making noise about buying it again, but Matt resisted. He'd fought too hard and long to own a ranch of his own and his stay here at the Flying M was temporary. Just until things calmed down, Thorne was back on his feet again and Randi was out of the woods. Then he'd leave Grand Hope and any lingering fascination he had with Kelly Dillinger behind him.

"You mentioned that Randi was writing a book," Thorne

said as Juanita unwrapped herself from several layers of coats and sweaters.

"*Sí.*" She hung her wraps on hooks near the back door and fussed with her hair, tucking a few wayward strands from the braid she pinned to the base of her neck.

"You saw it?"

"No."

"But you think it existed?" Another dead end in Matt's estimation. He stood and refilled his coffee cup from the glass pot warming on the coffeemaker.

"She said it did. The last time she was here." Juanita poured herself a cup of coffee, took one long gulp, placed her mug on the counter and started searching through the pantry. Her voice was muted as she said, "Señorita Randi, she worked on it for hours, sitting on the couch in the living room."

Thorne's eyes met Matt's as he lounged against the counter by the coffeepot. "So where is it? Her laptop computer?"

From the depths of the pantry, Juanita snorted. "How would I know?"

"Maybe Kurt'll find it," Matt said to his brother.

"If he's as good as Slade says he is," Thorne scoffed as Juanita reappeared, paused to take another swallow of coffee, then slid into an apron and tied it around her waist.

"He figured out another vehicle was involved in Randi's accident before the police did," Matt pointed out. "My money's on him."

Juanita was starting to bang some pans on the stove and the sounds of tiny scurrying feet approached. Thorne's harsh expression melted as the twins raced into the room, their footed pajamas sliding on the worn floor.

"I wondered when you two would wake up," he said with a chuckle.

"The baby was crying!" Molly wrinkled her nose and put her hands over her ears.

Mindy, who had crawled onto Thorne's lap, copied her sister, placing her chubby palms to the sides of her head and making a face as if she'd tasted something disgusting. "He cried and cried."

At that moment Nicole walked into the kitchen carrying little J.R. Her eyelids were still heavy, her normally crisp steps dragging. "We're up," she said around a yawn. "Whether we want to be or not." She was dressed in a fluffy white robe and pink scuffs, her hair mussed, her face devoid of makeup, but she radiated a quiet beauty that came from deep inside. And Thorne was captivated. Never in a million years would Matt have thought his older brother—a harsh, determined businessman hell-bent to make his next million—ever capable of falling in love and settling down, but this lady doc with her twin scamps had captured his heart.

"I'll take the baby," Thorne offered, and she shook her head and smiled.

"You've got your hands full already." She motioned toward the twins, both of whom decided they wanted to climb onto Thorne's lap.

"Here, sit down. Have a cup of coffee. I'll take over," Matt said, standing and reaching for the tiny bundle that was his nephew. Bright eyes stared up at him. "Don't panic," he ordered the little one. "No matter how clumsy I appear, it's just an act. I'm really a complete and utter idiot when it comes to taking care of a baby."

"You certainly instill confidence," Nicole observed as she poured herself a cup of coffee from the glass carafe. "Hey, girls, what do you say to pancakes?"

"With blueberries and syrup?" Molly asked.

"Well...syrup for sure. I don't know if we have any berries."

"In the freezer. I'll get some," Juanita said as she wiped her hands and walked into a small alcove by the pantry.

"You want the same?" Nicole asked her other daughter.

Mindy nodded vigorously. "Yeth."

"Easy deal," Thorne said, and Matt wondered about Thorne and his built-in family. It appeared to work. He was nuts for those kids and crazy about Nicole, acting as if she was the only woman on this entire planet for him.

Matt had trouble swallowing it. For years Thorne had dodged marriage, though many a beautiful and smart woman had set her matrimonial sights on him. But he'd never been interested and certainly hadn't committed. Until Nicole. And then all bets had been off.

Matt settled into a chair. He couldn't blame Thorne. Nicole was beautiful, smart, ambitious and a helluva mother. A catch.

Without preamble Kelly Dillinger's image sparked unexpectedly through Matt's mind. She, too, was beautiful...well, he supposed she would be if she ever shed her uniform and cop attitude, and she was smart as a whip, could handle herself in most situations, suffered no fools and, even in uniform, was sexy as hell. Too bad she lived here, so far from his ranch on the western Montana border, he thought, then caught himself up short. What the hell was he thinking? He wasn't even close to settling down, and certainly not with a woman—a cop—who lived hundreds of miles away from his home.

"So is that the consensus?" Nicole asked, searching the faces around the table. "Pancakes?"

Thorne nodded. "And bacon, eggs—"

"Cholesterol, fat..."

"Exactly." Thorne winked and Nicole laughed, a deep husky laugh.

"Well, okay. I know a great heart surgeon just in case we have a problem."

"Load me up!" Thorne said as the twins scrambled out of his lap. For the first time in his life Matt felt a touch of envy. What Thorne shared with Nicole was deep. True. With the kind of bond Matt hadn't believe existed. His father and mother, Larissa, had split up when Penelope had come into the picture. John Randall had married the younger woman, becoming a father again within six months of the wedding date, and that union, too, had crumbled, unable to stand the test of time.

Restless, Matt watched as his brother hobbled into the kitchen, gave Nicole a playful swat on her rump, then actually helped make breakfast around Juanita's sharp protests.

The self-made millionaire and CEO, playboy in his own right, was flipping flapjacks as if he'd done it all his life. Matt's gaze caught Juanita's and he saw that she was just as surprised as he. She didn't say it, but the words *will wonders never cease* came to mind as surely as if the housekeeper had sent them via mental telepathy.

Holding the baby and letting his cup of coffee grow cold, Matt stared through the window where ice had collected and snow gathered in the corners of the panes. What about his own life? He'd never considered marriage, had thought it all a waste of time, and children, well, there was plenty of time before he needed to become a father. And when he did, he'd find a homebody, not a career woman, someone who would want to live on his ranch, someone who cared as much for the land as he did, a woman who would want to share his life the way he wanted to live it. But that was someday. Not today. He just wasn't ready for a family.

He glanced down at the baby snuggled in his arms and for the first time second-guessed himself.

Maybe he'd been wrong.

"I think it was one of the brothers," Karla asserted as she worked on her last client of the day. Standing in the first station of her small salon, she swiped the strands of Nancy Pederson's hair with a small brush dipped into a red color, then wrapped the lock in foil until Nancy's head looked like it could pick up radio signals from Pluto.

Nancy, while twisting her head this way and that to accommodate Karla's ministrations, was doing a crossword puzzle. The pounding beat of a Shania Twain song underscored the sound of Karla's popping gum and conversation. Plants grew in profusion near the windows at the front of the shop, and on an antique armoire painted salmon-pink, bottles of shampoo and conditioner were displayed. The faint odors of a recently developed perm mixed with traces of perfume. The counters were a deep purple, the walls brown, and head shots of celebrities adorned the area around each individual station. Karla had been a beautician for ten years. She'd owned this shop for two.

"You think one of the McCafferty brothers tried to kill his sister?" Kelly said as she leaned against the manicurist's table and stared at the bottles of polish.

"One of them, two of them, maybe all three." Karla glanced into the mirror and met Kelly's dubious gaze.

"A conspiracy, I see." Kelly couldn't keep the sarcasm from her voice.

"Don't mock me." Karla waved a rattail comb at her sister. "Those brothers never liked Randi, and don't let them tell you any different. She was the reason their father divorced their mom and married Penelope. And then he left each of his sons one sixth of his ranch, a measly *sixth,* while she got half. Is that fair?" Karla rolled her expressive eyes and sectioned off another lock of Nancy's wet mane.

"Then why are they so adamant that I locate the killer?" Kelly asked as the song faded and a country deejay gave a weather report.

"To throw you off track, of course. Jeez, Kelly, don't be so dense. You're a detective, for crying out loud. The McCaffertys need to *pretend* that they're concerned for Randi or how would it look?"

"I'm not buying it." Kelly fingered a bottle of Pink Seduction nail polish and shook her head.

"Hey, I'm just telling you what I think, and I'm not the only one. I've had three clients sitting in this very chair and Donna's had four." Karla pointed toward the second station where Donna Mills, pregnant with twins, was sweeping up snippets of blond curls from the floor around her chair.

"That's right," Donna said with a smile.

"Everyone's talking about the attempt on Randi's life. I mean, the attempts. *Plural,*" Karla continued, managing to hold up two condemning fingers before she picked up another tiny piece of aluminum foil. "I even overheard a couple arguing about it at Montana Joe's when I was picking up a pizza for lunch. They were standing in line and started to argue over which one of the brothers actually did the deed."

"That's ridiculous."

"Maybe. Maybe not. Alexis Bonnifant, she grew up with Slade. I gave her a perm not two hours ago. The way she tells it, he hated Randi. They're in it together, I tell you, just so they can provide one another with alibis!"

"I doubt if they'd want to kill their sister."

"Murder's been committed for a lot less than half a Montana spread."

"Amen," Nancy added, looking up from her puzzle for just a second. "Who else would want Randi dead?"

Who else indeed, Kelly thought as she left a few minutes later. She'd just dropped by the Bob and Weave to offer to watch her sister's kids if Karla needed a night out, but she figured it didn't hurt to listen to gossip and see what the townspeople thought of the case. So far the odds were stacked against the McCafferty brothers.

She walked three blocks to the Pub'n'Grub and ordered a sandwich and bag of chips to go from a kid she'd sent to juvenile court on more than one occasion. He gave her correct change, but avoided eye contact as he placed the order in a computer. As she waited she stood on one side of a brick planter and couldn't help overhearing conversation from a booth on the other side of the silk philodendrons and ferns.

Over Reuben sandwiches and clam chowder two women were deep in conversation about the biggest news to hit Grand Hope since the mayor's wife had run off with one of the city councilmen.

"Always out for themselves, those McCafferty boys. Chips off the old block, if you ask me," Roberta Fletcher said, nodding her head emphatically, her earrings catching in the shivering fluorescent lighting overhead.

"Never got along with their stepmother or little sister. Never tried. Blamed them for their parents' divorce and well...you know, their mother had her share of problems. The drinking, you know. Probably all started when she was married to John Randall. I would've drunk, too, if that son of a gun was my husband." Kelly didn't know the other woman by name, but thought she was married to one of the insurance men in town…she also helped out with the local rodeo association.

"And what if he was your father?" Roberta clucked her tongue as she reached for her cola. "Poor girl—grew up with all those hellions, and now look. It's a shame, I tell you. When I think about that baby, with no father, at least none that we know of, his mother in a coma, three bachelors trying to raise him… Someone should call Child Services."

"If one of the brothers is a killer."

"Hard to believe, but stranger things have happened. The poor baby. He's the cutest little guy you've ever seen, I've heard," Roberta added. "My daughter's a friend of Jenny Riley's. Jenny, she looks after the baby and the Stevenson twins when Nicole's working, you know. Jenny says little J.R. is the most adorable baby in the world."

"Well the McCaffertys always were a good-looking lot. Every last one of 'em."

"Too handsome for their own good." Roberta swirled her straw in her cola. "It's always been a problem."

"But you'd think that baby's father would step forward." Roberta's friend rolled expressive eyes as she bit into her sandwich.

"Maybe the father doesn't know about the little tyke."

"Why wouldn't she tell him?" Roberta asked.

"Maybe they weren't together."

"Or maybe she doesn't know who the father is." Roberta cackled nastily, and the other woman hadn't commented on the gossip. Kelly had tried to turn a deaf ear as she waited for her order.

Later, back at the office, Kelly picked at her sandwich while she cruised through the notes she'd entered into her computer files. Dozens of questions burned through her brain. Who wanted to kill Randi? Why? Because of the baby? Because of her work? A love affair gone wrong? Did she owe someone money? Did someone take offense to her column? Who were her enemies? Her friends?

She studied the list of people who knew Randi—co-workers in Seattle, people she'd grown up with and gone to school with around Grand Hope, people she'd dated or befriended throughout her life. Nothing made any sense. Randi McCafferty had been a tomboy, probably because of her older half brothers. She'd been adored by her father and mother, a "princess" who had managed not to become too spoiled. She'd graduated from high school here in Grand Hope, gone to college at Montana State and eventually become a journalist. She'd worked on her father's ranch as well as having a part-time job at the *Grand Hope Gazette* while in high school, and eventually, after a series of jobs, she ended up in Seattle, where she'd landed the job with the *Clarion*. Her column had become syndicated, picked up by a few other papers, and she'd done some freelance work.

Then she'd had the accident.

Kelly bit into the pickle that came with her ham and cheese and scanned her notes again. Juanita Ramirez, the housekeeper and the one person who seemed to have kept in contact with Randi in the past few months, claimed Randi was writing a book, that the reason that she was returning to the ranch was to finish the book—wherever the blazes it was. If it existed. Juanita, for all her communication with Randi, hadn't known she was pregnant. So maybe she'd gotten the book thing wrong as well.

If only Randi McCafferty would wake up.

Before the killer tried to strike again.

Kelly tossed her hair over her shoulder and scowled at her

computer screen. There wasn't anything new. Even the recent lab reports hadn't helped much. The hospital room where Randi was attacked had heretofore given up no clues as to the identity of the person who had sneaked into her room and slipped a deadly dose of insulin into her IV. Interviews with everyone on duty had provided no new information and no one had witnessed anything suspicious aside from Nicole Stevenson's claim that she'd seen someone—man or woman— she didn't recognize near Randi's private room. According to hospital records and the pharmacy on the first floor, no insulin was missing from the locked cabinets, but records could be falsified and someone could have had enough in a vial hidden deep in a pocket.

Not much to go on. Not much at all. Kelly wadded up the uneaten portion of her sandwich in the sack from the Pub'n'Grub and tossed it into the wastebasket in frustration. "We'll get you," she promised, as if the perpetrator was in her office and could hear her. "And it's gonna be soon. Real soon."

She spent a few hours in the office returning phone calls and catching up on paperwork, then decided to finish the interview she'd tried to start with Matt McCafferty in the cafeteria the night before.

He wouldn't be happy to see her, as she didn't have any more information on the case, but that was just too bad.

She threw on her jacket and grabbed her gloves. What was it about that guy that got to her? Sure he was handsome in that cowboy, rough-and-tumble way that so many women found irresistible, and yes, he had a certain charm, but she'd met tons of charming cowboys over the course of her life and she'd never felt this attraction—and that's what it was—before.

Maybe she was just another silly woman who couldn't resist one of the McCafferty brothers, still the most eligible bachelors in the county. "Oh, give me a break," she mumbled to herself as she buttoned her jacket, yanked on her gloves and walked outside to the parking lot where her car was parked.

Don't do it, Kelly. Don't fall for him. He's the worst possible choice. She pulled out of the lot and eased into the sluggish traffic. What was she even thinking? She wouldn't fall for a McCafferty; she wouldn't fall for anyone.

Cautious by nature, she'd always protected her heart. She didn't trust easily and she had only to look at Karla's failed marriages and twice-broken heart to keep a rein on her emotions. No man, especially a McCafferty, was worth the heartache. But the image of Matt, tall, broad-shouldered, chiseled features, beard-darkened jaw, came to mind. She envisioned him in the saddle upon a racing horse, moving easily with the animal, looking for all the world as if he belonged astride a stallion galloping hell-bent-for-leather. Her mouth went dry at the image and she glanced in the rearview mirror. "You're a fool, Dillinger," she growled, disturbed, as she trained her attention to the road again.

She drove north, through the outskirts of town where pumpkins and cornstalks, leftovers from Halloween or precursors of Thanksgiving, adorned some of the porches. Eventually the houses gave way to wide, snow-covered fields.

The McCafferty ranch was located twenty miles out of town, and Kelly fought the weather all of the way. Snow swirled from the heavens, blowing across the highway and melting on her windshield as she squinted against the few oncoming headlights heading toward town. The sky was dark, the hills invisible, the wintry night cold enough to chill the bones.

She listened to the police radio, though she was officially off duty, and reminded herself that Matt McCafferty was only the brother of a crime victim. Nothing more. Her fingers shouldn't be sweating at the thought of him, her pulse should return to its normal, steady rate. She shouldn't be feeling one drip of anticipation.

And yet she did. Oh, Lord, she did. Even her stupid stomach knotted, and she imagined what it would be like to feel his arms around her, his anxious lips on hers…and…she shifted down before her wayward thoughts could take her into forbidden territory.

Eventually, thank God, she reached the turnoff.

So this is the Flying M, she thought as she wheeled into the snow-covered lane. She'd driven past it a million times, of course, but had never once turned down the twin ruts leading to the heart of the ranch. Until now. A few hardy dry weeds poked through the snow to scrape the undercarriage of her car, and she passed fields where cattle huddled against the wind and snow.

The lane widened to a large lot and a series of paddocks around a barn, stables and several other sheds. On a rise, the ranch house overlooked it all. Tall and rambling with weathered siding and windows glowing bright against the wintry night.

Kelly parked near a few other vehicles, flipped up the hood of her jacket and braved the elements, hunching her shoulders against the wind as she dashed to the front porch and climbed the steps. Stomping the snow from her boots, she rang the bell and the door swung open immediately.

"Detective Dillinger," Matt McCafferty drawled, his dark eyes silently appraising. Dressed in faded jeans and a denim work shirt tossed over a navy T-shirt, he stood in stocking feet. Some of the animosity had disappeared from his expression and a dark stubble covered his jaw. He was, without a doubt, sexy as hell.

And she was far from immune. Her heart was racing, her knees unsteady.

He swung the door open and stepped to one side. "Come in."

Suddenly she felt as if she'd just been invited into a viper's lair.

She cleared her throat. "I wanted to talk to you, ask a few more questions."

"Well, isn't that a coincidence?" His brown eyes held hers. "As it just so happens, I've got some for you."

Chapter 5

"*You* have questions?" Standing toe-to-toe with him on the porch, she lifted an eyebrow, encouraging him while trying to ignore his innate sexuality. "Shoot."

"Obviously you haven't found the person who tried to kill Randi."

"We're still working on it."

"Put more men and women on the job." His gaze intensified, left Kelly a little breathless.

She forged on. "It's not the only case we have, you know."

"Yeah, but someone bull-bustin' through a neighbor's fence, or…kids using mailboxes as target practice aren't quite in the same league, now, are they?"

"Trust me," she assured him, though she sounded more forceful than she felt beneath his assessing glare, "the attempt on your sister's life is top priority."

He stepped out of the way and threw the door to the ranch house open a little wider. "It had better be."

Kelly didn't respond, just scraped her boots on the porch mat, then walked inside. She turned her attention away from the cowboy and inspected the place where he'd grown up, the house Randi McCafferty had called home.

Inside, the old ranch house was warm, and despite its size, had a cozy feel. Soft golden light splashed upon pine-paneled walls and plank floors that had withstood three generations of McCaffertys. A faded runner covered stairs that wound upward from the entryway, and the aromas of burning wood, roasting pork and ginger tinged the air. From the floor above high-pitched giggles erupted. Young voices. Girls. Nicole's twins, Kelly deduced.

"Is there somewhere we could talk?" she asked as she unbuttoned her coat. He helped her remove it, the tips of his fingers brushing the back of her neck. She tried not to notice, it wasn't much contact, but still she felt an unwanted tingle as he hung her jacket on the hook near the door.

"This way." He led her around a corner to a living room where Thorne McCafferty, one leg bound in a cast and elevated on the extension of his recliner, was talking with a tall, blond man who hadn't bothered to take off his jacket and was holding his hat in one hand. "Larry Todd, Detective Dillinger," Matt introduced. "Larry's the foreman here and Detective Dillinger is with the sheriff's department, trying to find out who attempted to kill Randi."

"Any luck?" Larry asked.

"Not enough," she admitted, noticing a cheery fire burning in the grate of a river-rock fireplace. Mounted above a mantel strewn with framed photos was an expansive set of antlers holding an antique rifle. An upright piano filled one wall while worn chairs, tables and the leather couch surrounded a braided rug.

"Get the son of a bitch." Thorne was struggling to get to his feet.

Kelly held up a hand, indicating that he shouldn't bother standing. "We will."

"Make it soon," Matt persisted, and her back went up a bit.

"That's why I'm here. As I said, I'd like to ask you a few more questions. You, too," she added, motioning to Thorne.

"Well, it looks like you've got some business to take care of, so I'd better shove off." Larry hitched his pants up. "Think about trading some of the yearlings for Lyle Anderson's brood-mares. I think it would really improve the herd."

Thorne glanced at Matt.

Matt nodded. "I'm in favor of introducing new bloodlines in the stock."

"Then do it," Thorne said to the foreman. "I'll go along with whatever you and Matt decide."

"Done." Larry started for the door.

"Wait a minute, Mr. Todd," Kelly interjected. "Since you're here maybe you could give me some insight." She reached into her pocket and found a small notepad. While Thorne pushed himself out of the chair and braced himself with a crutch and Matt folded his arms over his chest, she said, "A couple of weeks before her accident, Randi McCafferty let you go, isn't that right?"

The big man flushed. His lips flattened over his teeth. He rubbed the back of his neck nervously. "Yep. That's just about how it happened," Larry admitted, not bothering to hide his irritation. "And it pissed me off royally. I'd been running this place ever since her father died and all of a sudden, out of the damned blue, she calls me and says she doesn't need me anymore."

"Did she give a reason?"

He shook his head. "Nope. I'd always gotten along with her and the last I'd heard she was satisfied with my job—liked having me look over things. I guess she changed her mind," he added, frowning slightly. "She didn't bother to explain, but I had the feeling that she was moving back here and that she had someone else in mind to run the spread. She didn't say so, but it was just the way she handled the conversation. She was nice enough, I suppose," he added, glancing at the brothers. "Even paid me for an extra three months, which was supposed to be my severance package, then she thanked me and basically showed me the door. And that was that. Years of work, down the drain. I was pretty mad about the whole thing, but figured there wasn't much I could do about it. She was the boss as she owned half this ranch."

"But she didn't ask any of her partners before letting you go," Kelly clarified.

"Not that I know of."

"None of us heard a word," Matt said. He grabbed a poker from the blackened tool set on the hearth and jabbed at the logs in the fire. Flames crackled and embers spit sparks. "Since Dad died, Randi was in charge. She's always been pretty independent."

"To a fault," Thorne grumbled.

"And since each of us—Slade, Thorne and I—only owned a sixth of the spread apiece, we let her do her thing. We— well, at least I figured if she needed my help, she'd ask for it." Matt's mouth tightened and he seemed a bit ashamed as he tossed a chunk of mossy oak onto the old andirons. "To tell you the truth, I thought she'd give it all up after one winter of ranching. Even though she was in Seattle, working at the newspaper, she was responsible for what went on here. I figured she'd want to sell out."

"To you?" Kelly asked.

"To whoever would buy, but yeah, I thought she'd come to either me or one of my brothers." He let out a disgusted breath. "Guess I was wrong."

Larry's anger had dissipated. "It's a helluva thing," he said, his lips folding in on themselves. "She fires me, then within two weeks ends up having a baby and fighting for her life."

"And you took your old job back."

"The brothers asked me." His green eyes narrowed a bit. "It took a little persuadin', let me tell you. I don't like bein' let go."

"I understand. Did you ask her who would be handling the place after you left?" Kelly asked. "This is a pretty big ranch, and since she didn't live here, how did she expect to keep things running smoothly?"

"Good question. One I didn't ask. Guess I was too hot under the collar." He took a step closer to Kelly and a shadow of concern darkened his gaze. "You know, I have this feeling… and it's nothing she said, mind you…but just a sense that she wanted to just hole up and be alone. She didn't fire the hands, just me, so maybe she thought she could run the place herself, but—" he hesitated as he squared his hat upon his head "—I guess we won't know until she wakes up."

"Hell's bells," Thorne grumbled as he reached for a single crutch tucked to the side of his recliner.

Larry checked his watch. "I'd better get home."

"If you think of anything else she may have said, call me." Kelly slipped her wallet from her jacket pocket and handed him a card.

"Will do." Larry nodded curtly, then swept his gaze to Thorne and Matt. "I'll see you in the morning." Within seconds the door was slamming shut behind him.

"I don't suppose either of you can shed any further light

on why your sister fired him?" Kelly asked, hitching her chin toward the window. Through the icy glass she watched Larry climb into a king-cab pickup. The sound of an engine rumbling to life reached her ears just as the truck's headlamps blazed through the swirling snow.

"Neither of us had talked to Randi in a while," Matt admitted, and Thorne scowled darkly. Larry Todd's truck tore off, plowing through the drifts.

"What about the father of her baby?"

"We're still trying to locate him—whoever he is. Kurt Striker is looking into it." Thorne hobbled to the fireplace and, bracing his shoulders on the mantel, picked up a photograph of his sister that had been propped against the old bricks. Sighing, Thorne shook his head. "Striker's supposed to be back here tomorrow."

"I'd like to talk to him."

Matt hesitated. "Is that standard procedure?"

Kelly's temper snapped. "Listen, Mr. McCafferty, nothing about this case is standard."

"I thought we established that you could call me Matt."

"Whatever," she said, bristling. "Now, what about her boyfriends?"

"I never met any of the guys she was dating, even if she was…well, obviously there was someone in her life." The lines bracketing his mouth became more pronounced. "But I don't have a clue as to which one of the men she'd been seeing is little J.R.'s father." Matt raked his fingers through his near-black hair and frustration was evident in the tension of his muscles and set of his jaw.

"J.R.'s father might be someone that no one knew about, a man she was seeing on the sly," Thorne said as the fire popped and bright sparks and smoke floated up the chimney.

Matt swore under his breath. "The truth of the matter is we all feel foolish, not knowing this basic stuff about our sister."

"I have several names of people she dated." Kelly flipped through her notes. "Joe Paterno, who worked freelance for the *Seattle Clarion,* Brodie Clanton, a lawyer whose father is a judge, and Sam Donahue, an ex-rodeo rider who ranches outside of Spokane, Washington." She glanced up and noticed the thunder in Matt's stare.

"I don't know the other two guys, but Donahue's a miserable piece of work," he growled, dusting his hands then shoving them into the front pockets of his jeans. "But I still can't believe that Randi was ever involved with him."

"You don't know that she was," Thorne rebutted. From his expression, Kelly guessed he didn't like the idea of Randi and Donahue any better than Matt did. Using the crutch, he hitched his way across the braided carpet to the bookcase. "Kurt Striker is checking blood types, which should help. Even if we can't determine who is the father of Randi's kid, we can rule out those who aren't."

"Exactly. We're working on the same premise," she said as a clatter of footsteps on the stairs caught her attention.

Nicole Stevenson, twin girls tagging behind her, and baby— presumably Randi McCafferty's infant—in her arms, made her way down the stairs.

Gone was the all-business, tough doctor whom Kelly had run up against. In her stead was a smiling mother listening to the little girls babble and giggle as she tended to the baby.

Kelly's heartstrings pulled a bit just as Nicole, who had reached the bottom of the stairs, looked up and caught sight of a policewoman in her home. Her jaw hardened just a fraction before a smile tugged the corners of her mouth upward. "I think I owe you an apology," she admitted, striding into the room. "Last night I was very upset when hospital security had been breached and Randi was attacked. I shouldn't have taken it out on you."

"It was tense for everyone."

"I know, but it wasn't very professional on my part." She was sincere. Kelly decided her apology was heartfelt.

"It's fine. Really." Even though she reminded herself not to be suckered in by anyone in the McCafferty family, Kelly couldn't help but warm to the slim woman with her forthright gold eyes and proud lift of her chin. In other circumstances, Kelly thought, she and Nicole might be friends.

"Thank you."

"This is Randi's baby?"

Matt crossed the room to peek at his nephew. "Yep. He's what all the fuss is about." To Kelly's surprise, Matt plucked the baby out of Nicole's arms. Big, calloused hands drew the infant to his chest, and though he seemed a tad awkward with J.R., Matt smiled down at the boy. "If only he could talk."

Or his mother could, Kelly thought, amazed at the transformation in both McCafferty brothers. Matt was ranch-tough and no-nonsense, but his leathery touch-me-not exterior softened as he gazed down at his nephew. Thorne, with the use of a crutch, had crossed the room and stood by Nicole, his free arm slung over her shoulder, the edgy, hard-as-nails corporate executive evaporating into a proud, caring husband-to-be. He ruffled one twin's crown with his free hand while the other twin, a shier girl, hid behind his cast. For the briefest of seconds, Kelly felt an emotion akin to envy for this tightly knit family.

Nicole's gaze moved from Thorne to Matt. "Hasn't either of these gentlemen, and boy, do I use the term loosely, offered you anything? Coffee...tea...a glass of wine?"

"I'm fine, really."

"I wants a drink," one of the girls said, tugging on her mother's blouse. "I wants a drink."

"In a minute, Molly. Now—" she eyed the men speculatively "—which uncle is on J.R. duty?" Nicole asked. "The baby could use a bottle, and then, no doubt, he'll need to be changed. Uncle Thorne? Uncle Matt?" From Matt's arms the baby let out a soft little coo that had the amazing effect of pulling on Kelly's heartstrings.

"I think it's my turn," Thorne grumbled good-naturedly, reaching for the child as Matt handed the baby to him. "But you'd better carry him into the kitchen and get me settled in with a bottle."

"I do it!" One of the curly-haired girls, Molly, Kelly guessed, volunteered, then she dashed down the hall.

"Me, too." Her sister raced after her, tiny feet pounding on the hardwood floor. Two bright-eyed dynamos.

"I think I'd better supervise. I'll meet you in the kitchen," Nicole said to Thorne as she took the baby from his arms and started out of the living room, only to pause midstep. "Oh, but one last thing." She was looking at Kelly. "Has it been proved that something was slipped into Randi's IV? I haven't been back at the hospital since last night."

"Insulin," Kelly supplied. "It can kill if the victim overdoses. Remember the Sunny von Bulow case? Where her husband was accused of trying to kill her by injecting her with insulin?"

"He got off, right?" Matt asked.

Kelly nodded. "But his wife remained in a coma. Alive, but hospitalized. Nearly dead. For years."

"Damn."

Nicole frowned and sighed. "I suspected as much. From the symptoms. Any ideas who could have done it?"

"Not yet," Kelly admitted.

"Well, do me a favor, will you?" she asked. "Nail the bastard who did this."

"We will," Kelly said fervently.

There was a crash and a wail at the far end of the hall and Nicole, still carrying the baby, took off toward the sound. Thorne was on her heels, hurrying after her on one crutch.

"*Dios, niña!* Look what you've done," a husky woman's voice cajoled, then muttered a Spanish phrase Kelly didn't understand.

Within seconds there was the sound of sobbing from one small girl and a series of denials from the other. "I didn't do it!" one of the twins cried.

"Did, too," the other responded.

One side of Matt's mouth lifted as he listened to the exchange from the living room. "Never a dull minute around here, I'm afraid."

"It seems that way."

Nicole, now carrying one of the twins, winked at Kelly and Matt as she reached the bottom of the stairs. The little girl had her head burrowed in her mother's shoulder and wouldn't look up, just sobbed as if her heart was breaking. "Good thing I'm an emergency room doc," Nicole confided, swallowing a smile as she toted her daughter upstairs. "Mindy might need major surgery."

The girl, aware that her mother was teasing, buried her tear-streaked face in Nicole's neck even further and muttered, "No."

"Is she okay?"

Nicole nodded. "Fingers got smashed when the sugar jar broke. I'm not sure how it happened—"

"Molly did it!" the girl insisted, finally lifting her head in self-righteous indignation. She sniffed loudly and her lower lip quivered. "She pushed my chair."

"Did not," the other twin denied as she streaked from the kitchen to proclaim her innocence. "You falled."

"I think Mindy will live," Nicole said as she turned at the landing and disappeared up the remaining stairs.

"You falled, you falled, you falled," Molly chimed, clambering up the remaining stairs.

"Damned three-ring circus," Matt grumbled as he checked his watch. "Look, I've got to check the broodmares." He slid her a glance that was unreadable. "You have any more questions?"

"A few."

"Then come along." He walked through the foyer, snagged a jacket and hat from a tarnished brass coatrack, then continued toward the back of the house through a hallway adorned with pictures of the McCafferty family at different stages in their lives—Thorne in a football uniform, Slade tearing down a mountain on skis, Randi in a long dress with her arm linked through that of a tuxedoed beau, and Matt astride a rodeo bronc. The buckskin horse, front feet planted firmly in the sod of an arena, head ducked, back legs shooting skyward, had been frozen in time trying to throw his rider—a lean, hard-muscled cowboy who seemed as determined to stay on as the stallion was to send him skyrocketing. Matt's right hand was lifted to the sky, his other buried in the strap surrounding the buckskin's chest.

"Who won?" she asked, motioning toward the glossy eight-by-ten.

"I did."

"Of course."

"Not always, especially when I drew Zanzibar." He motioned toward the picture. "He was a tough one." A nostalgic gleam sparked in his eye and Kelly suspected that he missed the excitement and thrill of the rodeo. From all accounts, though he often wore a wide belt buckle depicting a bucking bronco, Matt had given up the rodeo circuit years ago and contented himself ranching on a spread he owned in the western hills of Montana.

Through an archway, they stepped into a large kitchen where the fragrance of roasting pork and cooling pies tickled her nostrils. A battered butcher-block counter surrounded a stainless steel sink and electric range where pots were simmering, steam rising to the copper bonnet. In a corner, shards of delft-blue pottery and white crystals were gathered together in a dustpan, testament to the accident with the twins. Thorne was seated at the table, the heel of his cast on a nearby chair, the baby in his arms suckling at a bottle and staring up at him.

Matt clucked his tongue as he shrugged into his jacket. "I never thought I'd see the day—"

"Don't say another word," Thorne warned Matt, but there was a twinkle in his gray eyes, as if the millionaire CEO enjoyed his newfound role of temporary father.

"Who's gonna stop me? A man with a broken leg holding a baby?"

"Try me."

"Anytime, man. Anytime."

"Enough!" A hefty, dark-skinned woman with flashing black eyes and a strong chin emerged from the pantry. She placed bags of onions and potatoes on the counter. "You two are like two old...*toros*. Always pawing at the dirt and snorting... *Dios!*" She threw up a hand. Her gaze fastened on Kelly. *"Policia?"*

"Detective Kelly Dillinger, with the sheriff's office," Matt explained. "Our cook, housekeeper and angel of mercy, Juanita Ramirez."

"Angel?" Juanita snorted her disdain, but smothered a smile as she rounded the counter and picked up the dustpan, then shook it into the trash. "You two, you could have taken care of this…" she admonished as she dusted her hands. "So you," she said to Kelly, "you are searching for the person who is behind Randi's trouble?"

"Yes."

"But you have not found him?"

"Not yet."

Juanita sighed heavily, her ponderous breasts heaving at the injustice of the world. "So much trouble for that one. The baby. Her job…and the book." She reached for a knife and began skimming the skins off onions with expert dexterity. "If you ask me, this is about her *libro.*"

"You've read it?" Kelly asked.

"Me?" Juanita glanced up, the knife poised over the onion that oozed juice. "No." Shaking her head, she tossed a pile of thin, paperlike skins into a trash basket.

"But you saw it, know that it existed."

"She talked about it. She was here for a few days and she was on the phone all the time."

"Because of the book?" Kelly asked, trying to follow the older woman's line of reasoning.

"*Sí.* With her…" She snapped her fingers, as her forehead wrinkled in thought. "*Dios,* her…her…*agente.*"

Thorne's head snapped around. "Her agent?" he repeated, his eyes narrowing thoughtfully. "Randi had an agent?"

"*Sí.*"

"Who?" Matt demanded, and Kelly's heartbeat accelerated. Here was a fresh clue, one no one had picked up on before.

"I don't know." Juanita shrugged. "You will have to ask her when she wakes up."

"When was this?" Kelly asked. "How long before the accident?"

"Oh…let me see…the middle of summer, I think," Juanita said, and Kelly scribbled frantically in her notebook. "Yes, not long after Señor John passed on." Deftly, not bothering to drop the knife, she made the sign of the cross over her chest. "She came for a visit."

"And you didn't see that she was pregnant?" Matt asked, unable to hide his incredulity. "She would have been five or six months pregnant."

"No. *Sí*, she was…rounder…heavier…but I thought she had just gained weight."

"Did you see her working on the book?" Kelly asked.

Juanita cut thick slabs of the onion, frowned and blinked against tears that were probably brought on by her task rather than her ragged emotions. "I saw her working on something on her computer. She said it was a book. But no, I did not read any of the pages."

"So we're back to square one," Matt said, sliding his arms through the sleeves of his rawhide jacket in disgust.

Kelly disagreed. Now they had more information to work with. It could very well turn out to be another blind alley, but it was something. She stuffed her notebook into her jacket pocket and followed Matt through the back door and across the porch.

Outside the air was sharp. The wind slapped her face and snow swirled in the dark night. She trudged through the path Matt broke to the stables. He threw open the door and snapped on the lights.

One horse nickered nervously. Another snorted at the intrusion, poking a large head over the top rail of the stall. "How're ya, girl?" Matt asked, and scratched the blaze that ran crookedly up the mare's broad nose. Outside the raw winter wind raged and howled, but in this old building with its ancient siding, hayloft overhead, tack room visible through an open door, the stables felt warm and safe, filled with the scents of horses, oiled leather, dust and straw. Cobwebs hung from the support posts, surrounded the windows and feathered in the corners. Barrels of oats and mash were stacked in an old bin, and pitchforks, shovels and buckets were held by nails pounded into the siding years ago.

"These are the ladies of the Flying M," Matt explained to Kelly as other mares stretched their necks over the gates. "Expectant mothers."

Curious eyes blinked from the heads thrust over the railings. One mare seemed skittish, another jerked away as Kelly approached, but others allowed her to pet their muzzles.

Matt checked feed and water, patted each velvet-soft nose and spoke in low, soft tones as he scratched an ear or patted a sleek shoulder. All the while his eyes moved from one mare to the next.

It was hard to imagine him or any of his brothers as a murderer intent on killing their half sister for her share of the Flying M. No, that was just gossip whispered around the coffee shops and taverns of Grand Hope, nothing more. In Kelly's estimation the harsh talk was far-fetched and probably fueled by jealousy. Despite her own family's run-ins with the McCafferty family, she found it difficult to believe that Thorne, Matt or Slade was a potential murderer.

All of the brothers seemed more than concerned for their sister's well-being. They were clamoring for the police to find Randi's assailant.

And they all doted on the baby.

Now, as she watched Matt's ease with the mares, his strong hands gentle as he patted a shiny neck or scratched beneath a strong equine jaw, she was more certain than ever that someone outside the McCafferty family was behind the attacks on Randi and possibly Thorne.

"So what is it you wanted to ask me?" Matt glanced over one shoulder as he poured oats from a coffee can into the empty mangers.

She climbed onto the top rail of a stall and hooked the heels of her boots on a lower slat while bracing herself with her hands, the way she used to do years ago at her grandmother's farm. "I hoped you could tell me about why your father left half the ranch to your sister."

He slid her a troubled glance she didn't understand.

"Each of his sons got a sixth, but Randi inherited half of it, the half with the house and outbuildings, right? While you boys each got a sixth."

"That's about the size of it. I guess Dad felt he had to take care of Randi, more than he did with the rest of us."

"Because she was a woman?"

"Bingo." His lips thinned.

"Did she know anything about ranching?"

"Not enough."

"So how do you feel about that? I mean, don't you and your brothers resent the fact that she inherited the lion's share?"

He lifted a shoulder and something stirred in his gaze. "She was always Dad's favorite."

"Why?"

"Because she was Penelope's daughter," he said coldly. "He would have gone through hell for that woman, and in the end, she tossed him over. Kinda tit for tat, if ya think about what he did to Mom." His jaw tightened. "But it's all water under the bridge now. Doesn't matter a whole helluva lot."

"So you think John Randall didn't split things equally because of favoritism?"

"Probably, but I can't second-guess my old man. At the time the old man realized he was facing the grim reaper, Thorne was already a millionaire, I had my own place, Slade...well, Slade plays by his own rules, never gave Dad the time of day, and Randi, she had a job in Seattle, yeah, but Dad never approved. Not that it mattered. She did pretty much as she damned well pleased."

"A family trait."

"You noticed." He walked to a ladder built into the side wall and climbed up to the hayloft. Kelly dragged her gaze away from the faded buttocks of his worn jeans as he disappeared through an opening overhead.

Thud!

One bale of hay landed on the floor.

Thud! Thud!

More bales rained from above. Within seconds Matt had swung down to the main floor again and cut the bailing twine with his jackknife. As he leaned over, her eyes were drawn again to his hips and strong legs. Her blood heated and she turned her attention to the mare in the stall behind her. Lord, what was wrong with her? Why did she wonder what he wore, if anything, beneath those disreputable Levi's? Why did she envision hard, muscular thighs and strong calves? She'd never in her lifetime ever so much as contemplated what a man would look like naked. Until now. And now she wondered what his body would feel like stretched out over hers, touching, sweating, tasting...

He clicked his knife shut and she started, brought back to the here and now. Matt snagged a pitchfork from its hook on the wall and began shaking huge forkfuls of hay into the mangers.

"You know," he said, his shoulders moving fluidly beneath his shirt as he worked, "I hadn't seen Randi in a while. Neither had Slade nor Thorne and we all feel bad about it. We should have kept up with her."

"So, as you said, you didn't know about the men in her life, right?"

"Well, of course I knew Randi had boyfriends, not only here when she was growing up but also when she was away at college. But I never heard that she was ever serious about any one guy, not even lately." He jabbed the pitchfork into a fresh bale and looked over his shoulder, his gaze meeting Kelly's in the light from the few iridescent bulbs suspended from the ceiling. Her throat went dry, but she managed to concentrate on the conversation. "For someone who tosses out advice, she's pretty private," Matt added. "The independent kind. Well, you know about that."

"We're not talking about me," she retorted, stung a bit.

"No, but I thought you could relate." He leaned on the pitchfork and sighed. "It really doesn't surprise me that she was involved with a man who I didn't know about, but it's strange that she didn't tell any one of us, not me, or Thorne, or Slade that she was pregnant."

"Maybe she planned to give the baby up for adoption," Kelly suggested.

He shook his head. "I doubt it. It's not like she's a teenager who hasn't finished school and doesn't know what she wants in life, or that she couldn't afford a baby. No, I'm sure she intended to have the baby and keep him, but there was something she had to do before she told us about him."

"Write a book?" Kelly suggested.

"More likely deal with the father." He turned and faced her, and she noticed the lines of irritation pinching the corners of his eyes. "What's the deal with that guy? Where is he? If he cared a lick about my sister he would've shown up by now."

"If he knows about her accident."

"He should, dammit. If he cared enough…enough to get her pregnant, then he damned sure should be hanging around."

"Maybe they broke up before he found out she was pregnant. Maybe she didn't tell him just like she didn't tell you. Maybe she doesn't want him to know." She thought long and hard, avoiding staring into Matt's angry eyes. "Or maybe you're right, he just doesn't care."

"Damn it all." Matt kicked at a bale of hay as he walked up to her, and as she balanced on the top rail, he pressed his nose close to hers. "Let me tell you, if my woman was in the hospital and that kid was mine—" he jerked his thumb in the general direction of the ranch house where, presumably, little J.R. was sleeping "—things would be a lot different. A whole lot different." Matt's lips had thinned, his nostrils flared and one fist was clenched in impotent rage. He smelled of horses and hard work. A vein near his temple became more pronounced. Tiny crow's feet fanned from eyes set deep behind a ledge of thick black eyebrows.

Kelly's heart took off. She licked suddenly dry lips. Matt McCafferty was just too damned sexy for his own good.

Her stupid, feminine heartbeat accelerated to the rate of hummingbird's wings and she noticed the corners of his mouth, where anger pulled the skin tight. In another surreal moment, she wondered what it would feel like to kiss those blade-thin, furious lips and have his big, work-roughened hands rub against her skin. Just what kind of a lover would he be?

The best.

She caught herself up short.

This was silly.

Ridiculous.

Damned unprofessional.

His gaze caught hers for a second and held. Something dark and dangerous sizzled in those scorching brown depths, connected with a part of her she didn't want to examine any too closely. He was dangerous. Emotionally. But not a killer. Not a man who would plot to murder his half sister, no matter what the stakes.

The moment stretched long. Horses shifted and snorted in their stalls. Kelly heard her heartbeats count off the seconds.

Her throat was arid as a windswept Montana prairie.

His gaze flicked to her mouth, as if he, too, felt the sudden intimacy, sensed the unseen charge in the air.

This couldn't be happening. She...couldn't want him to gather her into his strong arms, pull her off the top of the stall, drag her close and kiss her until...oh, dear...

As if he, too, felt the atmosphere in the musty building thicken, he took a step back and cleared his throat. But his dark gaze still held hers and she saw sex and promise in his eyes.

Oh, God, no.

With more agility than she thought possible at the moment, she dropped to the cement floor. "If...if..." She licked her lips, felt a wash of heat stain her cheeks, realized with disgust that her legs had gone weak. What in the name of God was she thinking? "If you think of anything else, call me," she added, her voice louder than she'd intended.

He hesitated.

"I'm talking about the case."

"I know."

Her heart galumphed. Somewhere nearby a horse whinnied softly. Kelly tore her gaze from his. Dear Lord, what was wrong with her? This never happened to her. *Never.* She worked with dozens of men, interviewed witnesses, suspects and victims on a regular basis, and she'd never even brushed the emotions that were battling within her now.

"And you keep me posted on the investigation," he said.

In your dreams, she thought as she reached for the door. Yes, the family would be informed, but some of the evidence the department collected would be kept under wraps, privy only to law enforcement until the investigation was closed, used for the purpose of trapping the assailant.

As if he read her mind, Matt grabbed the crook of her elbow and spun her around.

"I mean it," he said with a quiet, deadly determination. "I want to know what's going on every step of the way in this investigation. And if there's anything I can do to nail the son of a bitch who did this to Randi, I will." His jaw was set, his eyes on fire, his skin tight over his cheekbones. "This guy can't get away."

"I know."

"Otherwise I might be forced to take the law into my own hands."

"That would be a mistake."

"Just be sure it doesn't have to happen. Get the creep."

"We will," she promised.

The fingers around her arm tightened. "I'm not kidding, *Detective,* I want this murdering bastard caught and punished. Big-time. And I'm tired of waiting around while my sister's life is in danger. Either you arrest the son of a bitch, or I'll find him, and when I do, I won't wait around for the courts to decide what to do with him. I'll handle it myself."

Chapter 6

"I just don't know why they don't have a man in charge of the investigation," Matt grumbled as he sat at the table cradling a cup of coffee two days later. It was only a few days until Thanksgiving. Juanita, Nicole and Jenny, the babysitter, had been bustling around, planning a big spread, inviting friends and relatives and decorating the house with those stupid accordion-pleated turkeys and pumpkins, gourds and squash. Randi's condition had stabilized but not improved much, little J.R. was getting cuter by the minute, and Mike Kavanaugh had called again, trying to press Matt into selling the place he'd thrown himself into the last six years.

On top of all that, he was losing sleep. Ever since Kelly Dillinger had been at the house the other night he'd been bothered with thoughts of her. Big-time. While working with the stock, his wayward mind would bring up the image of her face. At night he'd tossed and turned, dreamed of kissing her, woken up with an ache in his groin just as hard as it had been in high school. During the days, whenever he was at the hospital, he'd looked for her, hoped to run into her, found himself concocting excuses to call her.

So far he hadn't.

It was stupid. She wasn't even his type. He liked softer, quiet women with round curves, long blond hair and dulcet-toned voices. Whenever he'd considered settling down, which hadn't been all that often until Thorne had decided to marry, Matt had thought he'd like a nice, home-grown woman who wanted nothing more than to be a rancher's wife and a mother to his children. Never once had he considered that he might fall for a career woman, a gun-toting, no-nonsense, sharp-tongued cop, for crying out loud, one who lived too far from the ranch he'd bought with hard work, sweat and determination. He'd paid a hefty price for that scrap of land that signified his independence and he wasn't going to give it up for any woman, especially a detective.

Not that he was falling for anyone, he reminded himself, and took a gulp of coffee that burned the back of his mouth. He sputtered and coughed. Where the hell had that wayward thought sprung from?

"A man is in charge of the investigation," Thorne said. "Last I heard, Roberto Espinoza was leading the team."

Slade leaned low on his back and observed his brothers over the rim of his mug. "That's not what this is all about. Unless I miss my guess, I'd say the lady detective bothers you for the same reasons Nicole being Randi's doctor got under Thorne's skin."

"What's that supposed to mean?" Matt growled, not liking the turn of the conversation.

"Face it, brother, you're attracted to her."

His gaze bore straight into his younger brother's eyes. "No

way. She's a cop. I'm *not* interested in a woman detective. It's just that she's working on the investigation."

Slade slid a wide grin toward Thorne, silently inviting him in on the razzing. Ignoring Matt's protests, he feigned deep thought and said solemnly, "I think I know what it is. You've got yourself a reverse authority-figure fascination going on here."

"What?" Matt had to keep himself from shooting to his feet. His hands clenched his cup tightly.

"Oh, you know how they always say that women get off on men in uniforms…maybe that's what's going on with you— you like the idea of having some woman boss you around."

Matt snorted in disdain. "Don't you have something constructive to do?" Matt asked, draining his cup and not wanting to examine Slade's theory too closely.

"Yeah." The youngest McCafferty brother scraped his chair back. "I suppose I'd better put in another call to Kurt Striker. He said he'd be back in Grand Hope this afternoon. Maybe he learned something while he was in Seattle." He carried his cup to the sink and tossed the dregs down the drain. "I'll ask him to stop by this evening."

"Good." Thorne pushed out his chair. "The sooner we get to the bottom of this, the better."

Amen, Matt thought.

"No medications were missing from the cart, cabinets or pharmacy," Kelly said, tossing a file onto the corner of Roberto Espinoza's desk. It landed next to a picture of Espinoza's son's baseball team from last spring.

"I'd guess that someone brought the insulin in." Espinoza was leaning back in his chair, staring through windows reinforced with wire and glazed with ice.

"So the hospital staff is clean?"

"Or smart."

"Or both," she said, resting one hip on the corner of the desk and pointing to the file folder. "We'll check anyone connected with the McCaffertys. See if there's a diabetic in the crowd, and then find out if he's missing any medication."

Kelly made a mental note to herself, then asked, "What about fingerprints?"

"None that can't be accounted for, but given the amount of latex gloves floating around St. James that's not a big surprise." His eyebrows drew into a heavy single line. "But the good news is that Randi McCafferty is out of immediate danger and has been moved from ICU to a private room."

"With a guard?"

"You bet. I don't want to risk another attack or the McCafferty boys slapping a lawsuit our way." His eyes met Kelly's. "They're a passel of hotheads, y'know. All three of them were on their way to juvenile detention when they were in school. Their old man bailed 'em out, time and time again, and in my opinion it didn't do any of 'em any good."

"That was a long time ago."

"Yeah, I suppose." He cocked his head to one side and regarded her as if he had the right to. "They've got reputations. Broke more than their share of hearts around this town in their younger days."

"That's not relevant to the case."

"No?"

"Don't tell me, you think I need some advice, right?" she asked, deciding to take the bull by the horns. Espinoza was leading up to it. "So what're you trying to do? Warn me? About what?" Kelly braced herself for the lecture she saw brewing in his eyes. Every once in a while, Espinoza took on the role of older brother or uncle, probably because he'd worked with her father years before she'd joined the force.

He tented his hands under his chin and his eyes narrowed a fraction as if he wasn't sure he should share his thoughts.

"You started this," she said. "You may as well finish it. If you've got something to say to me, just spit it out."

"Okay." He leaned back in his chair until it creaked, but he never took his eyes off Kelly. "My sister, Anita, had a thing for the middle McCafferty boy. It was a long time ago, probably fifteen years ago. She was in her senior year of high school when she hooked up with Matt."

Matt, Kelly thought wryly. Of course it had to be the middle son of John Randall. She fought a prick of disappointment, but managed to hide it as she stood.

"McCafferty took her out a few times and it got pretty hot and heavy, at least from Anita's point of view. He acted interested in her, and then, out of the blue, took up with the rodeo circuit again and within a month had moved on. It was kind of a whirlwind thing, but my sister was crushed." Espinoza's jaw tightened.

"Let me guess. You've held a grudge ever since."

He clicked his pen. "Let's just say I wouldn't want it to happen again to anyone I know."

"Wait a minute. Are you talking about me? Are you warning me off Matt McCafferty?" Kelly demanded, her spine stiffening.

"Just making an observation."

"Well, observe something else, okay? It's none of your business who I see."

"Are you seeing him?"

"No! I mean, only professionally—not that it's any of your damned business." She was overreacting and knew it, but couldn't stop the sharp edge of her voice or the color she felt climbing up the back of her neck. "Let's get back to the case, okay? What about the men Randi McCafferty was interested in?"

He nodded. Apparently the older-brother-type lecture was over, at least for a while. "The three men we've linked to her—Paterno, Donahue and Clanton—have alibis, if that's what you mean. All of 'em were miles away from Grand Hope at the time she was forced off the road. They were also elsewhere when the attack at St. James occurred. Now, I'm not saying they have watertight alibis, but there are people who say they saw them during the dates of the attacks. Seattle PD's double-checking, though, to make sure."

"What about paternity?"

"Still checking." Espinoza's scowl deepened and he dropped his feet to the floor. "As far as blood types go, all three men—Joe Paterno, Brodie Clanton and Sam Donahue—could be the kid's father. It'll take paternity tests to narrow the field down and then maybe none of these guys would end up being the father."

"What have they got to say for themselves?"

"They're not a very talkative group, but a detective in Seattle is interviewing them. We really don't have a helluva lot to go on." He leaned forward and reached for the file she'd brought in. "I'm thinking about sending someone to Seattle to interview the men, just so we have a better handle on it."

And because the McCaffertys are breathing down our necks, demanding answers. He didn't have to say it.

"Are you interested?"

"Sure," she said quickly, eager to do anything to keep the investigation moving forward. She plopped down in the one chair on the opposite side of his desk. "When?"

"This week. Before Thanksgiving." He picked up the file folder and tapped it on the desk as if he'd just made the decision final in his mind.

"Count me in."

"Good. Now, we've still got a guard posted at the hospital. So far, there's been nothing suspicious happening, thank God, so if Randi McCafferty would just cooperate and wake up, maybe we'd get some answers."

He opened the file folder. Leafing through the pages, he scanned the lab reports on the crime scene about the latest attack on Randi McCafferty, though Kelly suspected he knew the contents by heart.

"What about Thorne McCafferty's plane?" she asked as he flipped to the final typewritten page. "The McCafferty brothers seem convinced that foul play was involved."

"Again, the jury's still out." He slapped the manila folder onto his desk. "There was one helluva storm that day. The crash could have been the result of pilot error or equipment malfunction. Or maybe it was just coincidence that his plane went down. It doesn't make a lot of sense to me that someone is trying to bump off the entire McCafferty family one at a time, and there hasn't been another attempt on his life." He clicked his pen again and shook his head, gray hairs catching in the fluorescent bulbs that hummed overhead. "Nope. I'll bet my badge that McCafferty just had a run of bad luck on that one."

"But Randi's another matter."

"Yep." Espinoza stuffed his pen into a mug labeled Coach Espinoza. "Someone's definitely trying to make sure that she doesn't wake up. We just have to figure out who."

"And why."

"Yeah." His thick eyebrows elevated a fraction. "A motive

would be nice. Some people around town think the brothers are involved, that Thorne staged the plane crash just to throw us off guard and that Randi and her son are the primary targets."

"No way. They could have come up with better ways to kill her off if they really wanted to." The thought soured her stomach and fired her blood. "They're three big, strapping men whom she trusted, they could have been one another's alibis, and as for the baby... I've seen the uncles with little J.R. They'd defend him with their lives."

Espinoza nodded. "Agreed. So who does that leave?"

Who indeed, Kelly wondered off and on for the rest of the day. She helped investigate an accident scene, interviewed witnesses in a hit-and-run, and took statements from the owners of a mom-and-pop grocery that had been vandalized. In between calls, she tried to work out the knots in the Randi McCafferty case.

It was after eight when she filed her last report and, hiking her jacket around her neck, climbed into her car. The windows fogged with the cold temperature, but the night was clear, stars visible above the lights of the town. She started for her row house, but changed her mind at a red light and turned toward the hospital where Randi McCafferty lay comatose.

There was no longer any evidence of the press as Kelly made her way to the fourth floor to Randi's private room. Seated on a folding chair, flipping through a magazine, the beefy policeman whose job it was to protect John Randall's daughter looked up and recognized Kelly. "Don't suppose you're my relief," he said with a toothy grin. He checked his watch. "If you are, you're early."

"Not me, Rex, but I'll take over if you want to take a break and refill that." She pointed to an empty paper cup that sat at his feet.

"You don't have to ask twice. You're on." He swiped the empty cup from the floor and swaggered down the hall. As Rex disappeared around the corner, Kelly walked into the private room where the lights were dimmed and Randi McCafferty lay on her back, her breathing regular, her lips slightly parted, her eyes closed.

"Wake up, Randi," Kelly said softly. "You've got some brothers who are worried sick about you and a baby who needs you." She touched the back of one of Randi's hands. Her skin was cool and soft. "You know, I could use some help here, too. I've got questions only you can answer." She bit her lip, wondering about this woman who seemed to be a mystery even to her brothers. No one in Grand Hope knew the ins and outs of Randi's life—who were her friends, what project she was working on, who was her lover? Maybe the answers were in Seattle. Maybe if Kelly was sent there for just a few days she could find answers to the dozens of questions surrounding this case. "Come on, Randi. Wake up, would you?"

"Y'know, she *still* can't hear you. No more than she could the last time you tried to talk to her."

Kelly froze, fought her instinctive reaction to reach for her sidearm and silently cursed her luck as she recognized Matt McCafferty's deep, condemning voice. So he'd caught her again. She dropped Randi's hand and turned to find him framed in the doorway, his shoulders nearly touching each side of the doorjamb, his athletic body silhouetted by the backlight of the hall.

Kelly's stupid heart skipped a beat. Her pulse jumped. She met cold censure in his chocolate-brown eyes. "Are you the guard?"

"No. His relief for a few seconds."

"You didn't hear me come in. I might have been the killer," he said, his voice tight. "I could've got the jump on you."

"Or my presence could have scared you off," she said. "I'm still in uniform."

His gaze raked down her body. "That you are."

"And I've got a weapon."

He didn't comment.

Rankled, she stepped closer to him and kept her voice low for the patient's sake. "So, are you through dressing me down? Because I'm not in the mood for it."

"What *are* you in the mood for?" he asked, and for the fleetest of seconds she thought he was making a pass at her. But she was probably imagining things.

"I just thought I'd see how your sister was doing and let Rex use the rest room and get a fresh cup of coffee. He's the guard on duty. You have a problem with that?"

Matt seemed to cool off a tad. He glanced quickly around the room, as if seeing for himself that it was secure. "I guess not."

"Good."

He strode to the bedside, bringing the scents of horses, hard work and the cold outdoors with him. "I heard you talking to her."

Now her embarrassment was complete.

"But it doesn't seem to work. We've all tried communicating with her. Over and over again, but she doesn't move. Not so much as a blink." He drew in a whistling breath, then sighed. "Sometimes I don't think she'll ever wake up."

His jaw was tight, his eyes trained on his half sister, frustration evident in the strain tugging at the corners of his mouth.

"It's just going to take more time."

"So I've heard. About a million times." He rubbed the back of his neck, his fingers delving beneath the collar of his suede jacket. "I'm not sure I believe it." Matt's gaze moved from Randi's bed to Kelly. "And don't give me any lectures about having patience or faith, okay? It's all been stretched thin. Real thin."

"It could be that she can hear all of us," Kelly said. "Maybe she just can't respond."

He lifted a dark eyebrow, then nodded curtly. "I s'pose." He reached for his sister's hand and Randi's palm seemed small and pale in his long, work-roughened fingers. "Come on, Randi gal," he said, seeming awkward in the role of doting brother. "Come on." Kelly's heart ached when she saw the pain etched across Matt's rugged face. He was a complex man, she realized, capable of a hundred emotions, ranging from anger, to guilt and love. Beneath his ranch-tough exterior was a good heart.

If only his sister's eyes would flutter open.

Realizing she was an intruder in a very intimate scene, Kelly started for the door.

"You don't have to go." Again his voice seemed loud and out of place in a hospital where hushed conversation and the faint strains of piped-in music were the backdrop.

"I'll just be outside." Kelly offered him a smile over her shoulder. "I think you need to be alone with her." Then she slipped through the doorway and eyed the nurses' station a few doors down a wide corridor. Two nurses, both women, were on duty, one talking on the telephone while looking at a computer screen, the second writing in a fat binder. An aide pushed a cart stacked with towels and blankets toward the elevator and one older man was strolling down the hallway, his IV stand in tow.

Quiet.

Peaceful.

Nothing strange or sinister.

"Hey, thanks for spelling me," Rex said as he ambled toward his chair. "I brought you a cup of coffee…hope you drink it black."

"Perfect." She accepted the second cup and took a sip of the scalding brew.

"It's supposed to be French roast, whatever the hell that is." Rex touched the lip of his cup to hers. "Here's to police work, which, in this case, includes babysitting." He shook his head, a few gray hairs catching the light. "Personally I think this is a big waste of time. I know someone tried to kill her before, but they'd have to be flat-out stupid to try it again. The hospital's beefed up security, and frankly, I haven't seen one suspicious character in this place."

"Let's keep it that way," Matt said as he overheard the last part of the conversation. He was frustrated with the situation, and seeing a big man in uniform sharing a cup of coffee and complaining to Kelly about the guy's duty irritated the hell out of him.

The policeman nodded as his eyes met Matt's. "I intend to," he said. "Rex Stanyon." He shot out a beefy, freckled hand that Matt reluctantly shook.

"Good." Matt squared his hat on his head and tried to ignore the spurt of jealousy that raced through his blood. His reaction to Kelly was all wrong. Way out of line. So she was pretty, so she filled out that drab uniform in all the right places, so what? She was a policewoman, for God's sake.

Ridiculously he felt a tightening in his groin, as he always seemed to whenever she was around. Hell. He clamped down his jaw. She was investigating the attempts on his sister's life; he couldn't think of her as a woman.

"We'll take care of your sister," Rex was saying.

"See that you do." He started for the elevator before he said something to the cop that he might regret.

From the corner of his eye he saw Kelly drain her cup, say something to Rex, then take off to catch up with him as the elevator doors parted and an attendant pushed an empty wheelchair into the hallway.

"That was uncalled-for." Kelly strode into the elevator and swatted the button for the ground level.

"What?"

The doors closed and with a groan the elevator car began its descent.

"Rex is a damned good cop."

"If you say so."

"Look, McCafferty," she said, stepping closer to him and jabbing a long finger at his chest. "Everybody's doing the best they can, and believe me, we all want to see the creep who attacked Randi behind bars. But that doesn't mean we don't have the right to grumble a bit."

"I just asked the man to do his job."

"You insinuated that he wasn't." Her lips pursed in fury, her nostrils flared and a soft blush colored her cheeks.

"Cops are supposed to have thick skins."

"So are cowboys!"

Without thinking, he grabbed her. His hands surrounded her upper arms and he dragged her close. "Cowboys are just like cops. Flesh and blood."

"And they have feelings, too. Is that the sorry line you were going to throw at me?"

"No, lady, I wasn't. In fact, I wasn't going to say a damned thing." Without really thinking about it, he yanked her closer still, lowered his head and kissed her. Hard. Full on the mouth while she was gasping and sputtering and probably reaching for her gun. Her lips were firm and warm, the starch in her spine not giving an inch. If he expected her to melt against him, he was disappointed.

She flung herself out of his arms as the elevator landed and her eyes flashed indignant fire. "Don't you ever—"

The doors parted and Slade McCafferty started to step inside. "Oh. Matt, I was looking..." Blue eyes focused full on Kelly and then, as if he read the situation perfectly, Slade had the nerve to grin, one of those crooked, I-know-what-you've-been-up-to smiles that had irritated the hell out of Matt while growing up. "Well, what's going on here?" he drawled, and Matt wanted to lunge at him.

"Nothing." Kelly found some shred of her pride. "I was just explaining to your brother that we're doing everything possible to locate the person who attacked your sister."

Slade's eyes danced and again Matt wanted to knock his block off.

"Well, I was trying to track you down, 'cuz we just got a call from Kurt Striker. He's on his way to the ranch from Seattle. Should be there in an hour."

"Let's go," Matt said.

"I'd like to talk to him," Kelly said as they headed along the hallway to the wide front doors of the hospital.

"I don't think—" Slade started to protest.

"Why not?" Matt nodded, as if agreeing with himself. "Maybe you could share some information with him and he could do the same for you." Slade was about to argue the point further, but Matt cut him off. "We just have to catch this bastard. If the police are willing to work with Striker, all the better." He glanced at Kelly. "You want to ride with me?"

"I've got my car."

He lifted a shoulder and ignored the unspoken accusations in his brother's eyes. "I'll catch up with you at the ranch," Slade said. "I just want to look in on Randi first." Turning on his heel, he started for the elevator.

The electronic doors opened to the cold night. "You were about to tell me where to get off," Matt reminded her as they strode across the parking lot and snow blew across the asphalt.

"Don't ever try to manhandle me, okay?" She zipped her jacket and glanced up at him. "It could be dangerous."

"What? Were you going to handcuff me? Pull out your .38? Use a billy club and knock some sense into me?"

"That's not what I was talking about," she said soberly, then, unexpectedly, chuckled. When she glanced up at him, snowflakes caught on her eyelashes. "But it's not a bad idea. Watch out. I graduated from the police academy with honors in billy-clubbing."

So she did have a sense of humor. Beneath Ms. All-business-I'm-a-member-of-Grand-Hope's-finest-team, the lady appreciated a joke. "I didn't mean to offend."

"Of course you did," she said, reaching her car.

"I just kissed you."

"No way. That wasn't a kiss. That was a slap in the face. You were trying to let me know who was boss. Period. Neanderthal tactics, McCafferty. In case you didn't get the word, they went out with the Stone Age." She yanked a key ring from her pocket and started opening the door.

"No one's ever complained before."

"Have you ever done a poll?"

"Ouch." He winced.

"Just telling it like it is."

The door unlocked, and Matt, his pride stung, wanted to

haul her into his arms again but didn't dare. "What is it with you?"

"What do you mean?"

"You're...different."

"From the women in your life? Let's hope." She started to slide into her vehicle when he grabbed the crook of her arm.

"Wait a minute."

She glanced down at his hand and disdainfully peeled his fingers from their grip on her elbow. "I don't go for the ma-cho-man tactics."

"No? Then what?"

She hesitated, bit her lip and studied him through night-darkened eyes. "Since you asked..." Stepping around the door of her four-wheel drive, she held his gaze. "I know I'm going to regret this, but you did bring it up...." She reached upward and placed her chilled hands on either side of his face. Stand-ing on her tiptoes, she pressed her lips to his, softly at first, just brushing her skin over his, and then, as her fingers warmed against his cheeks, she deepened the kiss, ever so slowly slip-ping her arms around his neck and molding her lips to his. Deep inside, the fire that had been banked for so many years ignited, warm ashes sparking to life. With a groan, he closed his eyes and slid his hands to her waist. Desire licked through his blood and the combination of the frigid night air and the warm woman in his arms was so damnably erotic. He wanted so much from her. Body and soul and— She pushed him away quickly, and though she tried to cover it up, he saw the quick-ness in her breath, noticed that her eyes were nearly black, her skin flushed.

"That...that was just a demonstration," she said, her voice husky. She cleared her throat. "So the next time you think about using caveman tactics you might want to think twice."

Chapter 7

Matt wasn't going to let some woman…some lady cop…best him. Grinning crookedly in the night, he drew her to him again. The ethereal lamplight glistened in the snow covering the parking lot and caught in her eyes. "You're not so tough, are you, Detective?" he asked, knowing he was stepping into dangerous territory. He should just leave well enough alone, but the challenge in her eyes, the defiant lift of her chin, the passionate woman hidden beneath that cop's uniform zeroed in on his male pride. "Don't lecture me about caveman tactics," he warned, "or I might just accuse you of being a tease."

"That wouldn't destroy me."

"No?" His fingers tightened over her arms. "And I'll bet it's not true."

"Wait a minute. I was just—"

"You were just curious and it backfired. You're not as immune as you thought you were. You're not an ice woman after all."

"And you're not a gentleman."

"Never said I was." He let her go then, dropped his hands and turned toward his pickup parked two rows over.

Kelly climbed into her rig and bit her lip. He was right, dammit. She had reacted to him. She slammed the door shut and jabbed her key into the ignition with trembling fingers. How long had it been since she'd felt any response to a man? Two years? Three? Five? She couldn't remember, not that there were all that many to consider. She'd only fallen in love twice, and both times when the man started talking marriage, she'd bowed out.

Maybe she hadn't really been in love.

Or maybe love didn't exist.

She kicked herself as she flipped on the wipers. She knew better. Her parents' marriage was proof enough of the commitment and bond that can exist between a man and woman.

Good Lord, what was happening to her? What was she doing thinking about love? Just because Matt McCafferty had kissed her, she shouldn't go off the deep end. Besides, any Mc-Cafferty brother, Matt included, was off-limits. Definitely off-limits. Not only was he the brother of a victim, but he was the son of John Randall McCafferty, the man who had single-handedly ruined her mother's life.

"This is nuts," she told herself as she watched him through the windshield. With the athletic prowess that had tamed more than one bucking bronco, Matt climbed into his truck and started the rig. She threw her own car into gear and followed the glow of his taillights as he drove through town toward the main highway leading north to the Flying M. "Stupid, stupid woman," she chastised herself. What had she been thinking? Why had she kissed him? Oh, yeah, feminine and professional pride, that had been her reasoning, she thought as she braked for a red light, then caught up with Matt's truck at the out-skirts of town. She didn't like any man coming on to her and McCafferty had been trying to teach her a lesson, so she'd thrown it back at him, only to have it blow up in her face, as he'd so ineloquently pointed out.

Matt drove a good five miles over the speed limit and she wondered if he was taunting her. She thought of pulling him over just to prove that she could, that he couldn't get away with breaking any law, but she tamped down the urge. It wouldn't get her anywhere and she'd already experienced one emo-tional dressing-down for the night. But...but, if he got reck-less or pushed the speed up another five miles an hour, she'd nail him. She'd have to.

Kurt Striker was already at the house, a cup of coffee cradled in his hands as he sat on the edge of a worn-looking chair. Ni-cole was seated on the piano bench near Thorne, who leaned back in the recliner. The twins and the baby were already in bed, the house quiet aside from the group clustered in the liv-ing room around a coffee table, where an enamel coffeepot, several empty cups and a plate of crackers and cheese were situ-ated. A fire crackled and the odors of coffee and smoke wafted in the air. Kelly stood at the fireplace, warming the back of her legs, and accepted a cup from Matt, who handed it to her and stood next to her, his shoulders braced against the mantel.

"Do you think this is a good idea?" Thorne asked, his eyes moving from Kelly to Kurt. Kelly understood what he meant. Kurt was working for the McCaffertys privately; he reported to them rather than the police. Kelly was the law.

"It's fine, as long as the sheriff's department agrees to share information." Kurt leaned back in his chair and eyed Kelly. He could have been Hollywood's version of a cop. Rugged

good looks, straight brown hair, hard-edged features and intense green eyes, he seemed like a man who would bend the
law if need be, just to get what he wanted. There was a se-
cretive shadow in his eyes, the kind that Kelly often thought
better belonged to criminals. Kurt was lanky and lean, dressed
in denim and cowboy boots—as if he were ready for the next
take on a weekly detective series.

"We just want to get to the bottom of the attacks on Randi
and possibly Thorne as quickly as possible," she said, "and, of
course, arrest the assailant and bring him to trial."

"Then we're all on the same page." Thorne flipped the recliner to a more upright position.

"I assume you've already checked my credentials." Kurt was
still staring straight at Kelly, and from the corner of her eye,
she saw Matt inch a little closer to her.

"Of course we have." Kelly nodded. "We've scrutinized
everyone involved."

"Good. Then let's get down to business." He set his cup on
the table. "I just flew in from Seattle where Randi worked. I
dealt with the Seattle PD while I was there."

He said it, Kelly guessed, to put her at ease, to let her know
that he was working on the right side of the law, but his eyes
narrowed slightly, as if he was trying to size her up. "Everything I discuss with you here tonight will be squeaky clean.
All according to police procedure. You don't have to worry
that your professionalism will be compromised."

"Just so we lay out the ground rules." She didn't believe him
for a second, but he seemed savvy enough to know where she
was coming from. "If you broke any laws, you won't tell me
about them and I'm supposed to ignore, not question them,
is that it?"

"For the record, I didn't."

"Duly noted," she replied, though she suspected he was lying. She whipped out a pen and notepad just in case he said anything she might want to check into later. "So what did you find when you were in Seattle?"

He reached into the pocket of his jacket. "To start with, this…" He withdrew a computer disk. "It's a copy. The Seattle PD have the original."

"That you found where?"

"Surprisingly the door to Randi McCafferty's apartment was unlocked. I knocked, no one answered and I walked inside."

"And found a computer disk that the police had overlooked?" she asked skeptically. She wanted to accuse him of being a bald-faced liar, tell him she damned well knew that he broke into the apartment, but saw no reason for it. Hadn't she used the same tactics herself? But then she'd bent the law while wearing a badge. This guy was a civilian. She was a cop. Which was worse?

"Not exactly. Let's just say I found a key to a locker."

"What locker?" Kelly asked.

"One at the train station."

"And the disk was in the locker?"

"That's right."

"Did you find anything else?"

"Not so far."

"What's on it?" Nicole asked, eyeing the computer disk as if it were evil.

"The start of a book. An outline and about three chapters."

Thorne shoved himself upright. "The book Juanita kept mentioning. I thought it was all just talk." He struggled onto his crutches and balanced near the bookcase. "Ever since she was a little kid, Randi had a dream of writing a novel of some kind. When she was in grade school, she kept a diary and was always making up little stories, but I thought she gave all that up when she was in junior high and started showing interest in boys and the rodeo. I figured getting a degree in journalism and writing a column for the newspaper was good enough."

"But she wrote magazine articles as well," Nicole added, pushing up from the piano bench and standing near Thorne. She ran a finger over a dusty volume of an outdated set of encyclopedias. "I'm sure I read one that was so much like her style, written under the name of R. J. McKay."

"I checked it out," Kurt said with a quick nod. "It looks like she did a little moonlighting. Every once in a while she wrote articles under a pseudonym—probably because she didn't want her publisher to find out and give her some grief about it."

"What's the book about?" Kelly asked.

"It's the start of a novel."

"Not a collection of anecdotes and advice from her column with the *Clarion?*" Thorne asked.

"Doesn't seem like it. There's a story, and if I were a gambling man, I'd think it was a blend of fiction and fact."

"Autobiographical?" Matt asked.

"I don't think so. It's certainly not about her life, but it could have been inspired by someone who wrote in and asked advice, or someone she knew personally, or someone she read about. I don't know. At this point everything is conjecture. As I said, the Seattle PD has the original disk and the laptop."

"But you have copies of everything," Kelly guessed. "This isn't the only one."

Kurt's slow grin confirmed her theory. "I said I'd work with you, not give up all my secrets."

Kelly didn't press the issue.

"I'll print it out," Thorne said.

"Already done." Kurt reached into his briefcase and pulled out a sheaf of papers just as Slade burst through the front door. Rubbing his hands together, the youngest McCafferty brother walked into the living room, clapped Kurt on the back and was brought up to date. Within minutes he'd poured himself a cup of coffee and, along with the brothers, Kelly and Nicole, scanned the pages of Randi's book.

"Who's this about?" Slade asked.

"Beats me," Matt muttered under his breath.

Kurt lifted a shoulder. "I'd say the names have been changed to protect the guilty."

Kelly agreed. The first three chapters were rough, and the remainder of the story compressed into a stripped-down idea surrounding a shady rodeo rider who was being blackmailed into throwing competitions. The main character was a poor boy from the wrong side of the tracks, who had all his life scraped to get by. Eventually he'd been forced by circumstances to step outside of the law and was sucked into a world of drugs and crime. The upshot was that no matter how hard he tried to free himself of the vicious cycle of crime and dependence, he failed.

"What an upper," Slade muttered sarcastically as he scanned the last page.

"Overblown melodrama," Matt snorted as he finished reading and tossed his share of the manuscript to Thorne.

Kelly glanced at Matt. "Or a real story that someone doesn't want published."

"Who would know about it?" Kurt asked.

"I suppose her agent. Maybe he's already shopped it around to publishers." Thorne slung his arm around his fiancée's shoulders.

"Maybe," Matt agreed. "Or maybe not. The trouble is, none

of us knows what was going on in Randi's life. But these—"
he motioned to the pages that were being passed from brother
to brother "—are pretty much nothing. So she was writing a
book. Big deal. So it might have had some basis in fact?" He
lifted his eyebrows. "So what?"

"You didn't find any notes?" Kelly asked Kurt.

"Other than what's on the disk?" He shook his head.

"Or reference books? Research materials?"

"There were books all over her den. Hundreds of 'em. And
a stack of magazines in one bookcase. I didn't see anything
that I thought significant."

Kelly didn't belabor the point. The Seattle police had already
been in the apartment and they'd either missed or dismissed
the fact that Randi was writing a book. It was something to
check when she got to the city on Puget Sound.

They discussed the case until there was nothing left to say,
then Kelly decided to call it a night. "I'll keep you posted if I
find anything," she said to the group in general, then, to Kurt,
"and I'll expect the same consideration."

"You got it," he assured her, though Kelly wasn't confident
she could trust him.

"Good night." She headed for the door, then thought twice
about it. Turning to Matt she said, "Could I see her room?"

With a shrug of his shoulder, Matt showed her upstairs and
quietly opened the door to a small room that had been trans-
formed into the nursery. The baby was sleeping soundly, his
breathing audible, and Kelly smiled as she looked down at him.
Matt glanced at his nephew and the hard lines of his face softened. "Such a little guy and such a big fuss," he whispered,
tucking a blanket closer to the baby's chin.

Kelly's heartstrings pulled so tight she suddenly couldn't
breathe. Matt's big hands seemed out of place fingering the

dainty satin-hemmed blanket. His tanned, work-roughened fingers should have been awkward but weren't, and the tenderness with which he adjusted the bedding was surprising. Someday, whether he knew it or not, Matt McCafferty would make one helluva father.

She darted a look to his face, caught him watching her reaction and, clearing her throat, stepped away from the crib. In the dim glow from the night-light, she searched the walls of the room. A bulletin board that hung near the closet still displayed some of Randi's childhood treasures: a dried, faded corsage, yellowed pictures of friends splashing in a creek and seated around the remains of a campfire, a couple of shots of Randi astride a black quarter horse, tassels from a graduation cap, a lacy garter and several blue-and-red ribbons tacked haphazardly over the corkboard surface.

A desk had been shoved into the corner, and in the bookcase resting above the walnut surface were trophies of various sizes all dedicated to horsemanship.

There was also a dusty cowgirl hat with a rhinestone tiara as the hatband. She fingered the dusty jewels.

"Randi was a rodeo princess in high school," Matt explained.

"So your sister had rodeo fever, too."

"It's in our blood," Matt admitted. "Every one of us but Thorne. He didn't have much use for anything to do with ranching or horses or that whole part of Western culture." He slid a glance in her direction. "He was more interested in making money—in fact, it was his only interest until he met Nicole."

"She changed his life."

"In a big way."

Kelly studied the books on the desk, mostly about horse care and grooming, then with one last sweeping glance, decided she'd learned all she could about Matt's half sister. If only she would wake up—there were so many questions only Randi could answer. "I guess that's about it," Kelly said, with one last smile for the baby as he sighed in his sleep.

"I'll walk you." Matt followed her down the stairs and zipped up his jacket as he walked her through the snow to her rig.

"For the most part, you were pretty quiet in there," he observed, hitching his chin toward the ranch house, his breath making a fine cloud in the night air.

"I suppose." She glanced over her shoulder to the two-storied building where the windows glowed in bright patches against the chill of the winter night. "I wanted to hear what Striker had to say."

"So what did you think?"

She met his gaze in the darkness. "It's all well and good, but I'm going to double-check everything when I get to Seattle."

"You're leaving?" He was surprised.

"For a day or two. Compliments of the department." At the SUV, she paused, sent him a mischievous glance. "I know, you're gonna miss me," she teased, but she'd struck closer to home than he wanted to admit.

"I'll try to survive."

"Do that, cowboy."

She smiled and that was all it took. Before he had a chance to think, he grabbed her, hauled her into his arms and slanted his mouth over hers. She gasped and he took advantage of her open mouth, his tongue sliding into her mouth to find hers. There was a second's resistance, her muscles tensing, and then he felt her melt, her body leaning into his for just a second. Matt closed his eyes, drew her closer still, his hands splaying upon her back, his heart pounding, blood thundering through his ears.

Somewhere he heard a door open and voices. Kelly froze in his arms, then pushed away. "I don't think this is a good idea," she said, and glanced to the porch. Slade and Kurt stood under the porch light, Slade lighting a cigarette, Kurt standing with his hands in the front pockets of his jeans. Both men were staring at them.

"Great," Matt said, knowing he was going to catch hell from his younger brother.

"I think we should keep this professional," she said as if reading his thoughts. She opened the door of her SUV and slid inside.

"And I think you're a liar." He leaned closer to her. "Face it, Detective," he said, his voice low. "You want me."

"You're insufferable."

"So I've heard." His grin was cocksure and irreverent.

"Good night, cowboy." She hauled the door shut and gritted her teeth. What was it about that man that got under her skin? Why had she let him kiss her again? He was right.

Jabbing her key into the ignition, she twisted her wrist and the engine sparked on the first try.

Face it, Detective, you want me.

Oh, if he only knew. The taste of him was still on her lips and her blood was thundering through her veins. Oh, yes, she wanted him, but she couldn't have him. The whole idea was ludicrous and completely out of character for her. She switched on the headlights and wipers, then pushed the heater's control lever to high.

Nimbly, she swung her car into reverse, her headlights slashed across the lot to land on Matt, standing feet spread apart, arms crossed over his wide chest, eyes trained on her vehicle. She threw the car into drive and stepped on the throttle. *Yes, damn it, I want you, but that's as far as it's gonna go. You, Mr. McCafferty, are strictly taboo!*

Matt braced himself as he walked back to the house. He saw the censure in Slade's dark gaze. "What the hell was that all about?" Slade demanded. He flicked his cigarette butt into the air and the red ember arced in the darkness to sizzle in a snowbank.

"What?"

"You and the policewoman, and don't try to deny it. I thought you were keeping your eye on the police department to see that they were doing their job."

"I am."

"By kissing the detective investigating the case?" Slade snorted. "You're trying to get her into bed, for God's sake."

"Back off, Slade. I'm handling things."

"You're stepping over the line. She needs to be thinking about the attacks on Randi and nothing else. And you—" he poked a thick finger at his brother's chest "—keep your head on straight."

"Don't worry about it," Matt said sharply, his back muscles tightening.

"You have a job to do!"

Matt grabbed his younger brother by the shirtfront. "I said back off and I meant it." He pushed his face so close to Slade's that in the porch light he could see the color throb in the scar running along the side of his brother's face.

"Hold on. Both of you." Kurt's eyes were narrowed and he was gazing down the lane where the taillights of Kelly's rig had so recently disappeared. "I think this could work out."

"How?" Matt demanded, turning his attention onto the detective, though he still wanted to throw a punch.

Kurt's eyes narrowed and he rubbed the stubble of his jaw. "Pillow talk." His gaze took in both brothers.

Slade's lips thinned. "I don't like it."

"Neither do I." Matt's fist uncurled and he stepped away from his brother, only to level a killing glare at Striker.

Kurt didn't back down. "Before you do something we'll both regret," he said, "hear me out. We all know that some-times women say things in bed that they wouldn't otherwise. This could definitely work to our advantage, as Detective Dillinger is so involved with the case."

"That's not the point," Matt argued.

"It's precisely the point. We're all working together, right? Toward a common goal. To find out who the hell's trying to kill your sister, and I figure we can do it by any means pos-sible. So you kiss the woman, so you bed her. Big deal. It's not as if you have to fall in love with her. She's here, you live far away, but for the meantime, you could enjoy yourself for a while. At least you'll find out whatever it is the police might be holding back."

"If she talks," Slade interjected.

"She will if given the right motivation. They all do." With that Kurt took off and jogged across the snowy parking lot to his four-wheel drive vehicle, leaving Matt with a bad taste in his mouth.

"I don't like him," he said to Slade.

"You don't have to. Just do what he says." His lips were compressed, his blue eyes harsh. "You want to bed Ms. Dill-inger, anyway. Now you've got an excuse."

Chapter 8

Kelly stomped on the accelerator and told herself she'd just won the medal for moron of the century. What had come over her? What was she thinking, flirting so outrageously, *kissing* Matt, for crying out loud? It was just plain nuts! She couldn't, *wouldn't,* let herself fall for Matt McCafferty. To let him kiss her was bad enough, but had she let it go at that? Oh, no, she had to challenge him, and even now, ten minutes later, she felt the heat, tingle and impression of his lips against hers.

"Idiot," she growled, clenching the steering wheel hard. She drove to Grand Hope as if possessed, parked and stormed up the flight of stairs to her living area. This damned case was making her crazy, that was it. She was losing her perspective.

She spent the rest of the night going over the computer printout of Randi's novel, making notes, drumming her fingers, reading passages over and over again, trying to gain some insight into the mind of Matt's half sister. The McCaffertys' housekeeper seemed to think this book was important; Kelly didn't see how. As far as she could tell it was fiction. She found no clues as to the identity of Randi's attacker, nor did she discover a hint about little J.R.'s father.

But the rodeo scenario bothered her. Not only had Randi's father followed the rodeo circuit, but two of her brothers, Matt and Slade, as well. And then there was Randi herself, into barrel racing and crowned a rodeo princess.

Kelly tapped her pencil against her teeth. So Randi found the whole cowboy thing fascinating, to the point that she'd been involved recently, however briefly, with Sam Donahue, a man who had grown up around these parts and joined the rodeo circuit soon after he'd graduated from high school.

So how did it all tie into Randi's book? Or did it? Was it significant? Or another false lead? One of far too many.

"It's a waste of time," she told herself, stretching in her chair at the kitchen table and eyeing the clock. It was well after midnight. She couldn't keep her eyes open and tumbled into bed where she spent a restless night, tossing and turning and dreaming of a rangy cowboy whose kisses stole the breath from her lungs.

By the time she'd walked into the office the next morning and dropped the rough draft of Randi's manuscript on the corner of Espinoza's desk, she'd tried and failed to push Matt McCafferty out of her mind.

"This is about all Striker found," she said as Espinoza picked up the rough draft of the manuscript and riffled through the pages. She placed the disk on top of the printout.

"Does it mean anything?"

"Just that she has a vivid imagination." Kelly leaned against the file cabinet and gave him the blow-by-blow of the night before.

He skimmed the pages and shook his head. "It bothers me that the Seattle police didn't find this."

"Me, too."

"I think you'd better check with them, ask them about Striker when you're there." He reached into the top drawer of his desk and withdrew a thick envelope, then slapped it into Kelly's hand. "Airline tickets," he explained. "You leave tomorrow."

"Son of a bitch!" Matt slammed down the receiver and caught a warning glare from Thorne, who was seated at the kitchen table with Nicole, J.R. and the twins as they all were trying and failing to play Go Fish. Nicole was balancing the baby on her lap while the twins slapped cards willy-nilly. Thorne was attempting to teach the four-year-olds the basics of the game while half-drunk cups of cocoa steamed and the bowl of popcorn had been reduced to a few unpopped kernels sitting in a pool of melted butter.

The scene was way too domestic for Matt. Who would have thought Thorne could become such a family man? But there he was discussing the upcoming wedding with his fiancée, laughing with the twins and taking the time to relax.

"Trouble?" Thorne asked.

"Yeah, there was a major storm in the mountains and it took out a lot of the power and phone lines. I can't get through to Kavanaugh." He glanced out the window to the dark night beyond and silently swore. He'd worked damned hard for that scrap of land near the Idaho border; it had been his pride and joy, his proof that he could make it on his own, without John Randall's help. Without anyone's. He always figured he'd eventually find a good woman to settle down there, raise his family and die on the land he'd claimed as his own. When the time came, he figured his ashes would be scattered in the wind, near the pond by the barn.

But lately he'd been thinking of giving it all up, relinquishing his dream.

For what?

For Kelly Dillinger.

Hell, what had happened to him in the past couple of weeks?

"You'll just have to be patient." Thorne picked up a card from the discard pile and tossed off another. "Mike will call when he can."

Matt didn't like it. He poured himself a cup of day-old coffee he didn't want and glared out the window. He needed to get back to his own place, to check on his stock, to reconnect with what was his. Day by day he was feeling less a part of his own spread and more entrenched in life back here in Grand Hope. His brothers, the kids, Randi...and, though he hated to admit it, Kelly Dillinger, all played a big part in his newfound roots at the Flying M.

"Go fish!" one little voice yelled proudly.

Matt took a swig from his cup, scowled at the bitter taste, tossed the remainder down the sink and tried to fight the restlessness that seemed to be his constant companion these days. "I think I'll go into town," he said, striding to the back door and grabbing his jacket. "I'll check on Randi."

"You don't wants to play?" one of the twins—Mindy, he thought—asked.

"Not right now, darlin'," he said, smiling and tousling her dark curls. "I'll take a rain check." Her face pulled into a little knot of confusion. "I mean I'll play with you another time, okay?"

"'Kay," she replied, and he felt a tug on his heart. Yep, he was getting way too tied up here. He grabbed his jacket off a hook near the back porch.

A chorus of "byes" followed after him until the door slammed shut. On one level he was glad his older brother was getting married. It was about time, and Nicole, even with her ready-made family, was a helluva catch, a beautiful woman who could handle Thorne like none other. That they loved each other was obvious to everyone. They planned to stay here at the house, rent Nicole's cottage in town and, eventually, once Randi woke up, build nearby.

If Randi ever woke up. Matt scowled into the night as his boots crunched through the crusted snow. Clouds covered the moon and stars, but so far the snow had held off. He slid into his truck and tore out of the lot. First he'd drive to the hospital, check on Randi, then he'd cruise by the station and see if Detective Dillinger was working and if not...

What then?

He pulled onto the two-lane highway and headed south toward Grand Hope without coming up with an answer.

"So I was gonna invite you over for a glass of wine, but since you're out, it'll have to wait until I get back from Seattle," Kelly said, leaving a message on her sister's answering machine. "I'll be back the night before Thanksgiving. See ya then."

Kelly hung up and stretched. She'd poured herself a glass of wine and had hoped that her sister would join her, but since she couldn't reach Karla, she'd have to alter her plans slightly. Instead of girl talk around the fire, or playing a board game with Karla's boys, Kelly decided on a bath and a good book. She hadn't soaked in the tub in ages, rarely had enough time. Instead she showered in the morning and, if she needed it, again at night. Fast, easy, done in five minutes. But tonight, after being chilled to her bones from working all day outside investigating accident scenes and vandalism to property, she decided she deserved the luxury of soft music.

She stripped off her uniform, twisted her hair into a loose knot, lit two white tapers and filled the tub with hot water. She left her glass of wine and book on the rim of the tub, then settled into the warm, scented water.

It felt like heaven.

She sank lower, half closing her eyes as the candles flickered and the heat seeped into her bloodstream, loosening the tension from her muscles. Her mind ran in slower and slower circles, winding down to eventually stop dead center at Matt McCafferty. Despite her warnings to the contrary, she thought about kissing him and her response. Deep. Heart-stopping. Breathless. He'd left her with her knees weak and an ache beginning to throb deep inside her.

Oh, she was playing with fire with that man. Kissing him was a luxury she couldn't allow herself again. At least not until the mystery surrounding his half sister was solved, and God knew when that would be. Soon...it had to be soon. She sipped her wine and tried to get into the mystery, but as she read one paragraph over and over again, she thought of Randi McCafferty's unfinished novel and she wondered at its significance. Rodeos. Barrel racing. Bareback broncos. Matt McCafferty. She could nearly picture him, lean body tense and rigid, one hand raised, the other tight around the strap surrounding a muscular, headstrong rodeo horse. With a sigh she gave up on her book and set it on the ledge. "Forget him," she chided. Closing her eyes, she nearly drifted off when she heard the doorbell chime softly over the music playing on the radio.

Her eyes snapped open.

Who in the devil would be dropping by?

Karla.

Her sister had gotten home, heard the phone message and hurried over.

"Coming!" she yelled as she stepped out of the tub, threw on her bathrobe and cinched the belt tightly around her waist. She slipped into scuffs and hurried down the stairs to the door, where she peeked through the peephole. Karla wasn't anywhere around, but Matt McCafferty, larger than life through the fish-eye lens, was staring back at her.

Her silly heart skipped a beat. She threw the bolt and swung open the door before she realized she was wearing nothing— not one solitary stitch—beneath the yellow terry robe.

His eyes widened just a fraction and for a second he actually seemed tongue-tied as he looked down at her. "I didn't realize it was so late," he said, and she swallowed a smile. Obviously he was expecting *Detective* Kelly Dillinger to answer the door, that he would be face-to-face with a no-nonsense officer of the law, dressed in full uniform and probably packing heat.

"Is there something I can do for you?" she asked.

He nodded, his eyebrows knitting into one dark line. "I was in town and I thought I'd…well, I guess I should have called." His lips compressed together and his glance shifted to one side. "I thought maybe you'd like to go out for a drink or a cup of coffee or something."

"Or something?" she prodded, amused and flattered.

"I should have called."

"That's usually the way it's done, yes," she said, not giving him an inch. Her pulse fluttered ridiculously and her heartbeat cranked up a notch as she stood in the doorway.

God, she was gorgeous, Matt thought, wondering what had compelled him to her doorstep. He'd told himself it was because he was keeping an eye on the sheriff department's investigation, that it was all business, but deep inside, he knew there was more to it, more than he cared to admit. He'd argued with himself as he'd driven to her row house, tried to convince himself to turn back to the ranch, but here he was, the victim of his own sexual drive, for that's what it was; he wanted to see her because she was an intriguing, sassy, beautiful woman. He'd expected to find a slim, all-business policewoman dressed in her uniform…but this…this fascinating lady was even more irresistible. Kelly appeared smaller, more vulnerable, incredibly feminine and damned sexy in that thick yellow duster. Her hair was piled onto her head, some strands escaping to curl in damp ringlets around a flushed face with incredible cheekbones, dark-fringed, mocking eyes and a saucy mouth curved into an amused smile.

"I suppose it's too late."

"For a date? Tonight?" she asked, folding her arms under her chest and allowing him just a peek at cleavage where the lapels of her robe overlapped. "I think so."

He felt like a schoolboy as he worked the brim of his hat between his fingers. "Maybe tomorrow."

"I'll be out of town. It's a working vacation. I'll be back in a couple of days…."

"Maybe we can get together then."

"I don't think that would be a good idea."

"No?" He couldn't help himself. Something in the defiant tilt of her chin challenged him.

"Well, you know, it might not be the proper thing to do."

"You're worried about propriety?" He didn't believe it.

"I wouldn't want to do anything where my professionalism or objectivity might be questioned."

Was it his imagination or did her eyes twinkle with a dare? The scent of jasmine reached his nostrils and he couldn't help himself. "The hell with professionalism," he growled. His arms surrounded her.

She gasped. "Now, wait a second."

"And damn objectivity." He slanted his mouth over hers. Her lips were warm and tasted faintly of wine. She moaned quietly and he kissed her harder, rubbing his mouth over hers, wrapping his arms more tightly around her body, feeling her melt against him.

The fire in his blood ignited. His fingers curled in the soft folds of her robe. He felt her quiver and it was his undoing. Deftly, he reached down, picked her off her feet and crossed the threshold.

"Hey," she said breathlessly. "What do you think you're doing?"

With a heel he kicked the door closed. "What I've wanted to do from the first time I saw you," he said, carrying her up the stairs and unerringly to her bedroom. Candles from the adjoining bath gave off a soft, glimmering illumination that reflected in the foggy mirrors and windows as he tumbled with her onto an antique bed covered with a plush comforter.

Kelly knew she should object, that she should resist the temptation of his touch, but his lips were magic, his hands warm and persuasive. He kissed her eyelids, her cheeks and neck as he somehow shrugged out of his jacket and let it drop to the floor. Work-roughened fingers scraped her robe open and he pressed his lips against the curve of her suddenly bare shoulder.

Flames of desire licked through her blood.

He untied the knot of her belt and lowered himself onto the bed. His breath was hot against the cleft between her breasts and she tingled inside, felt the first dark stirrings of want.

Don't do this, Kelly. Don't. This is the biggest mistake of your life! Think, dammit.

But she couldn't. His hands and mouth were seductive, chasing away all doubts, and try as she might, she couldn't find credence in any of the reasons she called up that might put an end to his lovemaking. She knew that her father and mother would disapprove, that her boss would consider this an act of betrayal insofar as she would compromise the investigation and her badge, that her sister would remind her that a McCafferty was the worst possible choice of a lover and yet... and yet...his lips were so warm and seductive, the ache deep within her impossible to deny.

He pulled the pins from her hair with his teeth just as the knot holding her robe together gave way, parting as his hand skimmed her skin beneath the rich cotton. A jolt of desire shot through her bloodstream. Kissing her cheek, he glanced down at her body. "I knew you'd be beautiful, Detective," he said, touching one nipple with the flat of his hand. "I knew it." He squeezed the dark bud gently and her entire breast began to ache. Oh, she wanted this man. She bucked up and he leaned forward, his mouth surrounding her nipple, his teeth lightly scraping her skin, his tongue laving.

Damn, but she was melting inside, feeling warm, moist heat coiling between her legs. As if he understood, he trailed one hand lower, fingers skimming her abdomen to delve deep into the curls where her legs joined. Lower still he probed, searching her cleft expertly, finding the nub that drove her wild, kissing her breasts as lust stormed through her blood. She moaned deep in her throat and shifted, anxiously wanting more...so much more...everything he could give...everything he would. Her skin was on fire, sweat dampening her forehead.

Her fingers tore at the buttons of his shirt, delving beneath the cotton to touch a hard-muscled chest covered in springy black hair. She touched taut, sinewy muscles, felt him tremble, but it wasn't enough. She needed to feel him, all of him, rubbing against her—skin on skin, heartbeat to heartbeat. And still he touched her deep inside. She gasped. Gripped his shoulders hard.

"Oh…oh…" She swallowed hard and felt as if her entire being was centered in that small spot that he rubbed intently. She writhed, sweated as if in a fever, felt the storm brewing hotter, and wilder.

"That's a girl," he whispered across her breasts, fanning the flames. "Just let go…"

The world seemed to spin. His lips found hers again, his tongue rimmed her mouth, his breath hot and wild against her already flushed skin. "Please," she murmured, her voice so low she didn't recognize it. "Please… Matt…oh, please…"

"Anything for you, darlin'."

She reached for the waistband of his jeans, felt his erection straining against the worn denim. "Then…"

With his free hand he grabbed her wrist. "In time, darlin', in time." His ministrations increased and she lolled back, closed her eyes, writhed and cried out as the first spasm jolted her, sending her skyrocketing through space, her soul streaking through the heavens.

"Oooh," she sighed, gasping, trying to take in any air.

But he wasn't finished. His fingers delved again, deeper, faster, pushing her to the limits again. Her fingers dug into his bare shoulders and she cried out as convulsion after convulsion ripped through her.

"Matt…oh…Matt…" She couldn't breathe, couldn't think, but knew she needed him, all of him, wanted the feel of his hard body joining with her.

She found his belt and her fingers fumbled with the huge rodeo buckle that held the strap together. Before he could protest, she kissed him, touched the tip of her tongue to his, invited him to enter her.

Groaning, sweat sheening his skin, he stretched out beside her, giving her better access, no longer fighting her.

Click.

The buckle was open.

Pop. Pop. Pop.

His fly gave way.

He felt a rush of cool air against his skin and bit his lips as her fingers brushed over his bare shaft.

Ding.

Somewhere a bell began to chime. A doorbell.

"Oh, no." Kelly's hand fell away. She turned a dozen shades of red.

"Expectin' someone?" he asked lazily, amused.

"No."

The bell chimed again. Insistently.

"Someone wants to see you real bad."

"Oh, damn. Karla! I—I left her a message earlier, on her machine...she's probably got her sons with her." She shoved her hair out of her eyes.

"Who's Karla?"

"Oh. My sister. Just...just wait." Kelly hurled herself off the bed, dashed to the closet, grabbed a shirt and a pair of jeans, then darted to the bathroom.

Matt zipped up his pants. Hooked his belt. The damned bell rang again and this time a woman's worried voice followed after it. "Kelly? Are you there? It's me."

"I know. I know," Kelly grumbled as she emerged from the bathroom. Barefoot but dressed, she was snapping her hair into a rubber band. Then, spying Matt still lounging on the bed, she hissed, "You, go sit in the living room for goodness' sake and pour yourself a glass of wine or something. Look like you've been in there all the time. Make it look…like we've been discussing the case, for crying out loud, and then…and then—" she stopped short at the foot of the bed and sighed loudly, then sent him a rueful glance "—and then brace yourself."

She disappeared out the door of the bedroom and he heard her footsteps hurrying down the stairs.

Matt hitched up his jeans, sauntered into the living room and, finding an open bottle of wine, went to a cupboard, plucked a long-stemmed glass from the shelf and heard the door open somewhere downstairs. Female voices reached him.

"Jeez, Kelly, didn't you hear the doorbell ring? I darned well froze my tail off waiting for you!" Footsteps pounded up the stairs. "What took you so long to…" A small woman with short red-blond hair and wide green eyes that landed full force on Matt appeared. "Uh-oh." She stopped dead in her tracks and the playful smile that had been tugging at the corners of her mouth faded. "Kelly…what's going on here?" Her eyes narrowed a fraction and zeroed in on the wineglass in Matt's hand.

"Oh. Well. Matt came over to discuss the case."

"Matt?" the woman repeated.

Kelly entered the room and despite the circumstances seemed cool. "Yes. Matt McCafferty, this is my sister, Karla."

"Pleased to meet ya," Matt drawled as Kelly's sister seemed all the more disconcerted. He had the manners to reach across the counter and clasp Karla's reluctantly offered hand.

"Oh, yeah, me, too," Karla said, rolling her expressive eyes before catching a hard look from her sister. "Wait a minute, is this for real?"

"What do you mean?" Kelly said. "Is what for real? Matt and I were going over—"

"Whoa." Karla held her hands up, the fingers of her right pointing into the palm of her left. "Time out, okay?" She skewered both Kelly and Matt in her hard glare. "Don't give me any garbage about the case. I've got eyes, Kelly." She gave her sister an exaggerated once-over. "I just hope you know what you're doing."

"Of course I do."

"Care for something to drink? A glass of wine?" Matt offered as he grabbed another stemmed glass from the cupboard and began to pour from the bottle of chardonnay.

"I think I need something stronger, but yeah, okay."

"There isn't anything stronger. I already asked."

Karla didn't so much as blink, just took the drink from Matt's hand and, with one last condemning glare at her sister, plopped down in a rattan chair covered with a plump green cushion. "So how is the investigation going?" she asked with more than an edge of sarcasm.

"There are some snags, of course, and we keep coming up against dead ends, but I think we're making progress."

"Ummm." Karla swirled her wine but obviously wasn't buying her sister's story.

Matt emptied the bottle into another glass and gave the drink to Kelly.

"I'm leaving for Seattle tomorrow," she explained, and fielded the questions Karla shot at her. From the gist of the conversation he gathered that Karla, after hearing Kelly's open invitation left on her answering machine, had decided to stop by. The younger Dillinger sibling had pawned her kids off on her folks and driven over, only to find Matt already here. For some reason his presence rankled Karla, and there was more to it than disappointment at having to share her sister for the evening. No, there were undercurrents of resentment running through the conversation and pooling in her eyes.

Rounding the kitchen bar, he joined the women in Kelly's small living room. He'd expected her apartment to be neat and tidy, functional yet spartan, but, as with everything about this woman, he'd been dead wrong. The row house wasn't cluttered but definitely had a lived-in feel. A raised counter separated the living room from the kitchen. Along with the rattan chair, there was an antique rocker, a tan couch with floppy pillows and a beveled-glass coffee table that appeared to match a lawyer's bookcase, crammed with all manner of paperbacks and criminology texts. A fussy walnut secretary occupied one corner and a collection of candles and photographs graced the mantel of a small fireplace.

"You said in the phone message that you'd be back in time for Thanksgiving," she said to her sister.

"That's the plan."

"Good." Kelly's sister relaxed a bit, sipping from her wine as Kelly took a seat on the couch and Matt leaned against the counter. "I wouldn't want to explain to Mom and Dad that you weren't going to show up at the house because of work."

"Dad would understand. He was a cop."

"Eons ago."

"So you come from a family tradition of fighting crime," Matt observed.

"Mmm. Dad, his father and, I think, my great-grandfather."

"It beat mining," Karla said. "Until Dad got shot and had to retire early. Disability." She finished her glass of wine with a flourish. "So, how about you?" she asked him, though she expected she knew a lot more about his family than he did about hers. Like it or not, the McCafferty name was nearly legendary around this part of western Montana, and Karla was fishing. The smile on her face was about as warm as the bottom of a Montana well in the middle of winter. "What is it your family does?"

She didn't bother to hide the bite in her words.

"Dad was a rodeo man turned rancher, bought the Flying M over fifty years ago and expanded that to include some other businesses around Grand Hope."

Karla's lips compressed and she cast a hard, darting glance at her sister. "He doesn't remember, does he?"

"Remember what?" Matt demanded.

Little lines of irritation surrounded Karla's lips but it was Kelly who answered. "Mom worked for your dad for a few years."

"Not just a few," Karla said, setting her empty glass onto the table. "She dedicated her life to that man, to her job as his secretary, or personal assistant, yeah, that's what he called her." She snorted. "And what happened when things started to go bad for your father's businesses? Mom was history. Just like that." Karla snapped her fingers for emphasis and her cheeks had turned a bright, hot scarlet. "No job, no retirement fund, no damned golden parachute. Nothing."

"Wait a minute—you said she was his secretary?"

"And more. She was like his right-hand woman, his executive assistant. Surely you remember her. Eva. Eva Dillinger."

"Eva?" The name did have a familiar ring, but Matt had never spoken to the woman. He'd only heard her name a couple of times in passing when John Randall had mentioned her, but Matt hadn't paid much attention. He was too self-involved at the time. "I guess Dad did mention her once in a while."

"Once in a while? I hope to shout he did," Karla said with a shake of her head. She glanced at the open bedroom door where Kelly's yellow robe was sliding off the messed bed. Her lips puckered even more. She seemed about to say something, then thought better of it and stood. "Maybe I'd better leave," she said, and some of her anger dissipated. "I think I interrupted something."

"You stay." Matt glanced at his watch. "It's time I was heading back, anyway." He drained his glass and set it on the edge of the counter. Reaching for his jacket, he said to Kelly, "Just let me know if you learn anything else about what happened to my sister."

"I will." Kelly walked him to the top of the stairs where he paused to zip his jacket.

"I'll talk to you later, oh..." He held up a long finger. "There is one more thing."

"What's that?" she asked, visibly tensing.

"Have a good trip."

"I will."

He turned to Karla. "Nice meetin' ya."

"You, too," she said, though the words seemed to strangle her. She was watching him as if he were the devil incarnate and Matt couldn't let it go.

With an exaggerated wink toward Karla, he turned on his heel, slipped his arms around Kelly's waist and dragged her close to him. "Thanks for the hospitality, Detective. Now, don't you forget me." He leaned forward and kissed her. Hard. Like he intended to ravish her body and never stop. She stiffened, then slumped slightly. He let her go, she stumbled back a step, then he winked at Karla again and headed down the stairs.

"Oh, my," Karla whispered, her gaze following him as he disappeared. Her eyes rounded and one hand covered her heart. "Oh...my."

Kelly steeled herself for the barrage she was certain was headed her way.

"You're in love with him, aren't you?" Karla accused, but some of the fury had left her voice and it was replaced by an emotion akin to awe.

Downstairs the front door opened, then slammed shut. Matt McCafferty was gone. A few seconds later an engine sparked to life.

"Well...you are, aren't you?" Karla demanded.

"No, of course not," Kelly snapped, stunned as she found her wineglass, polished off the last drops of chardonnay and gathered her wits. In love? With Matt McCafferty? Her heart pounded a million beats a minute at the thought. Oh, God, was she? Could she possibly have fallen for the smart-aleck, rogue of a cowboy? "That's ridiculous."

"I see it in your eyes," Karla countered as she walked to the window and peeked through the blinds to the wintry night outside. "I can't believe it, Kelly. Someone's managed to melt the ice around your heart and he's a damned Mc-Cafferty." Folding her arms across her chest, she clucked her tongue, cocked her head and eyed her sister as if she'd never seen Kelly in such a state. "Another time, I'd say we should celebrate, but since the man of your dreams is John Randall's son, I think it would be a better idea if I called a priest and asked for an exorcism."

"Very funny," Kelly grouched.

"It's not, I know, but *really,* are you out of your ever-lovin' mind? Mom and Dad are gonna flip when they find out and your boss will probably fire you. I mean, come *on,* what about the investigation?"

"Mom and Dad don't run my life, my boss can't tell me

what to do when I'm not on duty and the investigation is still ongoing. I haven't compromised anything."

"Yet," Karla said, unconvinced. She walked to the bedroom door and looked pointedly inside. "But it wouldn't be long."

"It's none of your business and you're borrowing trouble." Kelly carried the wineglasses to the sink and her sister padded after her.

"I don't think I have to borrow any. You've got enough to last us both for the rest of our lives. Oh, Kelly, don't be dumb, okay?" Karla rapped her fingers around her sister's upper arm. "The McCaffertys are bad news, all of them. You can't trust any one of them as far as you can throw them."

"I've heard this lecture before."

"Excuse me, I thought *you* were the one who gave it. Just listen, for God's sake. Whatever you do, Kelly," Karla advised with all the wisdom of someone who'd made more than her share of mistakes when it came to affairs of the heart, "don't fall in love with Matt McCafferty."

"I won't."

"It would be a devastating mistake."

"I said, 'I won't.'"

"And I think you're a liar. It's probably already happened." Karla held up her hands as if to ward off any further protests. "But if you are in love with him, you're in trouble. Deep trouble. All you'll get out of it is a broken heart. That, I can guarantee."

Chapter 9

"Where are you going?" Slade asked as Matt, hiking the strap of his duffel bag over his shoulder, hurried down the stairs. Slade was standing by the fireplace in the living room with a clear view of the foyer and bottom step. Standing in stocking feet, warming the backs of his calves by a slow-burning fire, he cradled a cup of coffee in his hands and had been paying attention to Larry Todd, who, Matt gleaned from the tail end of the conversation, was explaining the need for a new pole barn.

"So it wouldn't cost that much, as it's basically a roof on poles. It would just give the stock some more shelter and make feeding easier."

"I don't see why not," Slade replied, then looked past Larry to the bottom of the stairs.

Matt paused in the archway and explained, "I hope you and Thorne can hold down the fort. I'm gonna be spending a couple of days in Seattle."

"Don't tell me, the lady detective is there." Slade's smile was downright evil, and with the scar running down one side of his face and the antlers mounted over the mantel seeming to be growing out of his head, he looked even more fiendish. "Right? Detective Dillinger is there."

Matt didn't bother to answer. "On my way back, I'll stop by my place, check in with Kavanaugh, and be back by Thanksgiving."

"That's only few days away. And Nicole mentioned something about both of us going into town to make sure our tuxes for the wedding fit."

"Did she?" Matt wasn't deterred.

"She'll be mad as a wet hen if you don't take care of this. The wedding's set to go as soon as Randi wakes up."

"The tux will fit fine, the wedding will go on without a hitch, and they'll get married," Matt bit out, his temper starting to control his tongue. "Tell her not to get her knickers in a knot. Randi is not even conscious yet. As I said, I'll be back in a couple of days." He clomped down the hall toward the kitchen and the seductive scent of coffee. He'd woken up in a bad mood, having slept poorly, his dreams peppered with images of Kelly—sexy, hot images that had forced him to a shower that felt sub-zero this morning.

He passed the den. From the corner of his eye, he saw Thorne, his casted leg propped by a corner of the desk, a phone crammed to one ear, his black eyebrows pulled into a thick line of consternation as he read the monitor of his computer.

"I'm outta here," Matt said, and Thorne, absorbed in his conversation, took a second to glance up. He held one finger aloft, signifying Matt should wait a second. Probably for orders. Matt wasn't in the mood. "Be back in a couple of days."

"Hold on, Eloise, looks like I've got a crisis here," Thorne said into the receiver, then turned all of his attention on his middle brother. "Where the hell are you going?"

Matt repeated himself. "Striker says I should keep an eye on the police, and since the sheriff's department is sending Kelly Dillinger to Seattle, I decided that I should tag along."

"Does she know it?"

"Nope."

"Thanksgiving is in three days."

"I know, I know, and Slade was already on my case about the tux. I'll take care of it when I get back."

"You'd better." Nicole's voice preceded her, and Matt inwardly groaned as he turned to face his soon-to-be sister-in-law. Her hair was pinned back and she was wearing a crisp white blouse, dark slacks and a wide belt. A briefcase swung from her fingers, as she was on her way to the ER at St. James Hospital. She took her place in the doorway next to him. "If you don't," she warned, her lips quirking as she fought a smile, "I'll just have to tar and feather you, *then* skin you alive."

"Thanks, *Doctor.* Anything else?"

"That should do it. For now."

"Are you always this much fun?" Matt grumbled.

"Only when I want something." She smiled sweetly, then rested a shoulder against the door frame and turned her attention to Thorne. "I'll look in on Randi, and Jenny should be here any minute to see to the twins and the baby. Juanita's feeding him right now. I kissed the girls goodbye, but they both fell back to sleep, so they shouldn't give you too much trouble."

"I wouldn't count on it," Thorne grumbled, but his eyes had brightened at the sight of Nicole.

She chuckled, the sound deep and low. "I'll call them later."

Sliding a glance at her brother-in-law-to-be, she added, "You might want to say goodbye to your nephew."

"I will."

"Good." She blew a kiss to Thorne, then walked briskly down the hallway toward the kitchen.

Thorne's gaze followed her, his important call temporarily forgotten as he watched the sway of her hips. Boy, did he have it bad. When the lovebug bit Thorne McCafferty, it wasn't just a tiny nip. Thorne had been swallowed whole.

"I'll call," Matt said, and followed his future sister-in-law to the kitchen. As Nicole stated, Juanita was cradling the downy-haired baby in her arms and singing something that sounded like a Spanish lullaby to J.R. The baby blinked his round eyes and stared at the housekeeper-cum-nanny as if he was mes-merized.

Matt poured himself a cup of coffee from the pot simmer-ing on the coffeemaker. Juanita was doing a helluva job with the kid, and Jenny Riley, Nicole's babysitter, was a godsend. But, by rights, little J.R. should be with his mother. Right now Randi should be the one singing to him, cuddling him, even nursing him. The muscles in the back of Matt's neck tight-ened as he thought of the bastard who'd tried to kill his sister. Not once, but twice. Who the hell was he? Could he possibly be J.R.'s missing father? That would be a bitch. The poor kid would be screwed up for life. Matt couldn't imagine saying, *Yeah, J.R., we didn't know who your father was, but it turned that he didn't claim you and tried to kill your mother while she was preg-nant with you, and when that didn't work, tried again when she was in a coma in the hospital.*

Still in a black mood, Matt took two long swallows from his cup, then tossed the dregs into the sink.

"You're leaving?" Juanita asked, eyeing his duffel bag.

"*After* he gets fitted for his tux," Nicole said. She was half-serious, half-teasing. She sipped from her coffee cup and rested a hip against the counter.

"I'll take care of it." Tapping J.R.'s button of a nose, Matt said, "Don't give anyone any trouble, okay?" The baby cooed and Matt felt that familiar pull on his heartstrings that had become a part of his life here at the Flying M, new emotions that both J.R. and Kelly evoked in him.

Damn it all, anyway, what was happening to him? Ever since he'd heard the first news of Randi's accident, he'd changed. Angry at himself and the whole damned world, he squared his hat upon his head and ignored Juanita's protests that he needed a real breakfast before he left.

A broken heart indeed, Kelly thought the next day as she slid behind the wheel of her rental car at the Sea-Tac airport. *That would be the day.* But as she drove through the tangle of traffic toward downtown Seattle, flipping on her windshield wipers against the steady rain, she knew there was a smidgen of truth in her sister's concerns. She was falling in love with Matt Mc-Cafferty and it was a monumental mistake. Mon-u-men-tal.

But, no matter how she tried to talk herself out of seeing him again, she knew she wouldn't. It was all part of that moth-and-flame scenario where she was attracted to something that would ultimately burn her. "Fool, fool, fool," she admonished as she switched lanes, brake lights flashed in front of her, and someone honked loudly. She found the address of the Seattle PD, and after scouring the parking lot, squeezed the rental into a tight spot. Dashing through the rain, she headed into the building.

She spent the next five hours at the police station talking with a friendly, heavyset detective who had been handling information on Randi McCafferty. Oscar Trullinger told her that so far no one could see that the book Randi had been writing was connected to the attacks upon her in any way and that they had no new information. Of the men she'd been associated with, none seemed likely to hold a grudge against her. Sam Donahue was currently living in western Washington on a ranch outside of Spokane; Joe Paterno, the photojournalist, was on assignment in Alaska; and Brodie Clanton, whose great-grandfather had founded the *Clarion,* was out of the country, vacationing in a villa in Puerto Vallarta, Mexico.

How convenient that all of the men Randi McCafferty had dated weren't anywhere near Seattle. *Too convenient,* she thought as she drove to the offices of the *Seattle Clarion.* Located on the third floor of a brown brick building near Pioneer Square, the offices of the newspaper weren't much different from what she expected. Inside, the once-open rooms were broken up by modular units of soundproof walls where cluttered desks were occupied by a dozen or so reporters all typing on keyboards of computers, or talking on the phone, or scanning news reports on small television sets. Through the windows, views into other buildings and a few glimpses of the gray sky and green waters of Puget Sound were visible.

"Can I help you?" a sober receptionist with doelike eyes asked.

"I'd like to speak to Bill Withers," Kelly said, and flashed her badge. "Detective Kelly Dillinger. I'm from Grand Hope, Montana. I have some questions about Randi McCafferty."

The receptionist offered what might be considered a smile. "Mr. Withers isn't in right now."

Kelly wasn't surprised. "How about Joe Paterno or Sara Peeples?" she asked, though, again, she anticipated the answer.

"Joe's on assignment, won't be back until tomorrow. But

Sara's in. I'll let her know you're here." Without waiting for a reply, she pushed a button and left the appropriate message.

Within two minutes a small woman with a long face, oversize features and tousled blond curls appeared. She wore a short fitted dress, boots, jacket and half a dozen bracelets that jangled as she walked.

"You're Detective Dillinger?" Sara asked. "I'm Sara, and I'm really glad you're here. How's Randi?"

"Holding her own."

"Come on back, my desk is a mess, but we can talk there." She led Kelly through a maze of desks and past a fax machine and copy center to a desk in the corner, near what appeared to be an adjacent office dedicated to photography. "I heard Randi's still in a coma. That someone might have tried to kill her."

"That's what we're looking into," Kelly admitted.

"Wow." Sara's smile twisted at the irony. "You know, the paper reports this kind of thing all the time, but it doesn't really touch you until it's someone you know. Someone who's your friend or relative."

"I know. I was hoping you could tell me a little about Randi. Who she hung out with, who she was dating, who were her friends and enemies."

"And who the father of her baby is," Sara said. "That's the million-dollar question, isn't it? And I don't know." She seemed earnest, her eyebrows knitting, her lips pursing as she thought. "You know, I don't know who would want to hurt Randi and I would hope it wouldn't be the father of her kid, but the world is made up of all kinds...."

For the next two hours Kelly talked to Sara and others in the office and left without much more information than she came in with. No one had any idea who would want to hurt her, who the father of her baby was, who she'd inadvertently ticked off. She had girlfriends from college, one in particular, Sharon Okano, whom she was close to, an aunt and female cousin on her mother's side who weren't related to any of Randi's brothers, and it was generally thought that she was writing a novel, a fictional story against a backdrop of the rodeo circuit. Aside from her regular column, she occasionally wrote a freelance piece.

It was dark by the time Kelly checked into a hotel overlooking Elliott Bay, where she made her way to her room and tossed her purse onto the table.

She stood at the window, stared at the gray water for a few seconds, then placed a call to Randi's friend, Sharon, who, according the recorded message, would call her back "as soon as possible." Kelly left her name and the number of her hotel along with the telephone number of the sheriff's department in Grand Hope, then called the department and left a voice-mail message for Espinoza. Those tasks completed, she decided to explore the city. Windows ablaze, skyscrapers knifed upward from the steep hills, traffic whizzed past, and pedestrians huddled in raincoats and, carrying umbrellas, hurried along the wet pavement.

Kelly made her way to the waterfront, where a stiff breeze blew across the white-capped sound and ferries chugged through the dark water. Though it wasn't quite Thanksgiving, there were already hints of Christmas in the store windows, and there was a buzz in the air, an electricity that seemed to charge the night.

She bought a cup of chowder from a small restaurant located on Pier 56 and hiked back to her hotel, feeling wound tight and wondering what Matt McCafferty was doing. She thought about the fact that she'd nearly made love to him and knew in her heart that given a second chance, she'd do it again. Jamming her fists into her pockets, she considered the consequences of that one fateful act.

What would be the harm?

She was an adult.

He was an adult.

But you're a cop and he's the brother of a victim, perhaps even a suspect. Not that she believed the local gossip. Her hair was wet by the time she reached the hotel, her cheeks chapped and her fingers icy. She walked through the rotating door and started for the elevator when she sensed, rather than saw, someone fall into step with her. A hint of musky aftershave, and just the wisp of the scent of leather and horses. "How did you find me?" she asked, her heart skipping a beat as she caught his reflection in the elevator doors.

"A little detective work."

She nearly laughed. "Oh, yeah, right."

The doors parted and she stepped into the waiting car. Matt was beside her and she looked up into his dark eyes. They sparked with humor and something decidedly more dangerous.

"You think you've got the market cornered on snooping?"

"I don't think of it as snooping."

He pressed a button for the top floor of the hotel and she reached forward to poke a different one, but he grabbed her hand. "I thought you might want to come up to my room for a while. Have a drink."

Her throat tightened. "Did you?" She shook her head. "I know that we got a little carried away the other night, but it's really not a good idea for us to…" She lifted her shoulders and one hand as the elevator rumbled ever upward. "Well, considering the circumstances, it just wouldn't be smart for us to get involved."

"We already are." He was standing next to her, not touching her, just seeming to fill the whole damned car. Kelly felt claustrophobic, as if she couldn't breathe.

"Okay, then, maybe not any *more* involved. Until this case is solved, I don't have any business losing my objectivity."

"Too late." He grabbed her then, and though she knew she should tell him to go jump in the proverbial lake, she didn't. Instead she tilted her chin upward and met his warm mouth with her chilled lips. His arms wrapped around her, and as the elevator car landed on the uppermost floor, he kissed her. Hard. Long. With enough passion to send tingles to the deepest part of her.

The battle was over and she knew it, didn't bother to protest or resist as he lifted her from her feet and, like a groom carrying a bride on his wedding night, carried her over the threshold of the penthouse suite.

She closed her eyes and lost herself in him. They were alone, and what would one little night together harm? Groaning, he worked at the zipper of her jacket, peeling the unwanted garment from her easily as he kissed her. First the jacket, then her sweater, her boots and jeans, all piled onto the plush carpet, and she didn't stop him, just kissed him as fervently as he kissed her.

She was vaguely aware of the dimmed lights, hissing fire and flowers scenting the room as she stripped him of his clothes, but those images were lost in the touch and feel of his work-roughened hands caressing her body, his lips and tongue touching and tasting her, the length of him pressed hard against her. Slowly he pressed her backward onto the satin comforter stretched across a king-size bed.

"How...how did you find me?" she asked again as they tumbled together.

"When I want something, I go after it." He caressed her

chin with one long finger. "You told me you were leaving, I decided to follow."

"Seattle's a pretty big city."

His smile was wickedly delicious. "I'm a pretty determined guy."

"With connections."

"Lots of 'em." He kissed her shoulder and she shivered with want.

"And you use them."

"When I have to." He leaned toward her, kissing the top of her breast and lowering her bra strap, exposing more of her. Kelly swallowed hard as his hands sculpted her ribs, sliding behind her back, drawing her closer, and he finally took her nipple into his mouth.

She thought she would die.

He suckled and she arched her back.

"Kelly," he whispered across her abdomen, and lowered himself, brushing his mouth across her skin, touching her, tasting her, teasing her, dragging her panties down her legs and tossing them onto the floor. She writhed at his ministrations and she felt herself melting, wanting, aching for more of him. The corners of the room began to fog and she knew only the sensations he evoked from her.

Sweat dotted her body and her blood pounded through her veins, pulsing in her eardrums, thundering through her brain. She heard a moan before she recognized her own voice. Heat spread from the back of her neck through her extremities and she moved against him, wanting so much more.

"Matt, please…" she whispered throatily, and he came to her, slid up against her and somehow kicked off his jeans. His lips found hers, muscular arms circled her body as he poised above her for a heart-stopping moment. In one thrust, he entered her and she gasped against his skin. He began to move and she caught his tempo, her blood on fire, her heart thudding. Her fingers scraped his back and he held her tight, breathing in counterpoint to her own ragged gasps, his rhythm increasing, his sinewy body straining with each rapid thrust.

She stared into eyes that looked down at her, deep brown, intense, searching her soul. Deep inside she convulsed, and behind her eyes a thousand colors splintered, a million lights danced, and she was certain the universe collided. He let go and with a roar as untamed as the wild Montana wind, he fell against her, wrapped his arms around her and buried his face in her neck. "Kelly," he whispered. "Oh…Kelly."

They lay spent, entwined until at last their breathing had calmed. She nestled against him, resting her cheek on his bare shoulder as he caressed her face and brushed the hair off her cheek.

A dozen recriminations assailed her, but she ignored them. Instead, she slid him a mischievous glance. "So…tell me, cowboy," she teased. "What do you do for an encore?"

He barked out a laugh. "You want to see?"

"Mmm." She ran fingers through the curling hairs of his chest. "If you've got it in you?"

"You're asking for it, lady."

"Again. I'm asking for it again," she clarified with a giggle.

Quick as a rattler striking, he surrounded her, pressed his mouth against hers, and as she gasped, said, "Then you're gonna get it."

"Wait a second—" But her protest was cut off by his kiss, and within a heartbeat her blood had heated again, her heart was pounding and she lost herself all over again, realizing as she did so that there was no doubt about it, she was hopelessly, helplessly in love with him.

Chapter 10

"Randi's awake." Slade's voice echoed through the telephone wires and pounded through Matt's brain the next morning. Matt glanced to the side of the mussed bed where Kelly, her red hair splayed around her face, was stretching, yawning, those beautiful brown eyes blinking out of a deep sleep.

"When?"

"Just a little while ago."

"Has she said anything?" he asked, and Kelly was instantly alert, all traces of slumber disappearing. She'd reached over the side of the bed for her clothes.

"Not yet. I'm on my way to the hospital now."

"We'll catch the next flight out."

"We?" Slade repeated, and Matt winced.

His brother chuckled and the sound grated on Matt's nerves. "You can tell me all about it when you get back to Grand Hope, brother." Slade hung up and Matt reached for his clothes.

"Randi?" Kelly asked.

"She's awake."

She was suddenly all business. "What are we waiting for?"

"Maybe you'll tell me what's going on," Randi said as Matt and Kelly walked into her already-crowded hospital room. Slade, Thorne and Nicole surrounded the bed where Randi was ready to spit nails. "I want to see my baby."

Not only awake, Randi was ready to tear into any doctor or brother who made the mistake of keeping her from her child from limb to proverbial limb. In a private room, the top half of her bed elevated, she was glaring at the small gathering of people around her bed, and Matt felt as if a ton of bricks had been lifted from his shoulders.

Randi's brown eyes were clear, her face only slightly swollen, her short mahogany-colored hair sticking up at odd angles. Her jaw, which had previously been wired, was now working with some difficulty as the wires had been removed, and she winced as she lifted her right arm as if her broken ribs still bothered her. However, it was easy to read her expression: she was ticked. Big-time.

"Is there any reason she can't see J.R.?" Matt asked, his gaze landing on Nicole.

"We're arranging it."

"Well, arrange it faster," Randi insisted as she read the name tag pinned to her lab coat. "Who are you?"

"Dr. Stevenson," Nicole answered as Randi's eyes narrowed on her.

"I can see that, but I already met two other doctors who claim to be taking care of me." She was speaking with some difficulty, only forcing out the words by sheer will. They sounded a little muffled, but the message was clear: Randi

McCafferty was awake, angry and not about to be bullied. Good. That meant she was definitely getting better.

"I was the admitting doctor when you were brought in," Nicole explained, "and you were in pretty bad shape. Aside from being comatose, you had a concussion, punctured lung, broken ribs, a fractured jaw and a nearly shattered femur. Some of your bones have knit, you can talk, but it'll be a while before you can walk, I'm afraid, and then there was the complication that you've just had a C-section. And don't forget to factor in that someone slipped some insulin into your IV and you nearly died, so I think it would be best if you just took your time, listened to the doctors' orders and tried to get well before you start making too many demands."

"So are you the one in charge? My physician of record?"

"You have several. In fact, an entire team. I'm just interested because you were my patient and…and I'm involved with your family."

"Involved?" Randi repeated, her eyes narrowing. "What does that mean—'involved'?"

"Nicole's my fiancée," Thorne explained, stepping closer to the bed rails and linking his fingers through Nicole's. "And believe me, we'll bring the baby in as soon as the pediatrician and your doctors agree."

"Fiancée?" Randi whispered, then winced as if a sudden pain had slammed through her brain. "Wait a minute, Thorne. You? You're going to get *married?*"

"That's right. We've only been waiting for you to recover so that you could attend the wedding."

"Hold on a sec. This is a little too much for me to process. Just how long have I been out of it?"

"Over a month," Slade said.

"Holy Toledo!" She lifted her hand palm outward to stop

the flow of conversation. "Now, wait a minute," she said, finally zeroing in on Thorne's cane and cast. "What happened to you?"

"An accident. I was lucky. My plane went down."

"What?"

"And you..." She turned her eyes in Slade's direction. "Were you hurt, too?"

Slade touched the fine line that ran from his eyebrow to chin. "Nope. Skiing accident. Don't you remember?"

She shook her head slowly.

"It happened last winter, not quite a year ago. You saw the scar at Dad's funeral."

Her eyes clouded. "There's a lot I don't remember," she admitted, then turned her attention to Matt. "Is the whole family falling apart? What about you? Seems like everyone named McCafferty is cursed, so what's happened to you?"

"Nothing," he said.

"No near-death experiences, no injuries, no engagement?"

"Not so far," he drawled, and saw Kelly's shoulders stiffen slightly.

"Good. As for you," Randi said to Thorne, "I'll catch up on your love life later. For now, what I want is to see my son, so you can either bring him to visit me, or I'm walking out of here."

"Hang in for a while, okay?" Slade requested, his voice surprisingly tender. "We named him, J.R., like junior or after Dad. He's with Juanita at the ranch, and as soon as we can we'll get you two together."

"Just don't waste any time, okay?" Randi was adamant, but obviously starting to tire. "And we'll discuss the name thing. I don't think I want to stick with J.R. I mean, come *on*. After

Dad?" She swept a skeptical gaze over her brothers. "Whose brilliant idea was that?"

"Mine," Thorne said.

"Figures. You always were a Dudley Do Right. Even though you couldn't stand the guy."

Thorne started to argue but held his tongue, and Kelly stepped forward, closer to Randi's bed. "I'm Kelly Dillinger, with the sheriff's department," she said clearly as she offered an encouraging smile. Matt had a quick mental flash of another grin, one much more naughty, that she'd rained on him last night. His thoughts strayed for a second to their passionate night in Seattle, but he forced himself into the here and now. With Randi. "When the doctors agree," Kelly was saying, "I'd like to speak to you about the accident."

Randi's eyes clouded. "The accident..." she said, and shook her head.

"Up near Glacier Park. You were forced off the road, we think," Thorne added.

"You mean you think that someone purposely tried to kill me?"

"It's a possibility," Kelly said. "Or possibly it was a hit-and-run accident and the guilty party took off. But that seems unlikely, since someone walked into your hospital room and injected you with insulin. We're approaching this as an attempted homicide."

Randi's gaze traveled from one somber-faced half brother to the next. "Tell me she's exaggerating."

"'Fraid not," Matt replied, his blood cold at the thought of how close the would-be murderer had come to snuffing out Randi's life.

"Oh, God." The starch seeped from Randi's body and she leaned back on her pillow. "I...I can't remember...." Her eyebrows slammed together in concentration. "In fact...I don't remember much," she admitted. "I mean, I know all of you and realize I'm in a hospital and I know that I'm a writer, that I usually live in Seattle, but...so much else is blurry."

Thorne's shoulders stiffened. "How about the father of your child?" he asked, and the room was instantly so quiet that the noise from the hallway—the rattling gurneys, carts and the hum of conversation—seemed suddenly loud and intrusive. "Who's J.R.'s dad?"

Randi swallowed and turned suddenly pale. She glanced down at her hands, one strapped to an IV, the other bound by plaster and tape, her left hand bare, no wedding band surrounding her third finger. "The baby's father," she whispered, biting her lip. "I...I can't remember...I mean...oh, damn." She blinked rapidly, as if fighting a sudden wash of tears.

"That's enough," Nicole interjected. "She needs to rest."

"No!" Randi was adamant. "Are you a mother?" she asked her soon-to-be sister-in-law.

"Yes. I have twin girls."

"Then you understand. I want to see my baby. And as for you—" she swung her gaze to Kelly "—I'll answer anything I can, but right now I can't remember a thing. Maybe seeing my baby will jog my memory."

Matt knew a con when he saw one, and unless he missed his guess, his half sister was conning all of them, bargaining by trading on their emotions. Randi wanted to be reunited with her child, and she'd pull out all the stops, including lying about what she remembered, to attain her goal. Matt didn't blame her. The best medicine in the world for baby and mother was to get them together. "I'll take care of it," he said.

"Wait a minute." Nicole was suddenly in his face. Nicely,

but with emphasis on each syllable, she added firmly, "Of course we'll bring J.R. here as soon as possible."

Matt glanced over Nicole's shoulder to the battered, determined woman lying on the bed. "I'll see to it," he said to Randi, and he meant it. To hell with hospital procedure and damn the police investigation. Right now, all that mattered was to get J.R. into Randi's eager arms.

"So that's about the size of it," Kelly reported to Espinoza later in the day. He, too, had visited St. James, only to be rebuffed by hospital personnel. He hadn't gotten so much as a word with Randi and now sat in his chair, one leg crossed over the other, fingers tented under his chin, as Kelly told him about her dealings with the Seattle PD, the people at the *Clarion* and later, her short conversation with Randi McCafferty.

"You think she's an amnesiac?"

"I don't know." Kelly was seated on the corner of a visitor's chair on the other side of his cluttered desk. She lifted a shoulder. "Randi obviously remembered her brothers, her job, where she worked, but the accident seemed to elude her. Any references to foul play stopped her short, but she was bound and determined to see her child. Until she and J.R. are reunited, I don't think we'll get much out of her, including the name of the baby's father."

"Odd," Espinoza commented, clicking his pen as he concentrated. He was beginning to grow a mustache again, his upper lip darker than it had been a few days earlier.

"Not really. I think the motherhood instinct is the strongest on the planet."

He sent her a look silently begging the question *How would you know?* but had the presence of mind not to ask it. They talked for a while longer and he asked her how she'd gotten the information on Randi, as he'd tried to call her hotel room and no one had answered. Kelly couldn't dodge that one, admitting that she'd heard the information from Matt McCafferty, whom she'd bumped into in Seattle. Espinoza's eyebrows had lifted, inviting further details, but Kelly hadn't offered any. She was still trying to sort out her own emotions on her involvement with Matt. She didn't want or need any fatherly or brotherly advice from anyone. Especially not her boss, who seemed edgy and out of sorts.

"Some people still think one or maybe all of the McCafferty men should be suspects."

"Why?" She couldn't keep the snap from her voice.

"Because the half sister inherited so much, for starters. She was obviously the old man's favorite. If she was out of the way, everything would be left to her child, and since there's no father stepping forward, Randi's brothers would probably be appointed guardians."

"I think I told you before that theory's way off base."

"Just reminding you."

"Fine. I'm reminded," she snapped, then caught the censure in his eyes. He'd been testing her and she'd risen to the bait like a stupid trout to a salmon fly.

Irritated at Espinoza, her job, herself and life in general, she left her boss's office without slamming the door, collected a cup of coffee, received the local gossip and phone messages from Stella, then holed up in her office where she typed reports, returned calls and generally caught up. She worked through lunch, then spent the afternoon following leads in the McCafferty case. Who was trying to kill Randi or terrorize the McCaffertys and why? Something Espinoza had said triggered her to search through her notes. Motive. That's what they needed. Who besides the brothers would benefit by Randi's death?

Was there someone angling for her job? A boyfriend who'd been jilted? J.R.'s father, whoever he was? Someone with an old grudge against the family?

Like your own mother?

John Randall had made his share of enemies during his lifetime, but he was dead. Certainly no one would seek revenge against his progeny. But what about Randi? Had she offended someone in her columns, inadvertently triggered a homicidal response in someone who had written to her seeking advice? What about the book? Did someone know that she was writing about graft and corruption, and if so, who?

With more questions than answers, she finally gave up and stretched, her back popping as she shut off her computer and climbed out of her desk chair. The night crew had arrived and she waved to some of the officers she knew, then, zipping up her jacket and yanking on her gloves, made her way to her four-wheel drive.

The temperature was nearly ten degrees below freezing and she didn't want to think what the windchill added. Snow was beginning to fall again, dancing in front of her headlights and sticking to the windshield.

Adjusting the heater, she listened to the local news, only to be reminded by a newscaster that Randi McCafferty, the local woman who'd been in a coma for over a month, had woken up.

It was after seven by the time she reached her house, climbed up the stairs, peeled off her clothes and took a long shower. She'd just opened a can of soup when the phone rang. Her heart skipped a ridiculous beat at the thought that it might be Matt, and when she answered, she was disappointed to hear her sister's voice.

"About time you got home," Karla reprimanded.

Kelly stretched the phone cord so that she could stir her soup as it heated on the stove. "I do work for a living."

"So do I."

"It wasn't a dig."

"I know that," Karla said quickly.

"I'm just in a lousy mood."

"And I thought you'd be euphoric what with Randi Mc-Cafferty waking up."

"So you heard."

"Everyone's heard. I wondered what she had to say," Karla said.

"Not much." Kelly turned the burner down. "Come on, Karla, you know I can't discuss a case with you."

"Yeah, but I heard over at the Pub'n'Grub that Randi hasn't told anyone who the father of the baby is."

"You shouldn't listen to gossip."

"Oh, right. I work in a beauty parlor, Kelly."

"Then you should know everything already."

"Very funny. Besides, I heard a report on the television at noon. The anchors were hinting that there would be more information, even an interview with Randi on the evening news."

Kelly leaned a shoulder against the wall of her kitchen and looked out at the snow swirling around her window. "They'll have to break through a barricade of half brothers and hospital security to get to her, and then, believe me, she won't have a lot to say."

"What do you mean? Why not?"

"Look, I've said more than I should already." Then, hoping to change the subject, Kelly asked, "How're my favorite nephews?"

"In trouble. *Big* trouble," Karla said, as if her boys were hovering nearby and could hear the conversation. "Aaron found some extra tubes of hair dye here at the house and Spencer took it upon himself to give the bunny a new hairdo. He tried to change the color of Honey's fur from tan to red—I think the official name of the color is Heavenly Henna or something like that, but let me tell you, it's more like Hellish Henna. You should see the poor thing—all those red blotches. This year we won't be dyeing Easter eggs, we'll color rabbits for Thanksgiving instead," Karla joked.

"But Honey's okay?"

"Yeah. Just as embarrassed as all get out. I think she might have to go to one of those animal psychiatrists, she's so traumatized. I'm afraid Honey Bunny will be in therapy for years to come." Kelly chuckled and Karla added, "I guess I should count myself lucky the boys didn't decide to give her a perm. Think how that would've turned out." She sighed. "It's really not funny. They could have gotten some of that stuff into her eyes. I took all my supplies down to the shop and I'll have some more closets built—better yet, safes with combination locks, but, enough about all this, tell me about your love life."

"What?" Kelly should have expected the question from her straight-shooting sister, but it still caught her off guard.

"You were in Seattle yesterday, right? And so was Matt McCafferty. I happened to overhear that bit of news at the coffee shop. I figured it wasn't just a coincidence."

"You're fishing again."

"And you're dodging the question."

"Since when is my love life any of your business?"

There was a pause, then all of the humor left Karla's voice as she said, "Since you fell in love with that son of a bitch, Matt McCafferty."

★ ★ ★

Thanksgiving was a nightmare. Though Kelly enjoyed being with her family, she felt distant, somewhat removed from the festivities. Her mother and father had each other, Karla had the boys, and though Kelly was a part of it, she also felt alone.

Because of Matt.

A part of her wanted to share the holiday with him and his family. She'd ordered an apple pie and pumpkin pie from the local bakery, and had spent the morning helping her mother stuff the turkey and prepare the sweet potatoes, but still there was something missing.

The family had prayed together, and her father had made a big show of carving the bird, but Kelly felt, for the very first time in her life, as if she belonged somewhere else, which was just plain stupid.

"Something's bothering you," her mother said as she loaded the dishwasher. Karla was wiping the table and couldn't help but overhear the conversation as her boys were in the den with their grandfather, making out their Christmas lists. One holiday was about over, so on to the next.

"I'm okay," Kelly argued as she angled a serving dish into the overloaded washer.

"Is it the case?" Eva Dillinger prodded.

Karla snorted. "Not exactly."

"What does that mean?" Her mother's smooth forehead furrowed with concern. "Kelly...?"

"It's nothing, Mom."

Karla snapped her dish towel, then folded it over the handle of the oven door. "Kelly's in love," she said.

"You are?" The worry lines disappeared and Eva Dillinger's mouth curved upward in anticipation. This was news she'd been hoping to hear for years.

Kelly shot her sister a warning look.

"Who's the lucky guy?" Eva persisted.

"Karla shouldn't have said anything. I'm not in love," Kelly lied.

"But you're seeing someone. Who?"

Kelly squared her shoulders. "It's nothing serious, okay, so don't freak out." She wanted to strangle her sister, and if looks could kill, Karla would be six feet under.

"I wouldn't…" But Eva's voice faded with her smile and she glanced to the doorway.

"What?" their father said, rolling into the room. "What are you talking about? Kelly's got a boyfriend?"

Inwardly groaning, Kelly lifted a hand. "Not a boyfriend. Not really. I've just been spending time with Matt McCafferty. Because of the case."

No one said a word. From the den the sound of the television could be heard. Other than that, nothing. Karla had the sense to wince, as if she finally understood the magnitude of her faux pas. "I shouldn't have said anything."

"No. No, it's good you did." Ronald's face had turned scarlet, while his wife had paled to the point that she had to lean a hip against the counter for support. "You know, Kelly girl, your mom and I, we only want the best for you and…and I can't imagine why you would take up with—"

"Hush, Ron. Don't. Kelly's old enough to make her own decisions," her mother reprimanded softly, and her support of her daughter along with the wounded look in her eyes cut Kelly to the bone. She wanted to apologize, and yet she knew she had no reason to offer up any kind of "I'm sorrys." Her father clamped his jaw and wheeled in silent agony back to the den.

"Happy Thanksgiving," Karla muttered under her breath,

then added, "I'm sorry. I should have kept my big mouth closed."

Amen. But Kelly didn't say it out loud. Instead she said, "At least it's out in the open."

The rest of the evening was tense, conversation revolving around Aaron and Spencer, and Kelly couldn't wait to escape. She felt claustrophobic and restless and, for the first time in her life, undecided about her future. She'd grown up always knowing she wanted to be a cop, and she'd never let anything deter her. No man had derailed her from her objective. But then she'd never let any man as close as she'd let Matt. She drove home hardly aware of the city lights or the traffic. On autopilot, she pulled onto her street and hit the button of her remote garage door opener.

Somehow, she'd have to figure out what she was going to do with the rest of her life. Worse yet, she thought, as she steered into the garage, she'd have to figure out if Matt McCafferty would be a part of it. But how was that possible? His home, his *love,* was his ranch. She couldn't, *wouldn't,* ask him to give it up and her life was here. The situation was impossible.

She got out of her car and climbed the stairs to the main floor of her home, tossed her jacket and scarf over the back of her couch and saw the red light blinking on her answering machine. Kicking off her boots, she hit the play button and waited, then heard Matt's voice. Her heart skipped a beat.

"Hi, it's Matt. I thought maybe you'd like to join me and my family for Thanksgiving dinner." Her heart plummeted as she glanced at the clock. After nine. Too late. "We're celebrating in about three days or so, I'm not quite sure yet, but whenever Randi's released from the hospital. It just didn't make sense to go through all the folderol twice. Anyway, I'll let you

know when we pick a day…and…well, I'll be talkin' to ya."
The machine clicked and automatically rewound.

Kelly played the message again.

So he was inviting her to a family get-together. "Heavy
stuff," she muttered under her breath, and caught her reflection in the mirror. She saw the glint of hope in her eyes, the
flush on her cheeks that couldn't be entirely attributed to the
cold weather she'd just endured.

"Oh, Dillinger," she said on a sigh. "You've got it bad. Real
bad." She'd have to steel her heart. No matter what happened,
Matt would eventually leave. He was tied to his ranch hundreds of miles west of Grand Hope and this was her home.
There was no future with him for her. Absolutely none.

Yet, what they'd shared was nice. Intimate. But it meant
nothing in terms of commitment. He was a cowboy who lived
a nearly solitary life in the wilds of western Montana; she was
a cop, a dedicated officer of the law, whose ties were here in
Grand Hope. Fleetingly she thought of her mother and father,
Karla and the boys. They were her family.

She glanced at her left hand and her ringless third finger.
Did she really harbor the ludicrous notion that she would some
day marry Matt McCafferty?

Because they slept together?

She knew better.

Squaring her shoulders and tossing her hair off her face, she
told herself it didn't matter. For the moment, if not the rest of
her life, she'd enjoy the sensation of falling in love.

Even if it was one-sided.

After all, what was the worst that could happen?

Chapter 11

Matt forked hay into Diablo Rojo's stall and the two-year-old eyed him warily.

"Still don't trust me, do ya, boy?"

The Appaloosa snorted and pawed the straw.

"Then that makes two of us. I don't trust you as far as I can throw you."

Diablo lifted his head and shook it, jangling his halter and causing a nervous nicker from the bay in the box next door.

"Now look what you've done," Matt grumbled, but Diablo, ever the headstrong colt, didn't appear the least bit sheepish. Not much intimidated, that one. Maybe why Matt felt a connection with the beast.

He finished feeding the stock and walked outside. It was early morning, not yet light, the moon giving off a ghostly light that created shadows on the snow. Matt's breath fogged and his boots crunched as he followed the path he'd broken from the back porch. At the back door, he paused long enough to stomp the snow from his boots and walk inside, where a solitary light over the range was the only illumination. He'd gotten up early after a restless, sleepless night. When he had dozed, he'd dreamed of Kelly, and when he'd been awake, his brain had run in dizzying circles of memories of making love to her over and over again. In his mind's eye he'd seen her flawless white skin, her pink, puckered nipples, the teasing spark in her eyes and the way her red hair had spilled over her shoulders. Only pausing long enough to throw on clothes and plug in the electric coffeemaker, he'd trudged out to the barn and stables, intent on working out Kelly's image.

But it hadn't happened. With every lift of the pitchfork or ration of oats he'd poured into the mangers, he'd thought of her and the fact that he was, whether he would admit it to himself or not, falling in love with her.

He ground his back teeth at the realization and poured himself a cup of coffee from the carafe steaming in the coffeemaker. Kicking out a chair by the window, he drank his coffee and wondered what he'd do about her. He'd always planned to marry. Someday. When the time was right. He figured he'd find a local woman who was pretty, yes, and smart, but certainly not one so headstrong and career-minded. Never a cop. Never.

And not a woman who was tied so closely to Grand Hope. Her entire family lived here. She would never leave her home for a remote outpost in the western hills. And then there was the bad blood between the families.

Too much baggage.

Too much water under the bridge.

Too much…oh, hell.

He just couldn't get any more involved with her than he already was. He didn't want a long-distance love affair, nor, he guessed, did she. She was the wrong woman for him and that was all there was to it.

But even now, as he was trying to talk himself out of falling in love with her, his pulse jumped a notch and his groin tightened. Hell, he was horny as a schoolkid, always fighting his damned arousals. He hadn't felt this way in years. Or maybe ever. Not about one woman.

Nor had he ever in all of his thirty-seven years invited a woman to share the holidays with him. He'd considered it a time or two, but never had extended an invitation, always figuring the woman would see it as a sign of some kind of commitment or intent to commit. He'd also never accepted an invitation to be a part of some woman's family celebrations, either. Yet, even with the trouble between the McCaffertys and Dillingers, he'd be willing to take that step. And he'd make it right with Kelly's family. Somehow. Yep, this time it was different.

He took one final scalding swallow and forced his mind to other issues. Randi was coming home this morning, going to meet her son for the very first time. He'd have to concentrate on that reunion, of getting Randi into the house. Some of the staff at St. James weren't happy that she was being released, but she'd been adamant and chomping at the bit. Since Nicole was living on the ranch, all the release papers were being signed by the appropriate docs. The empty guest room on the main floor was being converted to Randi's bedroom, and a hospital bed was being transferred this morning before the guest of honor arrived.

Hopefully then, she'd be safe and get well. At least being close to the baby should help her peace of mind, maybe even jog her memory…if in fact she was telling the truth about her amnesia. Matt wasn't so sure. Randi had been John Randall's favorite child, the only one conceived with his second wife, Penelope, and the only girl to boot. Though she'd been raised in part as a tomboy, probably more because of the fact that she lived with three older half brothers than anything else, she'd also been pampered, the "princess," as John Randall had often referred to her. She'd grown up believing she could do anything she damned well wanted and that everyone in the world would treat her with the same regard and adoration as her father.

And she'd been proved wrong. Whatever had happened between her and little J.R.'s father couldn't have been good. Not good at all. That was the trouble with relationships—even with the right intentions, they usually went sour. His father had had two marriages and two divorces to prove Matt's point.

Headlights reflected against the side of the barn and shortly thereafter Juanita's station wagon slowed to a stop near the garage. Within minutes she hurried into the house. Blowing on her hands, she shivered, then unwound the scarf covering her head.

"You are up early," she said, and poured a cup of coffee.

"Big day."

Her smile was wide. "Señorita Randi will come home."

"That's the plan." He stretched from his chair. "I guess I'd better start moving some of the furniture out of the guest room to make room for some of the other stuff."

"And then, once she is home, we can have the wedding." Her dark eyes shone at the thought of the first McCafferty nuptials. *"Sí?"*

"Sí." Matt nodded. "You bet."

"And you, perhaps you will be next."

"To what? Get married?" He shook his head quickly, by

habit, as he always did when anyone brought up the subject of him getting married. "I don't think so."

Juanita didn't comment as she hung up her coat, but he didn't miss the smile that played upon her lips and the knowing glimmer in her eyes. In her mind, he was only one step away from the altar. Was it so obvious?

He thought of Kelly. God, he wanted her. Ached for her, but he couldn't imagine that she would ever want to be a rancher's wife, marry and settle down so far away...no, he concluded for the dozenth time, it just wouldn't work.

He heard the sound of a baby crying and made his way to the nursery where J.R. was starting to wind up, his little voice making coughing-hiccuping noises. "Hey, big fella," Matt said, picking up the baby and holding him to his shoulder. "What's wrong, hmm? Hungry, are ya?" While the baby stared up at him, Matt carefully placed him on the changing table and, with more dexterity than he ever thought possible, unsnapped the tiny pajamas, removed the wet diaper, cleaned the baby and fastened a clean diaper in place. J.R. kicked while Matt refastened the pajamas and carried him downstairs where Juanita was heating a bottle. She handed it to Matt and he carried the baby into the living room, plopped down in the old rocker and sat by the banked fire in the old stone grate. J.R., eyes bright, suckled hungrily as Matt stared down at this little wonder. "Mama's coming home today," he whispered, and the baby moved one tiny fist beside the bottle. "And then watch out. She's gonna take one look at you and melt." But that wasn't all, he decided, keeping his thoughts to himself. When Randi returned home, he was certain all hell would break loose. "You and I, we'll have to take care of her, won't we?"

He leaned back in the chair and rocked, wondering if he'd ever do the same for his own infant. Thinking of Kelly, he imagined a baby—maybe a girl—with bright red hair and wide, curious brown eyes.

Surprisingly the thought wasn't frightening at all. If anything, it was downright seductive.

"Listen, I've told you and Roberto Espinoza everything I remember," Randi McCafferty insisted. Her hospital bed was propped up and she was no longer attached to an IV. Wearing a jogging suit, peach lipstick and a don't-mess-with-me attitude, she skewered Kelly in her stare. "I'm going home and meeting my son for the first time, tomorrow my family's celebrating a belated Thanksgiving, and right now I'd like to forget all this for a little while, okay? I know you're just trying to do your job, but give me a break."

"Detective Espinoza and I are just trying to help," Kelly said, unswayed. "Trying to protect you and your baby."

"I know it. Really. But please, don't give me any lectures about taking care of myself or my baby or my safety, okay? Believe me, I've heard all the reasons I should stay in the hospital, comply with the police and live my life a virtual prisoner until whoever it is that's taking potshots at me is caught, a million times over from my brothers. But that's not going to happen." She stopped suddenly, sighed and jabbed stiff fingers through her short locks. "Look, I don't mean to come off ungrateful, or like some kind of bitch. I do appreciate what you're trying to do." She let her hands drop into her lap. "It's just that I want to see my son. I'm going crazy sitting here. I haven't had the chance to be a mother yet and he's over a month old. I think the most important thing for me to do is bond with my baby." The honesty in her dark eyes got to Kelly. "Would it be too much of a hassle for you to drop by the ranch in a few hours, after I've settled in and he and I have…well, you know, started to get used to each other?"

Kelly wasn't immune to what Randi was feeling. Espinoza wouldn't like it, but Kelly wasn't feeling particularly interested in keeping on his good side. She was still stung by his insinuations about her love life the other day.

Not a love life, she reminded herself. *Don't kid yourself. You had a good time the other night, but it was sex, nothing more. At least to Matt.*

She'd just finished the thought when he strode through the door, larger than life, bringing with him the scents of leather, musk and memories that she should best forget. His dark eyes found hers, and for a second she felt the same heat, the intensity that she had before. Her stomach tightened and she swept her gaze in Randi's direction again. "I understand. I'll drop by later. After dinner."

"Thanks," Randi said. "I'm sure my brothers will take care of me until then."

"We'll try," Matt drawled, then offered Kelly a smile that silently reminded her of the passion they'd shared. Ridiculously, she felt her cheeks stain. She was a cop, for crying out loud, she couldn't let some macho cowboy make her act like a silly schoolgirl. "How're you doin'?"

"I'm fine. I just want to get the heck out of here…oh, you weren't talking to me," Randi said.

"I was talking to both of you."

"I'm fine," Kelly replied. "I'll be in the hall, and I'll see that she gets to the car without any problems with the press."

"We can handle it. Slade's making sure all the discharge papers are ready and we've parked near a rear entrance."

"All right." She gave Randi a professional smile. "I'll be over about seven tonight, will that be okay?"

"Yes. And thanks."

Kelly walked out of the room stiffly. Why did she feel so awkward around Matt? So she'd spent a night with him. So they'd made love. So what? This was the twenty-first century, for heaven's sake. She was thirty-two years old, had graduated from college years ago and was a detective. She had every right to do whatever she wanted, sexually or otherwise, and yet she'd never been promiscuous, hadn't believed in sex for sex's sake, hadn't let herself have "flings" without any emotional attachment. In fact, other than a boyfriend in high school, another in college and one man since, she'd never been emotionally involved. While her sister had fallen in love a dozen times and been married twice, Kelly had been cautious and had lived her life by using her head instead of listening to her heart.

Until now.

Until Matt, damn him, McCafferty.

He caught up with her before she could leave. "I just wanted to double-check. We're planning a belated Thanksgiving celebration tomorrow and you're invited. Six o'clock."

"I don't get off until five, but, yes, I'd love to come."

"Good. And then..." He shifted his weight from one foot to the other. "Saturday night's the wedding. Thorne and Nicole are going to tie the knot. I thought you might want to be my date."

"You did, did you?" she teased.

"Unless you have other plans."

She laughed. What was it about this man? One minute she was tongue-tied and felt awkward around him, the next she was flirting as she'd never done in her life. "I'll cancel them," she joked, and started to walk off, before he caught her by the arm, spun her around and kissed her until she couldn't breathe.

"Do that," he whispered, and turned on his heel to disappear into Randi's room. Kelly cleared her throat, saw two nurses look quickly away, pretending they hadn't seen the open display, then caught sight of Dr. Nicole Stevenson striding down the hallway.

"Arrogant S.O.B., isn't he?" Nicole said as Kelly tried to regain some of her professional integrity.

"The worst."

"Like his brothers," Nicole said, and then managed a smile. "I know that I've come on a little strong sometimes, especially when it comes to my patients. I hope you understand it's nothing personal."

"I do."

"And I hope you'll come to the wedding. I know it's short notice, but Thorne and I wanted to wait until Randi could attend. It's this Saturday night."

"I'll be there," Kelly promised, and refused to second-guess herself.

She returned to the office and holed up, closing the door and the blinds so that she could plow her way through some paperwork on various cases, but as usual ended up flipping through Randi McCafferty's file. The same old names leaped out at her—friends and family, college roommates, peers and associates, but none leaped off the page as potential enemies. Aside from her half brothers she had an aunt, Bonnie Lancer, on her mother's side, and one cousin, Nora, who was Bonnie's daughter. Her friends were a small group who stayed in touch primarily through e-mail and an occasional phone call. Kelly had talked to everyone who had called or e-mailed Randi in the three months prior to her accident and had come up dry. The maroon Ford product that was thought to have been used to force her car off the road had so far proved to be a bust, and she couldn't figure out how Randi's book could possibly come into play. What had she written that would make someone angry enough to try to kill her?

She was about ready to call it a day when Stella buzzed. "Detective Dillinger...Kelly, there's someone here to... Oh, no, don't you do it again—" She had a visitor just as the door to her office burst open and Matt strode in.

"You really have to stop doing this," Kelly admonished, ignoring her elevating pulse as Stella, once again sheepish, filled the doorway and lifted her palms. "It's all right," Kelly said to the receptionist before the poor girl had a chance to apologize, and Stella hurried back to her desk.

"This is the sheriff's department, you can't just keep barging in here," she said, centering her gaze on the cowboy who in his sheepskin jacket, snow-dusted Stetson and faded jeans seemed to fill up the entire office. "I mean, you're giving poor Stella fits."

"We need to talk."

Her throat constricted. "I assume this is business."

His nostrils flared a little. "Partly."

"I'm at work," she reminded him as she leaned back in her chair, and waved him into a seat on the other side of her desk. "It's got to be all business. A hundred percent."

"Does it?" he challenged, and she saw the glint of a dare in his dark eyes. Her heart nearly stopped and she knew in an instant that he was remembering the night they'd been together. Her throat went dry at the memory of his hot skin, fevered touch, deep groans.

"Yes, well, I think that would be best." She cleared her throat, tossed an errant lock of hair over her shoulder and flipped open Randi's file. "What can I do for you?"

The man had the audacity to smile. Slowly. One side of

his mouth lifting into a crooked and decidedly wicked smile. "Now, that's a loaded question."

"I assume you have a reason, and it had better be a good one, for barging in here, bullying Stella and taking up my time," she said.

Leaning against the file cabinet, he said, "I heard you say that you were coming out to the house."

"Later. Around seven."

"How about now?"

"Why?"

"It's Randi. She's not cooperating."

"Meaning?" Kelly prodded.

"She doesn't seem to be taking the attacks on her seriously. She's refused to have a bodyguard and has been snapping everyone's head off. She claims we're all paranoid and that everything's just hunky-dory."

"Even though someone forced her off the road and then slipped insulin into her IV?"

"Yep."

"Why?"

"I don't know, probably just that damned McCafferty stubborn streak, but I thought maybe you could talk some sense into her. She seemed to listen to you at the hospital."

"Not much, she didn't."

"She's always been headstrong, but I thought a woman might be able to get through to her. Nicole's at the hospital, Jenny's watching the twins, but she's too young, really a kid herself, so...how about it?"

"Give me ten minutes. I'll follow you."

"Fine." He started for the door, and not knowing what got into her, she caught the crook of his elbow, spun him around and, standing on her tiptoes, kissed him hard on the lips. He gasped and she took advantage, slipping her tongue between his teeth for just the briefest of seconds. His arms tightened around her.

"You're asking for trouble," he warned as he kissed her.

She pulled back and skewered him with a vampish look. "And who's gonna give it to me?"

"Just watch."

"Slow down. I was only giving you a little of your own back," she said. To her surprise, he laughed, a deep warm sound that rippled through the offices.

"Don't lose that thought." With a tip of his hat and a low, mocking bow, he exited. "I'll see you at the ranch."

That you will, cowboy, she thought, and reached for the phone and flipped through her notes until she found Kurt Striker's number. She needed to get in touch with the P.I., just in case he'd come across any new information. She dialed his motel, waited and left a message when he didn't answer.

She'd get back to him later, she decided, hanging up and reaching for her jacket and gloves. As she left her office she ran into Roberto Espinoza striding through the front doors of the building. The scent of cigarette smoke clung to him and snow covered the shoulders of his down jacket. "Don't tell me, you're on your way to the Flying M, right?" His lips were compressed, his eyes dark, and his gaze landed like a ton of bricks on Kelly.

"Randi McCafferty was released from the hospital today and now she's not cooperating with her doctors, her brothers or anyone."

"And lover-boy thought you could talk some sense into her, right?"

Kelly bristled. "I need to question her again."

Espinoza looked about to spit nails. His dark eyes flashed and he sighed loudly. "As long as it's business."

"And what if it isn't?" she said. Who the hell did Espinoza think he was? "I am a professional, Bob."

"I know, it's just that…" Whatever it was he was thinking, he let the idea drift away. Frowning, he took off his hat, hung it on an ancient hook and raked stiff fingers through his hair. "It's your funeral, I guess."

"I'll remember that." Fuming, she held on to her temper. Blowing up now would only make things worse. For the moment, she had to maintain her composure, meet with Randi McCafferty and try to figure out how much the woman honestly didn't remember, because Kelly had a gut feeling that Randi knew a lot more than she was saying.

It was Kelly's job to find out just what it was and she was damned well going to do it.

Chapter 12

"I told you, I don't remember," Randi insisted, but Kelly wasn't buying it. Propped up in a hospital bed in the guest room of the ranch, her baby cradled in her arms, Randi McCafferty was lying through her teeth. And she wasn't particularly good at it. Then again, Randi wasn't interested in anything but her son. Cradling and cooing to her baby, Randi couldn't have cared less who had tried to kill her. She probably wouldn't have paid any attention if the world stopped spinning.

As Kelly stood near the bed, Matt filled the doorway, leaning a broad shoulder against the frame. He sent Kelly an I-told-you-so look as Harold sauntered in and circled a few times before lying on the rug at the foot of the bed.

"You asked me to stop by and promised you'd answer some questions," Kelly reminded Randi.

"I will, when J.R., and that's *not* his name, goes to bed. And don't look at me like I'm insane, okay? Lots of people go home without naming their babies first." At her brother's skeptic lift of an eyebrow, she amended, "Well, okay, not *lots,* but some. And I want the right name for my son. So don't give me any grief. Go ahead and call him J.R. if you want, but as soon as I come up with the perfect name, we're changing it."

"It might be too late," Matt drawled.

"Never. I've dealt with this in some of my columns," she said, then added, "the value of a name and all that."

"Didn't you have one picked out?"

"Yeah. Sarah. Somehow it doesn't seem to fit. Oh." Randi grinned as Juanita brushed past Matt and hurried through the door carrying a warmed bottle of formula. "*Gracias,* Juanita. You're a doll."

The housekeeper flushed as Randi accepted the bottle, adjusted the baby in her arms and offered him something to eat. With wide eyes, little J.R., or whatever she was going to name him, stared up at her. He suckled hungrily, but stopped every so often to observe the woman beaming down at him.

"Isn't he beautiful?" Randi whispered, awestruck at her infant, and Kelly, feeling just the trace of envy, silently agreed.

One side of Matt's mouth lifted. "And smart as the devil and no doubt athletic as all get out. I figure Harvard will be cablin' any day now."

Randi giggled. "I wouldn't be surprised. How about you, pumpkin?" she asked her baby as Juanita, too, smiled down at mother and child.

"Oh, no, you can't call him that. 'Sport' or 'big fella' or something else, they're okay, but not 'pumpkin' or 'precious' or any of those cutesy-sissy names, okay?" Matt insisted.

"You hush," Juanita snorted. "He is an angel. *Perfection.*"

"And the least you two will give him is a big head," Matt grumbled. "Look what happened to Slade."

"I heard that," the youngest McCafferty brother grumbled as he paused at the door by his brother.

Kelly realized she wouldn't get any more information until she was with Randi alone. "I'll talk to you later, once he's—" she hitched her chin in the baby's direction "—asleep."

"Thanks." Randi was more than appreciative.

"And I...I had better look in on the pies for tomorrow," Juanita said, bustling off toward the kitchen.

Kelly stepped out of the room.

"See what I mean? She's not taking anything seriously," Matt growled, walking into the foyer with her.

"She just wants to take care of her child."

"And bury her head in the sand. If we don't find out who tried to kill her and he strikes again, she won't be worrying about anything, baby or no." He rubbed the back of his neck in agitation.

"You don't feel she's safe here?"

"No, actually, it's better than the hospital. Not so many people coming and going. No strangers. No reporters."

"So far," Kelly said, "but that might not last."

"Damn. The problem is that Randi doesn't realize that the most important thing right now...the *only* thing, is finding out who's got it in for her. *Nothing* else can be a priority."

"Not even a baby?"

Matt's jaw turned to granite. His lips thinned. "This is all about the baby and keeping him safe. What do you think would happen if Randi lost him?"

"Let's not even consider that," Kelly said, her heart stopping at the thought.

"No matter what it takes, we have to find whoever's behind this." Frantic footsteps pounded overhead and echoed on the stairs. Over the thunder, the phone jangled somewhere in another room as the twins appeared.

Nicole, carrying two small pairs of jeans, was trying to shepherd her two rambunctious daughters, who, once they reached the bottom step, flew by in a blur of dark curls, rosy cheeks and mischief sparkling in two sets of bright eyes. Neither was wearing anything but a sweatshirt and panties.

"Never a dull minute around here," Nicole said, shoving her hair from her eyes as her daughters tore down the hall. "All I want them to do is try on their dresses for the wedding and you'd have thought I'd asked to handcuff and shackle them."

Matt's grin spread wide. "Maybe you should let their stepfather handle that."

"Now, that's a great idea!" Nicole said as Thorne, appearing in the hallway from the doorway to the den, called, "It's Kavanaugh on the phone for you, Matt."

"Excuse me," Matt said, and hurried off toward the den.

"I'll be right back, after I corral the girls." Nicole added, "Why don't you meet me in the kitchen and we can get to know each other?"

"In a minute," Kelly promised, thinking she might try to speak with Randi one more time. Matt was right. Finding out who was trying to kill his half sister was her top priority. It was also her job, something she was losing sight of a bit. Because of her feelings for Matt.

All her life she'd wanted to follow her father's footsteps and become a cop. She'd been focused. Determined. Hadn't even let any relationships deter her. Until now.

God, she was hopeless.

Loving Matthew McCafferty had changed everything.

She lingered at the doorway, hoping Slade would say his goodbyes and exit. From the kitchen she heard the twins talking and giggling as the scents of cinnamon and nutmeg mingled with the fragrances of baked apples and pumpkin. She couldn't hear what Matt was saying, but every once in a while heard the low rumble of his voice. It had been so easy, *too* easy, to fall in love with him.

She stared at the pictures mounted on the wall—the McCafferty photo gallery—and stopped at the one of Matt astride the bucking bronco. He was much younger then, of course, a wild cowboy, as untamed as the animal he was astride. A hell-raiser. And a heartbreaker. Anita Espinoza was just one of many women who'd hoped they'd be the one to capture his wayward heart.

Just like you.

As the noise from the kitchen muted, Kelly couldn't help but overhear the conversation between Randi and Slade through the open doorway of her bedroom.

"I mean, what's going on?" Randi was asking. "I was out of it for little more than a month and I wake up not only with this precious little guy, but to find out that Thorne, *Thorne of all people,* is head over heels in love and planning to get married! Who would have thought? He was as confirmed a bachelor as anyone I've ever seen. And then there's Matt—what in the world's going on with him? I was under the distinct impression that the ranch he fought so hard to buy was the most important thing in his world, that nothing and no one could hold a candle to it, at least not in his estimation. He practically sold his soul to Satan to buy the damned thing. Now all that's changed."

"He's just worried about you," Slade said, and Randi laughed.

"My eye! I see the way he is around that detective—the one who was in here earlier."

"Kelly," Slade supplied, and Kelly stiffened.

"Yes, Kelly. Matt's a different man around her. In fact, you'd think she was the only woman on the planet from the way he looks at her."

Kelly smiled and silently reprimanded herself for eavesdropping. Yet, she couldn't help herself.

"It might not be as serious as you think."

"What, because of that woman…Nell, in the town where he lives?"

"That's been over for months."

Kelly froze. Matt had never mentioned another woman. No one had. *But you knew he'd had lots of affairs, didn't you? He's a virile man. Why wouldn't there be a woman back home? Damn it, why wouldn't there be half a dozen, considering that you're thinking about Matt McCafferty?*

"I have eyes, Slade. The guy's in love, whether he knows it or not."

"Or it's an act. You know how he is with women. One comes along and he's in love, head over heels for a few weeks until…until…"

There was a long pause. Kelly felt her chest constrict.

"Until she becomes just another notch in his belt."

"I wasn't going to say it that way."

Kelly's heart plummeted.

"Okay, so let's say a scratch on the bedpost, a conquest, a quick roll in the hay, any way you say it, it comes out the same, doesn't it? All part of the old, sick double standard." Randi's voice inched up an octave and fairly shook with outrage at her brother's actions. Meanwhile, Kelly wanted to die.

"Hey, wait a minute, what's got you so riled?" Slade demanded.

"I just don't like the whole idea."

Amen, Kelly thought.

"It's degrading. Demeaning to women. In my job I see it every day. Women write me in reams about men who use them, pretend to be interested, make the woman think he's falling in love, then up and turn tail and run the other direction the minute she starts to get serious. It's age-old, Slade, and it's common."

"I'm just filling you in, but I thought you didn't remember much about your job. About your life. You know, I'm starting to think that's a crock, little sis. Don't tell me, let me guess, someone did a number on you. Right? Like maybe the baby's father?"

There was a tense, thick moment and Kelly wished she could witness Randi's expression. Despite her own embarrassment, Kelly still needed to know about the father of Randi's child. "We were talking about Matt and his women...I was hoping he was over all that love-'em-and-leave-'em adolescent garbage."

"It was Striker's idea," Slade explained. "He thought one of us should stay in tight with the police, keep an eye on the investigation."

"Why? Because you don't trust the police?" she asked, just as the baby started to cry.

"We just want to know what's going on. Sometimes the cops can be pretty closemouthed."

"So Striker *suggested* that Matt fall in love with...no, wait a minute, that Matt get the policewoman into bed... Oh, God, Slade, tell me that's not what it was all about. Tell me that Matt isn't using that detective, because she's pretty damned clever and she won't fall for any of that, besides which, it's just...just disgusting."

Kelly wanted to drop through the smooth patina of the old plank floorboards.

"He was hoping there might be a little pillow talk," Slade said over the baby's wail.

Sick inside, Kelly felt her knees start to go weak. *Don't do this, Dillinger. Chin up. Spine stiff. Shoulders square. You're a professional. A detective.*

"Then he's an idiot, because that woman impresses me as way too sharp to fall for that. In fact, she's probably too good for him!" Randi added, obviously furious. "And whether he knows it or not, he's falling in love. I'd like to throttle him and you and Striker and whoever else is involved."

You and me both. Heat flooded up Kelly's cheeks and she was mortified. What a fool she'd been.

The baby was still crying, and Randi must've turned her attention to her child, because she said, "Now, now...shh." Kelly had heard more than enough. On silent footsteps she moved into the living room and pretended interest in some farming magazine as Slade strode out of the bedroom. From the corner of her eye she caught him send her a dark glance, then take off toward the kitchen just as Matt emerged from the den into the hallway.

Her heart wrenched and she silently called herself the worst kind of fool imaginable.

"Sorry about that," he said, and there wasn't a glimmer of a smile in his voice. "The guy who's supposed to be taking care of my spread called from his place. He slipped, fell and broke his leg, so it looks like I'm going to be taking the next plane home."

She forced a smile she didn't feel. "I understand." *More than you know, McCafferty. A helluva lot more.*

"I won't be around here tomorrow for the belated Thanksgiving festivities."

And your invitation is withdrawn. He didn't say it, but it was there hanging in the air between them.

She grabbed her jacket from the hooks near the door. Shoved her arms through the sleeves. Reached into a pocket for her gloves. "Don't worry about it. I already celebrated," she said, inwardly cringing when she heard the drip of ice in her voice. *Get over it, Dillinger. It wasn't that big of a deal.* She pulled on her gloves. "I'd better shove off. Randi's not interested in talking to anyone in the sheriff's department right now. I'll be back."

She started for the door, and when he tried to reach for her elbow, she yanked her arm away from his outstretched fingers; she'd fallen for that trick one too many times as it was. Then she remembered how she'd turned the tables on him, spun him around by his arm just a few hours earlier and kissed him hard. Oh, what an idiot she'd been.

"Kelly?"

"I'm wise to you, McCafferty." She reached for the door, not bothering to explain. Let him think that she was talking about his little trick of whirling her into his arms. It didn't matter that she meant something much more serious.

With a hard yank she opened the door and walked into a biting wind that snatched the breath from her lungs and rattled the panes of the windows. But she didn't care. The sting of the icy blast felt good against her hot cheeks, shook her out of her dark reverie, reminded her that she wasn't dead, though she was beginning to feel hollow inside.

"I'll walk you." He was beside her, not bothering with his jacket and matching her short, furious strides with his longer ones.

"Don't bother."

"It's no bother."

"I'm a cop, McCafferty. I can make it to my rig alone."

"Wait a minute."

She didn't; she just kept walking, plowing through the crunchy blanket of white, barely noticed that small, icy crystals were falling from the dark sky again.

"Kelly, what the hell happened?" he demanded when she threw open the door of her SUV.

"I woke up," she said as she climbed behind the steering wheel. "Look, Matt, I've got to go. I'll be back to talk to Randi and I'll keep you posted on everything that's happening with the investigation, but I've done some thinking and I really don't think it's a good idea for either of us to become too involved right now."

"Wait a damned minute—"

"Look, Seattle was nice, but I think I'd better keep my perspective." *And my distance.* She ignored the questions in his dark eyes, the play of night shadows across his strong features, the pain ripping through her heart. "I'd hate to do anything to compromise my professionalism."

"I thought we'd talked this through already."

"And I rethought it. The thing is that you and I have different interests. We're at different places in our lives."

"This sounds like a canned speech."

"It's not. I've got my job. You've got your ranch."

"So?"

"That's all there is to say. I'm going to wrap up this investigation or die trying, and you're going back to the Idaho border." She twisted the keys in the ignition. "Goodbye, Matt." Her heart wrenched at the words and she saw the mixed emotions crossing his features. Disbelief, distrust and a seething anger evident in the throb of a vein at his temple.

Tough.

He'd get over it, she decided as she jammed the SUV into gear and cranked on the steering wheel.

He always did.

What in the hell just happened? Matt threw a couple of pair of jeans, two shirts and his shaving gear into his duffel bag and couldn't make heads nor tails of Kelly's change in attitude. One minute she'd been flirting with him and he'd been coming close to being envious of Thorne and Nicole, because they, not he and Kelly, were getting hitched; the next minute, after he'd taken the call from Kavanaugh, she'd been as cool as the proverbial cucumber, telling him in so many words that their love affair—so hot and torrid only days before—was over.

He wasn't buying it.

No woman would respond the way she did, then turn away. Not without a reason, and a damned good one.

He yanked the zipper closed and slung the strap of his bag over his shoulder. With one last glance around the room he'd reclaimed, he ignored the feeling that he was leaving more than a scarred old double bed and a collection of ancient, dusty rodeo trophies.

Nope, there was more here. Not only his brothers and half sister, but the twins, the baby and Kelly. God, why did it hurt to think that he wouldn't see her for a few days, and worse yet he might never get to kiss her again, touch her, make love to her?

Get over it, she's just a woman, he tried to tell himself, but the pep talk didn't work. Because that was the crux of the problem. She wasn't just a woman.

Hell.

He didn't have time to second-guess himself. He had to go back to his spread tonight. He'd put it off too long already, and Striker was camping out here at the ranch. Along with Thorne, Slade and their father's arsenal supplied by Remington and Winchester, Randi and the baby should be safe.

And Matt was coming back. Soon. Because of his family. Because of the unanswered questions surrounding the attempts on Randi's life, but most important, because of Kelly.

"What do you mean you're not going to the wedding?" Karla asked, checking her watch and shoving the remainder of the pizza she and Kelly shared across the table toward her sister. They were seated in Montana Joe's, not far from the glassy-eyed bison head, while the noon lunch crowd swarmed the counter, stomping snow from their boots and unwrapping their scarves to expose red noses as they tugged off gloves and ordered from plastic-covered menus. An old Madonna song played over the buzz of conversation and the shout from a loudspeaker for an order to go.

"I thought you were all hot to trot to do anything you could with the McCafferty clan."

"You make it sound like I'm a traitor."

"Are you?" Karla lifted an eyebrow, then reached across the table and pulled a piece of ham off the leftover pizza.

"I don't think so. But I did think that mixing business and pleasure wasn't such a hot idea."

Sighing, Karla plopped back on the cushions of the booth. "That's depressing!" She tossed her napkin on the remaining slices of the Hawaiian Paradise they couldn't quite finish.

"I didn't think you approved."

"I didn't. Don't. But...oh, damn, I was beginning to believe that there was such a thing as true love again, you know? I mean...it was kind of like one of those star-crossed-lovers things with the feuding families. Kind of a Romeo and Juliet scenario."

"In your rose-colored dreams."

"I thought maybe I'd just been unlucky and that there was still a chance. You know, that if you found love, maybe I would, too, and that the third time would be the charm."

"Sorry to dash your hopes," Kelly said, then sighed as she checked her watch. "You know, Karla, you're a hopeless romantic."

"I know it's my one serious character flaw."

"You've only got one."

"Absolutely."

"More bad news. It's ten till one."

"Oh, damn. I gotta run. I've got a wash and set for one of my regulars." Karla scrambled out of her side of the booth and threw on a wool poncho and floppy-brimmed suede hat.

"You look like a bad guy out of one of those old, old Clint Eastwood movies."

"Make my day."

"Older," Kelly said, "one of those spaghetti Westerns."

"Guess I missed it on the late-late show," Karla said as she adjusted the string. "But seriously, Kelly, you might want to rethink this Matt McCafferty thing. Mom and Dad will get used to the idea. No one's had a heart attack or a stroke over it. Well, not yet, anyway."

"What's with the turnaround?" Kelly asked, standing and reaching for the jacket she'd slung over the back of the booth.

"It's simple. I just want you to be happy, and these past few weeks you've been a whole lot more lighthearted. It's nice to see you smile."

"I do."

"Not all the time. The job gets to you whether you want

to admit it or not. And you're alone. That's not good. Your work is your life, I know. You practically work twenty-four-seven and that's also not good. It's bringing you down, Kell. You look half dead as it is."

"Thanks a lot."

"I'm not kidding. You can't be a policewoman day in and day out."

Kelly wanted to protest but didn't. For once, Karla was making a lot of sense. And she had been working long hours. Ever since leaving Matt at the Flying M the other night, she'd thrown herself body and soul into the case, digging up information on friends and family of the McCaffertys', searching out anything she could about Randi's job and her work acquaintances. Someone wanted her dead. Kelly was determined to find out who it was. And soon. She'd had less than five hours' sleep in two nights, but she was getting closer to the truth, she could feel it.

"It's a hard job and you're good at it, but it's bleeding you dry," Karla was saying. "I've seen it. You need some fun in your life. We all do. I don't think it's a coincidence that you lightened up about the same time that Matt McCafferty rode bareback into your life!"

"So now you know what's best for me."

"I always have." Karla flashed her a smile as they walked through the heavy doors to the outside. "I just wish I could figure out what's best for *me*."

With a wave, she jaywalked back to her shop and Kelly, surprised at her sister's turnaround, unlocked her four-wheel drive and drove out of town. She had avoided the Flying M on the day the McCaffertys had designated for Thanksgiving, but she wasn't giving up on talking to Randi. She still had a job to do, and it would be considerably less difficult with Matt out of the picture. If she was lucky, she could avoid him altogether.

At that thought her throat tightened and the heaviness in her heart, the ache she'd tried to ignore, throbbed painfully. "You'll get over it," she told herself as she took a corner a little too fast and felt her rig shimmy before the tires took hold. "You've got no choice."

With her own words ringing in her ears, she drove to the Flying M and made her way into the now-familiar ranch house. Jenny Riley, a slim girl with a nose ring and tie-dyed tunic over a long skirt, let her inside. "Randi's in the living room, and Kurt Striker is talking with Thorne in the den," she explained when Kelly stated her business.

Great. The P.I. who didn't trust the police and who had egged Matt on to get some "pillow talk." Kelly would like nothing better than to strangle that lowlife. He might be a hell of an investigator, but he was the one who'd suggested Matt get close to her to glean information about his sister's case.

"Do you want me to tell them you're here?"

"No. I'd rather speak to Randi alone."

"Then could I get you something? Coffee, tea or cocoa? I'm on my way to take the girls to their ballet lesson, but I have time to bring you a cup, and Juanita will skin me alive if I don't offer you something."

"I'm fine. Really. Just ate," Kelly said, and as a shriek from one of the twins soared to the rafters of the kitchen, Jenny took off down the hall while Kelly, hauling her briefcase with her, walked into the living room.

Randi was half lying on the couch, a small cradle near her side where the baby was sleeping quietly. Kelly couldn't help but smile at the crown of reddish hair peeking from beneath an embroidered quilt. "He's adorable," she said, wishing she had a child of her own.

"Isn't he?" Randi waved Kelly into a chair near her, one that faced the fireplace where embers glowed red and flames crackled and hissed. "Sit," she ordered and, as Kelly dropped into the chair with its back to the foyer, asked, "Would you like something?"

"Just answers, Randi." Kelly sat on the edge of one of the rockers and leaned forward, her gaze locking with the new mother's. "I know you want to keep the baby safe, and I think you know more than you're saying. Either you're covering up or afraid to say the truth, or don't realize how much danger you and your boy are in, but I've got to tell you that without your help the investigation is stymied." Randi glanced away, her gaze traveling from Kelly to the window and beyond, where snow was drifting against the fence and barn.

She hesitated. Tapped her fingers on the edge of the couch.

"Do you know anyone who would want to kill you?"

"You mean other than my brothers?" Randi joked.

"I'm being serious."

"I know." Her smile disappeared. "I probably have some enemies, but I don't remember them."

"Do you remember the man who fathered your child?"

Randi stiffened, picked at a scratch in the arm of the leather couch. "I'm...I'm still working on that."

"It won't help to lie."

"I said I'm working on it." Randi's index finger stopped working on the scratch.

"Okay, so what about the book you were writing?"

Was it Kelly's imagination or did Randi pale a bit?

"It's fiction."

"About corruption in the rodeo circuit."

"That's the backdrop, yes."

"Does it have anything to do with your father or your brothers?"

"No. Other than I got the idea for it from Dad, I think—Look, this is all kind of fuzzy."

"How about Sam Donahue? He's a cowboy and was involved in rodeo work. He still supplies stock to the national competitions, doesn't he?"

"I said it was fuzzy."

"You and he dated."

"I...I think that's true. I remember Sam."

"Could he be the father of your child?"

Randi didn't answer, and in true McCafferty fashion, her jaw slid forward in stubborn defiance.

"Okay, so what about your job? Do you remember anything about it? Anything that you might have been working on that would have caused someone to want to kill you?"

"I wrote advice columns. I suppose someone could have taken offense, but I don't remember them."

"What about Joe Paterno? The photojournalist you worked with? Do you remember him?"

Randi swallowed hard.

"You dated him."

"Did I?"

"When he was in town. He's gone on assignment a lot. Rents a studio over a garage in one of those old homes in the Queen Anne's district of Seattle when he's in the Northwest."

"As I said, I really don't remember. Not details. Names are familiar, but..." Kelly was ready. She snapped open her briefcase and slid three pictures across the coffee table. One was of Joe Paterno, his camera poised as he was about to snap a shot, while someone took a picture of him. The second was a color copy of a photo from a newspaper in Calgary. The grainy shot was of Sam Donahue, a rangy blond with a cowboy hat tilted back on his head and his eyes squinted against a harsh, intense sun. In the background penned horses and cattle were visible. The third photo was a glossy eight-by-ten of Brodie Clanton. Wearing a suit, tie and the thousand-watt grin of a lawyer with political ambitions, he stared into the camera as if it were his lover.

"Well," Randi said, leaning forward and separating the photos and eyeing each one. "You've certainly been busy."

Chapter 13

"I want to find the bastard who tried to kill you, Randi, but I can't do it without your help," Kelly said. "So tell me, who do you think it is?"

Randi eyed the pictures on the table. She chewed her lower lip as Kelly felt eyes on her back. At that moment, Randi turned her attention to the archway that separated the foyer from the living room. She froze.

"Who are you?"

Kelly glanced over her shoulder and found the private investigator standing at the foot of the stairs. "Kurt Striker."

"The private detective," Randi said, her eyes snapping and her chin inching higher. "My brothers hired you to try and figure out who's trying to kill me."

"That's right." Kurt sauntered into the room and extended his hand. Kelly gritted her teeth to hold her tongue.

Randi didn't bother shaking his hand. Her lips flattened over her teeth and she said, "I don't know what my brothers were thinking, but we don't need anyone investigating the accident."

"It wasn't an accident," Kurt asserted.

Randi's gaze zipped back to Kelly. She asked, "You're certain?"

"Fairly." Kelly nodded.

Randi shot a look at the private detective. "I think the police can handle it."

Kurt smiled crookedly and had the audacity to sit on a corner of the coffee table, placing his tough-as-leather body directly in front of Randi. "You got a problem with me, lady?"

"Probably." She reached over and adjusted the edge of the blanket near her baby's chin. "I just want things to be calm. Peaceful. For me and him. And for the record, don't call me 'lady' again. I consider it demeaning."

"I meant it as a compliment."

"I have a name."

He ignored the jab. "Okay, you want things to be back to normal, then let's wrap this up. The detective was asking a good question when I walked in. Who do you think tried to kill you?"

"I...I honestly don't know," Randi admitted.

"But you should remember the father of your child."

"I should."

Kelly smiled inwardly. Randi wasn't giving an inch for Striker. She leaned closer to the youngest McCafferty heir. "This is important. We think the vehicle that ran you off the road was a maroon Ford product. Maybe a van or SUV. Do you remember anything about the day of the accident?"

"Just that I was in a hurry. I had this feeling of urgency," Randi said, leaning back on the couch and looking at the fire. But Kelly suspected she wasn't seeing the hungry flames licking at the mossy chunks of oak, or the charred bricks in the grate. Her eyes were turned inward.

"I remember I was in a hurry. I was just a few weeks before term and I had a lot to do." Her brow furrowed and her eyes squinted as she thought. "I wanted to get to Grand Hope without going into labor."

"But your OB-GYN is in Seattle."

"I know. That was a problem. I mean, I think it concerned me, but I thought if I could…could spend some time here and finish the synopsis, you know, an outline, kind of, for my book, then once the baby was here, while I was on maternity leave, I thought I could polish the first few chapters and send them to my agent. He thought he might be able to find a publisher who would be interested…but that's about all I remember."

"No car or truck following you or pushing you onto the shoulder?"

She shook her head slowly. "No."

"You don't know anyone who had a maroon car?"

"Not that I can remember." She glanced at the three pictures still spread upon the table. "Do you know something else? Do any of these men… No, surely not someone I dated…but… do any of them own the car that pushed me off the road?" she asked, her color draining as she considered the possibility.

"None of these men has ever owned title to anything resembling what we're looking for," Kelly admitted, "but that doesn't mean the culprit couldn't have borrowed a friend's car or stolen one. The department has done a pretty thorough search of all the local body shops, in a wide arc around Glacier Park, Grand Hope and Seattle. Sure, there are some vehicles that needed repair that *could* have been the car or truck involved, but so far, we haven't been able to make a connection." She reached into her briefcase again and handed Randi a list of names. "Do you know any of these people? Do any of the names jog any kind of memory?"

Randi looked over the computer printout. "I don't think so," she said. "I mean, I don't remember any of them."

Kurt reached for the printout. "Mind if I have a look?"

Kelly wanted to tell him to go jump off the highest bridge, but didn't. There was a chance he could help. "See for yourself."

He eyed the report and Kelly envisioned the gears turning in his mind as he scanned the documents. When he finished he looked over the sheets at Kelly. "Good work."

"Thanks," she said, nearly choking on the word. She didn't trust this guy a bit. He had no scruples as far as Kelly could tell.

"I'm looking for a partner."

In your dreams. "I've got a job."

"I could probably make it worth your while."

"Not interested."

"A lifer, eh?"

She didn't respond, just said to Randi, "Let me know if you remember anything else. And you can keep those—" she motioned to the pictures and printouts "—I've got copies."

"Thanks. I'll let you know."

"I'll walk you out," the P.I. offered.

"It's not necessary."

But he was with her stride for stride, and as the front door shut behind them, he said, "I don't know why you've got a burr under your saddle when it comes to me, but it's not helping anything. We can work together or separately, but it might be easier, faster and damned more efficient if we pooled our resources."

"You mean I should give you all the information I have, all

the access the sheriff's department has, and make your job a whole lot easier, so you can 'solve,' and I use the term loosely, the case, take the credit and the money for it, without putting in the hours and the effort."

"I just want to get to the bottom of it," he said, and his expression was as dark as the night.

"Right," she muttered under her breath. "I'll keep it in mind."

She was down two steps when his voice caught up with her. "You know, Detective, unless I miss my guess, you're ticked off and it doesn't have so much to do with me as it does with Matt McCafferty."

She bit back a hot retort and just kept walking. There was just no reason under heaven to rise to the bait. Because, damn him, he was right.

"I'll give you top dollar, McCafferty. I already had the place appraised by two local real estate firms, but if you don't like what they've come up with, you can have someone else do it."

Mike was seated in his old pickup, the engine idling, with his crutches and old hunting dog, Arrow, on the front seat beside him. Matt stood in the snow-crusted lane of his house talking through the open window, his breath fogging in the clear air. Kavanaugh reached into a side pocket of the truck and withdrew a manila packet.

"What makes you want this place so badly?"

Kavanaugh grinned as he handed the thick envelope to Matt. "Carolyn's expecting and we're outgrowing my place. I figure we can live there while I remodel the farmhouse." He nodded toward the rustic house Matt called home. "It'll take some doin', but I'll finish off the top story, add a bath and let Carolyn decide what she wants to do downstairs. By the summer after next, about the time the baby will be on his feet, we'll be ready to move and I'll rent out my place to my foreman."

"You've got one?"

The grin in Kavanaugh's freckled face widened a bit. "I will have by then. If things go right. You know, I would have bought this the last time it came up for sale, but you beat me to it. Now I've come into a little money, you're never here, anyway, and I figure it's the right time." He stared through rimless glasses and the open window. "You're not telling me I'm wrong, are ya?"

Matt frowned and glanced around the hilly acres he'd ranched for the past few years. The house was big enough, two stories, but the upstairs had never been finished; it was three rooms separated by a framework of two-by-fours. Downstairs the kitchen needed to be gutted. Ditto for the bathroom, which was little more than a closet by today's standards. And the whole place needed new wiring, plumbing and a helluva lot of insulation.

It had been fine for him. He liked roughing it. But it probably wouldn't do for a wife and kids. Along with two barns, one a hundred years old, the other five years old, there were rolling acres backdropped by dark forests. The creek that ran through the property eventually meandered over to Kavanaugh's place.

He opened the envelope and saw Mike and Carolyn Kavanaugh's offer. It was fair. He knew what his place was worth, at least in terms of dollars and cents. And emotionally, he was ready to move on. He owned the spread outright.

"Now, I'd need a contract. It's all outlined in the offer," Kavanaugh said, "but I'd make a balloon payment in five years, either pay you off out of my pocket or get a real mortgage."

Matt's jaw slid to one side and he eyed his place one last time. "All right, Mike. You've got it." He stuck his hand through the open window and Kavanaugh's fingers clasped his.

"Just like that?"

"Just like that. I'll call the attorneys who drew up the papers when I bought this place, a firm named Jansen, Monteith and Stone in Missoula. Thorne worked there when he first got out of high school and they handled all my dad's legal work."

Kavanaugh gave a curt nod. "I've heard of 'em. See what you can work out."

They talked for a few minutes, then Kavanaugh took off. Matt wandered up the short walk and the three steps to the front porch. Inside he listened as the old furnace growled and the windows rattled with each gust of wind. His furniture was used, most of it had come with the place, and there just wasn't much to tie him here any longer. He didn't waste any time, but dialed the number of the law firm. After going through two receptionists, he was connected with Bill Jansen, the man who had handled splitting up the Flying M in accordance with John Randall's wishes.

"So what is it I can do for you?" Bill asked after a few polite preliminaries about health, the weather and the NFL.

Matt outlined his request. What he wanted, he explained, was to take the money he made on this property and offer to buy out his brothers for their share of the Flying M, and he wanted to set up some kind of trust for Eva Dillinger, in accordance with whatever agreement his father had made when the woman worked for him.

"That might be tougher than you know," Bill admitted. "I understand John Randall and Eva had spoken about some kind of retirement, but it was never drawn up legally."

"But you heard about it, right?"

"He'd mentioned it."

"Then let's figure out how to make it right. I'm not trying to set Eva up for life, just give her what's due. I'll talk to
my brothers. And this has got to be anonymous. Completely."

"I don't think that's possible."

"Anything's possible."

"Not really. Not only will the recipients want answers but
the government, as well."

"Can't you dummy up some blind corporation?" Matt said,
then laughed as he heard himself, talking like some big corporate hot shot. "Never mind. I just didn't want to deal with it
now," he admitted. It was the truth; he had too much to think
about, didn't want to stir up that particular hornet's nest. But
he had to. If he was going to right his father's wrong. "Don't
worry about it. I'll explain."

"Then it's not anonymous."

"Right. I'll handle it," Matt said. "Is it possible to get the
paperwork to me in the next few days? Fax it to the ranch
and I'll see that my brothers sign it. Can you work that fast?"

"Unless we encounter unforeseen problems."

"You shouldn't."

"One of the junior partners is going to be in Grand Hope
in a couple of days. I'll tell her what's going on, and if there's
any problem, you can meet with her while she's in town. Her
name is Jamie Parsons and she spent her senior year of high
school there. Maybe you know her."

The name was slightly familiar, but Matt couldn't recall
why. "I don't think so."

"I'll have her give you a call when she gets into town. She'll
be staying there for a few weeks, as she's going to be selling
her grandmother's place."

"Parsons," Matt repeated.

"Her grandmother was Nita Parsons."

"As I said, the name's vaguely familiar."

"Nita passed away a couple of months ago. Your father might have known her."

"Possibly."

"Anyway, I'll get on the sale and transfer of property right away. All I'll need is your brothers' signatures."

"You'll have them," Matt said, though he hadn't mentioned his plan to either Thorne or Slade. He was certain it wouldn't be a problem. Thorne had already mentioned moving to a spread close by and Slade wasn't one to put down roots. Matt was the rancher of the lot. He'd buy out his brothers and own half of the Flying M.

Matt hung up and his gaze swept the interior of the old house. He'd spent a lot of years here. Alone. And it had been fine. But he wanted something more from life right now, and that something was a red-haired lady cop.

There wasn't any reason not to start the ball rolling. Quickly he dialed the number of the Flying M, connected with Thorne and stated his business. "Get Slade on the extension. I've done a lot of thinking while I've been gone. Kavanaugh's buying my place, so I want to transfer my operations to Grand Hope. Come up with a fair price. I'll buy the two of you out."

"Just like that?"

"If you'll sell," Matt said.

Thorne hesitated, then said, "I don't see any problem. Let me get Slade on the phone and we'll work something out."

"Just like that?" Matt threw back at him.

"Yep. It's the way I do business."

Kelly was burned. Big-time. The last place she wanted to be was at Thorne McCafferty's wedding, but she didn't have much of a choice. Espinoza had insisted.

"Look, the investigation is still wide open," he'd told her while smoking a cigarette in his office. "The potential killer could be there. This is a chance for you to meet those people closest to the family."

"At a wedding?" she'd protested.

"At a wedding, dressed as a guest, mingling at the reception, keeping your ears and eyes open." He'd drawn hard on his smoke, exhaled and looked up at her through the cloud. "Do you have a problem with that, Detective?"

"No problem at all," she said aloud to her reflection, repeating the exact phrase she'd spoken to Espinoza less than three hours earlier. So here she was wearing a midnight-blue silk dress, braiding her hair and wrapping it into a thick chignon at the base of her neck and dreading the thought of seeing Matt again.

You'll get through it; it's just business. But as she dusted her nose, applied brown mascara and touched up her peach lipstick, she felt like a fraud. Her stomach was tense, her skin felt flushed. She—a girl who had taken on men twice her size while training for her job, a female officer who had been known to take a bead on a suspect and demand "Drop it" when she'd been threatened with a weapon, an officer who wasn't afraid to drive more than a hundred miles an hour if a high-speed chase was necessary—was intimidated by a simple wedding and reception.

It was only one night. Somehow she'd get through it. As she reached for her coat and checked to see that she had her car keys, the phone rang. She nearly ignored it, then picked up on the third ring.

"Kelly?" her sister said breathlessly, as if she'd been running.

"This is my house. You called. Right?"

"What do you know about some trust being set up for Mom?" Karla asked, undeterred.

"A trust?"

"That's right. She got a letter from an attorney in Missoula, Jamie Parsons, that says she's the recipient of some trust fund."

"Why?"

"That's what I'm asking you."

"Didn't they say?"

"No, and when Mom called the law firm and talked to the lawyer, he was evasive, wouldn't give her any information. Said it would be coming in a few weeks. Isn't that strange?"

"Very."

"I told Mom and Dad not to look a gift horse in the mouth, but you know how they are. They're certain there's been some mistake. What do you think?"

"What's the name of the law firm?"

"Jansen, Monteith and Stone." Karla hesitated just a second, then added, "Mom said that when she worked for John Randall McCafferty, that was the firm he used. You think it's a coincidence?"

"I'm a cop, Karla. I don't believe in coincidence."

"I'm a beautician, Kelly. I believe in past lives, reincarnation, split personalities, winning the lottery and, in case I forgot, coincidence."

"I'll check it out for the folks."

"Figured you would. Now, have fun at the wedding."

"It's *not* going to be fun."

"You're right. If that's the attitude you're wearing. Come on, Kell, lighten up. It wouldn't kill ya."

Kelly wasn't so sure.

Matt hooked two fingers under the collar of his tuxedo shirt and twisted his neck to give him some breathing room. Small places made him claustrophobic, and this anteroom off the chapel where Thorne was about to be married was barely big enough for the minister and the three McCafferty brothers. Maybe it was because Matt didn't have such a great relationship with God, maybe it was because the thermostat in the room must've been broken and the heater was pumping out air that felt at least a hundred degrees, or maybe it was because he was faced with the fact that he'd be seeing Kelly again.

Kelly. Detective Kelly Ann Dillinger.

The woman who hadn't returned his calls.

He'd been back in Grand Hope all of twelve hours, and in that time he'd left three messages for her. He'd gotten no response, but Nicole was certain Kelly would show up.

Good.

Because he wanted answers.

"So we'll sign the papers next week," Slade said as he glanced in a small mirror, frowned and brushed a wayward lock of black hair off his forehead.

"As soon as the lawyer contacts us."

"Bill Jansen?" Thorne said, though it was obvious his thoughts were elsewhere.

"No, his associate. A woman. Jamie Parsons."

Slade froze. "Who?"

"Jamie Parsons. She's here on business as she's going to sell her grandmother's house." He caught a shadow chase across Slade's blue eyes. "Do you know her? She lived here her senior year of high school. Her grandmother was named Anita."

"Nita."

"Yeah, that was it. So you've heard of her."

"It was a long time ago," Slade admitted, his lips thinning as the sound of organ music filtered through the walls. "This is it," Slade said to Thorne, as if eager to change the subject. "Your last few seconds as a single man."

Thorne's grin was as wide as the whole of Montana.

"You can still take off," Slade offered.

"I don't think so." Thorne laughed and Matt wondered if he'd ever seen his brother so happy. Joy came with difficulty to Thorne; it wasn't an emotion Matt would have attributed to his eldest brother. Until Nicole. He'd changed since meeting his fiancée. And the change was definitely for the better.

The door to the chapel creaked open and the minister, a tall scarecrow of a man with wild gray hair, rosy cheeks and thick glasses, walked into the anteroom. "Are we ready?"

Thorne nodded. "You bet."

"Then let's go."

Thorne only hesitated long enough to predict, "It'll happen to you two, too. Your days as bachelors are numbered."

Slade snorted.

Matt didn't comment.

"Not for me," Slade argued.

"The bigger they are, the harder they fall."

"Well, maybe for Matt, he's already half-hitched as it is."

For once, Matt didn't argue. Yes, he was ready, but the woman he wanted for his wife seemed to be avoiding him.

"Don't they say something like pride goes before a fall?" Thorne said, adjusting his tie. "You might remember that, Slade." Squaring his shoulders, he led his brothers through the arched doorway and stepped into the candlelit chapel. It was small, more than a hundred years old, and the stiff-backed, dark wood pews were packed with family and friends.

Matt zeroed in on Kelly and his heart skipped a beat at the sight of her. The rest of the crowd seemed to disappear. Even when Matt's attention should have been drawn to the two bridesmaids, Randi and a woman doctor, Maureen Oliverio, Matt could hardly drag his gaze away from Kelly. God, she was beautiful. He forced his eyes to the back of the church as Nicole, dressed in a long cream-colored gown that shimmered in the candlelight, walked slowly to the front of the church to take Thorne's hand. Yet, from the corner of his eye, he noticed Kelly.

This should be me, he thought ridiculously. *Kelly and I should be up here exchanging vows.* He remembered the day his father had studied him trying to break Diablo Rojo and how the old man had advised him to settle down, to start a family, to ensure that the McCafferty name would go on.

Matt swallowed an unfamiliar lump in his throat.

The old man had been right.

He'd found the woman he wanted to live with; he just had to find a way to make her his wife.

Somehow he got through the ceremony. He watched tears spring to Nicole's eyes as Thorne slipped a wide gold band over her finger and felt a deep jab of envy as Thorne kissed his bride in front of all their guests. The ceremony completed, Matt followed the bride and groom outside and into the cold winter air.

He fell silent as Slade drove him to the Badger Creek Hotel where the reception was to take place. Built on the banks of the stream for which it was named more than a century earlier, the hotel had once been a stop on the stagecoach line and had enjoyed a colorful past. In its hundred-and-twenty-year history, the hotel had been renovated and updated every other decade and now had been restored to its original nineteenth-century grandeur.

Slade stopped for a smoke in the parking lot, but Matt hurried up the stairs to the ballroom, hoping to catch up to Kelly. He was surprised to see her at the wedding and hoped that she would come to the reception.

A crowd had already gathered in the cavernous room with its coved ceiling nearly thirty feet high. Tall windows ran the length of the room and thousands of tiny lights glittered from three immense chandeliers that sparkled with cut glass and dripped crystal. A small combo played music from an alcove in one corner while a fountain of champagne bubbled near an ice sculpture of a running horse.

He saw her the minute she entered. Without her coat, in a long shimmery gown of dark blue, she was exquisite. A silver necklace adorned her long neck and her hair was pulled away from her face, not severely, but with an element of sophistication that got to him.

Snagging two long-stemmed glasses from a linen-draped table, he walked up to her. "Well, Detective," he drawled, "you look...fantastic."

She cocked a reddish brow. "Oh, come on, McCafferty, you miss the uniform. Admit it."

So she still had a sense of humor. "I miss you."

"I don't understand."

"Liar." He handed her a glass and she started to take a sip.

"Wait. I think a toast is in order."

"To the bride and groom?"

"That'll come later." He didn't explain, just took hold of her hand and drew her through a draped French door and onto a snow-covered veranda.

"Wait a minute."

"Nope. I've waited too long." Balancing his glass in one hand, he wrapped his other arm around her and drew her close. Before she could protest, he kissed her, waiting until he felt her loosen, her bones melt against him. Only then did he lift his head. "Isn't that better?"

"No, I mean…look, Matt, I've been trying to tell you that it's over. You can drop the charade."

"Charade?" he asked, and felt the first drip of premonition in his blood.

"I know that you courted me just to get close to the investigation."

"No, I—"

"Don't deny it. I overheard a conversation between Randi and Slade." Anger surged through his veins. "I know that this flirtation or whatever you want to call it was because Kurt Striker told you to play up to me. To get me into bed."

"You believe that."

"Yes."

Anger roared through his blood. He opened his mouth just as she looked up at him with sad eyes. "Don't play me for a fool, okay? It's just not necessary."

"I wouldn't."

"Good. Then we can go on and forget what happened between us."

"Nope."

"Matt, really." She turned toward the door, and he didn't bother reaching for her.

"I'll never forget it, Kelly. Never." She'd reached the door but turned to face him. Tears glistened in her eyes.

"Don't do this," she whispered.

"I love you."

She closed her eyes. A tear, caught in the moon glow, wove a silent course over the slope of her cheek.

"You don't have to—"

"I love you, dammit."

She leaned against the door. "I don't want to do this, Matt.

I only came tonight because my boss asked me to. Because of the investigation."

"Have you seen any suspicious characters?"

"Just the groom and his brothers," she said, but the joke fell flat. "Look, I know that you set up some kind of trust fund for my mother, probably because of a guilty conscience over what your dad did to her, and...and that's all well and good, really, but you shouldn't have. It was your father's problem, not yours."

"You're mine."

"A problem...I imagine I am."

"That's not what I meant!"

"The past is over and done. My family is fine...we can take care of ourselves. We don't need any kind of Johnny-come-lately charity."

"That's not what it is."

"It doesn't matter."

"Like hell!" He dropped his champagne glass and his shoes crunched through the snow as he walked to her. "You came here to see me. I did what I did for your mother to right a wrong, my brothers agreed to it, and as for leaving well enough alone, I can't. Not until you tell me that you'll be my wife."

"What? Oh, God, your ego just won't quit."

"I love you," he said again, and Kelly felt her heart rip into a thousand pieces. If only she could believe him, trust him, but she knew better. She opened her mouth to protest again but he snatched the glass of champagne from her fingers, flung it over the rail toward the creek, and pulled her into the circle of his arms. "What will it take to convince you?"

"You can't."

"Sure I can. We'll elope tonight."

"You're crazy."

"I'm serious."

Her throat felt as if it were the size of an apple. Could she dare believe him? Trust him?

"I—I don't believe that's possible," she whispered.

"Anything is." He stared at her long and hard. "I sold my ranch. I'm moving back to Grand Hope. For good. And I want you to be my wife and the mother of my children. You do love me?"

"Yes."

"Then we'll get married."

"I—I'd like that."

"Then that's settled." He smiled down at her with his crooked, damnably sexy thousand-watt grin.

"I...I don't...I don't know what to say," she whispered, stunned at the turn of events.

"Then don't say anything, just kiss me."

She nearly laughed through her tears, but tilted back her head and felt his mouth cover hers. Music filtered through the open door and he started moving, dancing with her, alone on the snow-blanketed veranda with the cold winter air swirling around them, and high overhead the stars twinkled in the night-darkened Montana sky.

Kelly leaned against him. She thought of the investigation, of the danger still surrounding the McCafferty brothers and of Randi and little J.R. Now, knowing she would soon marry Matt, she was more determined than ever to find the culprit who was terrorizing his family...her family.

But...for tonight, she'd dance with Matt, laugh with him and know that whatever fate had in store for them, they would face it together.

"Should we make the announcement?" he asked.

"Tonight?"

"Why wait?"

Why indeed?

"Let's wait until tomorrow. Tonight belongs to Thorne and Nicole," Kelly said as she glanced through the windows and saw the bride and groom gliding around the dance floor. Nicole's eyes were bright, her cheeks flushed, and as the song ended Thorne swept her into a back-breaking dip. The crowd clapped.

"Then tomorrow," Matt agreed.

"Yes, tomorrow."

He kissed her then and she wound her arms around his neck. "All right, Detective. Let's join the party. It looks like you lost your champagne. Besides, aren't you supposed to be looking for the bad guys tonight? Wasn't that your assignment?"

"Right you are, cowboy."

"I don't supposed you've seen any suspicious characters."

"Only the McCafferty brothers," she teased, linking her arm through his as they walked into the ballroom. "And you'll never meet a sexier, more disreputable bunch of *hombres* in your life!"

"I suppose you're right." Matt laughed, then gave her a conspiratorial wink. "Welcome to the gang."

"My pleasure," she assured him as he wrapped his arms around her and they joined the other guests, who were dancing under the dimmed lights of the chandeliers. Her heart pounded, her head spun and she fought to keep tears of happiness from sliding down her cheeks. As he guided her easily across the floor, she smiled up at the man she loved, the man she'd been waiting for all her life, the man who would soon be her husband, a cowboy after her own heart.

Mrs. Matt McCafferty.
Detective Kelly McCafferty.
Either way, the name sounded right.

Epilogue

A horse nickered softly as Matt entered the darkened stables. He flipped on the first switch, allowing only half the bulbs to illuminate the musty interior. Mares and colts rustled in their stalls and the wind whistled outside. Diablo Rojo stuck his head over the stall door and snorted.

"Yeah, yeah, and I'm glad to see you, too." Matt reached into his pocket for a bit of apple he'd pilfered from the kitchen as he walked to the Appaloosa's box. He tipped his hat back a bit to look the feisty colt square in the eye. "Juanita's making a pie, but I figured she didn't need this." Opening the flat of his hand, he added, "However, she might just disagree, and if she did, we both know she'd skin me alive." Soft lips swept the morsel from his palm. "So we're friends, are we, Devil?"

The horse tossed his head. His dark eyes were still bright with a fire no man would ever tame. Not even a McCafferty.

"That's what I thought."

He rubbed the colt's wide forehead and surveyed the stock.

A few of the broodmares were penned within, their swollen bellies indicating that they'd soon deliver the next generation of McCafferty foals.

Matt smiled as his boots rang on the concrete aisle between the stalls. God, he loved these animals. In the spring he'd transfer his own herd here. By that time he'd be married, maybe have a child of his own on the way.

The door creaked open and Kelly slid inside, bringing in a rush of bitter cold air. Snowflakes collected on the shoulders of her jacket and melted in her red hair. Matt's heart pumped at the sight of her, just as it did every time since the first time he'd laid eyes on her.

"I figured I might find you here," she said as she made her way between the boxes, her fingers trailing along the top rails. When she reached him she stood on her tiptoes and planted a kiss on his cheek.

Not good enough. Before she could pull away, he wrapped his arms around her and dragged her tight against him, his lips finding hers instinctively. Her perfume invaded his nostrils and her warm body caused his to respond with a dire need to have all of her. Every day. For the rest of his life. "You came in here so we could have some privacy," he charged when he finally lifted his head and noted the flush on her cheeks.

Her laughter rang to the dusty cross beams high overhead. "Well…that, too, I suppose, but I just wanted to check on you, see how you're doing."

"Fine. Why wouldn't I be?"

She lifted a shoulder. Wrinkled that damnably cute nose of hers. "I want to make sure that selling your place is something you want to do." She was suddenly serious. "I mean, I could move if you wanted to keep your ranch and—"

"No way. This is home." Still holding her, he glanced

around the boxes filled with horses and, high above, to the hay mow. "I did what I had to. Proved my point that I could make it on my own. Now I want to be here." He stared deep into her eyes. "With the woman I love."

"Who's that?" she teased, one side of her mouth lifting.

He barked out a laugh and squeezed her. "Besides, I'm not the only one making sacrifices." He was talking about her decision to quit the police force and take a position as junior partner with Kurt Striker. They'd aired their differences and Kelly was convinced this was the right move. She needed more free time, a more flexible schedule, and less stress on the job as she became Mrs. Matt McCafferty. "How did Detective Espinoza take the news?"

"Not well," she admitted.

"Tried to talk you out of it?"

"Mmm. Offered me a promotion."

"And you turned him down?"

"In a heartbeat. Roberto knew it wasn't going to happen, anyway. My mind was made up. I think he realized he couldn't change it."

"But he gave it a try."

She grinned.

"How about your folks?"

"They're another story." She giggled, snuggled closer to him. "They're adjusting. And even though they're grateful for the trust fund, they're not sure they can trust anyone named McCafferty."

"Even their daughter?"

"We'll see. It'll take some time."

He pressed a kiss to her forehead and she sighed. "Will they come to the wedding?" he asked.

"With some arm twisting."

"Really?"

"No...I'm kidding." Her breath was warm against his chest. "Neither one of my parents would miss my wedding for the world and Karla's excited about being my maid of honor, though she did have a few choice words about marriage and broken dreams."

"Funny, my family's all for it," he said as Diablo stretched his neck, stuck his head over the stall door and, with nostrils flared, searched Matt for another piece of apple.

"Your family is just grateful to marry you off."

"Very funny."

"They thought you were hopeless."

"They were probably right, but it could be something else, you know. It could be that you captivated my brothers and sister."

"Oh, right," she countered, but seemed to glow under the compliment. She checked her watch and sighed. "Got to run."

"You just got here."

"I promised Randi I'd babysit. Does he have a name yet?"

"She's, and I quote, 'working on it.' Until she does, we're all still calling him J.R. She doesn't like it too much, but she's going along with it. Doesn't have much choice."

"I haven't given up on finding who's been threatening her," Kelly said, her eyes darkening thoughtfully as she twisted a button on his jacket. "I'll just be working with Kurt instead of the sheriff's department."

"We'll get him," Matt said, and meant it. "Together." He pushed a lock of hair from her face. "Just like we'll do everything."

"Everything?" she teased, her brown eyes sparkling in that mischievous way he found so intoxicating. One arched brow lifted in naughty anticipation.

"Everything." He meant it. To prove his point, he pressed her against the wall, let her feel the want in him.

"Oh…oh…" He kissed her and she melted, sagged against the old siding.

"Wh-what about when we have children, and the baby needs to be fed or diapered and it's one in the morning?" she asked breathlessly as he lifted his head.

"No problem."

"Spoken like a true man. What about running them all over the map when they've got piano and soccer practice and you're dealing with a sick horse or cattle that have escaped through a hole in the fence?"

"Bring it on," he said.

"What about—"

"What about this?" he said, wrapping his arms around her more tightly. "You and I, we should quit worrying about what will happen when we have the kids and start concentrating on making a baby."

"Now?" she asked as he kissed the side of her face.

"Now."

"Here?"

"Anywhere." His lips brushed over hers, and as he bent down to lift her off her feet, he felt his father's rodeo belt buckle press into the muscles of his abdomen. "Anywhere. Anytime. Anyhow. Just as long as it's you and me."

"You got it, cowboy," she whispered into his open mouth, and removed his hat, before dropping it onto her own head and kissing him as if she'd never stop.

* * * * *

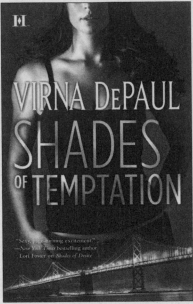

**Nothing can shake a cop from pursuing justice—
except a beautiful witness marked for death.**

**A fearless and sensual new romance from
New York Times bestselling author**

LORI FOSTER

When Detective Logan Riske goes undercover to find Pepper Yates,
a potential link to his best friend's unsolved murder, he vows to gain
her cooperation by any means necessary. But the elusive beauty is
more suspicious—and in far more danger—than he expected.
And the last thing Logan needs is to start caring for her....

RUN THE RISK

Available today.

"Steamy, edgy and taut."
—*Library Journal* on *When You Dare*

Celebrate the holidays with a brand-new McKettrick tale by beloved #1 *New York Times* bestselling author

LINDA LAEL MILLER

With his wild heart, Sawyer McKettrick isn't ready to settle down on the Triple M family ranch in Arizona. So he heads to Blue River, Texas, to seek a job as marshal. But in a blinding snowstorm he's injured—and collapses into the arms of a prim and proper lady in calico.

The shirtless, bandaged stranger recuperating in teacher Piper St. James's room behind the schoolhouse says he's a McKettrick, but he looks like an outlaw. As they wait out the storm, the handsome loner has Piper remembering long-ago dreams of marriage and motherhood. But how long is Sawyer willing to call Blue River home?

AN OUTLAW'S CHRISTMAS

Available in hardcover today!

www.Harlequin.com

PHLLM701TR

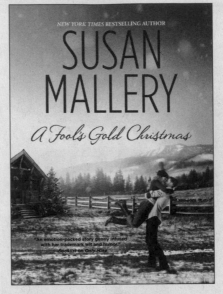

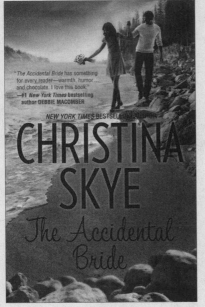